"One of the all-time winners..."
—*Sunday Times* on *Cousin Kate*

❧ ❧ ❧ ❧

"Philip! Have you come to stay?"

Torquil eagerly clasped his cousin's hand.

"For a day or two. Am I unwelcome?"

"You will be, with Mama!" replied Torquil. His eyes fell on Kate and he said, "Oh, Philip, this is Cousin Kate!"

"Ah, yes!" said Philip, bowing slightly. "Cousin Kate!"

"I don't think I can claim even remote kinship with you, sir," Kate retorted, nettled by his tone.

"Can't you? Why not?"

"I am merely Lady Broome's half niece. I can only be, at the best—or worst—a *connection* of yours!"

This flash of spirit seemed to amuse him, a reluctant smile warmed his eyes; he said, "Bravo!"

Selected quotes on

GEORGETTE
HEYER

"Once again Georgette Heyer has demonstrated her amazing ability to make life in the late 18th century as real as today's news..."
—*Chicago Sunday Tribune* on
THE GRAND SOPHY

"I love her wit, her marvelous use of language, her complex, often quirky characters, her sense of place and the sheer Englishness of her stories."
—*New York Times* bestselling author
Mary Jo Putney

"Stylish, witty and bang up to the mark for all Heyer fans."
—*Punch* on *FREDERICA*

"If you don't know these delightful yarns, now is the time to start!"
—*Cleveland Plain Dealer*

GEORGETTE HEYER

Cousin Kate

With a foreword by
Teresa Medeiros

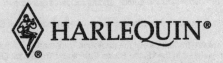

HARLEQUIN®

TORONTO • NEW YORK • LONDON
AMSTERDAM • PARIS • SYDNEY • HAMBURG
STOCKHOLM • ATHENS • TOKYO • MILAN • MADRID
PRAGUE • WARSAW • BUDAPEST • AUCKLAND

Special thanks and acknowledgment are given to
Teresa Medeiros for her contribution to the foreword for
COUSIN KATE.

ISBN 0-373-83446-2

COUSIN KATE

Cousin Kate

Foreword by
Teresa Medeiros

TERESA MEDEIROS

Teresa Medeiros wrote her first novel at the age of twenty-one and has since gone on to win the hearts of both readers and critics. All eleven of her books have been national bestsellers, climbing as high as #20 on the *USA Today* Top 50 and ranking in the Top 10 on the Waldenbooks, B. Dalton, Wal-Mart, Ingram and *Newsday* mass market lists. Her last four books were extended *New York Times* bestsellers.

She was recently chosen as one of the Top Ten Favorite Romance Authors by *Affaire de Coeur* magazine and won the *Romantic Times Magazine*'s Reviewer's Choice Award for "Best Historical Love and Laughter." She is a three-time RITA finalist, two-time PRISM winner and recipient of the 1996 Waldenbooks Award for her time-travel romance *Breath of Magic*, which was also voted one of the *100 Greatest Romances of the 20th Century* by an on-line poll conducted by the Florida chapter of RWA.

She lives in Kentucky with her husband, Michael, and four lovably neurotic cats. Teresa's first hardcover, *The Bride and the Beast*, will be released in June 2000.

The honorarium for this project will be donated to the Christian County Literacy Council in Hopkinsville, Kentucky.

Foreword

I have a confession to make that probably won't surprise most of my readers. I'm a complete sucker for style. I love a good story as much as the next reader, but if you can tell me that story with grace and wit in language that both dazzles and delights, then you've won my heart forever.

Between the years of 1921 and 1972, Georgette Heyer collected nearly as many hearts as did her dashing heroes. It seems like only yesterday that she first captured mine. Having exhausted the charms of Victoria Holt, Mary Stewart and Anya Seton, I was combing the shelves of my local library, searching for new treasures, when I stumbled upon a shelf and a half of books by an author I had never heard of. Their bindings were cracked, their pages yellowed and dog-eared, their covers outmoded, yet there was something irresistible about their titles: *Venetia, The Grand Sophy, Devil's Cub, The Black Moth, The Convenient Marriage, Faro's Daughter*. I left the library that day with a stack of books cradled lovingly in my arms, not realizing that I'd caught a glimpse of my own destiny.

When I began to write my own romances in 1984, I discovered that Georgette and I had much in common. We loved language and the pleasures it afforded. We adored dialogue that resembled a sparring match at Jackson's as much as a conversation. We had a highly refined appreciation for the absurd. We both appreciated the value of a well-timed kiss. And we couldn't resist the challenge of wooing those "bad boy" heroes—the unrepentant rakes, devilish dukes and roguish highwaymen who haunt every woman's secret fantasies.

Georgette's favored period may have been the Regency, but within the pages of the fifty-seven books she wrote prior to her death in 1974, she popularized all of the archetypes that still endure in my books and in the romances penned by my peers.

She used meticulous research to transport her readers to a world where passion and manners collide, with entertaining and often humorous results. When she died at the age of seventy-one, she left behind a research library of well over a thousand volumes, which included numerous sketches of clothing, carriages, maps, etc., drawn by her own hand. She shifted the focus from historical events to the development of a romantic relationship between a man and a woman. She used an astonishing variety of romantic plots and themes, including abduction, ugly ducklings who bloom into swans, the intellectual heroine who captures the heart and *mind* of a rake, dangerous highwayman and the ever-beloved marriage of convenience. She sprinkled those plots with adventure, mystery, social commentary and a generous dose of her own ironic humor. And she created unforgettable secondary characters, breathing fresh life into portly innkeepers, eager young stableboys and devoted abigails who were three-dimensional enough to have been penned by Dickens himself.

She was also one of the first writers to insist that strong heroines deserved men who were their match in both character and intellect. Her heroines may have been victims of circumstance, but they were never victims. She asked much of them, including a willingness to sacrifice naive romantic idealism for a genuine passion strong enough to last a lifetime.

Katherine Malvern in *Cousin Kate* is just such a heroine—intelligent, passionate and possessed of a wry wit that acknowledges both her strengths and her shortcomings. Relieved of her former position because she is deemed "too pretty" to be a governess, the penniless woman soon finds herself thrust into a web of intrigue and deceit within the forbidding halls of Staplewood Manor. As always, Georgette's characters are vivid and unforgettable: Phillip Broome, the handsome relation; Sarah Nidd, Kate's devoted nurse and Sarah's irascible father-in-law, Mr Nidd; Minerva Broome, who plays the role of doting aunt, yet seeks to use Kate for her own nefarious ends; and most haunting of all, Torquil, the brilliant and beautiful boy who may or may not be mad.

Although Georgette Heyer wrote a dozen straight mysteries during her illustrious career, *Cousin Kate* was a bit of a departure from her "high comedies." The book does a skillful job of blending elements of Gothic suspense with her trademark humor and romance. You're really not sure until you turn the last page whether the fancy young Torquil has taken to Kate will prove to be her salvation or her doom.

As a reader, I have another shocking confession to make. I've yet to read all of Georgette Heyer's books. I prefer to hoard them like boxes of fine, rich chocolates, to be opened only on a rainy Sunday afternoon after the candles have been lit and the phone has been unplugged. I know that when I turn the final page of that final book it will be with a sigh of mingled pleasure and regret.

So light the candles and unplug the phone and prepare to be transported back in time to an era when even the finest of gentlemen were sometimes rogues and the ladies liked it that way. Whether *Cousin Kate* is a treasured favorite or you're discovering the charms of Georgette Heyer for the first time, do remember that all of us who love the genre of romance, both readers and writers, owe her a tremendous debt. She spent her life giving voice to our dreams, and in the process gave all the writers who would come after her the power to make their own dreams come true.

Teresa Medeiros

Cousin Kate

Chapter One

At no time during the twenty-four hours was the Bull and Mouth Inn a place of quiet or repose, and by ten o'clock in the morning, when the stage-coach from Wisbech, turning top-heavily out of Aldersgate, lumbered into its yard, it seemed, to one weary and downcast passenger at least, to be crowded with vehicles of every description, from a yellow-bodied post-chaise to a wagon, with its shafts cocked up and the various packages and bundles it carried strewn over the yard. All was bustle and confusion; and for a few minutes Miss Malvern, climbing down from the coach, was bewildered by it, and stood looking round her rather helplessly. Until the guard dumped at her feet the small corded trunk which contained her worldly possessions and advised her to look sharp to it, no one paid the least attention to her, except an ostler leading out two horses, and adjuring her to get out of the way, and one of the inevitable street-vendors who haunted busy inn-yards, begging her to buy some gingerbread. The guard, assailed by demands from several anxious travellers to have their bags and bandboxes restored to them immediately, had little time to spare, but Miss Malvern's flower-like countenance, and her air of youthful innocence, impelled him to

ask her if anyone was meeting her. When she shook her
head, he clicked his tongue disapprovingly, and expressed
a hope that she might at least know where she was a-going
to.

A gleam of amusement lightened the shadows in Miss
Malvern's large grey eyes; she replied, with a tiny chuckle:
"Oh, yes! I do know that!"

"What you want, missy, is a hack!" said the guard.

"No, I don't: I want a porter!" said Miss Malvern,
speaking with unexpected decision.

The guard seemed to be inclined to argue this point, but
as a stout lady was tugging at his coat-tails, shrilly demanding to know what he had done with a basket of fish
consigned to his care, he was obliged to abandon Miss
Malvern to her fate, merely shouting in stentorian accents
for a porter to carry the young lady's trunk.

This summons was responded to by a burly individual
in a frieze coat, who undertook, for the sum of sixpence,
to carry Miss Malvern's trunk to the warehouse of Josiah
Nidd & Son, Carriers. Since this establishment was situated a bare quarter of a mile from the Bull and Mouth,
Miss Malvern had a shrewd suspicion that she was being
grossly overcharged; but although an adventurous youth
spent in following the drum had accustomed her to hag-
gling with Portuguese farmers and Spanish muleteers, she
did not feel inclined to embark on argument in a crowded
London inn-yard, so she agreed the price, and desired the
porter to lead her to the warehouse.

The premises acquired some years earlier by Mr Nidd
and his son had originally been an inn, of neither the size
nor the quality of the Bull and Mouth, but, like it, provided
with a galleried yard, and a number of stables and coach-
houses. Occupying a large part of the yard was an enor-
mous wagon mounted on nine-inch cylindrical wheels, and

covered by a spreading tilt. Three brawny lads were engaged in loading this vehicle with a collection of goods ranging from pack-cases to farm-implements, their activities being directed, and shrilly criticized, by an aged gentleman, who was seated on the balcony on one side of the yard. Beneath this balcony a glass door had once invited entrance to the coffee-room, but this had been replaced by a green-painted wooden door, flanked by tubs filled with geraniums, and furnished with a bright brass knocker, indicating that the erstwhile hostelry had become a private residence. Picking her way between the piles of packages, and directing the porter to follow her, Miss Malvern went to it, lifting its latch without ceremony, and stepping into a narrow passage, from which a door gave access into the old coffee-room, and a flight of uneven stairs rose to the upper floors. The trunk set down, and the porter dismissed, Miss Malvern heaved a sigh of relief, as of one who had accomplished an enterprise fraught with peril, and called: "Sarah?"

No immediate response being forthcoming, she called again, more loudly, and moved to the foot of the stairs. But even as she set her foot on the bottom step, a door at the end of the passage burst open, and a lady in a flowered print dress, with an oldfashioned tucker round her ample bosom, and a starched muslin cap tied in a bow beneath her chin, stood as though stunned on the threshold, and gasped: "Miss Kate! It's never you! Oh, my dearie, my precious lambkin!"

She started forward, holding out her plump arms, and Miss Malvern, laughing and crying, tumbled into them, hugging her, and uttering disjointedly: "Oh, Sarah, oh, Sarah! To be with you again! I've been thinking of nothing else, all the way! Oh, Sarah, I'm so tired, and dispirited, and there was nowhere else for me to go, but indeed I don't mean to impose on you, or on poor Mr Nidd! Only until I can find another situation!"

Several teardrops stood on Mrs Nidd's cheeks, but she said in a scolding voice: "Now, that's no way to talk, Miss Kate, and well you know it! And where else should you go, I should like to know? Now, you come into the kitchen, like a good girl, while I pop the kettle on, and cut some bread-and-butter!"

Miss Malvern dried her eyes, and sighed: "Oh, dear, would you have believed I could be so ticklish? It was such a *horrid* journey—six of us inside!—and no time to swallow more than a sip of coffee when we stopped for breakfast."

Mrs Nidd, leading her into the kitchen, and thrusting her into a chair, demanded: "Are you telling me you came on the common stage, Miss Kate?"

"Yes, of course I did. Well, you couldn't expect them to have sent me by post, could you? And if you're thinking of the Mail, I am excessively glad they didn't send me by that either, because it reached London just after four o'clock in the morning! What *should* I have done?"

"You'd have come round here straight! For goodness' sake, dearie, what's happened to bring you back in such a bang, with never a word to me, so as I could have met you?"

"There was no time," explained Kate. "Besides, I couldn't have got a frank, and why should you be obliged to pay for a letter when you were going to see me immediately? I've been turned off, Sarah."

"Turned off?" repeated Mrs Nidd terribly.

"Yes, but *not* without a character," said Kate, with an irrepressible twinkle. "At least, Mrs Grittleton wouldn't have given me one, but Mr Astley assured me his wife would, and was very sorry to lose me. Which, indeed, I expect she is, because we dealt very well together, and I did make the children mind me.''

"And who, pray, may this Mrs Grittleton be?'' said Mrs Nidd, pausing in the act of measuring tea-leaves into a large pot.

"A griffin,'' replied Kate.

"I'd griffin her! But who *is* she, love? And what had she to say to anything?''

"She is Mrs Astley's mother. She had everything to say, I promise you! She took me in dislike the moment she saw me. She said I was too young to have charge of her grand-children, and she told poor Mrs Astley that I had *insinuating manners!* Oh, yes, and that I was sly, and designing! That was because her detestable son tried to kiss me, and I slapped his face. Though why she should have thought that was being designing I can't conceive! Oh, Sarah, you never saw such a moon-calf! He is as silly as his sister, and not by half as agreeable! She may be a wet-goose—which, indeed, she is!—but the most amiable creature! And as for *my* being too young to have the charge of the children, *she* was a great deal too young to *have* three children! Why, she's no more than three years older than I am, Sarah, and *such* a featherhead! And now she has miscarried of a fourth child, and Mrs Grittleton set it at my door! And, I must say, I thought it pretty poor-spirited of Mr Astley not to have turned *her* out of the house, because he told me she never came to stay with them but to make trouble, and as for young Grittleton—'' She broke off, with a gurgle of laughter. "The *things* he said about him, Sarah! I couldn't but laugh! And the odious creature's intentions were most honourable! He made me an offer! That, of course, was what threw Mrs Grittleton into such a pelter, for, try as I would, I couldn't make her believe that nothing could prevail upon me to marry her detestable

son. She ranted like an archwife, and scolded poor Mrs
Astley into such a pucker that she fell into strong convulsions, and miscarried. So Mr Astley saw nothing for it but
to send me away. I own, he behaved very handsomely, for
he paid me for the whole year—not merely the six months
I had truly earned!—and sent me to the coach-stop in his
own carriage; but, considering he told me himself that he
held me blameless, I can't but think it was very poor-
spirited of him not to have sent Mrs Grittleton packing
instead of me!''

"Poor-spirited?" ejaculated Mrs Nidd, removing the lid
from one of the pots on the fire, and viciously stirring its
contents, "ay, and so you may, and so they are—all of
'em! Anything for peace and quiet, that's men!" She replaced the lid on the pot, and turned to look down at her
nursling, trouble in her face. "I'm not saying you should
have accepted that young Grittleton's offer, but—oh,
dearie me, what's to be done now?''

"I must find myself another situation, of course," responded Kate. "I mean to visit the registry office this very
day. Only—" She paused, eyeing Mrs Nidd uncertainly.

"Only what?" demanded that lady.

"Well, I have been thinking, Sarah, and, although I
know you won't agree with me, I believe I should be very
well advised to seek a situation in—in a *domestic* capac-
ity."

"In a—never while I'm alive!" said Mrs Nidd. "The
lord knows it went against the pluck with me when you
hired yourself out as a governess, but at least it was genteel! But if you're thinking of going out as a cook-maid,
or—"

"I shouldn't think anyone who wasn't all about in her
head would hire me!" interrupted Kate, laughing. "You
know I can't bake an egg without burning it! No, I believe

I might do very well—or, at any rate, tolerably well!—as an abigail! In fact, I daresay I could rise to be a *dresser!* Then, you know, I should be a person of huge consequence, besides making my fortune. Mrs Astley's housekeeper has a cousin who is dresser to a lady of fashion, and you wouldn't *believe* how plump in the pocket she is!"

"No, I wouldn't!" retorted Mrs Nidd. "And even if I did—"

"But it is perfectly true!" insisted Kate. "For one thing, a firstrate dresser commands a far bigger wage than a mere governess—besides being a person of very much more consequence! Unless, of course, the governess should be excessively well-educated, and able to instruct her charges in all the genteel accomplishments. And even then, you know, nobody slides sovereigns or bills into her hand to win her favour!"

"Well, upon my word—!" uttered Mrs Nidd explosively.

Kate's eyes danced. "Yes, isn't it shocking? But beggars can't be choosers, and I've made up my mind to it that to make my fortune—or, at any rate, to win an independence!—is of more importance than to preserve my gentility. No, no, listen, Sarah! You must know that I *have* no accomplishments. I can't speak Italian, or play the piano—far less the harp!—and even if people wished their children to be instructed in Spanish, which they don't, I don't think they would wish them to learn *soldiers'* Spanish, which is all I know! On the other hand, I can sew, and make, and dress a head to admiration! I did so once for Mrs Astley, when she was going to a ball, and her woman had made a perfect botch of her hair. So—"

"No!" said Mrs Nidd, in a tone which brooked no argument. "Now, you drink your tea, and eat your nice bread-and-butter, and no more nonsense! If ever I listened to such a pack of skimble-skamble stuff—! And I don't want to hear any more about *imposing* on me and Nidd, for there's no question of that, and I take it unkindly of you to say such a thing, Miss Kate!''

Kate caught her hand, and nursed it to her cheek. ''No, no, Sarah! You know better! How infamous it would be if I were to foist myself on you! When I think of all you have to do, with old Mr Nidd living here, and all those grandsons of his to feed, and house, I feel it's quite shameless of me to come to you even for a short visit! I couldn't stay here for ever, dear, dearest Sarah! You must own I could not!''

''No, you couldn't,'' acknowledged Mrs Nidd. ''It wouldn't be fitting. Not but what there's only three grandsons, and one of them lives with his ma—that's Joe's sister Maggie, and the most gormless creature you ever did see! Still, there's no harm in her, and I'm bound to say she's always ready to come and lend me a bit of help—if help you can call it! But a carrier's yard is no place for you, dearie, and well do I know it! We'll think of something, never you fear!''

''I have thought of something!'' murmured Kate wickedly.

''No, you haven't, Miss Kate. You're puckered, with that nasty stage-coach, and all the uproar that was kicked up by that Mrs Brimstone, or whatever she calls herself, and you'll feel different when I've got you tucked into bed which I'm going to do the minute you've drunk up your tea. You'll have your sleep out, and when you wake up you shall have your dinner in the parlour upstairs, and we'll see what's to be done.''

Kate sighed. ''I *am* very tired,'' she confessed, ''but I

shall be happy to eat my dinner *downstairs,* with the rest of you. I don't wish—''

''An ox-cheek, with dumplings!'' interrupted Mrs Nidd. ''I daresay! But it ain't what *I* wish, Miss Kate, and nor it isn't what Nidd or the boys would wish neither, for to be sitting down to their dinner in company with a young lady like yourself would put them into such a stew, minding their manners and that, as would turn them clean against their vittles! So you'll just do as Sarah tells you, dearie, and—''

''Believe that *Sarah knows best!*'' supplied Kate, submitting.

''Which you can be bound I do!'' said Mrs Nidd.

Miss Malvern was neither so young nor so guileless as her flower-like countenance frequently led strangers to suppose. She was four-and-twenty years old, and her life had not been passed in a sheltered schoolroom. The sole offspring of a clandestine marriage between the charming but sadly unsatisfactory scion of a distinguished family and a romantic girl of great beauty but somewhat inferior lineage, she was born in a garrison-town, and reared in a succession of lodgings and billets. The runaway bride whom Captain Malvern had captivated disappointed her scandalized relations by suffering no regret whatsoever at being repudiated by them; and falsified their expectations by remaining so ridiculously besotted that neither the discomforts of following the drum, nor the aberrations of her volatile spouse abated her love, or daunted her spirits. She brought Kate up in the belief that Papa was the personification of every virtue (the embarrassing situations in which from time to time he found himself arising not from any obliquity but from an excess of amiability), and that it was the duty of his wife and daughter to cherish him. She died, in Portugal, when Kate was twelve years old,

almost with her last breath adjuring Kate to take good care
of Papa, and, to the best of her ability, Kate had done so,
aided and abetted by her redoubtable nurse. Sarah cher-
ished no illusions, but, like nearly all who were acquainted
with him, she was a victim of his compelling charm. "Poor
dear gentleman!" Sarah had said, after his funeral. "He
had his faults, like the best of us—not that I'm saying he
was the best, because telling farradiddles is what I don't
hold with, and there's few knows better than me that you
couldn't depend on him, not for a moment, while as for
the way he wasted his money it used to put me into such
a tweak that there were times when I didn't know how to
keep my tongue between my teeth! He never took thought
to the morrow, and nor did my poor dear mistress neither.
You never knew where you was, for there wouldn't be
enough money to buy one scraggy chicken in the market
one day, and the next he'd come in singing out that the
dibs was in tune, and not a thought in his head or my
mistress's but how to spend it quickest. Well, he told me
once that it was no use ringing a peal over him for going
to low gaming-houses, because he was born with a spring
in his elbow, and there was no sport in playing cards and
such in the regiment, for nearly all the officers was living
on their pay, same as he was himself. But this I will say
for him! There was never a sweeter-tempered nor a kinder-
hearted man alive!"

"Ay," had agreed Mr Nidd, rather doubtfully. "Though
it don't seem to me as he behaved very kind to Miss Kate,
leaving her like he done with a lot of debts to pay, and
nobbut his prize-money to do it with—what was left of it,
which, by what you told me, wasn't so very much neither."

"He always thought he'd win a fortune! And how was
he to know he was going to meet his end like he has? Oh,

Joe, I wish he'd been killed at Waterloo, for this is worse than anything! When I think of him that was always so gay, and up to the knocker, no matter whether he was plump in the pocket or regularly in the basket, being knocked down by a common tax-cart, well, it makes me thankful my poor mistress ain't alive to see it, which is a thing I never thought to be! And my lamb left alone, without a sixpence to scratch with, and she so devoted to her pa! I never ought to have married you, Joe, and it weighs on me that I let you wheedle me into it, for if ever Miss Kate needed me she needs me now!''

"I need you too, Sarey," had said Mr Nidd, with difficulty.

Observing the look of anxiety on his face, Sarah had mopped her eyes, and implanted a smacking kiss on his cheek, saying: "And a good, kind husband you are, Joe, and if there was more as faithful as what you proved yourself to be the world would be a better place!"

Colouring darkly, Mr Nidd had uttered an inarticulate protest, but this rare tribute from his sharp-tongued spouse had been well-earned. Falling deeply in love with a much younger Sarah, who had been on the eve of accompanying her mistress and her nursling to Portugal, and had rejected his offer, he had indeed remained faithful. Seven years later ("Just like Jacob!" had said Kate, urging her nurse to the altar), when Sarah had come back to England with her widowed master and his daughter, he had renewed his suit, and his constancy had been rewarded: Miss Sarah Publow had changed her name to Nidd, and had lost no time at all in assuming the control of her husband's family, and vastly improving their fortunes. Within a year, she had bullied and cajoled her aged father-in-law into spending his jealously hoarded savings on the acquisition of the inn which now provided the firm with spacious headquarters,

and had transformed it from a single carrier into an establishment which, if it did not yet rival Pickford's, was in a
fair way to providing Pickford's with some healthy com-
petition. Her husband adored her; his father, while losing
no opportunity to get the better of her, had been known to
inform his cronies at the Cock, when mellowed by a suf-
ficient quantity of what he inelegantly termed belly-juice,
that she was a sure card; his sisters wavered between in-
effective resentment of her managing disposition, and a
comfortable dependence on her willingness to assist them
in any difficulty; and his nephews, all as inarticulate as he
was himself, said simply that you wouldn't get a more
bangup dinner anywhere than what Aunt Sarey would give
you.

Even Miss Malvern, for all her four-and-twenty years,
turned instinctively to her in times of trouble, and was
insensibly reassured by her air of competence. Tucked now
into bed, told that there was no need to get into high fidgets, and adjured to go to sleep, she thought, snuggling into
the feathered softness, that perhaps she had allowed herself
to become too despondent, and that Sarah really did know
best.

But Sarah, stumping downstairs again to the kitchen,
was feeling far from competent; and although the dinner
she presently set before her husband, her father-in-law, one
of her nephews, and two of the lads employed in the stables, in no way betrayed her inward perturbation, she ate
very little of her own portion, and was a trifle short in her
responses to the remarks addressed to her. This circumstance did not escape the notice of Mr Nidd Senior, or of
Mr Nidd Junior, but when the younger Nidd, a simple-
minded soul, began anxiously to ask if anything were
amiss his more astute sire cut him short, adjuring him not
to be a jobbernoll, and enquiring affably of Sarah if it

wasn't Miss Kate he'd seen crossing the yard a while back.
"Which I hopes it was," he said, mopping up the gravy
on his plate with a large lump of bread, "for she's been
first-oars with me from the moment I clapped eyes on her,
and she's heartily welcome. A prettier gal I never did see,
and nothing niffy-naffy about her! Sweet as a nut, she is,
but for all she don't hold up her nose at folks like us she's
a proper lady, and don't you forget it, young Ted!" he
concluded, rounding suddenly on his grandson with such
ferocity that the hapless youth dropped his knife. "If you
was to behave disrespectful to her, I'd lay your back
open!"

Such was the awe in which his descendants held him
that Young Ted, a brawny giant, saw nothing absurd in
this threat, but informed him, in stammering haste, that
nothing was further from his intentions than to treat Miss
Kate with disrespect. He accepted this assurance, but
caused the two hirelings to quake by saying: "And as for
you, you'll keep out of her way! Couple of clod-crushers!"

At this point, Sarah intervened, telling her father-in-law
that there was no call for him to rake the poor lads down,
and providing them with generous portions of apple-pie.
She spoke sharply, but she was not unappreciative of the
tribute he had paid her darling; and when the younger
members of the party had withdrawn, and Mr Nidd had
bade her empty her budget, she said in a much milder tone:
"Well, I don't mean to fall into the dismals, but I am in
a worry, Father: that I can't deny."

"Ah!" said Mr Nidd. "On account of Miss Kate. I sus-
picioned as much. What brought her back to Lunnon in
such a crack? Not but what you don't have to tell me,
because I ain't a cod's head! Someone's tried to give her
a slip on the shoulder, which is what I thought would happen, for it stands to reason a spanking beauty like she is,

which is allowed by them as should have known better to
go jauntering round the country unbefriended, is bound to
find herself in the briars.''

"Yes! And well I know it!'' cried Sarah, stung by this
palpable dig at herself. ''But what could I do, when her
mind was made up, and she was as poor as a Church rat?
I thought she'd be safe with that Mrs Astley!''

"That's where you was a woolly-crown, my girl,'' said
Mr Nidd, with a certain amount of satisfaction. ''Because
if Mrs Astley's husband is a rabshackle—''

"It wasn't him!'' interrupted Sarah, very much flushed.
"He behaved very proper to Miss Kate! It was Mrs Astley's brother! And he don't seem to have been a rabshackle, though he'd no business to go trying to kiss Miss Kate!
He made her an offer!''

"Now, that,'' said Mr Nidd, ''is something like! What
Miss Kate wants is a husband!''

"You needn't think I don't know that, Father! If this
young Grittleton had taken her fancy I'd have thanked God
on my knees, for all she'd have been demeaning herself,
she being above the Astleys' cut, but she didn't. A moon-
calf is what she says he is.''

"Well, such ain't a particle of use to her,'' said Mr
Nidd, abandoning interest in young Grittleton. ''What is
she meaning to do now, Sarey?''

"Hire herself out as a common abigail!'' replied Sarah
bitterly.

At this disclosure, the younger Mr Nidd looked very
much shocked, and said that she must not be allowed to
do it. He added diffidently: ''If she'd lower herself to live
here, with you to take care of her, we'd be proud to have
her, wouldn't we, Father?''

"It's no matter what we'd be: it wouldn't fit!'' responded Mr Nidd unhesitantly. ''If you'd ever had any

wits I'd be wondering where they'd gone a-begging! How I come to have a son that was no better than a chawbacon is something I'll never know, not if I live to be a hundred!''

"No! Nor I'll never know how you came to have a son with such a good heart!" snapped Sarah, rising instantly to Joe's defence. A mumbled remonstrance from him caused her to pat his hand, and to say in a mollified tone: "I'm sure I don't want to offend you, Father, but I won't have you miscalling Joe. Not but what he's right, Joe: it *wouldn't* fit! But how to stop her doing what's beneath her I don't know! Perhaps your father does, so long-headed as he is!''

"You can lay your life I do!" said Mr Nidd, a gleam of triumph in his eye. "To think I've a longer head than you, Sarey! What Miss Kate's got to have is a home with her own kin.''

"Ay! she did ought to have that!" agreed his son, much struck by this display of wisdom.

"I said it when the Major took and died, and I'll say it again," pursued Mr Nidd. "Her relations ought to be wrote to. And don't you pitch me any gammon about her not having none, like you did afore, Sarey, because it's hornswoggle! We all got kin of some sort.''

"Yes," said Sarah slowly. "But there's none left on my mistress's side but her sister, and if she'd lift a finger to help Miss Kate she's mightily changed since I knew her! What's more, Miss Kate wouldn't have anything to say to that set, nor I wouldn't wish her to, the way they behaved to her mama! I don't say she hasn't maybe got some cousins, but I don't know who they are, or where they live, or anything about them. And as for the Major, I never heard tell of any relations other than his half-sister, and he paid no more heed to her than she did to him. She married a titled gentleman that had a place called Staplewood, which made the Major laugh out when he read about it, telling my mistress that there was never anyone more ambitious than his sister, and the only thing that surprised him was that she was content with a baronet, instead of having set her cap at a Duke, or a Marquis, or some such. Still, I fancy he must be a high-up baronet, because the Major said: 'Well done, Minerva! Broome of Staplewood, no less!' And my mistress told me that it was a very old family, that had lived at this Staplewood since I don't know when, and all as proud as peacocks. But I don't know where it may be, nor it wouldn't signify if I did, for the Major said his sister had risen quite beyond his touch now, and if he got more than a common bow from her, if ever they was to meet again, he'd have nothing more to do than bless himself for his good fortune, supposing he didn't suffer a palsy-stroke!'' Her eyes filled. She wiped away the sudden tears, saying: ''He was always so full of fun and gig, poor dear gentleman! Whenever I think of the way— But it's no manner of use thinking of what's done, and can't be undone! The thing is that it isn't to be expected that *she'd* do anything to help Miss Kate, when she'd got to be too proud to behave civil to her own brother. Besides, I don't know where she lives!''

''That don't signify,'' said Mr Nidd impatiently. ''There's books as will tell you where the nobles and the landed gentry lives! Ah, and there's directories, too! What I'm thinking is that a starched-up lady wouldn't wish for her niece to be hiring herself out like Miss Kate means to— Now, what's the matter with you, Joe?''

The younger Mr Nidd, who had been sitting with his brow furrowed in painful cogitation, opening his mouth as if to speak, and shutting it again, gulped, and answered diffidently that he rather thought he did know.

"Know what?" demanded his progenitor irascibly.

"Staplewood," produced Joe. "Ay, that was it! Market Harborough! Leastways, it ain't there, but nearby, seemingly. Because the orders was to set the pack-case down at the Angel. Likely they would ha' sent in a cart, or a farm-wagon, maybe, to fetch it. I disremember what it was, but I got it in my head it was a *big* pack-case, such as you could put a pianny into—though I don't know it *was* a pianny, mind!"

"No, and it don't make any odds if it was a kitchen stove!" said Mr Nidd. "All we want to know—"

"You've hit it, Dad!" uttered Joe, his frown banished by a broad grin. "If you aren't a one!" he said, in affectionate admiration. "A Bodley Range, tha's what it was! It come back to me the moment you said *stove!*"

Mr Nidd cast his eyes upwards in entreaty. "Don't heed him, Sarey!" he begged. "He always was a knock-in-the cradle, and he always will be! What you got to do is to write a letter to Miss Kate's aunt, telling her as how Miss Kate's left properly in the basket, and meaning to get herself hired as a housemaid, or a shopwoman, very likely. You want to tell her who you are, and how the Major was took off sudden, which she maybe don't know, but mind you don't run on like a fiddlestick! If you was to cross your lines, it's ten to one she wouldn't be able to read 'em; and if you was to take a second sheet she'd have to pay for it, which is a thing that might get up her back, same as it would anyone's."

"But, Father!" protested Sarah. "I don't know if it would do any *good!*"

"No, and no more I don't neither," conceded Mr Nidd graciously. "There's no saying, howsever, but what it might, and if it don't it won't do no harm. You do like I tell you, my girl, and don't start in to argufy! I'll allow you got more rumgumption than most females, but you ain't got so much in your nous-box as what I have, and don't you think it!''

Chapter Two

The letter was written, and (under the direction of Mr Nidd, a severe critic) rewritten, but not without misgiving. Sarah knew very well how much Miss Kate would dislike it, and she was thereafter torn between the hope that it would win response from Lady Broome, and the dread that it would bring her under Miss Kate's displeasure. However, her father-in-law read her a lecture on the evil consequences of shrinking from one's duty, stood over her while she folded the single sheet, sealed it with a wafer, and laboriously inscribed it to Lady Broome, and then wrested it away from her, telling her that if Miss Kate nabbed the rust he would talk to her himself.

"I hope and trust you'll do no such thing, Father!" said Sarah, who viewed with disapproval, and a certain amount of apprehension, his predilection for Kate's society.

"Don't you get into a fuss!" recommended Mr Nidd. "There's no call for neither of us to say a word to her until you gets an answer to this letter; and if you don't get one she won't never know anything about it! And you don't need to worrit yourself every time her and me has a poker-talk!" he added, with asperity. "Her and me goes on very comfortable together."

"Yes, Father, I know!" Sarah said hastily. "But you do say such things!"

"I'll be bound she don't hear no worse from me than what she's heard from them soldiers of her pa's!" retorted Mr Nidd.

This being unarguable, Sarah subsided, and when she begged Kate not to encourage him to intrude upon her, boring her with his pittle-pattle, Kate merely laughed, and replied that she much enjoyed his visits to the parlour. "I like him!" she said. "As for *boring,* he keeps me in whoops, for he *is* such a funny one! He gives me very good advice, too, I promise you! *And* some scolds." Her eyes danced. "He says that I shall be no better than a nick-ninny if I leap at the first chance that offers, like a cock at a blackberry! Not that any has offered, alas! I ventured to ask him if cocks *do* leap at blackberries, but he said, without a moment's hesitation, that addle-brained ones do! He thinks, too, that I should be ill-advised to seek employment with a milliner, or a dressmaker, which was something that did occur to me, because I do know how to make stylish dresses, and I *can* fashion hats and bonnets, can't I, Sarah?"

Horrified to discover that her father-in-law's prophecy was already in a fair way to being fulfilled, Sarah said: "Yes, Miss Kate, but it wouldn't do—I promise you it wouldn't do!"

"Well, that's what Mr Nidd says. He says it would be the merest drudgery, unless I had the money to set up an establishment of my own, which, of course, I haven't." She wrinkled her brow. "He doesn't seem to think I could become a dresser either. I must own that that hips me a little—but perhaps he may be wrong!"

"No, dearie, he's right!" said Sarah emphatically. "Now, my precious one, you don't want to fall into despair just because that Mrs Lasham which you was sent to didn't engage you!''

''No,'' agreed Kate, a little forlornly. ''Well, to own the truth, Sarah, I don't *wish* to be a governess!'' She smiled, seeing the anxious look on Sarah's face, and added: ''I *will* be one, if I can find someone to hire me, but I am not at all like you, you know! You will be quite shocked, I daresay, but I think it a dead bore to be obliged to devote myself to children! Particularly other people's odiously spoilt brats!'' she added, with feeling.

''You won't think them a dead bore when they are your own, love,'' suggested Sarah fondly.

''Perhaps I might not. But I daresay we shall never know, for it is excessively unlikely that I shall be married,'' said Kate, not in a complaining spirit, but as one dispassionately considering the probabilities. Sarah cried out upon her, but she shook her head. ''Well, it's true that Grittleton offered for me, but he didn't in the least wish to, and I don't fancy he would have if Mr Astley hadn't given him such a trimming. And, of course, I did have offers when I was young. But—''

''Whatever next?'' exclaimed Sarah. ''When you were young, indeed! Why, you're no more than a baby now, Miss Kate!''

''But I'm not a baby, Sarah: I am four-and-twenty, and if I had had a come-out, in the ordinary way, this would be my *fifth* season, and everyone would be saying that I was an ape-leader!''

''Well, they wouldn't, because you'd have been married long since, miss! As for the offers you had when the Major was alive, a very good thing you didn't accept any of them, for they was none of them what your ma would have called eligible! Besides, you wouldn't have left the Major!''

Kate considered this, a rather rueful smile twisting her

lips. "You know, Sarah, I'm not such a saint as you choose to suppose! I think I might have left him, if I had formed a strong attachment. But I never have done so, and very likely I never will, which is a very good thing, because although Johnny Raws, like Grittleton, may want to kiss me, when it comes to marriage they wish for a girl with a dowry. Oh, don't look like that! *Pray* do not! It isn't a great tragedy, and I promise you I am not the victim of a blighted romance!" She gave a chuckle. "I'll even engage myself never to become one! Indeed, I don't think I could, for my disposition is *not* romantical! Oh, dear, I wish I were a man—or that females were permitted to engage in gainful occupations that are not of a domestic nature! I can't think of any, for it is useless to suppose that I might suddenly become a great singer, or write books, or even paint. Isn't it a lowering thought? Unless— Sarah, do you think I might become an actress? That would be something indeed!"

Since Sarah regarded all actresses as abandoned, this suggestion sank her spirits so low that she actually appealed to Mr Nidd to exert his influence over the orphan. He told her never to fear, but, as she knew how much there was to fear, this large reassurance quite failed to allay her anxiety. The stage now joined servants' halls and modistes' workrooms in the nightmares which rendered sleep hideous, for Kate, in her reluctant endeavour to obtain another governess's situation, was meeting with rebuffs. *Too Young!* was what prospective employers said, but Sarah knew that *Too Pretty!* was what they meant, particularly those whose families included sons of marriageable age. And you couldn't blame them, thought Sarah, thrown into deeper gloom, for anyone prettier, or with more taking ways, than Miss Kate would be hard to find. Not only Mr Nidd's three grandsons, but the stable-boys too, and even

Old Tom, who was notoriously cross-grained, and had charge of the stables, made cakes of themselves about her! "What," demanded Sarah of her sympathetic but speechless spouse, "is to become of her, if her aunt don't pay any heed to my letter? That's what I want to know!"

No answer, beyond a doubtful shake of the head, was forthcoming, but the question was rendered supererogatory, some ten days later, by the arrival, in an ordinary hack, of Lady Broome.

Mr Nidd, enjoying the spring sunshine at his favourite post of vantage on the balcony, observed the approach of this vehicle with only mild interest; but when a tall, fashionably dressed lady stepped down from it, and sought in her reticule with one elegantly gloved hand for her purse, he cast aside the shawl which was protecting his aged legs from quite a sharp wind, and nipped with surprising agility into the house, to give Sarah forewarning of the arrival of Miss Kate's aunt.

Emerging from the kitchen, with a rolling-pin in her hand and her arms generously floured, Sarah gasped: *"Never!"*

"Well, we ain't looking for no duchess to come a-visiting us, so if it ain't a duchess it's my Lady Broome!" replied Mr Nidd tartly. "Bustle about, my girl! She's paying off the jarvey, but she don't look to me like one as'll stand higgling over the fare, so you'd do well to stir your stumps!"

The advice was unnecessary: Sarah was already in the kitchen again, stripping off her apron; and, within a few moments of hearing the knocker, she was opening the door to her visitor, looking as trim as wax, and in very tolerable command of herself.

An imposing figure confronted her, that of a tall, handsome woman, wearing a velvet pelisse, bordered with sable, and carrying a huge sable muff. A close hat, of bronze-green velvet to match her pelisse, and trimmed with a single curled ostrich plume, was set upon a head of exquisitely dressed dark hair; her gloves were of fine kid; and her velvet half-boots, like her hat, exactly matched her pelisse. Her countenance was arresting, dominated by a pair of brilliant eyes, in colour between blue and gray, and set under strongly marked brows. Her features were very regular, the contour of her face being marred only by the slight heaviness of her lower jaw, and rather too square a chin. She looked to be about forty years of age; and, at first glance, Sarah found her intimidating. Her smile, however, was pleasant, and her manners, while plainly those of a lady of quality, were neither high nor imposing, but at once kind and gracious. She said, with a faint smile, and in a voice more deeply pitched than the average: "Good-morning! I am Lady Broome. And you, I think, must be Miss Sarah Nidd. Or should it be Mrs Nidd?"

"Mrs Nidd, if your ladyship pleases," said Sarah, dropping a curtsy.

"I beg your pardon! I have come—as you have guessed—in response to your letter, for which I am very much obliged to you. I was unaware of my brother's death, or of the uncomfortable circumstances in which my poor little niece finds herself. May I see her?"

"Yes, indeed, my lady!" replied Sarah, holding the door wide, and dropping another curtsy. "That is, she isn't here, not just at the moment, but I expect her to be back any minute. If your ladyship would condescend to step upstairs to the parlour, you will be quite private there, for only Miss Kate uses it."

"Thank you. And if you will bear me company I am persuaded you will be able to tell me a great deal about which I might hesitate to question Miss Kate for fear of

embarrassing her. You must know that since my brother's
unhappy estrangement from the family we lost sight of
each other: indeed, I was barely acquainted with him, for
there was considerable disparity of age between us. You
wrote of his death as of recent date: I collect it was not
the result of a military action?''

''No, my lady,'' Sarah replied, leading her up the stairs,
and throwing open the parlour door. ''He'd sold out,
which, at the time I was glad of, thinking it was time, and
more, that he settled down. On account of Miss Kate, my
lady—but I should have known better!''

''He did not, in fact?'' said Lady Broome, sitting down
in one of the chairs which flanked the fireplace, and indicating, with a smile and a gesture, that Sarah should
follow her example.

Sarah obeyed, but with a little reluctance, choosing the
extreme edge of the chair to sit on. ''No, my lady, he
didn't. And it's my belief he never would have, even if
he'd won a fortune, like he said he would, because he was
a gamester, ma'am, and I've often heard it said that such
can't be cured. He was knocked down by a common tax-
cart, and hit his head on the kerbstone, being not—not
tosticated, but—but muddled!''

Lady Broome nodded understandingly. ''And Miss
Kate's mother, I think you wrote, died some years previously? Poor child! Were her maternal relatives informed
of this sad event?''

''Yes, my lady, they was!'' said Sarah, her eyes kindling. ''Being as how I was Mrs Malvern's abigail before
ever she eloped with the Major—not that he was a Major
in those days!—I took the liberty of writing a letter to her
papa, but I never had an answer. I wouldn't wish to speak
ill of the dead, and dead both he and my mistress's mama
are, but it's my belief they didn't neither of them care a

straw what became of her, nor of Miss Kate! And as for
Miss Emily, that was my mistress's sister, she's as full as
a toad is of poison, my lady, *as* I know, and I wouldn't
write to her, not for a fortune!''

"Well, I am very glad you wrote to me, Mrs Nidd,"
Lady Broome said. "I shall certainly not permit my
brother's child to engage on any menial occupation—for
such, from what I have observed, seems to be the fate of
governesses!''

"Yes, my lady, and there's worse to be feared!" said
Sarah eagerly.

"Tell me!" invited her ladyship, so sympathetically that
Sarah plunged straightway into an account of the dire
schemes which had entered Kate's head.

In the middle of this recital, Kate came into the room,
pausing on the threshold, and looking in bewilderment
from her aunt to her nurse. "Mr Nidd—Mr Nidd tells
me—that my *aunt* has come to visit me!" she stammered.
"But I don't understand! *Are* you my aunt, ma'am? How
did you— Sarah! This must be your doing! How *could*
you?''

Lady Broome broke into a deep laugh, and rose, casting
aside her muff, and advancing with her hands held out.
"Oh, you *pretty* child!" she said caressingly. "Why, Mrs
Nidd, you didn't prepare me for such a little piece of perfection! My dear, I am happy to be able to tell you that I
am your Aunt Minerva.''

She folded Kate in her arms as she spoke, and lightly
kissed her cheek. Overwhelmed, Kate felt herself obliged
to yield to that soft embrace, but the look she cast Sarah
was one of deep reproach. This made Lady Broome laugh
again, giving her a little shake, and saying, in a quizzical
tone: "Was it so dreadful of Mrs Nidd to have written to

me? I promise you, *I* don't think so! She told me something I never knew before: that I had a niece!''

"Only—only a half-niece, ma'am!" Kate faltered. "And one who has no claims upon you!"

"Ah, you don't understand! How should you, indeed? You are too young to know what it means to have been an only child, when you reach my age, and have no close relations, and no daughter! I have always longed for one, and never more so than now! It's true I have a son, but a boy cannot give one the same companionship. Dear child, I've come to carry you off to Staplewood! I'm persuaded I must be your natural guardian!''

"But I am of age, ma'am!" protested Kate, feeling as though she were being swept along on an irresistible tide.

"Yes, so your kind nurse has informed me. I can't *compel* you—heaven forbid that I should—but I can beg you to take pity on a very lonely woman!''

At this point, Sarah, perceiving that her nursling was much shaken, effaced herself with a murmured excuse. Kate said: "You are very good, ma'am—Aunt! I am *excessively* grateful, but I couldn't—no, I *couldn't*—subsist on your generosity! Why, you know nothing about me— you might even take me in dislike!''

"So I might," agreed Lady Broome, looking amused. "So might you take me in dislike! If that were to happen there would be nothing for it but to part. You wouldn't be my prisoner, you know! Come! Let us sit down, and talk the matter over! You must tell me, if you please, how in the world you come to be unmarried, for it seems to me to be quite extraordinary. Your mama must have been very beautiful; I don't remember my brother very clearly, but I don't think you resemble him much, do you?''

"No," admitted Kate, blushing faintly. "That is, I was

thought to favour my mother, but she was *much* more beautiful than I am.''

"And she died when you were twelve? Poor child! I wish I might have known, but I was still in the schoolroom when my brother married her, and only a child when he first joined, so that he was almost a stranger to me. Do you blame me for not having tried, in later years, to better my acquaintance with him? Pray do not!''

"Oh, no!'' Kate said. "He did not, either.'' She glanced up into that handsome countenance, a tiny crease between her brows, and in her eyes a doubtful question. "*Don't* you remember him, ma'am? He remembered you!''

"Very likely: he was six-and-twenty when I was six-teen. I only wish he may have remembered something to my credit, but when I look back upon myself I realize that at that age I must have been a detestable girl, with a very good conceit of myself, and my head stuffed with every sort of ambitious notion, from making a brilliant marriage to winning the admiration of all by some improbable deed of heroism! I fear my governess was to blame: she was much addicted to reading sentimental romances, and she permitted me to do so too.''

Kate smiled, reassured. "Papa did say that you were very ambitious,'' she admitted.

"He might well! I hope he knew that I outgrew such nonsense, and instead of marrying a Prince or a Duke fell in love with my dear Sir Timothy. I must tell you, my dear, that *he* was almost as pleased as I was when he learned of your existence. He would have accompanied me to London if I had allowed him to do so, but I was obliged to forbid it. You see, I have to take great care of him: he doesn't enjoy good health, and the journey would have quite knocked him up. So he charged me with a message, that a warm welcome awaits you at Staplewood.''

"How kind—how *very* kind he must be!" Kate exclaimed, much moved. "Pray tell him how grateful I am, ma'am! But—"

"No, no, let us have no buts!" interrupted Lady Broome. "You shall come to Staplewood on a visit merely. You can have no objection to spending a month or two in the country. Then, if you are still determined to seek another situation, I must try if I can find one for you." She smiled at Kate's quick look of enquiry. "Yes, I can, you know—and a better one than you could discover for yourself. However, we shan't think of that yet. In another fortnight we shall be in May, and must hope that this odiously sharp wind will have blown itself out. Ah, you can't conceive of any place more beautiful than Staplewood in summer!"

It was too tempting; it would be too churlish to refuse. Kate stammered her thanks, was silenced, and found herself listening to a description of the household.

"Sir Timothy," said Lady Broome, "is many years older than I am, and has become very frail. I am his second wife, you must know, and my son, Torquil, is his only surviving child. He is some years younger than you." She hesitated, looking all at once a little stern; then she sighed, and continued quietly: "I am sorry to say that his constitution is sickly. It has never been possible to send him to school. He is under the care of Dr Delabole, who also attends Sir Timothy, and lives with us. So you see, my dear, why I have so much wished for a daughter! I am a very lonely woman."

Feeling all the embarrassment of one made the recipient of such a confidence, Kate murmured: "Yes. I mean, I see!"

Lady Broome leaned forward to pat her hand. "You don't of course, but never mind! you will! Now, we must decide, must we not, what it will be proper to pay your nurse for having housed you. Do you think—''

''Oh, no!'' Kate exclaimed, recoiling. ''No, no, ma'am! I beg you will not offer Sarah money! I shall give them all presents—Joe, and Mr Nidd, and the nephews as well!—but I must pay for them out of my own savings!''

''Very well!'' said her ladyship, rising, and drawing her pelisse about her again, and buttoning it at the throat. Her eyes ran over her niece; she smiled, and held out a gloved hand. ''*Au revoir,* then! I am putting up at the Clarendon. You will take a hackney coach, and join me there tomorrow: it is understood? Good! Now, do you think that Joe, or Mr Nidd, or even one of the nephews, could procure me a hack?''

''Yes, ma'am, on the instant!'' replied Kate, starting up from her chair, and running to the door. ''Only wait, I do implore you!''

Pausing merely to cram a hat over her dusky locks, and to huddle a cloak about her person, she darted down the stairs, and out into the yard, to be pulled up in her tracks by Mr Nidd, who, from his vantage-point on the balcony, saw her, and briskly commanded her to stop. Rising, not without difficulty, from his seat, he adjured her not to be a hoyden, but to come back into the house this instant. ''Ah, *I* know!'' he said. ''Going to summon a hack, ain't you? Well, you won't, see? You'll leave that to them as is better able than you to do it, my girl! Back with you into the house, miss! And take that nasty hat off your head!''

''It is not a nasty hat!'' retorted Kate indignantly.

But, as Mr Nidd had dived through a doorway out of sight, this reply fell on the ambient air; and a few minutes later Old Tom came grumbling out of the stables, and hobbled across the yard to the gateway.

"Oh, *Tom!*" uttered Kate, in remorseful accents.

"You let him be!" said Mr Nidd, emerging from the stables behind him. "Joe and Jos and Ted being gone off with loads, there ain't nobody but that gormless hunk, Will, in the stables, and likely he'd come back with the oldest hack in the rank. You get back up them stairs, missy, and go on gabbing to her ladyship!"

This, however, proved to be unnecessary, her ladyship having descended the stairs, and penetrated to the kitchen, where she found Sarah testing the heat of the oven with her hand, prior to inserting a large steak pie. "Oh, don't let me disturb you, Mrs Nidd!" she begged. "Dear me, how cosy it is in here, and *what* a good smell! I shall sit down on this chair, and watch you." She seated herself as she spoke and smiled graciously at her hostess. "Well! You will be happy to know that I have prevailed upon Miss Kate to pay us a long visit," she disclosed. "I wonder would you be good enough to let me know her measurements? And the colours she prefers? Ah, thank you! What forethought!"

She stretched out her hand, and Sarah put the list into it, looking frowningly at her. It seemed to Sarah that she had taken possession of the house; and the feeling that her mantle was cast over its inmates, and even over the stables, grew upon her, and could not be shaken off. You couldn't say that she was condescending, for she was very affable. Patronage! That's what it was: my lady stooping from her height to be kind to a carrier's wife! No doubt she would be just as kind to Joe, and would laugh easily at Mr Nidd's sallies. She was putting the paper away in her reticule, and had drawn out her purse. Sarah stiffened, but she only selected half-a-crown from amongst the coins it contained, and laid it on the table. "Will you give that to the stable-boy who has gone to summon up a hackney coach for me?'' she asked.

Sarah nodded, still frowning. But Kate looked in at that moment, seeking her aunt, and, at sight of her, said gaily: ''Why, ma'am, when I couldn't find you in the parlour I made up my mind to it that I had dreamt the whole!'' She saw Sarah's worried expression, and said, with a droll look: ''Oh, faithless one! I'll never forgive you! Or shall I? Yes, perhaps I shall! I can't tell! Aunt Minerva, Tom has procured a hack for you, and it is waiting in the yard.''

''Then you shall escort me to it,'' responded Lady Broome, rising, and holding out her hand to Sarah. ''I'll take my leave of you, Mrs Nidd. I daresay it may be impossible for you to get away, but if you *can* contrive to do so I hope I need not tell you that you will be welcome at Staplewood?''

''No, my lady,'' replied Sarah, with a slight curtsy. ''Oh, dear me, no!''

Lady Broome then preceded her niece out of the kitchen. Five minutes later, Kate came back, her eyes dancing, and her cheeks aglow. She clasped Sarah round the waist, and hugged her. ''Oh, Sarah, I've thrown my cap over the windmill, and whether I'm glad, or whether I'm sorry, I don't know, but I think I'm glad! To own the truth, it has been a struggle to know how to support my spirits, for the very thought of another situation as governess sinks me into gloom! Particularly now, when you have petted and cosseted me so much. Yes, but I'm a little frightened as well. How shall I go on in such a house as Staplewood seems to be? The Astleys' was nothing to it, I feel sure! There will be a butler, of course, and—do you think footmen?''

''Not more than two,'' answered Sarah decidedly. ''That's supposing there's an under-butler, which it's likely there will be. The housekeeper, her ladyship's dresser, the stillroom-maid, and four or five housemaids: that's all that need concern you, miss, or it's not to be expected that you'll have much to do with the gardeners, nor the grooms. When are you to go?''

"Tomorrow! At least, I am to join my aunt at the Clarendon tomorrow.'' She put up her chin, allowed her eyelids to droop, and said languidly: "I shall be spending the night at the Clarendon, Sarah: be good enough to pack my trunk!''

"You may be sure I will!'' replied Sarah grimly.

"You will not!'' cried Kate, abandoning her haughty pose.

"Indeed and I shall! Now, give over, Miss Kate! Who packed your trunk when you went to the Astleys, pray? I must get up your best muslin, too—which reminds me that you need to put fresh ribbons on it!'' She bustled across the room to the dresser, and took her purse out of one of its drawers. "Take this, love, and go and buy yourself some! Dinner won't be ready for above an hour yet, so you've plenty of time.''

Kate put her hands behind her back, vigorously shaking her head. "I'll go, but I won't take your purse. I have a *great* deal of money in my own—so much, in fact, that I shan't grudge the expense of a hack to Bedford House!''

"Did her ladyship give it to you?'' demanded Sarah.

"No, I saved it!'' said Kate, laughing, and backing to the door. "No, Sarah, no! I've had too much from you already. Keep some dinner for me, won't you?''

She vanished through the doorway, and was not seen again until nearly five o'clock, when a hack deposited her in the yard, laden with packages.

"Well!'' said Sarah. "A fine time to come home to

dinner this is, miss! And what may you have been wasting your money on, if you please?''

"I haven't wasted it—at least, I do hope I have not!" replied Kate, spilling her parcels on to the kitchen-table. "That one is for you, and this is a pipe for Joe, and—oh, goodness, where is the snuff-box I bought for Mr Nidd? It isn't *that*, or *that*—oh, I put it in my reticule, to be safe! Tell me, Sarah, do you think Jos will like—why, *Sarah—!*"

"I can't help it," sobbed Sarah, from behind her apron. "To think of you flinging your money away, and you with so little! Oh, you naughty girl, how could you? Didn't you buy nothing for yourself? Oh, I can't bear it!"

"But of course I did! Ribbon trimmings, just as you bade me, and—oh, all manner of things, to furbish me up a trifle!" said Kate merrily. "Sarah, do, pray, stop napping your bib!"

This had the desired effect. Sarah dropped her apron, ejaculating: "Miss Kate! How dare you? Where did you learn that nasty, vulgar expression? Not that I need to ask you! From Father, I'll be bound!"

"Not a bit of it! From Tom!"

"Oh, you did, did you? And how many times have I told you not to go near the stables, miss? Yes, and I'll tell you something else, which is that if you talk like that at Staplewood you'll be back here in the twinkling of a bed-post!"

"Yes, Sarah!" said Kate meekly. She tore the wrapping from the largest of her parcels, shook out the Paisley shawl it contained, and swept it round her nurse. "There! Please say you like it!" she coaxed, kissing Sarah's cheek. "It comes to you with my love, dearest."

Mr Nidd, entering the kitchen some minutes later, was revolted to find his daughter-in-law peacocking about (as he phrased it) in a handsome shawl, and instantly demanded to be told what she thought she was a-doing of, dressed-up like Christmas beef.

"Oh, Father, Miss Kate has given it to me!" said Sarah, dissolving again into tears. "The very thing I always wanted!"

"Ho!" said Mr Nidd. "I might ha' known it! Flashing the rags all over! Soon as I see her trapesing off, I says to myself: *Wasting the ready! that's what she's a-going to do!*"

"Did you indeed?" said Kate. "Well, in that case I won't give you your snuff-box, Mr Nidd!"

"You've never gone and bought me a snuff-box, miss?" he said incredulously. "You're gammoning me!"

"See if I am!" challenged Kate, holding the box out to him.

"Well, dang me!" said Mr Nidd, accepting it in one gnarled hand, and subjecting it to a close inspection. "Silver!" he pronounced, much gratified. "Well, I'm sure I thank you very kindly, miss—very kindly indeed I thank you! Ah, and whenever I helps meself to a pinch of merry-go-up out of this here box I shall think of you, and I can't say no fairer than that!"

Even Sarah felt that he had expressed his gratitude with rare grace. He then, and with great care, transferred the contents of his horn box into the new silver one, handing the old box to Sarah, with instructions to throw it away, since he had no further use for it. After that, he sallied forth, bound for his favourite hostelry, where, no one could doubt, he had every intention of offering his cronies pinches from his box. The discovery, later, that Kate had bestowed a handkerchief on his youngest grandson only abated his satisfaction for as long as it took him to assess the respective values of a silver snuff-box and what he designated a Bird's Eye Wipe.

Chapter Three

By five o'clock two days later, the chaise that bore Lady Broome, her niece, and her abigail, was nearing its destination, and her ladyship woke up. Miss Malvern, brighteyed and alert, had not slept, but had divided her time between reverently stroking the sleek ermine muff which Lady Broome had bestowed upon her, squinting down to admire the matching stole about her shoulders, observing with interest the country through which four fast horses were carrying her, and speculating on the sudden change in her fortunes.

From the moment of her arrival at the Clarendon Hotel, she felt that she had been pitchforked into another, and more affluent, world. Received with great civility, she was led upstairs to my lady's apartments, a large suite of rooms looking on to Albemarle Street, and welcomed affectionately by my lady, who kissed her, held her at arms' length, and exclaimed ruefully: "How *very* pretty you are! And what charming taste you have! I don't wonder at it that that horrid young man made up to you! Ah, Sidlaw, here she is—my little half-niece! My love, this is Sidlaw, my dresser, and once, like your Sarah, my nurse!"

Not for nothing had Miss Malvern spent six months in

a gentleman's establishment: Miss Sidlaw's mien might be forbidding, and her curtsy majestic, but Miss Malvern knew better than to offer her hand. She smiled, and acknowledged the curtsy with a gracious inclination of her head, well aware that by this manner of receiving an introduction she had risen from the status of Poor Relation to that of a Lady of the First Stare.

Dinner was served in my lady's private parlour: not a large dinner, but one of great elegance, beginning with a soup, going on with lobster, dressed in a sauce known only to Jacquard, reaching its climax in a capilotade of ducklings, and ending with a dish of peu d'amours. Miss Malvern, abandoning herself to the flesh-pots, enjoyed every mouthful.

While she ate, she lent an attentive ear to my lady's discourse, which was devoted to the glory of Staplewood and the Broomes. She learned that a Broome had been one of King James the First's braw new knights; and that ever since that day son had succeeded father in an unbroken line; she learned that while none had achieved fame, many had been distinguished; and she learned that each one had made it his business to enlarge, or to embellish, the original manor. Lady Broome promised to show her the sketches and plans of the house over more than two hundred years, adding: "My part—or, rather, Sir Timothy's—has been to improve the gardens, and to build a belvedere, commanding a view of the lake."

There was an appreciative twinkle in Kate's eye, but her aunt was choosing a peu d'amour, and she did not see it. It seemed to Kate that although Lady Broome might have outgrown a girlish desire to marry a Duke she still had her fair share of ambition. It was directed into worthier channels; her enthusiasm for the Broome family was certainly not assumed; and when she spoke of Staplewood it was with reverence, and a great deal of knowledge.

She sent Kate early to bed, warning her that she must be ready to start on the long journey at five in the morning. "You won't object to travelling all day, I hope? I don't care to be away from Sir Timothy for more than three nights—and I never sleep well in posting-houses."

"Of course I don't object, ma'am!" instantly responded Kate. "I have frequently travelled all day, in the Peninsula, and over shocking roads! In antiquated carriages, too, when I have had no horse to ride."

"Ah, I was forgetting! I am afraid parts of the road are very bad, but my chaise is particularly well-sprung, and I employ my own postilions. A sad extravagance, when I go about so little nowadays! But when one is obliged to travel without male escort trustworthy boys are a necessity. Now I am going to take you to your bedchamber, just to be sure that you have everything you want for the night."

She cast a keen, critical glance round this apartment, but Kate's gaze fell on the ermine stole and muff laid out on the bed, and remained riveted. "But—those aren't mine, ma'am!"

"What are not yours? Oh, the furs! Indeed they are! The first present I have ever given my niece: do you like them?"

"Oh, yes, yes, but—Aunt Minerva, I do thank you, but you mustn't crush me with benevolence!"

Lady Broome laughed. "Mustn't I? Foolish child, do you mean to throw them back at me?"

"No, I'm not so rag-mannered, and I like them too much!" said Kate naïvely, lifting the muff to her cheek. "Oh, how soft! How *rich!*"

She might have said the same about the chaise which bore her so swiftly north next morning, and did indeed say that so much unaccustomed luxury was putting quite unsuitable notions into her head. Lady Broome, with a significant glance at the back of Sidlaw's bonnet, smiled, but requested her not to talk nonsense. Sidlaw, occupying the unenviable forward seat, smiled too, but sourly. However, when my lady had fallen asleep, which she very soon did, and she heard herself addressed in a cautious undervoice, she unbent a little. "Tell me about Staplewood!" begged Kate. "You must know that I have spent almost all my life in the Peninsula, under the roughest conditions, and have never stayed in an English country house, or had a proper come-out, or—or anything! How shall I do?"

"You will do very well, miss—being as her ladyship has taken a fancy to you."

"I hope I may be worthy of her regard!"

"Yes, miss. My lady has had many crosses to bear."

"Does that signify that you hope I may not become another cross?"

After a moment's hesitation, Sidlaw replied, picking her words: "Oh, no, miss! Merely that you might disappoint her—but that I'm sure you won't do."

"I trust I shall not!"

"No, miss. My lady is kindness itself—to those she likes."

The inference was plain. Kate sat pondering it, a slight furrow between her brows. Instinct forbade her to enquire more closely, but the silence was broken by Sidlaw, who said: "I believe, miss—but I am not positive!—that my lady hopes you may provide Mr Torquil with the youthful companionship which he has missed, through no fault of his own."

The slowing down of the chaise as it approached the lodge-gates woke Lady Broome. She opened sleepy eyes, blinked them, and became aware of her surroundings. She sat up, gave her shoulders a little shake, and said: "So we arrive! My love, I do beg your pardon! So impolite of me to fall asleep! Ah, Fleet! You see me home again before you expected to! And is all well here? Very well? You relieve my mind! Go on, James!" She turned her head, and smiled at her niece. "This is Staplewood," she said simply.

The chaise bowled at a slackened pace through the park, allowing Kate plenty of time to see, and to admire. It had been a fine day, and the sun was setting redly. Kate's first view of the great house drew a gasp from her, not of admiration but of dismay, since it seemed to her for a moment, staring at the huge façade, whose numberless windows gave back the sun's dying rays in every colour of the spectrum, that the building was on fire. Shaken, but realizing that her aunt had not correctly interpreted her gasp, she murmured appreciation.

"Yes," said Lady Broome, in a purring voice that reminded Kate irresistibly of a large, sleek cat. "It *is* beautiful, isn't it?"

She put aside the rug that covered her legs as she spoke and prepared to alight from the chaise. A footman, hurrying out of the house, let down the steps, and offered his arm, and an elderly man, whose habit proclaimed his calling, bowed to her, and said: "Welcome home, my lady!"

"Thank you, Pennymore. Kate, dear child, you must let me make Pennymore known to you! Our good butler, who knew Staplewood before ever I did. How is Sir Timothy, Pennymore?"

"Quite well, my lady, and will be glad to see you home again. Mr Torquil too—as Dr Delabole will doubtless inform your ladyship."

She nodded, and led Kate into the house, saying: "You will think it difficult at first, I daresay, to find your way about, but you will soon grow accustomed. We are now in the Great Hall, and that is the Grand Stairway.''

''I can see that it is, ma'am,'' responded Kate. ''Very grand!'' She heard the sharp intake of breath behind her, and shot a mischievous look over her shoulder. The next instant, however, she had schooled her features into an expression of rapt interest, and was able to meet her aunt's eyes limpidly enough to allay suspicion.

Before Lady Broome could conduct her up the Grand Stairway to her bedchamber, a tall, Gothic door at one side of the Great Hall was opened, and an old gentleman came into the hall. His hair was white, his frame emaciated, and his skin the colour of parchment. His eyes struck Kate as the weariest she had ever seen; and when he smiled it was with an effort. He said, in a gentle voice: ''So you have brought her to Staplewood, Minerva? How do you do, my dear? I hope you will be happy with us.''

Taking the fragile hand he held out to her in her own warm clasp, she answered, smiling at him: ''Yes, sir, I hope so too. It won't be my fault if I am not.''

''Well, as it certainly won't be mine, you *will* be happy!'' said Lady Broome quizzically. ''Sir Timothy, I must take her up to her bedchamber! You, I see, have changed your dress, but *we,* I must inform you, are sadly travel-stained, and it wants but half an hour to dinner! Come, my love!''

Kate, meekly mounting the Grand Stairway in her aunt's wake, paused on the half-landing to look back. Below her lay the Great Hall, stone-paved, and hung with tapestries. A log-fire smouldered in the wide stone hearth, which was flanked by armoured figures, and surmounted by an arrangement of ancient weapons. A highly polished refectory-table supported a pewter dish; an oak coffer with brass hinges and locks, burnished till they shone, stood against one wall; an oak armoire against another; several high-backed chairs, also of oak, completed the furniture; the tall windows were hung with faded tapestry; and the Grand Stairway was black oak, uncarpeted. Kate, critically surveying the scene below her, found that her aunt was watching her, the corners of her mouth lilting upward.

"Well?" said Lady Broome. "What do you think of it?"

"It isn't very gay, is it?" replied Kate honestly. "Or even very cosy! No, I don't mean cosy, precisely—homelike!"

A chuckle from Sir Timothy brought her eyes to his face, a most mischievous twinkle in them. Lady Broome's triumphant smile vanished; she put up her brows, saying: "Cosy! Homelike? Not, perhaps, to our modern notions, but the Elizabethans would have found it so, I assure you."

"Ah, no, my love!" gently interpolated Sir Timothy. "The Elizabethans, whose taste was not to be compared with yours, would have covered the beams with paint, you know. My father had it stripped off when I was a boy." He added, dispassionately considering the tapestries: "And the hangings must have been very bright before the colours faded, and the gold threads became tarnished. *Eheu fugaces!*"

"My dear Sir Timothy, how absurd you are!" said Lady Broome, with an indulgent laugh. "Don't heed him, Kate! He delights in bantering me, because I care more for these things than he does."

She swept on up the stairs, and across the hall to a broad gallery, down which she led Kate. Opening one of the doors which gave access to it, she said archly, over her shoulder: "Now, pray don't tell me that you think this room unhomelike! I have taken *such* pains to make it pretty for you!"

"No, indeed!" exclaimed Kate, turning pink with pleasure. "I never saw a prettier room, ma'am! *Thank you!* A fire, too! Well, if this is the way you mean to use me you will never be rid of me! What can I do to repay so much kindness? I hope you will tell me!"

"Oh, you will find a great deal to do! But I don't wish to be rid of you. Good-evening, Ellen! This is Miss Kate, whom you are to wait upon. What have you put out for her to wear this evening?"

The young housemaid rose from her knees by Kate's trunk, and bobbed a curtsy. "If you please, my lady, the white muslin, trimmed with a double pleating of blue ribbon," she said nervously. "Being as it came first to hand!"

"Well, show it to me!" commanded Lady Broome, with a touch of impatience. She nodded at Kate. "A country girl! I hope you won't find her very stupid and clumsy." She surveyed the dress Ellen was holding up. "Yes, that will do very well. Put it down, and go and desire Sidlaw to give you the package I gave into her charge!"

"Yes, my lady!" said Ellen, curtsying herself out of the room.

"It is almost impossible to get London servants to come into the country," remarked Lady Broome. "When we gave up the London house I did make the experiment, but it didn't answer. They were for ever complaining that it was lonely, or that they dared not walk through the park after dark! Such nonsense! By the by, I do hope you are not nervous, my dear!"

"Oh, no, not a bit!" replied Kate cheerfully. "After all, I'm not at all likely to be snatched up by a party of guerrilleros, am I?"

"Extremely unlikely! Yes, that is the package, Ellen, but there is no need to enter the room as though you had been shot from a gun. My love, this is a shawl for you to put round your shoulders: I hope you will like it. I shall leave you now. When you are dressed, Ellen will show you the way to the Long Drawing-room.''

She moved towards the door, and paused before it, looking at Ellen with raised brows. With a gasp, the girl scurried to open it for her, curtsying yet again. Having carefully shut it, she turned, gulped, and said: ''If you please, miss, I haven't finished unpacking your trunk!''

''Well, you haven't had time, have you? Oh, pray don't keep on dropping curtsies! It makes me feel giddy! Have you found a pair of silk stockings yet? I think I should wear them, don't you?''

''Oh, yes, miss!''

''I bought them yesterday,'' disclosed Kate, rummaging through the trunk. ''My old nurse said it was a sinful waste of money, but I thought my aunt would expect me to have at least *one* pair. Here they are! The first I've ever had!''

''Oo, aren't they *elegant?*'' breathed Ellen, awed.

''Well, I think so! Tell me, how much time have I before dinner?''

''Only half an hour, miss. Being as it's half-past six, and dinner's at seven. Generally it's at six, but my lady had it put off, in case you'd be late. If you please, miss!''

Kate laid her furs down on the bed, and began to unbutton her pelisse, glancing thoughtfully round the room. ''It was very kind of her to make so many preparations for me,'' she said. ''Are those blinds new?''

''Yes, miss, *and* the bed-curtains, made to match!'' said Ellen, with vicarious pride. ''Such a time as we all had with them, Mrs Quedgeley, which is my lady's sewing-woman, saying as they couldn't be made up, not under a sennight! So we was all of us set to stitching, and Mrs

Thorne—that's the housekeeper, miss—read to us, to im-prove our minds.''

"Goodness! *Did* it improve your mind?"

"Oh, no, miss!" answered Ellen, shocked. "I didn't un-derstand it."

Kate laughed, tossing her hat on to the bed, and running her fingers through her flattened curls. "My aunt must have been very sure she would bring me back with her," she commented.

"Oh, yes, miss! Everything always has to be just as my lady says."

Kate did not reply to this, possibly because she was trying to unfasten her dress. Seeing her in difficulties re-called Ellen to a sense of her new duties, and she hurried to her assistance, even remembering, once Kate had stepped out of the dress, to pour warm water from a brass can into the flowered basin upon the wash-stand, and to direct her attention to the soap, which, she said simply, was a cake of my lady's own, from Warren's, with *ever* such a sweet scent.

Having washed her face and hands, Kate sat down at the dressingtable, in her petticoat, and vigorously brushed her hair, threading a ribbon through it, and twisting the ringlets round her fingers. Her handmaiden, watching with great interest, said: "Lor', miss! Is it *natural?*"

"Yes, quite natural!" Kate answered, amused. "Isn't it fortunate for me? Now, if you will do up my dress for me—oh, and open the package my aunt gave me!—Good God, what a beautiful shawl! It must be Norwich silk, surely!—Where is my trinket-box?" She dived into the trunk again, and dragged from its depths a small box, which she opened. After critically inspecting its contents, she selected a modest string of beads, and a posy-ring; and, having clasped the one round her throat, and slipped the other on her finger, disposed the shawl becomingly, and announced that she was now ready.

"Oh, miss, you do look a picture!" exclaimed her handmaiden involuntarily.

Heartened by this tribute, Kate drew a resolute breath, and stepped out into the corridor. She was led down it to the hall, and across this to a picture-gallery, where brocade curtains shrouded no fewer than fifteen very tall windows. Wax candles flickered in a number of wall-sconces, but did little to warm the gallery. Kate drew the shawl more closely about her shoulders, and was reminded of a draughty château near Toulouse, where she and her father had had the ill-fortune to be billeted for several weeks.

"This is the anteroom, miss!" whispered Ellen, opening a door, and walking across the room on tiptoe to where heavy curtains veiled an archway. She pulled one back a little way, signifying, with a jerk of her head and a frightened grimace, that Kate was to pass through the archway.

There were only two people in the Long Drawing-room, neither of whom was known to Kate. She hesitated, looking enquiringly from one to the other.

Standing before the fire was a well-preserved gentleman of uncertain age; and lounging on a sofa was the most beautiful youth Kate had ever seen. Under a brow of alabaster were set a pair of large and oddly luminous blue eyes, fringed by long, curling lashes; his nose was classic; his petulant mouth most exquisitely curved; and his pale golden hair looked like silk. He wore it rather long, and one waving strand, whether by accident or design, fell forward across his brow. He pushed it back with a slender white hand, and favoured Kate with the look of a sulky schoolboy.

His companion came forward, bowing, and smiling. "Miss Malvern, is it not? I must make myself known to you: I am Dr Delabole. Torquil, dear boy, where are your manners?''

This was uttered in a tone of gentle reproof, and had the effect of making Torquil get up, and execute a reluctant bow.

"How do you do?" said Kate calmly, putting out her hand. "I shan't eat you, you know!"

Light intensified in his eyes; he laughed delightedly, and took her hand, and stood holding it. "Oh, I like you!" he said impulsively.

"I'm so glad," responded Kate, making an attempt to withdraw her hand. His fingers closed on it with surprising strength. She was obliged to request him to let her go. "Even if you do like me!" she said, quizzing him.

The cloud descended again; he almost flung her hand away, muttering: "You don't like me!"

"Well, I find you excessively uncivil," she owned. "However, I daresay you are subject to fits of the sullens, and, of course, I don't know what may have occurred to put you out of temper."

For a moment it seemed as if he was furious; then, as he looked at her, the cloud lifted, and he exclaimed: "Oh, your eyes are laughing! Yes, I *do* like you. I'll beg your pardon, if you wish it."

"Torquil, Torquil!" said Dr Delabole, in an admonishing voice. "I am afraid, Miss Malvern, you find us in one of our twitty moods, eh, my boy?"

She could not help feeling that this was a tactless thing to have said; but before she could speak Sir Timothy, with her aunt leaning on his arm, had come into the room, and Lady Broome had exclaimed: "Oh, you are before me! Torquil, my son!" She moved forward, in a cloud of puce satin and gauze, holding out her hands to him. He took one, and punctiliously kissed it; and she laid the other upon his shoulder, compelling him (as it seemed to Kate) to salute her cheek. Retaining her clasp on his hand, she led him up to Kate, saying: "I will have no formality! Kate, my love, you will allow me to present you to your cousin Torquil! Torquil, Cousin Kate!"

Kate promptly sank into a deep curtsy, to which he responded with a flourishing bow, uttering: "Cousin Kate!"

"Cousin Torquil!"

"Dinner is served, my lady," announced Pennymore.

"Sir Timothy, will you escort Kate?" directed her ladyship. "She has yet to learn her way about!"

"It will be a pleasure!" said Sir Timothy, offering his arm with a courtly gesture. "A bewildering house, isn't it? I have often thought so. I should warn you, perhaps, that the food comes quite cold to table, the kitchens being most inconveniently placed."

Kate gave a gurgle of laughter, but Lady Broome, overhearing the remark, said: "Nonsense, Sir Timothy! When I have been at such pains to introduce chafing-dishes!"

"So you have, Minerva, so you have!" he replied apologetically.

The dining-room, which was reached by way of the picture-gallery, the Grand Stairway, a broad corridor, and an anteroom, was an immense apartment on the entrance-floor of the mansion, panelled in black oak, and hung with crimson damask. Several rather dark portraits did little to lighten it, all the light being shed from four branching chandeliers, which were set at intervals on the long, rather narrow table, on either side of a massive silver epergne. The chairs were Jacobean, with tall backs, upholstered in crimson brocade; and in the gloom that lay beyond the light Kate could dimly perceive a large sideboard.

"Not very homelike?" murmured Sir Timothy.

"Not like any home I was ever in, sir," she replied demurely.

Torquil, overhearing this as he took his seat beside her, said: "Bravo! Cousin Kate, Mama, has just said that this is not like any home she was ever in!"

Kate flushed vividly, and cast an apologetic look at Lady Broome, who, however, smiled at her, and said: "Well, I don't suppose it is, my son. Your cousin has spent her life following the drum, remember! She never knew *my* home. What have you before you, Sir Timothy? Ah, a cod's head! Give Kate some, but don't, I do implore you, place an eye upon her plate! Considered by many to be a high relish, but not by me!"

"Or by me!" said Torquil, shuddering. "I shall have some soup, Mama."

"Which leaves the cod's eyes to me, and to Sir Timothy!" said Dr Delabole. "*We* don't despise them, I promise you!"

Since he was seated opposite her, Kate was now at leisure to observe him more particularly. He was a large man, with a bland smile, and sufficiently well-looking to make the epithet *handsome,* frequently used to describe him, not wholly inapposite. He had very white hands, and his mouse-coloured hair was brushed into a fashionable Brutus; and while there was nothing in his attire to support the theory, he gave an impression of modishness. Perhaps, thought Kate, because his shirt-points, though of moderate height, were so exquisitely starched, and his neckcloth arranged with great nicety.

The cod's head was removed with a loin of veal; and the soup with a Beef Tremblant and Roots. Between them, side-dishes were set on the table: pigeons à la Crapaudine, petits pâtés, a matelot of eels, and a fricassée of chicken. Kate, partaking sparingly of the veal, in the foreknowledge that she would be expected to do justice to the second course, watched, with awe, Dr Delabole, who had already consumed a large portion of cod, help himself to two pigeons, and eat both, with considerable gusto.

The second course consisted of a green goose, two rabbits, a dressed crab, some broccoli, some spinach, and an apple pie. It occurred forcibly to Kate that Lady Broome's housekeeping was on a large scale. She was not so much impressed as shocked, for as one who knew that one skinny fowl could, skilfully cooked, provide a satisfying meal for three hungry persons, and who had seldom had more than a few shillings to spend on dinner, this lavishness was horrifying. Torquil had eaten two mouthfuls of the crab before pushing his plate away, peevishly saying that the crab was inedible, and toying with his apple pie; Sir Timothy, delicately carving a minute portion of rabbit for himself, had allowed her to place a spoonful of spinach on his plate, and then had left it untouched; Lady Broome, having pressed Dr Delabole to permit her to give him some of the goose, took a small slice herself; and Kate, resisting all coaxing attempts to make her sample the goose, ended the repast with the apple pie and custard. Throughout the meal, Lady Broome maintained a flow of small talk, and Dr Delabole one of anecdote. Sir Timothy, his world-weary eyes on Kate's face, talked to her of the Peninsular Campaign, to which she responded, at first shyly, and then, when he touched on battles that came within her adult memory, with animation. She drew a soft laugh from him when she described conditions in the Pyrenees, "when even Headquarters, which were at Lesaca, were—were *odious!*"

Torquil said curiously: "Were you there?"

"No, not at Lesaca," she replied, turning her head towards him, and smiling in her friendly way.

"Oh, I meant in the Peninsula!"

"Why, yes! You may say that I was bred in Portugal! Though, owing to the fact that I was only a child at the time, and was left with Mama and my nurse in Lisbon, I can't tell you anything about the retreat to Corunna. Indeed, the first campaign of which I have the smallest recollection is that of 1811, when Lord Wellington advanced from the Lines of Torres Vedras, and drove all before him, as far as to Madrid!"

"How much I envy you!"

"Do you? It was very uncomfortable, you know! And sometimes rather dangerous."

"I shouldn't care for that," he said, throwing a challenging look at his mother. "I bear a charmed life!"

"You talk a great deal of nonsense, my son," she said shortly, rising, and going to the door. One of the footmen opened it for her and she passed out of the room, followed by Kate, whose instinct bade her thank the man, but whose judgment forbade her to do so. She achieved a compromise between self-importance and the sort of familiarity she knew her aunt would deprecate, and smiled warmly up at him. He maintained his air of rigid immobility, but later rendered himself odious to his peers by saying that he knew quality when he saw it, and it didn't depend on a fortune, not by a long chalk it didn't, whatever ill-informed persons might suppose. "Sir Timothy's Quality," he said, pointing his knife at his immediate superior, and speaking a trifle thickly, "which you won't deny! And for why? Because he ain't so stiff-rumped that he won't thank you civil if you was to perform a service for him! And his lady ain't! For why? Because she's so top-lofty she don't so much as notice any of us servants! And that Dr Delabole ain't quality either, for *he* notices us too much! But Miss Kate *is!*"

Meanwhile, Kate, unaware of this encomium, had followed her aunt to the Yellow saloon, and was listening to her exposition of her son's character. According to Lady Broome, he had been (owing to his sickly childhood) too much indulged, to which circumstance must be attributed his every fault. "You won't heed him, I know, when he talks in that wild way," she said, with a slight smile. "I sometimes think that he would have made a very good actor—though whence he derives his histrionic talent I confess I haven't the remotest guess!"

"Oh, no! I shan't heed him," replied Kate cheerfully. "Any more than I heeded my father's subalterns!"

"Dear child!" purred her ladyship. "You have such superior sense! Torquil, I fear, has none at all, so you will be an excellent companion for him. I should explain to you, perhaps, that although it was found to be impossible to send him to school, I felt that it would be improper to admit him into our social life, and so set up an establishment for him in the West Wing, where he resides—or has resided, up to the present time—with Dr Delabole, and his valet, our faithful Badger."

A wrinkle appeared on Kate's brow; she ventured to ask how old Torquil was. She was told, Nineteen, and looked surprised.

"You are thinking," said her ladyship smoothly, "that he should be at Oxford. Unfortunately, his health is still too precarious to make it advisable to send him up."

"No, I wasn't thinking that, ma'am. But—but he is a man grown, and it does seem a little odd that he should be kept in the nursery!" said Kate frankly.

Lady Broome laughed. "Oh, dear me, no! Not the nursery! What a notion to take into your head! The thing is that having been reared in the West Wing he chooses to remain there—using it as a retreat, when he is out of hu-

mour. He is subject to moods, as I don't doubt you will
have noticed, and the least excitement brings on one of his
distressing migraines. These prostrate him, and there is
nothing for it but to put him to bed, and to keep him in
absolute quiet. Impossible, of course, if his room were in
the main part of the house.''

Never having had experience of sickly young men, Kate
accepted this, and said no more. When the gentlemen had
come into the room, the backgammon table was set out,
and Sir Timothy asked her if she played the game. She
responded drolly: ''Why, yes, sir! I have been used to play
with my father, and consider myself to be quite a dab at
it!''

He chuckled. ''Come and pit your skill against mine!''
he invited. ''Did you also play piquet with your father?''

''Frequently, sir!''

''We'll try that too. Delabole is no match for me, and
Torquil holds all such sports in abomination. In which he
takes after his mother, who can't tell a spade from a club!
Eh, Minerva?''

She smiled at him, but rather in the manner of a woman
who found little to interest her in the prattling of a child;
and signed to Dr Delabole to sit beside her on one of the
sofas. Him she engaged in low-voiced converse, while
Torquil sat down at the piano, and strummed idly. Glancing up momentarily from her game, Kate was forcibly
struck by the intense melancholy of his expression. His
eyes were sombre, his mouth took on a tragic droop; but
before she could speculate on this her attention was recalled by Sir Timothy, who said demurely: ''I *don't* think
you should accept a double, should you, Kate?''

Chapter Four

The following morning was spent by Kate in exploration. Torquil was her guide, and since he seemed to have thrown off the blue devils, an agreeable one. He conducted her all over the house, not excluding his own wing of it, and entertained her with his version of its history. "And here," he said solemnly, throwing open a door, "we have the Muniment Room! Why don't you bow profoundly? I warn you, my mama will expect you to do so! She has been at such pains to collect our records, and to store them here! I don't think Papa ever troubled himself to do so—or to have a Muniment Room—but pray don't tell her I said so!" He cast her a sidelong look, out of eyes brimming with laughter. "Isn't it odd that she, who was not born a Broome, should care so much more for them than Papa? She was ably assisted by Matthew—oh, Dr Delabole! I call him Matthew—who has also catalogued the library. Have you seen enough? Shall I take you out into the gardens?"

"Yes, please, but let me get a shawl first."

He accompanied her to her bedchamber, and stood in the doorway, leaning his shoulders against the wall, his hands dug into his pockets, while she changed her slippers for a pair of half-boots, and wrapped a shawl round herself.

His attitude was one of careless grace; his dress negligent, with the unstarched points of his shirtcollar drooping over a loosely knotted handkerchief, and a shooting-jacket worn open over a fancy waistcoat. A lock of his gleaming hair fell across his brow, and prompted Kate to say, with a twinkle: "You do study the picturesque, don't you? One might take you for a poet!"

"I am a poet," he replied coldly.

"No, are you? Then that accounts for it!"

"Accounts for what?"

"The windswept look, of course. Oh, don't poker up! Did no one ever banter you before?"

It seemed, for a moment, as though he had taken offence; but then he laughed, rather reluctantly, and said: "No, never. Is that what you mean to do, cousin?"

"Well, I don't precisely *mean* to, but I daresay I shall. You must remember that I have lived amongst soldiers! Very young officers, you know, are for ever cutting jokes, and poking fun at each other, and anyone making a figure of himself must be prepared to stand the roast! Come, let us go: I am quite ready!"

He muttered something which she did not catch, but she did not ask him to repeat it, feeling that he must be left to recover his temper. Not until they had left the house did she speak again, and then, perceiving a bed of spring flowers, she exclaimed: "Oh, how charming! Your mama told me that she had made the gardens her particular concern. Pray take me all over them! If it isn't a dead bore?"

"Oh, everything is a dead bore!" he said, shrugging up his shoulders. "Being a Broome—being the heir—being alive! Do you ever wish you had never been born?"

Suspecting him of dramatizing himself, she answered, after consideration: "No. I always think, when things are at their worst, that *tomorrow* will be better. And it very

often is—as when your mother, finding me, if not quite
destitute, at any rate at my wits' end, invited me to stay
with her. So don't despair, Torquil!''

She ended by impulsively pressing his thin hand, and
smiling up into his suddenly haggard face. He stared hun-
grily down at her for a moment, before shaking off her
hand, and saying harshly: ''Well, let us take a look at the
Italian garden—and the rose-garden—and the knot-
garden—and the belvedere—if that's what you wish! Oh,
and the herb-garden, and the shrubbery! Not that you will
see much in them at this season! But you won't care for
that, I daresay!''

She stood her ground, saying calmly: ''But I do care.
Take me, if you please, to the belvedere, which I have
already seen from the window of my room, and which
seems to command a view of the lake!''

Their eyes battled for mastery. Hers won, their coolness
quenching the flame in his; but the effort to withstand his
scorching gaze left her shaken. Before she could bring her
thoughts into order, the flame had shrunk, and he was making an exaggerated bow, and saying gaily: ''As you wish,
cousin! This way!''

She walked in silence beside him down a path which
led to the belvedere, and almost shrank from him when,
all at once, he stopped, compelling her to do so too by
gripping her arm, and swinging her round to face him.
''Are you afraid of me, Cousin Kate?'' he demanded.

''Afraid of you? No, why should I be?'' she countered.

''You jumped!''

''Well, so I should think, when you startled me so
much!'' she said indignantly. ''For goodness' sake, Torquil, don't play-act! At all events, not to me, for, whatever
your entourage may feel, I am quite unimpressed! Now, if

you will be so obliging as to let me go, we will proceed on our way to the belvedere!''

He gave a low chuckle, and released his painful grip on her arm. ''Strong, aren't I?'' He flexed his long fingers, regarding them with an admiring smile. ''I could strangle you one-handed, you know. Wouldn't think it, to look at me, would you?''

''No, but as I haven't had occasion to consider the matter there's nothing wonderful in that!'' she retorted, rubbing her arm. His chagrined face stirred her sense of fun; she broke into laughter, and said: ''Cry craven, Torquil! You have the wrong sow by the ear: I'm not so easily impressed!''

That made him echo her laughter. ''Kate, Cousin Kate, do you call yourself a sow? *I* should never dare do so! You are the most unusual girl!''

''I've had an unusual upbringing—and well for you if you don't call me a sow! Now, do come to the belvedere! My aunt will certainly ask if you showed it to me, and if you are obliged to say that you didn't, it will be all holiday with you!''

He threw a quick look over his shoulder, as though he feared to see Lady Broome. ''Yes. As you say! Come, let's run!''

He caught her hand as he spoke, and forced her to run beside him down the path. She made a snatch at her skirt, but arrived, breathless, laughing, and with a torn flounce, at the belvedere. ''*Odious* boy!'' she scolded, pulling her hand out of his. ''Just look at what you've made me do to my gown! Now I must pin it up!'' She opened her reticule, drew out a paper of pins, and, sitting down on the steps, began to repair the damage.

Watching with great interest, Torquil asked if she always carried pins.

"Yes, for one never knows when one may need them. There! I hope it will hold until I can stitch it—and that my aunt doesn't see me with a pinned-up flounce! She would take me for a regular Mab, I daresay. I may now enjoy the view—and, oh, yes, I do enjoy it! How very right your mama was to build a belvedere just here! May I enter it?"

"Do!" he said cordially.

She mounted the steps, and found herself in a summerhouse, which was furnished with a table, and one chair. A book lay on the table and a standish was set beside it. Kate said: "Is it private, this room? Ought I to be in it?"

"Oh, yes! I don't care."

"You may not, but perhaps your mama might!"

"Why? *She* doesn't sit here!"

"Is it yours, then? I'm very much obliged to you for letting me see it." She moved to the front of the round tower, and stood resting her hands on the stone ledge, looking out between the slender pillars to the lake below, and to the trees and the flowering shrubs beyond the lake. "It is very beautiful," she said, in a troubled tone. "Very beautiful, and yet very sad. Why should still water be so melancholy?"

"I don't know. I don't find it so. Come down to the bridge! *There is a willow grows aslant a brook, That shows his hoar leaves in the glassy stream*—only it isn't a brook! Just a deep lake!"

She followed him down the steps to the stone bridge which was flung across the narrow end of the lake. He went ahead of her to the middle of the bridge, and stood there, leaning his arms on the parapet, and watching her with a mocking smile. "Come along!" he coaxed. "I won't throw you in!"

She laughed. "No, won't you?"

"Not if you don't wish it!"

"I most certainly do not wish it!"

"Don't you? Not at all? I often think how pleasant it would be to drown."

"Well, it wouldn't be in the least pleasant!" she said severely. "Are you trying to make my flesh creep? I warn you, I have a very matter-of-fact mind, and shall put you to a non-plus! What lies beyond the lake?"

"Oh, the Home Wood! Do you care to walk in it?"

"Yes, of all things! If we have time? What *is* the time?"

"I haven't a notion. Does it signify?"

"I was thinking of my aunt."

"Why?"

"She may need me to do something for her!"

"Mama? Good God, she doesn't need anyone to do things for her!" he said impatiently. "Besides, she told me to take you all about!"

"Oh, then in that case—!" she said, yielding.

It was pleasant in the wood, sheltered from the slight but sharp wind, and with the sun filtering through the trees. There were several grassy rides cut through the undergrowth, and in a clearing bluebells had been planted. Kate exclaimed in delight at these, and could scarcely drag herself away. "How much I envy you!" she said impulsively. "I have never lived in the English countryside, until last year, and then, you know, it wasn't springtime. The autumn tints were lovely, but oh, how it did rain!"

"Where was this?" he asked.

"In Cambridgeshire, not far from Wisbech. I was employed as governess to two detestably spoilt children, and as the elder was only seven our walks were restricted. Thank God I left before the third could be handed over to me!"

"A governess!" he said, looking very much struck. "Does Mama know this?"

"Of course she does! You may say that she rescued me!" She glanced up at him enquiringly. "Didn't she tell you?"

"Tell me? Oh, no! How could you suppose she would? She never tells me anything!"

"Perhaps she thought I shouldn't wish it to be known."

"More likely *she* didn't wish it to be known! Very high in the instep, my dear mama! Keeps the world at a proper distance!"

Kate was shocked, for there was a note of venom in his voice. After a moment's hesitation, she said diffidently: "You should not speak so, least of all to me. Recollect that I have cause to be grateful to her! Indeed, she has almost overwhelmed me by her kindness!"

"Has she, by Jove? I wonder why?" he said ruminatively, his eyes narrowed, and gleaming strangely. "You may depend upon it that she has a reason! But what can it be?" His eyes slid to her face, saw in it a deep disapproval, and shifted. "Oh, are you shocked?" he said derisively. "Do you believe that one should love and honour one's parents? Well, I don't, do you hear me? I don't! I am treated like a child—not allowed to do this—not allowed to do the other—kept in seclusion—spied on—" He broke off, his face convulsed with rage. He covered it with his shaking hands, and said chokingly: "*She* is to blame! She has my father so much under her thumb—oh, you don't know! you can't know! We are all afraid of her—all of us, even Matthew! even me!"

He ended on a hysterical sob. As much moved as shocked, she ventured to lay a soothing hand on his arm, and to say: "You are her only child, and—and, I collect, not *robust!* Her care of you must spring from her love—don't you think?''

His hands fell; he showed her a distorted face, in which his eyes blazed. "Love?" he ejaculated. "*Love?* Mama? Oh, that's good! That's rich, by God!" Suddenly he stiffened, and grasped her wrist, listening intently. "I thought as much! Matthew, or Badger, spying on me! If they ask you what I've been saying to you, don't tell them—either of them! *Promise* me!"

She had only time to utter the desired assurance before his hand left her wrist. Dr Delabole stepped into the clearing, and waved to them, saying: "So here you are! 'Depend upon it,' I told her ladyship, 'Torquil has taken Miss Kate to see the bluebells!' My dear young people, have you the least notion of what the time may be?"

"Well, I did ask my cousin, when he suggested a stroll through the wood, but he said it didn't signify! And then we came upon the bluebells!" replied Kate gaily.

"Beautiful, aren't they? One could spend an hour, feasting one's eyes upon them! But it is past noon, and a nuncheon awaits you!"

"Past noon! Oh, we must go back instantly!" exclaimed Kate, stricken.

"On the contrary! We must go *on!*" said the doctor, laughing gently. "The wood dwindles into the park, and if we continue down this ride we shall find ourselves within a stone's throw of the house. And what, Miss Kate, did you think of the belvedere?"

He had fallen into step beside her, but it was Torquil who answered him, from beyond Kate. "How did you know I had taken her there?" he demanded suspiciously.

"Well, by the process of deduction, dear boy!" replied the doctor apologetically. "Having seen you set out from the house into the gardens, and having failed to discover you there, I naturally assumed that you had done so! When I drew another blank at the belvedere, it dawned on my powerful intellect that you must have crossed the bridge into the wood! And lo, here you are!''

''Oh!'' said Torquil, disconcerted.

In a few minutes they were crossing the park, within sight of the house. They entered it by the front door, and were met by Lady Broome, who threw up her hands, and said quizzingly: ''Oh, you abominable children! Where did you find them, doctor?''

''Where I thought I should find them, ma'am! Looking at the bluebells!''

''Ah, then I must forgive them! And should perhaps blame myself for not having warned you, Kate, that Torquil has no idea of time! Eh, my son?''

She pinched his chin as she spoke, and then slid her hand in his arm, and went with him into one of the saloons, saying over her shoulder: ''I don't stand on ceremony with you, Kate! Are you quite famished? You don't deserve it, either of you, but you shall have a nuncheon!''

The table in the saloon was set for two, and bore a selection of cold meats, and fruit. Lady Broome took her place at the head of it, and carved some slices of chicken for them.

''Not for me, ma'am!'' said Torquil.

''Just one slice of breast, to please me!'' she said, laying his plate before him.

He looked mutinous, and started to say something about not being hungry, but she interrupted him, meeting his eyes steadily, and saying in a calm tone: ''Eat it, Torquil!''

He reddened, hunching a shoulder, but picked up his knife and fork. Lady Broome chose an apple from the bowl in front of her, and began delicately to peel it with a silver knife. Addressing herself to Kate, she said: ''Well, my dear, and what did you think of the gardens? They are not looking their best so early in the season, but the azaleas and the rhododendrons round the lake must be coming into flower?''

Kate shook her head. ''Not yet, ma'am, though I did notice some buds.''

''Cousin Kate, ma'am, didn't like your belvedere,'' interpolated Torquil maliciously. ''She said it was melancholy.''

''I said,'' corrected Kate, ''that there was something very melancholy about still water.''

''Yes, I collect many people think so,'' agreed her ladyship. ''I have never been conscious of it myself. There, Torquil! I haven't lost my old skill!'' She showed him an unbroken spiral of apple-peel, and turned her head to tell Kate that when he had been a little boy he had eaten apples only for the joy of watching her peel them for him. ''As he will today!'' she said, cutting the fruit into neat quarters, and arranging them on a plate.

He accepted this from her without demur, for he had been struck by a sudden thought. His eyes lit; he said: ''Do you ride, cousin?''

''Indeed I do!''

''Oh, that's famous! Will you ride with me? Do say you will! I've no one to ride with except Whalley, my groom! Or Matthew! And they are both slow-tops!''

''Yes—with the greatest imaginable pleasure!'' she replied promptly. ''That is—if my aunt permits?''

''But of course!'' responded Lady Broome. ''Tell Whalley to put my saddle on Jupiter tomorrow, Torquil! My dear, have you a riding-habit with you?''

''Well, yes, ma'am! It so happens that I did bring it with me—in the hope that I might be granted the indulgence of a ride!'' confessed Kate. ''Oh, what a treat it will be! I haven't been on a horse since we came home to England!''

"Then you'll pay dearly for it!" said Torquil, chuckling.

"I know I shall—but I have an excellent embrocation!' she said hopefully.

But it seemed, on the following morning, as though the treat was going to be denied her. When she and Torquil came out of the house, not two but three horses stood saddled below the terrace, and to this Torquil took instant exception, saying sharply: "We shan't need you, Whalley!''

"Her ladyship's orders are that I should go with you, sir,'' said the groom apologetically. "In case of accidents!'' He kept a wary eye on Torquil's whip-hand, and added, in a soothing voice: "I shan't worrit you, Master Torquil, but if Miss was to take a tumble—or you wanted a gate opened—''

"Go to the devil!'' whispered Torquil, white with fury, his hand clenched hard on his whip. "If you go, I don't!''

Kate, feeling that it behoved her to intervene, said calmly: "Well, I don't mean to take a tumble, but if my aunt wishes your groom to accompany us it may be irksome, but not such a great matter, after all! Will you put me up, if you please?''

He glared at her, biting his lip, and jerking the lash of his whip between his hands; but after a moment's indecision came sulkily forward. She took the bridle from Whalley, and, as Torquil bent, laid one hand on his shoulder, slightly pressing it. He threw her up rather roughly, but she surprised him by springing from his grasp, and landing neatly in the saddle. While Jupiter sidled and fretted, she brought one leg round the pommel, adjusted the voluminous folds of her skirt, and commanded Torquil to shorten the stirrup-leather. He did so, with no very good grace, flung himself on to his own mount, and dashed off down the avenue. The next instant, Whalley, with an agility astonishing in a man of his years, had leapt into his own saddle, and had set off after him, leaving Kate to follow as best she might. This, since Jupiter was an incorrigible slug, was no easy task: he lacked the competitive spirit, and it was not until she had startled him with a slash from her whip that he broke into a gallop. By the time she overtook Torquil, he had reached the shut gates, and Whalley was remonstrating with him. "Give over, Master Torquil! give over!" Whalley implored. "Whatever will Miss Kate think of you?"

"The worst escort possible!" said Kate, not mincing matters. "How dared you, cousin, dash off like that, without warning me that you meant to make a race of it? Not that this animal has the least notion of showing the way! Is he touched in the wind, or gone to soil?"

"Neither! Just lazy!" answered Torquil, bursting into laughter. "Or perhaps your hand is strange to him!"

She was relieved to see that his rage had apparently burnt itself out, and said, in mock dudgeon: "Let me tell you, cousin, that I am held to ride with a particularly light hand, and an easy bit! Where are we going?"

"Oh, anywhere!" he said bitterly, leading the way through the gate, which the lodge-keeper was holding open. "All roads are alike to me, when I have a spy following me!"

She thought it best to ignore this. She said prosaically: "Well, they are naturally all the same to me, so take me where I can enjoy a gallop—if Jupiter can be persuaded to gallop!"

After this, she set herself to win him from his ill-humour, and succeeded pretty well, until a farm-gate was reached. He rode up to open it, and his horse, which seemed to be a nervous animal, sweating, fretting, and continually tossing up his head, shied away from it, and reared up, nearly unseating Torquil. He cursed him, getting him under control, but before he could make a second attempt to bring him up to the gate, Whalley had ridden up, and had opened it for him. He flushed angrily, and relapsed into the sulks, vouchsafing no reply to Kate's next remark. More than a little exasperated, she said: "Oh, do come out of the mopes! You are a dead bore, Torquil!"

"I'm not in the mopes! I'm angry!"

"Why should I be made to suffer? You are behaving like a peevish schoolboy."

His colour rose again; he said through clenched teeth: "I beg your pardon!"

"Muchas gracias!" she flashed, and urged Jupiter into a canter.

Torquil soon caught up with her, demanding to know what she had said. When she repeated it, he asked interestedly if it was Spanish.

"Yes, and it means thank you!"

"I thought it did. Are you a Spanish scholar?"

She laughed. "No, alas! I only speak soldiers' Spanish."

"What was it like, following the drum?" he asked curiously.

Glad to find that he had emerged from the sullens, she was very ready to encourage him. She favoured him with an amusing description of the conditions she had endured, several times making him laugh, and answering all his eager questions to the best of her ability. He was just demanding an account of the Battle of Vittoria when suddenly he broke off, and ejaculated: "Oh, here come the Templecombes! Famous!"

He spurred forward to meet the two riders who were cantering towards them, and Kate heard him call out: "Dolly!" and saw him lean forward to clasp the hand of a very pretty girl. Following at a more sedate pace, she had the leisure to observe the Templecombes. She judged them to be brother and sister, for there was a strong likeness between them, and although there was also considerable disparity of age the man was certainly not old enough to be the girl's father. Kate judged him to be in his late twenties; the girl, she thought, was not out of her teens. As she came up to them, she saw that the child was blushing adorably, and drew her own conclusions. Then Torquil turned his head, and summoned her to be introduced. "Kate, here is Miss Templecombe! And her brother! Dolly—Gurney, this is my cousin Kate!—Miss Malvern!"

Mr Templecombe bowed, sweeping off his modish hat; his sister smiled shyly, murmuring something about being "so pleased!" and Torquil, not allowing her time to say more, instantly intervened, saying, with a slight stammer: "How is this? I had supposed you to be in London! Has your come-out been postponed?"

"No—oh, no! but we don't go to London until the end of the month!" replied Miss Templecombe, in a soft little voice.

"When the balls will be in full swing!" said Kate, smiling at her. "Does your mama mean to present you, Miss Templecombe?"

"Yes—and I am to wear a hoop, and feathers!' disclosed Miss Templecombe.

"Antiquated, ain't it?' said her brother. "Can't see, myself, why females set so much store by these Drawingrooms. Or why," he added, with feeling, "they should wish to be escorted to 'em! Y'know, Miss Malvern, you have to rig yourself out in fancy-dress! No, no, I'm not bamming you! Knee-breeches, and chapeau-bras! Give you my word! Orders, too! Not that I have any, but don't it all go to *show?*''

"Oh, Gurney!" remonstrated his sister. "As though you hadn't worn precisely the same dress at Almack's!"

"The only time I ever went to Almack's," returned Mr Templecombe, "was on the occasion of my own come-out, Dolly, and I'll be vastly obliged to you if you don't recall it to my memory!" He shuddered eloquently. "The most insipid evening I ever spent in all my life!" he declared impressively. "Nothing to drink but lemonade or weak orgeat, and I sank myself beneath reproach—oh, *fathoms* beneath reproach!—by inviting a girl in her *first* season to stand up with me for the waltz! You may imagine the looks that were cast at me!"

"I can, of course," admitted Kate, "though I've never been to Almack's. I've never been presented either, so if you are thinking of asking my advice on the management of your hoop, I'm afraid you will miss the cushion!"

"Oh, no! Mama will show me, just as she showed my sisters," said Miss Templecombe simply. "And they all three made good marriages!"

Kate glanced apprehensively at Torquil, wondering how he would receive this naïve remark. He did not appear to have paid the least heed to it: his eyes were ardently devouring Dorothea's exquisite countenance, and there was a smile on his lips. Kate could not forbear the thought that they were a singularly beautiful couple, and stole a look at Mr Templecombe's face. It told her nothing, but she had a feeling that he did not view the very obvious attachment with complaisance. As though to lend colour to this presentiment, he pulled out his watch, exclaiming: "Dolly, if we don't make haste, Mama will be sending out a search-party! 'Servant, Miss Malvern! Yours, Torquil!''

"Oh, we'll go along with you!" said Torquil, wheeling his horse. He said, over his shoulder, tossing the words at Kate: "You've no objection, coz, have you?"

"No, none. And much good it would do me if I had!" she added.

Torquil did not hear her, but Gurney Templecombe did, and burst out laughing. Ranging alongside her, he remarked quizzically: "Well said, ma'am!"

"I'm afraid it was very ill said!" she confessed. "It fell on the wrong ears! And I know, of course, that every allowance ought to be made for him. My aunt tells me that he is not at all robust, besides suffering from severe migraines, so that it's no wonder he should be a trifle spoilt."

"'Mm, yes! Handsome boy, ain't he?" drawled Gurney, looking after the young couple with a frown in his sleepy eyes. "Much better-looking than Philip, I suppose, though for *my* money—" He stopped, seeing that she was puzzled, and said: "Are you acquainted with Philip Broome, ma'am?"

"No, who is he?"

"Torquil's cousin. Friend of mine!" he answered. "Beg pardon, but I don't perfectly understand! You can't be a Broome, surely? Well, what I mean is, never heard Philip speak of you!"

"Oh, no, I'm not a Broome! Lady Broome was my father's half-sister," she explained. "But owing to a quarrel in the family I didn't meet her until last week, when she invited me to visit Staplewood."

"Invited you to— Did she, by Jove!" he said, surprised. "I wonder why—" He broke off, reddening, and giving an embarrassed cough. "Forgotten what I was going to say!"

"You were going to say that you wonder why she did invite me," she supplied. "Torquil said the same yesterday, and *I* wonder what you both mean! She invited me out of compassion, knowing me to be a destitute orphan— and I can never be sufficiently grateful to her!"

He stammered: "No, indeed! Just so! Shouldn't think you could! Well, what I mean is— Did you say *destitute,* ma'am?"

"Forced to earn my bread!" she declared dramatically. She saw that he was quite horrified and gave a gurgle of laughter.

"You're shamming it!" he accused her.

"I'm not, but you've no need to look aghast, I promise you! To be sure, I didn't precisely enjoy being a governess, but there are many worse fates. Or so I've been told!"

"Yes—well, stands to reason! Though when I think of the pranks m'sisters used to play, and how m'mother always blamed the wretched female who had 'em in charge—well, *are* there worse fates?"

"Between ourselves, sir, no!"

"Thought as much." He was struck by a sudden idea, and added admiringly: "Y'know, you're a very unusual girl, Miss Malvern!"

Chapter Five

They parted from the Templecombes where the lane leading to Staplewood branched off the pike-road. As they rode away, Torquil said, with a sidelong look: "You needn't say anything to my mother, you know. Not that it signifies! Whalley will tell her fast enough!"

"If you mean that he will tell her we met Mr and Miss Templecombe, I am heartily glad of it!" said Kate directly. "I don't at all wish to deceive my aunt. Why don't you wish her to know?"

"She don't like Dolly," he answered shortly. "Doesn't mean me to marry her. That's why she won't let me go to London."

"Well, you are rather young to be thinking of marriage, aren't you?" she suggested reasonably. "I daresay you won't find her opposed to the match in another few years' time. Tell me, who are the Templecombes, and *what* are they?"

"Perfectly respectable!" he said, firing up.

"That was obvious. I meant, what does the family consist of!"

He was instantly mollified. "Oh, I see! They are landowners, like ourselves. Lady Templecombe is a widow,

and Gurney is her only son. She's bird-witted! A silly widgeon, who lets herself be nose-led by Gurney! And *he* is
nose-led by my dear, *dear* cousin Philip!''

She was startled by the suppressed venom in his voice,
but said matter-of-factly: ''Yes, he spoke of your cousin
Philip. He seemed surprised that I had never heard of him.
Tell me about him!''

''Philip, dear Kate, is my father's nephew, and, after
me, the heir to Papa's title and estates. He is also my chief
enemy. Oh, yes, I assure you! All the narrow escapes from
death I've had occurred when he has been staying at Staplewood!''

She could only gasp. He threw her a bright, flickering
smile, and said chattily: ''Oh, yes! A cope-stone once fell
from the pediment, missing me by inches. Wasn't it odd?
The branch of a tree, which I was climbing, broke under
me. I was thrown at a fence which had been wired. I
was—''

Recovering her breath, she interrupted: ''These surely
must have been accidents!''

''Yes, even Mama said so,'' he agreed affably. ''And
she don't love Philip! Papa does, though: positively dotes
on him! My Uncle Julian was employed in the Diplomatic
Service, wherefore Philip sent most of his holidays at Staplewood, ingratiating himself with my papa! He's ten years
older than I am, you know. Yes, does it not seem odd? It
is due to the circumstance of Papa's first wife having failed
to rear beyond infancy any of her numerous offspring. I
don't know whether to be glad, or sorry.''

Summoning to her assistance all her faculties, she said:
''I can't tell that, but I do implore you, Torquil, not to
refine too much on what may well have been accidents! If
your mama did not believe—''

''Oh, but she did!'' he told her, bright-eyed and smiling.

"That's why she places a guard about me! Philip has been her enemy from the outset!"

She was appalled into silence. It endured until the lodge-gates had been reached, when she said suddenly: "I don't believe it! No, I *don't* believe it!"

He laughed. "Don't you? Wait, cousin, wait! You will see!"

Feeling very much as if she had strayed between the marbled covers of some lurid novel, she said no more, but rode in silence beside him up the long avenue to the terrace-steps. Here she dismounted, gave her bridle into Whalley's hand, and went quickly into the house. There was no one in the hall, but as she went up the stairs Pennymore came through the door which led to the kitchen-quarters, and she was obliged to scold herself for thinking that she detected a look of relief in his face. "So you are back, miss!" he said, smiling up at her. "Did you have an agreeable ride?"

Of impulse, and to try him, she answered: "Why, no, not very agreeable!"

Was there a shade of anxiety in his eyes? It was impossible to decide. He said, in his gentle way: "Oh, dear, dear! How was that, miss?"

"My cousin was out of humour, and I was mounted on a slug!"

He coughed. "Well, miss, the truth is that her ladyship wasn't sure if you were clever in the saddle, so she mounted you on Jupiter—to give you a safe, comfortable ride!"

"What you mean is an arm-chair ride!" she said.

"Well, yes, miss!" he admitted, twinkling.

She laughed, and went on up to her bedchamber. It was only when she was taking off her riding-habit that she realized that he had not answered the first part of her complaint. Knowing that she should not have made it, she came to the conclusion that by ignoring it he had reproved her, and felt ashamed of herself.

She had just taken a cambric dress out of the wardrobe, and cast it on to the bed, while she searched for a spencer to wear with it, when a knock on the door heralded the entrance of Lady Broome, who was followed by Sidlaw, carrying various dresses in her arms.

"So I gave you an arm-chair ride, did I?" said her ladyship, laughing at her. "Pray, how was I to know that you could keep a horse in hand? So many people who are buckish about horses belong to the *awkward squad!* Never mind! Next time you go out you shall ride my own mare: a little spirited thoroughbred! A perfect fencer, but, alas, I don't hunt nowadays! Now, tell me, my love: do you like these few dresses which Sidlaw has made up for you? Your nurse furnished me with your measurements, but Sidlaw would wish you to try them on while they are still only tacked together. I purchased the materials in London, pretending that I was doing so for the daughter I never had, and I do *hope* I chose what you will like!"

"B-but, ma'am!" stammered Kate, quite overset. "You must not! You—you are *crushing* me with generosity!"

"Oh, pooh! nothing of the sort! You mean you *don't* like them!!"

"Oh, no, no, no!" cried Kate, distressed. "Only that I can't be so much beholden to you! I've done nothing to deserve such kindness, ma'am. *Oh,* what a truly beautiful evening-dress! Take it away, Sidlaw, before I lose my resolution!"

"It is to be worn, miss, with this three-quarter pelisse of pale sapphire satin, trimmed with broad lace," explained Sidlaw. "And I venture to say, miss, that it will become you to admiration! Though I say it as should not."

"Try it on, my dear!" coaxed Lady Broome. "Sir Timothy, I must tell you, likes the ladies of his household to be prettily dressed! If you don't choose to oblige me, oblige him!"

"Aunt Minerva! How *can* you suppose that I don't choose to oblige you?" protested Kate. "Only—"

She was silenced by a finger laid across her lips. "Only nothing!" said Lady Broome. She patted Kate's cheek. "Foolish child! What in the world are these crotchets? Because I have a few dresses made for you? Don't be so gooseish!"

Feeling quite helpless, Kate submitted, allowing Sidlaw to slip the evening robe over her head. While Sidlaw discussed with Lady Broome the alterations which should be made, she stood passive, studying herself in the long glass, thinking how well she looked, how often she had longed for such a gown, how impossible it was to refuse to accept it. She could only be grateful.

During the following week she had plenty of cause to feel grateful, and strangely oppressed, for Lady Broome showered benefits upon her. Her gifts ranged from trinkets unearthed from her jewel-box to ribbons, or scraps of lace. None of the things she gave Kate were very valuable, but they made Kate uncomfortable. It was never possible to refuse them. "My dear, I have been going through my lace-drawer, and came upon this set of collar and cuffs. Do you care to have them? They are of no use to me, but they would look very well on your fawn-figured dress, don't you think?" would say her ladyship, and how could you reply that you didn't think so? How could you say, when a necklace of seed-pearls was clasped round your neck, and your aunt told you that she was too old to wear it herself, that you preferred not to accept it? It wasn't possible even to refuse a new riding-habit, made by a

tailor in Market Harborough, for Lady Broome pointed
out, very gently, that her old one was woefully shabby.
"We shall have everyone thinking me a shocking pinch-
penny not to provide my only niece with a new one!" she
said.

"If that is so, I need not ride, ma'am!"

"That's being foolish beyond permission. What would
Torquil say, I wonder? When he looks forward so much
to the daily rides in your company! I must tell you, my
love, that you have done Torquil a great deal of good, so,
if you wish to repay me, continue to ride with him!"

"I do wish to repay you, ma'am, and surely there must
be more I can do for you than ride with Torquil?" said
Kate imploringly.

"Why, certainly! You can be my aide-de-camp, if you
will, and attend to all the details which I neglect! I shall
get you to write my letters for me, to arrange the flowers,
and to keep the servants up to their work. You will soon
be wishing that you hadn't offered yourself as *quite* so
willing a sacrifice!"

Kate had to be satisfied, but as it did not seem to her
that her aunt neglected any detail, and was far from being
a sad housekeeper, she found little to do, and was obliged
to content herself with such unexacting tasks as gathering
and arranging flowers, dusting ornaments, and playing
cards with Sir Timothy, whenever his health permitted him
to emerge from the seclusion of his own apartments. This,
as she discovered, was not often. Dr Delabole was in constant attendance upon him, and watched him without seem-
ing to. She was made aware of this when Sir Timothy
suffered a slight seizure one evening, after dinner. Before
she had realized it the doctor, who had been talking to
Lady Broome, was at his side, reviving him with strong
smelling-salts, and lowering him to a recumbent position.

Dismissed with Torquil to the billiard-room, she ventured to ask him what ailed his father, and was considerably daunted by the reply. "Oh, I don't know!" said Torquil indifferently. "He's been in queer stirrups ever since I can remember. I believe it's his heart, but no one ever tells me anything!"

After this, Kate added a postscript to the letter she had written to Mrs Nidd: *My cousin Torquil is the strangest boy, with the face of an angel, and the coldest of dispositions. I don't know what to make of him.*

This was not the first letter she had written to Mrs Nidd, but so far she had received no response to any of her previous missives. She was beginning to feel worried, and a little hurt. Since Sir Timothy was not a Member of Parliament, she had been unable to get a frank; but it seemed very unlikely that Sarah had repulsed her letters because she grudged the postage; nor, in a city, was she obliged to collect her letters from the receiving office: indeed, Joe Nidd even paid to have his mail delivered early each morning. It seemed even more unlikely that she could be ill: Sarah was never ill. And if she *had* been taken suddenly ill she would surely have scribbled a few lines, or instructed Joe to do so? When Kate had written her first letter, she had taken it to Lady Broome, and asked diffidently if it might be despatched. Lady Broome had replied: "Yes, dear child, of course! Put it on the table in the hall! Pennymore arranges for the letters to be carried to the Post Office in Market Harborough, and it will go with mine."

Kate had obeyed these instructions; but when no answer was forthcoming she asked Pennymore if her letters had in fact been taken to the Post Office. He said that if she had placed them on the table in the hall they had certainly been posted; and further disclosed that the incoming postbag was always delivered to her ladyship, who sorted out and distributed the letters it contained, most of which were directed to herself.

So when Kate had sealed her fourth letter to Sarah, she hesitated for a few moments, and then went in search of her aunt. She found her writing at her desk, and upon being invited, with a kind smile, to tell her aunt what she wanted, said frankly: "To own the truth, ma'am, I am in a worry! I haven't heard from Sarah—from Mrs Nidd!—though I've written to her several times. I can't help wondering whether—" She stopped, finding herself quite unable to continue, and tried again. "I collect, ma'am, that she hasn't written to me? I mean—you would have given me any letters that were directed to me?"

"But of course!" said Lady Broome, raising her eyebrows.

Thrown into a little confusion, Kate said stammeringly: "Yes. Well, of c-course you would, ma'am! Only it does seem so odd of Sarah…"

Lady Broome gave a soft laugh. "Does it? You must remember, my dear, that persons of her order find writing a great labour."

It was true that Sarah did not write with ease. Kate agreed doubtfully. Lady Broome continued in a smooth tone: "If you have given her an account of yourself she knows that you are well, and—I trust!—happy, and she feels, no doubt, that you are off her hands. So much as she must have to do!" She smiled. "After all, you haven't been here for very long yet, have you? I shouldn't get into a fidget, if I were you!"

"No, ma'am," said Kate meekly.

She turned away, and was about to leave the room when Lady Broome said: "By the way, my dear, I am giving a dinner- party tomorrow, so tell Risby to send suitable flowers up to the house in the morning! For the hall, the Crimson saloon, the staircase, the Long Drawing-room, and the ante-room. I suppose we had better have some for the gallery as well.''

"Yes, ma'am, but I had liefer by far pick them myself! Risby's notions of what is suitable are so—so nipcheese!''

"As you wish," said her ladyship. "Don't fag yourself to death, however!''

"I won't!'' promised Kate, laughing.

She went off, heartened by the prospect of a party to relieve what had begun, very slightly, to be every evening's boredom. She had been surprised to find her aunt leading almost the life of a recluse at Staplewood, for she had assumed her to be a woman of decided fashion, and knew that she took pleasure in being the great lady of the district. She supposed that Sir Timothy's ill-health accounted for it, but it did seem to her that a few small parties of young persons need not disturb him, and would have done much to reconcile Torquil to his lot. Then it occurred to her that Torquil had no friends, other than the Templecombes, and she wondered whether there was perhaps a dearth of young people in the neighbourhood. She ventured to ask Lady Broome if this were so, and was told that there were very few of Torquil's age. "He doesn't make friends easily, and I must own that I am glad of it,'' said her ladyship frankly. "He is somewhat above the touch of most of the people who live within our reach. Mere smatterers, my dear, to put it in straight words! Much given to romping parties, too: I daresay you know what I mean. I dislike such affairs, and they would not do for Torquil at all. He is so excitable, and his character is as yet unformed. You must have noticed that he suffers from unequal spirits: either he is in alt, or sunk in dejection! The one state invariably follows hard on the other, and although he is in a way to be very much better, Dr Delabole considers that he should still lead a quiet life.''

It did not seem to Kate that to be shut off from his contemporaries could be a cure for unequal spirits, and the suspicion crossed her mind that Lady Broome was a possessive parent. But nothing in her behaviour supported this theory. Her manner might be caressing, but she did not hang about her son, and she certainly did not dote upon him, however jealously she might guard his health. Little by little it was being borne in on Kate that, despite her manners and her generosity, Lady Broome was a cold-hearted woman, who cared more for position than for any human being. Scolding herself for harbouring so ungenerous a thought, Kate cast about in her mind for the real author of Torquil's enforced seclusion. She found it easily enough in the person of Dr Delabole. From the first moment of meeting him she had taken him in dislike. He spared no pains to make himself agreeable; he had treated her with every degree of attention; towards Sir Timothy he showed an engaging solicitude; towards Lady Broome a playful friendliness which never passed the line; and yet Kate could not like him. She suspected him of feathering his nest at Sir Timothy's expense. It then occurred to her that she might be thought to be feathering her own nest at Sir Timothy's expense, and she was obliged to scold herself for harbouring yet another ungenerous suspicion.

These ruminations led her inevitably to the reflection that Staplewood was a most extraordinary house, in that its three inmates led quite detached lives. Sir Timothy's apartments were in one wing of it; Torquil's in the opposite wing; and Lady Broome might have been said to occupy the central block. Unless Sir Timothy were indisposed, they met at dinner; but only rarely did Lady Broome intrude upon her husband's privacy, and still more rarely upon her son's. Kate knew herself to be ignorant of the customs prevailing in large establishments, but this state of affairs struck her at the outset as being very strange, for although, to all outward appearances, Lady Broome was a devoted wife and mother, it seemed odd to Kate that even when Dr Delabole reported Sir Timothy to be rather out of frame, she showed no disposition to remain at his bedside.

Torquil, incensed by the discovery that Kate was far too busy collecting flowers to ride with him, announced that he would dine in his own room, for the party would be the dullest entertainment imaginable. Since it had not taken Kate more than a few days to realize that he stood very much in awe of his mother, she was not surprised to find that this had been an empty threat. When she came downstairs to the Crimson saloon, sumptuously attired in white kerseymere, embellished with Spanish sleeves, and pearl buttons, she found him already in the saloon, very correctly dressed, and looking as sulky as he was beautiful. But at sight of her the cloud lifted from his brow, and he exclaimed: "Oh, by Jupiter, that's something like! Coz, you look slap up to the echo!"

She blushed, and laughed. "Thank you! So, I must say, do you!"

He made an impatient gesture, but Dr Delabole said: "Exactly so! It is what I have been telling him, Miss Kate: he is all in print!" He laid an affectionate hand on Torquil's shoulder, and added humorously: "And now you see, don't you, dear boy, why you should have been expected to dress yourself up to the nines!"

Torquil shook off his hand. "Oh, be damned to you, Matthew! What a bagpipe you are! I wish you will bite your tongue! I warn you, Kate, this will be one of Mama's

most insipid parties! In fact, you've rigged yourself out in
style to no purpose!''

She soon saw that he had judged the party to a nicety.
The guests were all elderly, and arrived in pairs, being
received by Lady Broome, splendid in crimson velvet and
rubies; and by Sir Timothy, looking like a wraith beside
her. Lady Broome made it her business to present Kate to
everyone, until, as she whispered to Torquil, when he took
his place beside her at the dinner-table, her knees ached
with curtsying. The Templecombes were not present, but
a moment's reflection sufficed to remind Kate that they
must, if they left Leicestershire at the end of April, be
established in London. She could not help wondering if
Lady Broome had known this when she sent out her cards
of invitation.

Dinner was very long, and very elaborate; and since
Kate had a deaf man beside her, who devoted his attention
to his plate, and she would not encourage Torquil to neglect his other neighbour, an amiable and garrulous dow-
ager, she had nothing to do but to admire her own arrangement of flowers in the centre of the table, while disposing
of her portions of soup, fish, and suckling-pig. When the
second course made its appearance, with its plethora of
vegetables, jellies, fondues, blancmanges, and Chantilly
baskets, she refused to allow her aunt to serve her from
the larded guinea-fowls which graced the head of the table,
or Sir Timothy to tempt her to a morsel of the ducklings
set before him, and ended her repast with some asparagus.
Beside her, Torquil accepted whatever was set before him,
ignored some dishes, toyed with others, drank a great deal
of wine, and endured the determined chattiness of his
neighbour. Kate could only be thankful that he did endure
it. He slipped away, however, when Sir Timothy brought
the gentlemen up to the Long Drawing-room to join the

ladies: a circumstance which, to judge by her expression, was far from pleasing to his mother. She shot a look at Dr Delabole, which caused him to cast a quick glance round the room, and another, of apology, at her, before he unobtrusively withdrew.

Except for those who played whist in the anteroom, where two tables had been set up, the evening, Kate thought, must have been extremely boring. Fortunately, it was not of long duration. The moon was not yet at the full, so that most of the guests, anxious to reach their homes in the last of the daylight, had bespoken their carriages at an early hour. By ten o'clock, even the inveterate lingerers had departed, and Lady Broome, yawning behind her fan, was saying: "What an intolerable bore country dinner-parties are! No one has anything to say that might not as well be left unsaid, and one is reduced to flowery commonplaces. My dear Sir Timothy, I was sorry to be obliged to saddle you with Lady Dunston at dinner, and can only trust that you were not worn down by her prattle!"

"Oh, no!" he replied. "She is always very amiable, and full of anecdote."

"A gabble-monger!"

"Why, yes, my dear, but gabble-mongers have this to be said in their favour: they provide their own entertainment! I find that few things exhaust me more than making conversation. I had an enjoyable rubber of whist, and passed a very agreeable evening. However, I *am* a little tired, so I'll bid you both goodnight."

He smiled vaguely at both ladies, and went away, leaving Lady Broome to thank God the party had broken up so early. "You see how it is, Kate!" she said. "The least thing exhausts him! That is why I so seldom entertain—and then only the people he knows, and who understand

how easily he can be knocked-up. Very naughty of Torquil
to have escaped, but I find it hard to blame him: I fancy
one of his headaches may be coming on. Don't be surprised if he keeps his bed tomorrow!''

Kate privately considered that it was boredom, not headache, which had made Torquil leave the party, but this she
naturally did not say. Nor, when her aunt recommended
her to retire to her own bed, did she say that she was not
tired. But the truth was that she was remarkably wide-
awake, and found the prospect of reading or sewing in her
bedchamber unattractive. She was young, healthy, and full
of energy; she was, furthermore, wholly unused to a life
of indolence. She had welcomed it, but after only a fortnight she had begun to feel enervated, and could almost
have wished herself back in the Astley household, where
there was at least plenty to do.

After sewing on two buttons, and exquisitely darning a
tear in a lace flounce, she was obliged to fold up her work,
for her candle, burning low in the socket, had begun to
flicker. Sleep was as far away as ever, and with an impatient sigh she went to the window, and pulled back the
blinds, looking wistfully out. The moon was not quite at
the full, and its light was rendered the more uncertain by
a cloudy sky, but Kate knew an impulse to slip out of the
house into the scented gardens. She knew very well how
improper this would be, and was just about to draw the
blinds again when she caught a glimpse of a figure emerging from the deep shadow of a yew hedge. It was only for
a moment that she saw it, but for long enough for her to
perceive that it was a man's figure. Then, as though he
became suddenly aware that he was being watched, he
vanished behind the hedge.

Kate was startled, but not alarmed. She had removed
her dress before she settled down to her stitchery, and she

now snatched up her dressing-gown, and hastily put it on before running along the gallery to her aunt's room. There was no response to the first tap on the door so she repeated it, rather more loudly. Then, as still there was no reply, she ventured to open the door, and to speak her aunt's name. Even as she did so she saw, by the light of the lamp burning on a table, that the great bed was unoccupied, its curtains undrawn, and its clothing undisturbed. Since Lady Broome had declared herself to be dropping with sleep, and had certainly gone to her room after bidding Kate goodnight, this was surprising. Kate was wondering what to do next when she saw a light approaching up the secondary stairway which lay at the end of the gallery. That did alarm her for an instant, but even as she caught her breath on a gasp Lady Broome came into sight, carrying a lamp. She had put off her rubies, but she was fully dressed, and was looking exhausted. When she saw Kate, she said sharply: "What is it? What are you doing here?"

"I came in search of you, ma'am. There is a man in the garden: I saw him from my window!"

"Nonsense! *What* man?"

"I don't know that: I had only a glimpse of him before he hid behind the yew hedge. I came to tell you! Should we rouse Pennymore, or, perhaps, Dr Delabole?"

"My dear child, I think you have been dreaming!"

"No, I haven't! I haven't been to bed!" said Kate indignantly.

Lady Broome shrugged. "Well, if you did indeed see someone it was probably one of the servants."

"At this hour?"

'It is not so late, you know! It wants twenty minutes to midnight. Do, child, go back to your room, and to bed!"

"But—"

"Oh, for heaven's sake, don't argue!" interrupted Lady

Broome, with a flash of temper most unusual in her. She stopped herself, pressing a hand to her brow, and said in a more moderate tone: "Forgive me! I have the headache."

The door at the end of the gallery which led into the West Wing opened, and Torquil came into the gallery. When he reached the light thrown by his mother's lamp, Kate saw that he was considerably dishevelled, but in high good humour. He was chuckling a little, and his eyes were sparkling. He said: "I have had a fine game! Hide-and-seek, you know! I led them *such* a dance!"

"Where have you been, Torquil?" asked his mother. She spoke with customary calm, and compellingly.

He giggled. "In the woods. I heard them coming, Matthew and Badger, and I escaped over the bridge. Famous sport! They are still searching for me!"

He sounded unlike himself. Remembering the wine he had drunk at dinner, Kate came to the conclusion that he was a trifle foxed. His speech was not slurred, nor was his gait unsteady, but he seemed to her to be decidedly well to live.

"Go back to your room, Torquil!" said Lady Broome coldly.

His mood changed. He stopped giggling, and glowered at her. "I won't! I won't be ordered about! I'm not a child! No, and I won't be spied on! I won't—"

"Torquil, go back to your room!" commanded Lady Broome, in a level voice.

Her stern eyes held his glittering ones for a few moments of silent struggle for mastery. It was Torquil who yielded. His angry glare shifted, and fell; as his mother advanced slowly towards him, he turned, and ran back into his own quarters, slamming the door behind him.

"You too, Kate," said Lady Broome, her iron calm undisturbed. "There is nothing to alarm you: the man you saw was probably Dr Delabole, or Badger. Goodnight!"

"Goodnight, ma'am," responded Kate, subdued.

Chapter Six

Torquil did not appear at the breakfast-table on the following morning. Kate was not surprised, for experience had taught her that when a man went bosky to bed he awoke with a splitting headache, and a general feeling of being quite out of curl. When Lady Broome apologized, rather stiffly, for the incident, she replied, with her engaging twinkle: "He was in a very merry pin, wasn't he, ma'am? No need to ask you in what sort of cue he is this morning!" She saw that her aunt was staring at her, and added: "No need to beg my pardon either! I have frequently seen men in their altitudes as the saying is. He wasn't more than half-sprung, you know!"

"No," agreed her ladyship slowly. "He wasn't, was he?" She smiled, and said: "I daresay it is unnecessary for me to warn you not to mention the matter to him?"

"Quite unnecessary, dear aunt!" Kate assured her. "I don't suppose that he will retain the least recollection of it!"

This, when Torquil rejoined the family circle before dinner, was seen to be true. He was lethargic, and his eyes, which had shone with such unearthly brilliance, were a little clouded. But he smiled sleepily at Kate, and seemed to be in an unusually docile mood, and with no remembrance of anything that had happened after dinner on the previous evening. Trying to recollect, he frowned, and gave his head a little shake, as though in an attempt to shake off the mists in his brain. Before he could succeed in doing so, Sir Timothy, who had been watching him in what seemed to Kate to be disproportionate anxiety, rose shakily from his chair, muttering: "I am unwell. I must go to my own rooms. Give me your arm, one of you!"

A footman was instantly at his side, but was ousted by Dr Delabole, who said soothingly: "Lean on me, sir! That's the way! You will soon be better—soon be better!"

Torquil had dragged himself to his feet, looking bewildered, but Lady Broome, who had not left her seat, said, without emotion: "Sit down, my son! You can do nothing to help him: it is not serious! He has been in a poor way all day, thanks to last night's party, but he *would* come to dinner!"

She smiled consolingly, and her optimism was soon justified by the return of the doctor, who said, as he resumed his seat at the table, and picked up his knife and fork again, that it was a mere faintness: he had given Sir Timothy a restorative, and had left him in the charge of his valet.

The evening surpassed in dullness all that had gone before it. Lady Broome was abstracted, and Torquil sleepy, and it was left to Dr Delabole to provide entertainment for Kate. He did this by challenging her to a game of cribbage. He said gaily that he was no match for her at backgammon, or piquet, but that he fancied himself to be a bit of a dab at cribbage. He enlivened the game with a constant flow of persiflage, and Kate could only be thankful when her aunt broke up the party soon after the tea-tray had been brought in.

Nothing occurred that night to disturb her rest, but on

the following morning the doctor reported that Torquil was a trifle out of sorts so she was deprived of her daily ride. As though to make up for this, Lady Broome took her out in her barouche, to visit the indigent sick, an unexciting occupation which made her think longingly of a busier if less comfortable life. She found herself wondering how long it would be before she could bring her visit to an end, but it was evident that Lady Broome had no idea of her leaving Staplewood until the autumn, and no suspicion that she might be bored there. Kat had begun to realize that her aunt had very little imagination: she was not herself bored at Staplewood, and could not understand how anyone (least of all an impoverished niece) could wish to be otherwhere. She had surrounded Kate with every luxury; she had clothed her expensively; she had bestowed gifts upon her; and while she brushed off any expressions of gratitude she did expect, perhaps unconsciously, that Kate should repay her with a grateful adoration.

Kate was grateful, but she could not love her aunt. In spite of her kindness, and her generosity, there was something in Lady Broome which repelled her. She more than once suspected that under the façade lay a cold and calculating nature; and tried to recall just what it was that her father had said about his half-sister. Something about her ambition, and how she was ready to go to all lengths to achieve it—but he had said it jokingly, not as though he had meant to disparage her. "She married Broome of Staplewood," he had said, and had laughed. "Not a peer, but pretty well for Miss Minerva Malvern!"

But Papa had not known how proud his sister had become of Staplewood, and the Broome heritage. To Kate, it seemed as if this pride had become an obsession: nothing, in her aunt's esteem, ranked above it. She had taken Kate to the Muniment Room, and had shown her its contents, and Kate had dutifully admired, and marvelled, and said all that was proper. But she could not share her aunt's enthusiasm. It did not seem to her that the unbroken line was of so much importance, but since it was made plain to her that Lady Broome considered it to be of the first importance she did not say so. Only she did wonder that her aunt should bestow so much more of her loving care upon Staplewood than upon her husband, or her son.

She was for ever talking about it, trying, as it appeared, to inspire Kate with something of her own feeling for the place. When she had discharged her errands of mercy, and had rejoined Kate in the carriage, she gave the order to drive home, and told Kate that few things afforded her more pleasure than to pass through the lodge-gates, and up the long, winding avenue to the house. "When I compare it to other people's houses, I realize how superior it is," she said simply.

The sublimity of this statement surprised a choke of laughter out of Kate, for which she immediately apologized, saying that she supposed everyone considered his own house to be superior.

Lady Broome put up her brows. "But how could they? Be it understood that I am not speaking of great houses, such as Chatsworth, or Holkham—though both are too modern for my taste! I daresay there may be some who admire them, but for my part I prefer the antique. I like to think of all the Broomes who have lived at Staplewood— for it dates back beyond the baronetcy, and although succeeding generations have added to it, nothing has ever been destroyed. That is an awe-inspiring thought, is it not?"

"Most sobering!" agreed Kate, a little dryly.

Missing the inflexion, Lady Broome said: "Yes, that is what I feel." After a pause, she said dreamily: "Sometimes I wonder whether my successor will share my feeling. I hope so, but I don't depend on it.''

"Your successor, ma'am?"

"Torquil's wife. She will be a very fortunate young woman, won't she?''

"Why, yes, ma'am! I suppose she will.''

"Position, wealth, Staplewood, a house in the best part of London—'' Lady Broome broke off, sighing. "That was a sad blow to me, you know: being obliged to shut it up. Before Sir Timothy's health failed, we were used to spend several months in London, during the Season. I won't conceal from you, my dear, that I enjoyed those months excessively! I don't think there can have been a single *ton* party given for which I didn't receive a card of invitation. I was famed for my own parties, and have frequently entertained the Prince Regent, besides other members of the Royal Family. You may readily conceive what it meant to me to be obliged to give it all up! But the doctors were insistent that London-life would never do for Sir Timothy. His constitution has always been delicate. Even when we were first married, he was used to become exhausted for what seemed to me to be no cause at all. He was bored by the balls, and the drums, and the race-parties, and the Opera-nights of which *I* could never have enough, but because he knew how much I enjoyed that way of life he concealed his boredom from me. And I was too young, and perhaps too much intoxicated by my success, to realize it.'' She smiled faintly. "I *was* successful, you know! *My* parties were always amongst the biggest squeezes of the Season! But, naturally, when Sir Timothy suffered his first heart attack, and the doctors warned me that a continued residence in London would prove fatal, I perceived that it was my duty to abandon the fashionable life, and to devote myself entirely to Staplewood. I've accustomed myself, but I do, now and then, envy Torquil's wife!''

Rendered vaguely uneasy by this speech, and acutely aware of the footmen standing rigidly behind her, Kate tried for a lighter note. ''You should consider, Aunt Minerva, that Torquil's wife may not share your sentiments! For anything you know, he may fall violently in love with a country-bred girl who would shrink from the town-diversions which to you are so desirable!''

The barouche, having passed through the lodge-gates, was now bowling up the avenue. After a moment's silence, Lady Broome said abruptly: ''Would they not be desirable to you, Kate?''

Since she had never considered the question, it took Kate aback. She took time over her answer, and, as the house came into sight, replied hesitantly: ''I don't know. They might, I suppose.''

Lady Broome seemed to be satisfied, and said no more. In another few minutes, the barouche drew up, and the ladies alighted from it. As they entered the house, Kate was impelled to say: ''Knowing myself to be quite ineligible, I have never permitted myself to think how it would be to become a fashionable lady. Which is just as well, perhaps, since I'm almost an ape-leader now!''

''What nonsense!'' replied Lady Broome, amused. ''Is there *no* gentleman for whom you feel a *tendre?*''

''Not one!'' replied Kate blithely. ''Oh, in my salad days I fancied myself to be in love with several dashing officers—and with one in particular! I've forgotten his name, but he was very handsome, and, I regret to confess, a very ramshackle person! I have heard that he married a woman of fortune—that, of course, was always an object with him!—and is now the father of a hopeful family!''

''I hope you don't mean to tell me that you have no

admirers! That, I must warn you, would be coming it very much too strong!''

"No, ma'am, I don't mean to tell you that," replied Kate, "but my admirers, owing to my want of fortune, think of me as an agreeable flirt, not as a wife. Only one of them ever made me an offer—and he was the most odious little mushroom!''

"Ah, the brother of your late employer! You told me about him, and very diverting I found it! But it is a sad fact, my love, that the lot of a single female who has no fortune is not a happy one. While she is young, and able to earn her bread, it may be supportable; but when one is old and unwanted—oh, let us not dwell upon such misery! It makes me shudder even to think of it!''

It made Kate shudder too, but inwardly. It was as though a cold hand had closed over her heart; and although, with the optimism of youth, she shook it off, it made her remember her unavailing search for employment, and ask herself if boredom was really so great a price to pay for security.

But the feeling that she was being enclosed in a silken net grew upon her during the following weeks; and, when she scolded herself for being so stupid, it occurred to her that she had very little money left in her purse, not enough to pay for the coach-fare to London, and something akin to panic seized her. She might write to Sarah, begging her to come to her rescue, but Sarah had answered none of her letters, and the seed sown by Lady Broome had borne fruit. She did not doubt Sarah's affection, but she had certainly been a charge on her, and it was possible that Sarah was thankful to be relieved of it. Things had changed since the days when Sarah had been her nurse: she was married now, and, besides her husband, she had his father and his nephews to care for. And even though she would probably still extend a welcome to her nursling, Kate recoiled from the thought of foisting herself on her again, and for heaven only knew how long a period.

Meanwhile, nothing happened at Staplewood to relieve the monotony of its ordered days, the only variation being Church-going every Sunday. The family attended Divine Service in the village Church, which was conducted by the Vicar, a middle-aged cleric, with obsequious manners, who stood in unbecoming awe of Lady Broome, and preached long, and very dull sermons. To these, however, the occupants of the Broome pew were not obliged even to pretend to listen, this pew being screened from the rest of the congregation by walls of carved oak, dating from Jacobean times, and reminding Kate irresistibly of a loose-box.

To reach it, it was necessary to walk in procession down the aisle; and, since his infirmity made Sir Timothy's progress slow, and Lady Broome inclined her head graciously whenever she perceived a known face, this was so like a Royal Visitation that Kate was torn between embarrassment, and an improper inclination to giggle.

Driving to Church in the first of the two carriages which set out from Staplewood, with his lady beside him, and the two footmen perched up behind, seemed to be the only expedition Sir Timothy ever took beyond his gates; and although Kate suspected that he would have been pleased to have lingered in the porch, after the service, greeting friends and tenants, he was never permitted to do so, Lady Broome discouraging any tendency to loiter, either because there was a sharp wind blowing, or because to stand about was what his doctor particularly deprecated. In this she was ably seconded by Delabole, who insisted on Sir Timothy's taking his arm, and conducted him tenderly back to the barouche. The party then drove back to Staplewood at a sedate pace, the second carriage being occupied by Kate, the doctor, and, when he was well enough to be dragged unwillingly to Church, Torquil.

But when the warmer weather came it brought with it a mild diversion, in the form of two al fresco parties, one being held at Staplewood, and the other at Nutfield Place, the residence of the Dunsters, where Kate was surprised to see Gurney Templecombe. He at once came up to her to ask how she did. "But no need to ask, Miss Malvern!" he said gallantly. "I can see you're in high bloom!"

"Thank you, but how comes this about, sir? I had supposed you to be in London, escorting your sister to Almack's!"

"No, no, I'm held to have done my duty, and have escaped! She's engaged to be married, you know: notice will be in the Morning Post next week."

"What, already?" she exclaimed.

He nodded, grinning. "Quite a triumph, ain't it? Mind you, I knew how it would be: even I can see she's a taking little thing! Amesbury popped the question before she'd been in town above a sennight! He's a friend of mine: a very good fellow! Of course, m'mother said they must wait, but anyone could see she was in high croak! Well, what I mean is, it's the best marriage she's made for any of the girls—not that she did make it: they fell head over ears in love with each other!"

Kate disclosed this information to her aunt, as they drove back to Staplewood. Lady Broome laughed, and said: "To Lord Amesbury! Well, I'm sure I wish her very happy. I must own that I have the greatest admiration for Lady Templecombe: how she contrived to find eligible husbands for four daughters, and all in their first seasons, really does command applause! They are no more than respectably dowered, too: I should doubt if they have more than ten thousand apiece, and I shouldn't have said that the elder girls had beauty enough to figure in London.''

"That can't be said of the youngest, ma'am!"

"No, very true: Dorothea is remarkably pretty," agreed her ladyship. "A lovely little pea-goose!"

Kate hesitated for a moment. "Mr Templecombe told me that the engagement won't be announced until next week, but I thought you would wish to know of it earlier, in case—in case you think it wise to warn Torquil, Aunt Minerva."

"My dear child," said her ladyship, mildly amused, "have you lived with us for several weeks without discovering that, with Torquil, it is *out of sight, out of mind*? Oh, I don't doubt this news will put him into a flame! After that he will glump for a day or two, before forgetting all about it. The case would have been different, of course, had I permitted him to dangle after her."

Kate's brow was wrinkled. She said: "Why didn't you, ma'am? It seems to me such a suitable alliance!"

"I have other plans for Torquil," replied her aunt lightly. "So, as is seen, had Lady Templecombe for Dorothea!"

Whatever Kate may have thought of this ruthless management of her son, she very soon saw that Lady Broome had exactly gauged the effect of the announcement on him. It did, at first wind him up; and he talked, in a theatrical way, of Dolly's having sold herself to the highest bidder; but he then fell into the mops, in which state of mind he was at outs with everyone, ripping up grievances, and subjecting his entourage to Turkish treatment, as Kate roundly informed him. It seemed, for a moment, that he would take violent exception to this reproof, but after staring at her for a blazing instant he suddenly burst out laughing, snatched her into his arms in a breath-taking hug, and exclaimed: "I like you! Oh, I *do* like you, coz!"

"Well," said Kate, disengaging herself, "I don't know why you should, but I'm very much obliged to you!" She saw that this rebuff had brought back the lowering look to his face, and added: "Now don't try to come the ugly with me, Torquil, for you'll be taken at fault if you do!"

He looked at her, queerly smiling. "Not afraid of me, are you, coz?"

"Not in the least!"

There was a spark kindling in his eyes; he said softly: "Shall I make you afraid? No, I don't think I will. And yet—and yet—!" His smile grew; he took her face between his slim, strong hands, and turned it up. An indefinable change came into his own face; his eyes grew brighter; his fingers slid down to her throat, and she felt them harden, and quiver.

From the doorway, a stern voice said imperatively: "Torquil!"

Torquil's hands fell; he lifted them again, but to press them over his eyes. Kate, flushing, found herself confronting a stranger, who looked her over rather contemptuously, and then transferred his gaze to Torquil. He seemed but just to have arrived at Staplewood, and to have come from some distance, for he was wearing a long, caped driving-coat, which brushed the heels of his top-boots, and he was carrying his hat and gloves in one hand. He was a tall man, with broad shoulders, and very regular features; and Kate judged him to be about thirty years of age.

A sigh broke from Torquil; he uncovered his eyes, and turned, blinking at the stranger. "Why—why—*Philip!*" he exclaimed, starting forward with every sign of delight.

The stranger smiled at him. "Well, bantling? How do you do?" he said, holding out his hand.

Torquil clasped it eagerly. "Oh, famously! But how is this? Did we expect you? Have you come to stay?"

"For a day or two. No, you didn't expect me. Am I unwelcome?"

"You will be, with Mama!" said Torquil, giggling. His eyes fell on Kate; he said: "Oh, are you there, coz! This is Philip, you know! Philip, this is Cousin Kate!"

She was too much surprised by his unaffected pleasure in his Cousin Philip's arrival to take more than cursory note of the artless surprise in his voice when he saw that she was still in the room. When she recalled how viciously he had spoken to her of Philip Broome, she could only marvel at him, and congratulate herself on not having believed his accusations.

"Ah, yes!" said Philip, bowing slightly. "Cousin Kate!"

"I don't think I can claim even remote kinship with you, sir," she retorted, nettled by his tone.

"Can't you? Why not?"

"I am merely Lady Broome's half-niece. I can only be, at the best—or worst—a *connection* of yours!"

This flash of spirit seemed to amuse him; a reluctant smile warmed his eyes; he said: "Bravo!"

"Philip, have you seen my father?" interrupted Torquil.

"No, not yet: Pennymore tells me that he's not in very plump currant, and doesn't leave his room until noon. Tenby is helping him to dress so I came to find you instead."

"Oh, yes! I'm glad you did: I have so much to tell you!"

Kate went quietly out of the room, her mind in turmoil. Although she had not believed that he could be responsible for the various accidents which had befallen Torquil, she had had no doubt that Torquil hated him, and she had been prepared to dislike him. But Torquil had astonished her by welcoming him with real pleasure; and she did not dislike him. He had given her every reason to do so; but when she had seen him standing in the doorway she had received the instant impression that she beheld a man in whom one could place one's trust, without fearing to be betrayed. Then she had read the contempt in his eyes, and she had been as much shocked as enraged. What right, she asked herself, had he to despise her? What cause had she ever given him? How *dared* he? she silently demanded, lashing herself into a fury.

It was in this mood of burning chagrin that she encountered Lady Broome, halfway up the stairs. Lady Broome barred her progress, laying a hand on her arm, and saying, with a lightness at variance with the keen glance she directed at her face: "Whither away, Kate? You look to be out of reason cross! Can it be that Mr Philip Broome has set up your hackles? Oh, yes! I know that he has descended on us, and I am heartily sorry for it! We go on very much better without him. Don't you like him?"

"No, ma'am, I do not!" replied Kate, with undue vehemence. "I—I think him an—an *odious* person!"

"Do you? Well, so do I—to give you the word with no bark on it! But it won't do to say so, you know: Sir Timothy dotes on him! His influence is one which I have always deprecated. He is a man of large ambitions, one of which, unless I much mistake the matter, is to succeed to the title and the estates. When I tell you that one life only stands between him and the realization of his ambition, you won't be astonished that I should regard him with—how shall I put it?—*dread* was the word which sprang to my tongue, but perhaps that is a little too strong! I'll say, instead, *apprehension.*"

Kate regarded her with painful intensity. "Torquil told

me once, ma'am, that all the accidents which had befallen him occurred when his cousin was staying at Staplewood. I didn't believe that Mr Philip Broome could have been responsible for any of them, but—but *was* he?''

Lady Broome seemed to hesitate before replying: ''It is hard to see how he could have been. You will not mention this, if you please!''

''No, ma'am,'' Kate said obediently. She lingered, frowning, and then said, turning her eyes once more upon her aunt: ''But I don't understand! I had supposed Torquil to hold his cousin in—in positive hatred, but when he saw him, just now, he was *glad!*''

''Was he? Well, that doesn't surprise me as much as it seems to have surprised you, my dear! Torquil is a creature of moods! He was used, when a child, to adore Philip, and I daresay some of that old feeling remains. Depend upon it, he will have come to cuffs with him before the day is out!''

He did not do so, but it was easy to see that his mood underwent a change, becoming steadily more uncertain as the day wore on. For this, Kate considered, Dr Delabole was a good deal to blame, for when Torquil dragged his cousin off to the stables he found an excuse to accompany them, showing, she thought, a sad want of tact. Nothing could have been more exactly calculated to set up Torquil's back! He told the doctor, very rudely, that he was not wanted, and it had been Philip's intervention which had averted an explosion. Philip had recommended him to try for a little conduct, and although he had flushed up to the roots of his hair he had subsided. It was obvious that he stood greatly in awe of Philip, which was not, thought Kate, at all surprising. It was a case of the weak character yielding to the strong: just as Lady Broome could with one word quell a sudden spurt of temper, so too could Philip.

When the party assembled for dinner, Sir Timothy came in leaning on Philip's arm. He was pathetically glad to see his nephew again, speaking fondly to him, and regarding him with a mixture of pride and affection. Kate could not wonder at it, for the affection was clearly mutual, and Philip treated him with the deference which was almost wholly to find in his son. The contrast between the man and the boy was painful: Torquil was beautiful, but his manners were those of a spoiled child. Towards his social inferiors he was arrogant, and although he was civil to his father and mother, his civility was grudging. Kate had never been able to discover a trace of affection in him for either of his parents, and had again and again been shocked by his indifference. He was obedient to his mother only because he feared her; his father he largely ignored. His temper was quite uncontrolled: the least thing would cause him to fly up into the boughs; and he could sulk for days. Philip, on the other hand, had good manners, and if his countenance was stern he had only to smile to make it easy to see why Sir Timothy loved him. There was nothing of the dandy in his appearance, but he dressed with a neatness and a propriety which cast into strong and unflattering relief Torquil's negligent style.

Sir Timothy, when Kate came into the room, welcomed her with a smile, and an outstretched hand. "Ah, here she is!" he said. "Come here, my dear, and let me make my nephew known to you!"

"I have already had the honour of making Miss Malvern's acquaintance, sir."

"Oh, that is too bad! I had promised myself the pleasure of introducing you to her. She is our good angel—a ray of sunshine in the house!"

Philip bowed politely. Kate, a good deal embarrassed, took the frail hand held out to her, but said: "Thank you sir! You are a great deal too kind, but you are putting me to the blush. Besides, if you make me out to be beyond the common Mr Broome will be disappointed!''

''By no means, Miss Malvern! I think you quite beyond the common.''

''Mr Broome—Miss Malvern—! What is all this formality?'' asked Sir Timothy playfully. ''Let me tell you, Philip, that we have decided that she shall be Cousin Kate!''

''Well, sir, I did so address her, but she refuses to acknowledge the relationship.'' He turned his head towards Lady Broome. ''I understand she is your half-niece, Minerva?''

''My half-brother's only child,'' she answered shortly.

''Just so! I own I haven't worked out the exact degree of our relationship, but she informs me that—at the worst—we can only be *connections!*''

''Oh, pooh! no need to stand upon points!'' said Sir Timothy, brushing the objection aside. He smiled up at Kate, as she stood beside his chair. ''She is the daughter of my old age, and that makes her your cousin.''

Kate could only be thankful that Pennymore chose at this moment to announce dinner. Sir Timothy, struggling to rise from his chair, found a strong hand under his elbow, and said: ''Thank you, my boy. Not as steady on my pins as I was used to be! Now, if you'll lend me your arm, we'll go down to dinner.''

It occurred forcibly to Kate that Torquil's support had been neither offered nor requested. He was lounging by one of the windows, his brow overcast; and it was not until Lady Broome called upon him to escort her that he was roused from abstraction. He got up, but muttered disagreeably that he wondered why she chose to go down on his arm rather than Matthew's.

While Kate sat in her usual place at the dinner-table, on Sir Timothy's right, Mr Philip Broome was on his left: an arrangement that brought them opposite each other. It seemed to her that whenever she looked up she found that he was watching her, until at last, considerably ruffled, she tried to stare him down. She might have succeeded if the absurdity of it had not struck her, and made her utter an involuntary chuckle. Then, as this drew everyone's attention to her, she lowered her gaze to her plate, and replied, in answer to her aunt's demand to know what had amused her: "Nothing, ma'am: I beg your pardon!"

Torquil, who had been pushing the food about on his plate, thrust it away suddenly, and said: "Philip, will you play billiards after dinner?"

Philip looked at him under his brows, frowning a little. "Yes, if you wish," he replied.

"Well, I do wish! I'm tired of playing with Matthew: he always lets me win. And Kate is a wretched player!"

"So you are obliged to let *her* win!" said the doctor quizzingly.

"No, I'm not," said Torquil, staring at him. "Why should I?"

"Chivalry, dear boy! Chivalry!"

"Oh, Kate don't care for that stuff, do you, coz?"

"No, and isn't it a fortunate circumstance?" she said brightly.

"Yes— Oh, you're joking me!"

"No."

"Have I put you into a miff?" he asked incredulously. "Oh, well, then, I'm sorry! If you care to join us tonight I'll give you a game, and I *will* let you win!"

"Very handsome of you, Torquil, but I am going to play backgammon with your father." She turned her shoulder on him as she spoke, and smiled at Sir Timothy. "You won't let me win either, will you, sir?"

"Not if I can prevent you, my dear! But you are growing to be so expert that I doubt if I can hold you at bay for much longer!" He glanced at his nephew. "You must know that Kate indulges me with a game of piquet, or of backgammon, every evening, Philip."

"Does she, sir?" said Philip dryly. "How very obliging of her!"

Chapter Seven

When Torquil and Philip came back to the drawing-room after their game of billiards, Sir Timothy was just about to retire to bed, and Kate was putting the backgammon-pieces away. Sir Timothy paused, leaning on his valet's arm, to ask how the billiards-match had gone. Torquil shrugged, and laughed. "Oh, he beat me, sir! I was quite off my game!"

"Were you? But you could hardly expect to win against Philip, could you? He and I were used to play a great deal together: indeed, I taught him to play, and I was no mean player, was I, Philip?"

"No, sir, you were very good—too good for me!"

Sir Timothy laughed gently. "At the start, of course I was! But we ended pretty evenly matched, I think. Kate, don't put the backgammon away! Why don't you have a game with Philip? She plays very well, Philip: she beat me three times tonight, let me tell you!"

"I had some lucky throws, sir. But you won the last of our games, and I don't care to risk my luck against Mr Broome tonight. I am going to bed too."

"Afraid, Cousin Kate?" Philip said.

"No, sir: sleepy!" she retorted.

He accepted this with a slight bow. "Another night, then, I shall hope to pit my skill against yours."

"De buena gana!"

There was a gleam of interest in his eyes, and a furrow between his brows. He said: "Where did you learn to speak Spanish, cousin?"

"My father was a military man, sir, and I passed my youth in the Peninsula," she answered, and turned from him to address Lady Broome, begging leave to be excused, and saying that she had a slight headache.

A gracious permission having been granted, she went away, in a mood of strange depression. Ellen's artless prattle, while she helped her to undress, did little to lighten it. Ellen was full of Mr Philip Broome's perfections; she thought it such a sad pity that he wasn't Sir Timothy's son. Everyone said so, even Mr Pennymore!

Kate dismissed the girl presently, but she did not immediately get into bed. It had occurred to her that Mr Philip Broome was at the root of her depression, and it was necessary to rid her mind of this absurd notion. There was no reason why he should like her; but similarly there was no reason why he should have taken her in dislike, which he undoubtedly had. Nor was there any reason why she should care a pin for his opinion of her. She told herself so, but she did care. Facing the abominable truth, she was forced to admit that from the first moment of setting eyes on him she had formed a decided partiality for Mr Philip Broome.

She arose on the following morning, rather heavy-eyed from the effects of a restless night, and went down to the breakfast-parlor. Mr Philip Broome was its sole occupant. She checked involuntarily on the threshold, but recovered herself in an instant, bidding him a cheerful good-morning, and advancing to take her seat opposite him. He was dis-

cussing a plate of ham, but he got up, at her entrance, and
returned her greeting. "May I give you some coffee,
cousin?" he asked.

"No, thank you, sir: I prefer tea," she replied politely.

"There seems to be none: I'll ring for Pennymore," he
said. "Meanwhile, may I carve some ham for you?"

"No, thank you, sir: I prefer bread-and-butter."

His lips twitched. "A bread-and-butter miss? I don't believe it!"

She said, stung into retort: "I'm no such thing!"

"So I knew," he said, resuming his seat, adding, after
a reflective moment: "Or so I thought, perhaps I should
say." Without giving her time to reply, he said abruptly:
"Why *did* you laugh last night at dinner?"

She looked up quickly, her eyes suddenly full of mischief. "Oh—! I've forgotten!"

"No, you haven't."

"Well, if you must have it, sir, I laughed because I
thought, all at once, that we must resemble nothing so
much as two cats trying to stare one another out!" she
answered frankly.

That made his lips twitch again. "Was I staring at you?
I beg your pardon, but can you blame me? I was unprepared to find myself confronting such a highly finished
piece of nature."

"I trust you will forgive me, sir, when I say that *I* was
unprepared to receive extravagant compliments from you!
I thought you were a man of sense."

"I am," he replied imperturbably.

"Well, no one would believe it who heard you talking
flowery commonplaces!"

"Don't you think yourself—a highly finished piece of
nature?"

"No, of course I don't!"

"An antidote?" he asked, with interest.

She gave a choke of laughter. "No, nor that either!—Good-morning, Pennymore!"

"Good-morning, miss," said Pennymore, setting a teapot and a dish of hot scones before her. "Have you any orders for Whalley?"

"No, no, it is far too hot to ride for pleasure! At least, it is for me."

"Yes, miss. Very sultry it is this morning. It wouldn't surprise me if we was to get a storm."

"Oh, I hope not!"

"Are you afraid of thunderstorms?" asked Philip, as Pennymore left the room.

"Yes, a little. I was once in a very bad one, in Spain, and I saw a man struck down." She broke off, shuddering. Summoning up a smile, she said: "Since when I have become shockingly hen-hearted!"

He directed a considering look at her, but said nothing, and, as Lady Broome came into the room at that moment, the subject was abandoned. She was shortly followed by Torquil, who wanted to know what were the plans for the day. On hearing that none had been made, he propounded that he, and Kate, and Philip should go on a picnic expedition to some place which, from what Kate could gather, was situated at a considerable distance from Staplewood. Lady Broome entered an instant veto, and was supported by Philip, who said that he, for one, did not mean to ride so far on what promised to be a very sultry day. "And, if Pennymore is to believed—which I think he is," he said, turning to look over his shoulder out of the window, "we are going to have a thunderstorm."

"Oh, pooh! What of it?" said Torquil impatiently. "One can always find shelter!"

"Not in my experience!" said his cousin.

"No, and not in mine either!" said Kate. "Besides, it's too hot for riding! I've told Pennymore so already, so pray exclude me from this expedition of yours, Torquil! Another day, perhaps!"

He set his cup down with a crash into its saucer. "Anything I want to do!" he said, in a trembling voice. "It's always the same tale! Always!" He jumped up from his chair, thrusting it back so violently that it fell over, and went blindly to the door.

Here he was checked by Dr Delabole, who was just entering the room, and who barred his passage, laying a restraining hand on his arm, and saying: "Whither away, Torquil? Now, what has happened to put you all on end? Come, come, my boy, this won't do! You will bring on one of your distressing migraines, and I shall be obliged to physic you!"

"Come back to the table, my son!" commanded Lady Broome sternly. "You are behaving like a child, and must be treated like one, unless you mend your ways! Pick up your chair!"

He gave a dry sob, and turned, white and wild-eyed, and stared at her for a hard-breathing moment. As Kate had seen once before, his eyes sank under Lady Broome's quelling gaze. Kate leaned sideways to pick up his chair, and patted it invitingly, smiling at him. "Come and sit down again!" she coaxed.

His smouldering eyes travelled slowly to her face, searching it suspiciously. Finding nothing in it but friendly sympathy, he yielded to her invitation, muttering: "Very well! To oblige *you* coz!"

"You shall be rewarded with one of my scones," she said lightly. "I'll butter it for you."

He said nothing, either then, or when she handed it to him, but he ate it. Lady Broome, turning her attention to

Philip, engaged him in conversation, while Kate talked in a soothing under-voice to Torquil, and the doctor applied himself with his usual appetite, to his breakfast.

Encountering Philip an hour later, in the hall, Kate would have passed him with no more than a nod, but he stopped her, and asked her where she was going. She replied: "To cut some fresh roses, sir. This hot weather has made the ones I gathered yesterday hang their heads, and they refuse to be revived."

"I'll accompany you, if I may—to carry the basket!" he said, taking it from her hand. "Where is Torquil?"

"I think he has ridden out with Whalley."

"Unfortunate Whalley!"

She was silent.

"You seem to possess the knack of managing him, cousin," he said, as they crossed the lawn towards the rose-garden. "My felicitations!"

"I don't know that. I have had some experience in the management of spoiled children."

"So that was true, was it? When I saw you, I supposed it to be one of Gurney's Banbury stories."

She looked round at him in surprise. "Did Mr Temple-combe tell you that I had been a governess?" He nodded. "I wonder why he should have done so?"

"He thought I might be interested. I was."

Her surprise grew. "I can't conceive why you should have been!"

"Can't you?" He raised a quizzical eyebrow.

"No. Unless—"

"Unless what?" he asked, as she hesitated.

She still hesitated, but presently confessed, with a tiny chuckle: "Well, I was going to say, unless you wondered how it was possible for my aunt to own an indigent relative! The thing was that she didn't know I existed, until a month ago.''

"I take leave to doubt that.''

"No, indeed it's true! You see, my father quarrelled with his family when Aunt Minerva was still in the schoolroom, and—and—they cut the connection!''

"And what brought it to Minerva's knowledge that you did exist?''

"My old nurse wrote to her, informing her of my circumstances.''

"I see.''

"And then my aunt swept down upon me,'' continued Kate, not perceiving his curling lip. "I was never nearer to pulling caps with poor Sarah! But she did it all for the best, and so it has turned out. For my aunt invited me to stay here, and has overwhelmed me with kindness.'' She paused, and then said, with a little difficulty: "I collect you don't like her, but you must not say so to me, if you please!''

He regarded her frowningly. "Oh, no, I won't say so!'' He stood aside for her to pass through the archway cut in the yew hedge that enclosed the rose-garden. "You have made conquests of them all, Cousin Kate—even of my uncle!''

"I am sure I have done no such thing.''

"But indeed you have. I hear your praises sung on all sides.''

"I expect I should be excessively gratified—if I believed you!'' she retorted, laying the two roses she had cut into the basket, and moving on.

"You may believe me—and accept my compliments!''

She turned to confront him, a spark of anger in her eyes. "That goes beyond the line of pleasing, sir! I am well aware that you've taken me in dislike, so pray don't try to flummery me!''

"I beg your pardon! But I don't think I have taken you in dislike. I own that I came prepared to do so, but you puzzle me, you know: you are rather unexpected!''

"Well, I know of no reason why you should say so, unless you expected to find I was inching my way into your uncle's good graces to—to batten on him! Was that it?''

"No. Not entirely."

"Not—'' She uttered an indignant gasp, and then, suddenly, laughed, and said: "I suppose it does look like that! Let me assure you that it *isn't* like that, sir!''

"In that case, I am sorry for you," he said. He glanced over his shoulder, and smiled sardonically. "Yes, I thought it wouldn't be long before Minerva came to discover what I have been saying to you." He waited until Lady Broome had come up to join them, and then greeted her with the utmost affability. "Do join us, Minerva! I've been attempting to flummery Cousin Kate, and without the least success."

"Absurd creature! Kate, my love, when you have finished picking roses, I want you to come and help me in the house. Dear me, how oppressively hot it is out here! And you without a hat! You will become sadly tanned! Nothing is more injurious to the complexion than to expose it to strong sunshine! There are some who say that contact with *all* fresh air is destructive of female charms— the natural enemy of a smooth skin. But that I don't agree with, though a wind is certainly to be avoided. I myself always wear a veil, or carry a parasol, as I am doing now."

"And who shall blame you, ma'am?" said Philip. "It throws a most becoming light on your face!"

"Are you now trying to flummery me, Philip? You are wasting your time!"

"No, merely paying a tribute to your unerring taste in choosing a *pink* parasol."

She cast him an unloving look. "You would say, I collect, that my face needs to be protected from the unflattering daylight?"

"I shouldn't say anything of the sort," he replied. "I am not so uncivil, Minerva."

She bit her lip, but returned no answer. They strolled together in Kate's wake, until she had cut enough blooms to replenish her vases. Lady Broome then bore Kate off to the house, and kept her occupied until she knew Philip would be out of the way. Since the tasks she found for Kate to perform were all of a trifling nature, Kate could not but feel that she had purposely interrupted a tête-à-tête, and wondered why.

Except for one or two flickers of lightning, and some distant rumbles, the storm held off all day, but it broke in the middle of the night. Kate was jerked awake by the first crash, which sounded to be directly over the house. Almost before its echoes had died away, she heard another sound, and this time, she was sure, inside the house. It was even more alarming than the storm, because it was a cry of terror. She sat up, thrusting back the curtains of the bed, and listened intently, her heart thudding in her breast. She could hear nothing, but the sudden silence was not reassuring. She winced as the thunder crashed again, but slid out of her bed and caught up her shawl. Hastily wrapping this round herself, she groped her way to the door, intending to open it, so that she could hear more clearly. She cautiously turned the handle, but the door remained shut. She had been locked in.

In unreasoning panic she tugged at the handle, and beat

with clenched fists on the panels. The noise was drowned
by another clap of thunder, which drove her back to her
bed, blundering into the furniture, and feeling blindly for
the table which stood beside it. Her fingers at last found
the tinder-box, but they were trembling so much that it
was some time before she succeeded in striking the spark.
She relit her candle, but even as the little tongue of flame
dimly illumined the room her panic abated, and was succeeded by anger. She climbed into bed again, and sat hugging her knees, trying to find the answer to two insoluble
problems: who had locked her in? and why? The more she
cudgelled her brain the less could she hit upon any possible
theory. She began to feel stupid, and, as the storm seemed
to be receding into the distance, blew out the candle, and
lay down.

When she next woke, it was morning, and the pale sun-
light, seeping into the room through the chinks in the
blinds, made the night's alarms ridiculous. She could almost believe that she had dreamt the whole, until her eyes
alighted on the chair she had overturned, and she realized
that her toes were bruised. She slid out of bed, and went
to try the door again. It opened easily, but she noticed, for
the first time, that there was no key in its lock. She went
thoughtfully back to bed, determined to demand an explanation of her aunt.

But Lady Broome, listening to her with raised brows,
merely said: "My dear child, if you wish to lock yourself
in, a strict search shall be made for the key! But why *do*
you wish to do so? Who, do you imagine, has designs on
your virtue?"

"No, no, ma'am, you mistake! What I wish is *not* to be
locked in!"

Lady Broome regarded her in some amusement, but

said, with perfect gravity: "Certainly not! But *were* you, in sober fact, locked in?"

Kate flushed. "Do you think I'm cutting a sham, ma'am?"

"No, dear child, of course I don't!" replied her lady-ship. "Merely of having allowed your mind to be quite overcome by the storm! Extraordinarily violent, wasn't it? That first clap, Dr Delabole tells me, made Torquil start up with a positive shriek!"

"Then it was he who uttered that cry of terror!" Kate exclaimed.

"Yes, did you hear it?" said Lady Broome smoothly. "He hates storms even more than you do! They bring on some of his worst migraines. Indeed, he is quite prostrate today!"

"Is he? I am sorry," said Kate mechanically. "But—but—my mind was not overset, ma'am! It wasn't the storm which made me get up, but that cry! And I couldn't open the door!"

"Couldn't you, my love?" said Lady Broome.

"No! I couldn't!" stated Kate emphatically. "I can see that you don't believe me, Aunt Minerva, but—"

"Dearest, I believe you implicitly! Your mind was all chaos! You were rudely awakened by that first clap; you heard Torquil cry out; you tumbled, half-asleep, out of bed; you tried to pull open your door, and failed! So you went back to bed. But when you woke for the second time, and again tried to open your door, you found that you could easily do so! Well—what interpretation would you wish me to put on that, my love, except the very obvious one that your senses were disordered?"

"I don't know," said Kate, feeling remarkably foolish. But when she recalled the cry she had heard she did not think that Torquil had made it. He had a boy's voice, and when he raised it it was rather shrill; what she had heard was unmistakeably a man's voice. She said nothing, however, because Mr Philip Broome walked in at that moment, saying: "Good-morning, Minerva—Cousin Kate! The storm did a good deal of damage: several tiles blown from the roof, a tree down, and enough wreckage in the gardens to keep Risby and his minions busy for days. Where's Torquil?"

"He has one of his migraines," answered Lady Broome. "Storms always affect him in that way, you know."

"I didn't, but I can readily believe it."

Kate looked at him in some surprise. "Why, are you so affected, sir?"

"No. I slept through it. Did you?"

"I'm afraid I didn't, but it hasn't given me a headache. But then I am not subject to headaches."

"Oh, you shouldn't have said that!" he told her reproachfully. "You made a headache your excuse for not playing backgammon with me the other evening."

The twinkle in her eyes acknowledged a hit, but she replied without hesitation: "You are very right: it was uncivil of me to have said it, sir!"

He smiled. "Well done, Cousin Kate! A homestall!"

Dr Delabole, entering the room in time to overhear this, asked playfully: "And what, may one venture to ask, is a homestall, Mr Philip?"

One of the few adjuncts of the dandy which Mr Philip Broome affected was the quizzing-glass. He used it to depress pretension. He now raised it to his eye, and through it dispassionately observed the doctor, allowing his gaze to travel slowly from Dr Delabole's feet to his head: a process which the doctor found to be strangely unnerving. After keeping it levelled for a few moments, he let it fall, and replied suavely: "Position, or place, sir—according to the dictionaries.'' He waited for the effect of this snub to be felt, and then said: ''May one—in one's turn—venture to ask how your patient does?''

''Do you refer to Sir Timothy, Mr Philip?'' countered the doctor, making a gallant recover. ''Not very brisk, I regret to say. His constitution, you know—''

''No, I refer to my cousin Torquil,'' said Philip, ruthlessly interrupting him. ''Lady Broome has just informed me that he is quite knocked-up by the storm, which has brought on one of his distressing migraines.''

''Alas, too true!'' said the doctor, mournfully shaking his head. ''One had hoped— But we know too little, as yet, about the effects of atmospheric electricity upon the system! I have been obliged to administer a sedative. Not, I confess, a thing one would wish to do, in the case of so young a patient, but when a blister applied to the head, and cataplasms to the feet, had failed to produce any alleviation of what you so justly term his *distressing migraines,* sir, I considered it proper to administer a paregoric draught. He is now asleep, but will, I trust, wake up in better cue.''

''Even if he should be rather drowsy. And how, doctor, is the faithful Badger?'' enquired Philip affably.

''Badger?'' repeated the doctor, apparently bewildered.

''Yes, Badger! I caught sight of him this morning, and he looked to be in very queer stirrups—almost as though he had been engaging in cross and jostle work, and had come off the worse for it.''

''Oh!'' said the doctor, laughing. ''One learns not to ask embarrassing questions of our good Badger when he has enjoyed leave of absence! If he has a fault, it is that he is rather too ready to sport his canvas when he has had a cup too much!''

''Indeed! He was never used to be so. Now that I come

to think of it, I can't recall that I ever saw him above his bend either,'' said Philip reminiscently. He smiled limpidly at the doctor, and said with even more affability: ''He was used to look after me, when I was boy, you know. Or perhaps you don't: it was before your time.''

Dr Delabole gave Kate the impression of one who was fighting with his back to the wall. She glanced quickly at him, wondering if his smile was a little less urbane, or whether she was indulging her imagination. It broadened as she looked at him, and he replied, with a creditable assumption of amusement: ''But that was many years ago, sir! Badger is not a young man, and I fear he does now, occasionally, feel in need of—er—stimulants!''

At this point, Lady Broome intervened, saying in a tone of displeasure: ''I hope you mean to tell me Philip, what concern of yours are Badger's failings—or the failings of any other member of my household?''

''Do you, ma'am?'' he replied, measuring her.

She shrugged. ''Oh, if you wish to stand upon points, no! it is not a matter of interest to me. Dr Delabole, I should like to have a word with you: will you come to my room, if you please? Kate, dear child, pray have the goodness to tell Mrs Thorne to bring her accounts to me presently!''

''Yes, ma'am,'' said Kate, slightly taken aback.

''That was really quite unworthy of her,'' remarked Philip, when Lady Broome had swept from the parlour, followed by the doctor. ''I can't think that Mrs Thorne needs to be reminded—*if* this is Minerva's day for settling the accounts! I can see, from your expressive countenance, that it isn't—and also that you mean to give me a heavy set-down.''

''No: merely to go upon my errand—thus putting it out

of your power to cut at my aunt behind her back!'' flashed
Kate.

She left the room as she spoke, but twenty minutes later
she encountered him on the terrace, looking up at the roof.
He said, as though nothing had occurred to provoke her:
"That chimney must have been hit. It's badly cracked."

Her eyes followed the direction of his pointing finger.
"Is it safe?" she asked.

"Probably not. I must warn my uncle to have it looked
to."

"Yes, pray do!" she said earnestly. "If it fell, it might
kill someone! Then you would be blamed, wouldn't you?"

He looked frowningly at her for a moment, then his
brow cleared. "Oh, are you thinking of the coping-stone
which once fell in front of Torquil? It gave him a sad
fright, and since he was at outs with me at the time he set
the accident at my door—though how he thought I could
have contrived it God only knows! Or why I should have
wished to do him an injury. Does he still remember it?"

"Yes. That is, when he is in one of his distempered
moods he does. I daresay you must know how he loves to
play-act! I believe it is not an uncommon fault in boys
who are romantically inclined. In general, they are the heroes of their dreams. Torquil isn't. At least, he is not a
conquering hero! He likes to think that he is persecuted.
And I must say," she added frankly, "I think he is! I don't
scruple to tell you, sir, that I consider Dr Delabole a persecution in himself! You know, one can't blame Torquil
for holding him in abhorrence! He *always* says the wrong
thing! You did me the honour to say that I seem to have
the knack of managing Torquil: well, I think I have! At
all events, he is never as horridly rude to me as he is to
everyone else! Naturally, I understand how anxious my
aunt must be, because his health is so indifferent, but I do

feel that he might be better if he were allowed more freedom, and—and more congenial companionship!''

"Your own, for instance?"

"Yes, in default of better. He seems to have no friends.
No one to laugh him out of his crotchets! I told him once,
joking him, that he studied the picturesque in his attire,
and instead of laughing, he took offence! He looked as if
he would have been happy to have murdered me, which
showed clearly that he was unused to being roasted. Which
he wouldn't have been, had it been possible to have sent
him to school, would he?"

"No, but it was not possible."

"Oh, I know that! But although he may behave like a
spoiled child he is now a man grown, and I can't but feel
that it is most unwise to keep him in leading-strings." She
recollected herself, and said: "But I shouldn't say so!"
She saw that he was frowning, and added cheerfully: "It
is a mistake to refine too much on the odd humours of
adolescents, particularly of those who don't enjoy robust
health. I daresay he will outgrow his aches and ails, and
become perfectly stout."

"I wish you may be right, but I fear you are not," he
replied, rather harshly. "I think him worse than he was
three months ago." He glanced down at her, a satirical
gleam in his eye. "And I don't think, Cousin Kate, that
you will be able to manage him for long!"

Chapter Eight

When Torquil emerged from seclusion, he looked jaded to death, and was in a mood of black depression. Kate was shocked, and needed no prompting from Lady Broome to try to raise him from his dejection. But she did venture to suggest that a change of scene would be of more benefit to him than her company.

Lady Broome vetoed this. She spoke in glib terms of his excitability, and the irritation of his nerves; she said that it suited him best to go on in a jog-trot way. Kate could not deny his excitability, or the imbalance of his spirits, but when she hinted that boredom and constant surveillance were at the root of the trouble, she received a crushing snub. "My dear Kate," said her ladyship, "I've no doubt you mean well, but you must really allow me to understand Torquil's constitution better than you do! You seem sometimes to forget that I am his mother."

There was no more to be said. Kate begged pardon, rather stiffly, and went off to tell Torquil that she had failed in her mission. As she had approached Lady Broome at his instigation, and knew that he believed her to have considerable influence with his mother, she was not surprised that he should sink instantly into gloom.

"I see what it is!" he declared, clenching and unclenching his fists. "I shall be kept here all my life!"

"No, you won't," said Kate, in heartening accents. "You will come of age in another two years, and then you may do as you choose."

"You don't know my mother!" he said bitterly. "She'll never let me go! *Never!*"

"Yes, she will. Even if she wished to keep you here, she couldn't do so!"

"I hate her!" he whispered. "Oh God, how I hate her!"

Kate was horrified, but she managed to speak calmly. "You must not say so, Torquil. You know it is untrue! How could you hate your mother? She may be over-anxious, but you can't doubt that she has your welfare at heart!"

"No, she hasn't! She only cares for the Broome heritage!" he said savagely. "Well, I *am* a Broome, which she isn't, and I don't care a straw for it! Sometimes I think I'll run away, but I haven't any money! She'd get me back, as sure as check! She'll drive me to put a period to my life!"

This was very much too melodramatic for Kate, and she nearly lost patience, and did, in fact, say with some severity: "When you talk like that, Torquil, you make it hard for me to sympathize with you! And—which is perhaps more to the point!—it lends a great deal of weight to what your mother says of you!"

"What does she say of me?" he demanded, searching her face with hungry eyes.

"That you are too excitable. And it is true, you know! Either you are *aux anges,* or blue-devilled! If you wish for enlargement, keep a stricter guard on your temper! Don't—don't fly into a pelter for trifling reasons! Show your mother that you have overcome the—the inequality of your spirits, and I am persuaded she won't keep you here against your will!'' She laid a quietening hand over his clasped ones, which writhed together, and said coaxingly: ''You know, Torquil, your constitution is not yet as robust as she could wish, and *she* knows, if you do not, that it needs very little to put you quite out of curl.''

He looked intently at her, and startled her by saying: ''How pretty you are! How *kind!* I like you so much, Kate!''

''Well, I'm very much obliged to you, but what has that to say to anything? I wish you won't fly off at a tangent!''

''I thought I wanted to marry Dolly,'' he said, disregarding her words. ''Now I think I'd rather marry you.''

''Oh, do you, indeed? Well, you can't marry me!''

''Why can't I?''

''For a number of excellent reasons!'' she replied tartly. ''One is that I am much too old for you; another that it would be a most unsuitable alliance; and a third is that I don't wish to marry you! Don't take an affront into your head! I like you very well, but if you mean to fancy yourself in love with me I shall take you in strong aversion— for it *is* only fancy, Torquil!''

Without paying the least heed to her, he said abruptly: ''I'll recite one of my poems to you, shall I?''

''Certainly! Pray do!'' she invited cordially.

He sat staring ahead of him for several moments, and then struck his fists against his knee, and exclaimed pettishly: ''No, I won't! You wouldn't appreciate it!''

''No, very likely I shouldn't. Let us go for a walk instead!''

''I don't wish to go for a walk! Where's my cousin?''

''I don't know. Probably with Sir Timothy.''

''Ay!'' he said, his eyes kindling. ''Bamboozling my father with his coaxing ways!''

"Nonsense!" she said impatiently. "He hasn't any coaxing ways! Merely, he feels an affection for Sir Timothy which you, Torquil, do not!"

"What cause have I to feel affection for my father?" he demanded. "Always—*always!*—he yields to Mama! Or to Philip! Oh, yes, certainly to Philip! And you may depend upon it that Philip won't recommend him to let me go!"

She was silent, not knowing what to say, because when she had asked Philip if he did not agree that Torquil would be better if allowed rather more freedom, he had shaken his head, and had said decidedly: "No, I don't!"

Stung, she had said: "I can't conceive what you have to gain by supporting my aunt in her determination to keep the poor boy cooped up here!"

"I have nothing to gain but one single object!" He broke off suddenly, and added curtly: "Which does not concern you!" Perceiving from her heightened colour and smouldering eyes that he had nettled her, he had laughed, and had said: "Oh, don't nab the rust, Cousin Kate! What I have to gain doesn't concern me either!"

In high dudgeon, she had turned on her heel, and left him. Thinking over his words, she could make nothing of them. She was reluctant to believe that he harboured designs against Torquil's life; and, even if he did, it was impossible to see how these could be furthered by Torquil's continued residence at Staplewood, as closely guarded as he was.

She was thinking of this passage when Torquil's voice intruded upon her reverie. "Have I nicked it, coz?" he asked jeeringly. "Have you spoken to Philip on this subject? What a goose-cap you are! I know what answer he gave you!" He sprang up, his face contorted. "I tell you I am surrounded by enemies!" he said violently.

"Are you?" she enquired politely. "I trust you don't number me amongst them?"

"How can I tell? Sometimes I think— No! No, I don't! Not you! But everyone else—Matthew, Philip, Badger, Whalley, my mother—even my father! They are all in a string!"

"Oh, *fiddle!*" she snapped, losing patience. "I wonder you will talk such moonshine, Torquil! You must know it don't impress me!"

He muttered something under his breath. She did not hear what it was, but guessed it to be an objurgation, for he was looking furious, and plunged away from her, almost running across the lawn towards the lake. She made no attempt to stop him, but remained where she was, seated on a rustic bench below the terrace and thinking that there was perhaps something to be said for those who considered him to be too excitable to be allowed to run loose.

Presently she was joined by Mr Philip Broome, who came down the steps from the terrace, and, upon catching sight of her, walked towards the bench, saying, with a smile: "Ruining your complexion, Cousin Kate?"

"Oh, it was ruined long ago, in the Peninsula!" she said lightly.

"A demonstrably false observation!" he said, seating himself beside her. "No, don't go! I want to talk to you."

"Do you? Why?" she asked, looking surprised.

"Because you interest me and I find I don't know very much about you."

"Well, there isn't very much to know. And it wouldn't be any concern of yours if there were!" she said, with relish.

His eyes gleamed appreciatively. "Giving me my own again, cousin?"

She could not help laughing. "I couldn't resist, sir! If I

was impertinent I beg your pardon, but you needn't have snubbed me so roughly!''

"I didn't mean to. You said you couldn't conceive what my object is in supporting Minerva—''

"And you told me it was no concern of mine!''

"Accept my apologies! I'll tell you now that my only concern is to spare my uncle anxiety, and—possibly—grief. He is old, and very frail, and he has borne a great deal of trouble in his life. He was passionately devoted to his first wife, but she was of sickly constitution. Two of her children were still-born, and the other three didn't survive infancy. He wanted a son, you know: any man must want a son to succeed him! That's why he married Minerva. Oh, I don't say that he wasn't petticoat-led! Minerva was a very beautiful girl, but she had only a small fortune. I was a child at the time, but—don't eat me!—the on-dit was that although everyone admired her no one of rank offered for her. So she married my uncle, and presented him with—Torquil.''

She had listened to him in attentive silence, the echo of her father's words in her ears, and for a moment she did not speak. Then she said hesitantly: "I am aware, of course, that Torquil is a disappointment to him. It could hardly be otherwise, for I suppose that no man wants a son who has to be kept in cotton, or—or who suffers from distempered freaks. But he may improve—indeed, my aunt tells me that he *has* improved! I collect that you think he might indulge in excesses, if he were allowed more freedom, and so cause Sir Timothy distress?''

"I think—'' He checked himself, and said curtly: "Never mind that! How old are you, Kate?''

"I'm four-and-twenty—and that's not a question you should ask any female past the first blush of her youth, sir!''

"Yes, from things you have said I'd gathered as much. But when I first saw you I took you for a girl just emerged from the schoolroom."

"Well, that was no less than the truth—only I was the governess, not the pupil! And I wish with all my heart that I *didn't* look like a schoolgirl! Whenever I apply for a post I'm told that I'm too young!"

"I imagine you might be!" he said, amused. "I know your father is dead, but your mother—?"

"I am an orphan, sir."

"I see. But you have other relations, surely?"

"Only Aunt Minerva. At least, I believe I have numerous relations, but I've never met any of them, and I don't wish to! They behaved very shabbily to my mother, and quite cast her off when she eloped with Papa."

"But you have friends?"

She sighed. "I've lost sight of all our friends in the Regiment, and—and circumstances have prevented me from making new ones. I have my old nurse, however. And my aunt, of course." She thought that he might suppose her to be repining, and added brightly: "She had proved herself to be very much my friend, you know! You don't like her, but when she came to invite me to stay here I was almost in despair, and thinking of hiring myself out as an abigail! Only Sarah wouldn't hear of it, which was why she wrote to my aunt. And although my aunt is so high in the instep—I mean," she corrected herself hastily, "although you might suppose her to place herself on too high a form she has been so kind to me that I feel I can never repay her."

"In fact, you are alone in the world," he said. "I begin to understand: that is an unhappy situation for a girl."

"Yes, but I am not a girl," she pointed out. "You must not suppose, because I said I was in despair, that I am not very well able to take care of myself, for I promise you that I am! I told you once before that I didn't come to batten on my aunt, but I think you didn't believe me!''

''No, I didn't, but I've changed my mind. Or, rather, I can't blame you for succumbing to temptation. In your circumstances—which must, if you are obliged to earn your bread, be uncomfortably straitened—it would have been hard to have refused the offer of a home.''

''Well,'' she said frankly, ''it *was* hard! Indeed, my aunt made it almost impossible for me to refuse her invitation. She said I might at least spend the summer at Staplewood. It seemed absurd not to do so, particularly when she said that she could use her influence to procure an eligible situation for me. So I came, meaning to make myself useful. But she gives me nothing to do but the most trifling tasks, showers gifts upon me, and when I protest, says that it was always her wish to have a daughter, and that if I want to please her I'll accept them.''

''Gammon!'' said Philip. ''I'm sorry if I offend you, but there's no other word for it. Minerva never had any such wish!''

''No, I don't think she had, but you will own that it is kind of her to say so. It is to put me at my ease, of course.''

''Has it occurred to you, Kate, that she is placing you under an obligation?''

''Oh, yes, indeed it has, and it is *crushing* me!'' she said earnestly. ''If only there were some way of requiting her—not arranging flowers, or entertaining Sir Timothy, or bearing Torquil company, but a big thing! Something that was vital to her, or—or even something that entailed a sacrifice! But there isn't anything that I can discover.''

There was a pause, during which he frowned down at his well-kept finger-nails. At length he said slowly: ''If she were to demand it of you, would you be prepared to make a sacrifice of yourself?''

"Yes, of course I should! At least, I *hope* I should!" She looked sharply at him. "Why, do you know of something? Pray tell me!"

Again there was a pause, while he seemed to deliberate. Then he said: "No, I can't tell you, Kate. I suspect that there may be, but while all is conjecture I prefer to keep my tongue. But this I will say to you!— You are not entirely friendless! You have a friend in me, and you may call upon me at any time. Believe me, I shan't play the wag!"

She laughed at this. "Does that mean that you won't fight shy? From what I have seen of you, sir, I am fully persuaded that you wouldn't! You would come—come *bang up to the mark*—is that right?—and positively *enjoy* sporting your canvas! I make no apology for employing boxing cant: you cannot have forgotten that I was reared in Army circles!"

"No," he agreed, his eyes warm with amusement, "I haven't forgotten that! Has anyone ever told you, Cousin Kate, that you are—wholly entrancing?"

"Since you ask me, sir," she replied, with great calm, "yes—several persons!"

"And yet you are still unmarried!"

"Very true! It is a mortifying reflection," she said, mournfully shaking her head.

"Cousin Kate, you are a rogue!"

"Yes, that's another mortifying reflection," she agreed. She turned her head to study him, and asked involuntarily: "I wish you will tell me, sir! *Why* does Torquil hate you so much? *Why* does he think you the author of the various accidents which have befallen him? He believes you to covet his inheritance, but you don't, do you?"

"No: there is nothing I covet less! I have an estate of my own, in Rutlandshire: my father bought it, and I wouldn't willingly exchange it for all Staplewood's grandeurs." His face softened. "I hope I may, one day, be able to show it to you, Kate! I think—no, I am certain—that you would be pleased with it! My father, foreseeing all the possibilities which attached to it, caused the original farmhouse to be demolished, and built upon the site a neat, commodious manor, which has been my home since his retirement, nearly ten years ago. Between us, we set about the task of improving the property. But he died before he could see the results of our efforts. My mother survived him by less than a twelvemonth, since when I have lived there alone—but too busy to be lonely! I farm my land, you know, and hunt with the Cottesmore. We pride ourselves on our hounds! They may not be so quick in the open as the Quorn, but they are the best of any on the line. They must needs be good hunters, for our country is very deep and rough. But you mustn't encourage me to bore on about hounds and hunting!"

"No, indeed you don't bore me!" she assured him. "I have hunted myself, in Portugal, and in Spain. Not, of course, with the Duke's pack, but several officers hunted their own hounds, and permitted me to join them now and then. I'm told that the country doesn't compare with the Shires, but I don't think you could call it *humbug* country, for all that!"

"I am very sure I couldn't! You must be a notable horse-woman, Kate!"

"Well, I don't think I'm contemptible, but I must own that I took a great many tumbles!" she said merrily. "Do you hunt here?"

"Oh, yes, with the Pytchley! That is to say, I was used to when I was younger. While my father was employed abroad, this was my home. My uncle mounted me on my first pony, and inducted me into all the niceties of the sport—and even burdened himself with me in the field when I was a clumsy schoolboy! I must have been a dead bore to him, but he never let me guess it.''

"You have a great regard for him, haven't you?" she said gently.

"A very great regard. He was a second father to me."

"It must be a grief to you to see him failing, as I fear he is."

"Yes. When I recall what he once was— But that serves no purpose! He abandoned the struggle a long time ago, and is content now to let Minerva rule the roast."

She could not deny the truth of this, so she was silent for a minute or two before turning the subject. "Does Torquil know that you don't covet Staplewood?" she asked him.

"Yes, in his more rational moments," he replied. "At such times, he doesn't hate me in the least. So far as he is capable of being fond of anyone, he is fond of me, I believe."

"Then why— Is he perhaps jealous of you? Because Sir Timothy loves you? Because he thinks Sir Timothy wishes you to succeed him?"

"My uncle doesn't wish that."

"But Torquil might think so, might he not?"

He shrugged. "Possibly." He looked round. "Where, by the way, *is* Torquil? I had thought he was with you."

"He was, but I pinched at him, and he flung away in rage. I daresay he is in the woods, or in the belvedere."

"Take care what you are about!" he warned her. "Torquil can be violent!"

"Oh, yes, I know he can!" she answered blithely. "He often puts me in mind of one of my late charges—a veritable demon, who became violent the instant his will was crossed! However, I managed him tolerably well, and, even though you don't think so, I believe I can manage Torquil. At all events, I haven't failed yet!" She got up. "I must go and see if my aunt has any errands for me to run."

He too got up, and possessed himself of her hand. "Very well, but don't forget what I have been saying to you! If you should want help, you may count upon me!"

"Thank you—I'm much obliged to you, but I can't imagine why I *should* want help. In any event, you won't be at hand, will you?"

"No more than thirty miles away: Broome Manor is near Oakham. But I am not returning there immediately. When I leave Staplewood I shall probably go to stay with Templecombe for a few days. Which reminds me I'm dining with him this evening: I must tell Minerva."

Lady Broome received this news with cold civility, but confided to Kate that she considered it pretty cool of Philip to treat the house as though it were his own. "I shall be thankful when he takes himself off altogether," she said. "I don't know how it is, but he always contrives to set everyone at odds. Now he has upset Torquil!"

"I'm afraid I did that, ma'am," said Kate guiltily. "I gave him a scold, for talking dramatic nonsense, and he went off in a huff."

"Oh! Well, I daresay he was very provoking, but young men, my dear, don't care to be scolded, and certainly not by young women! You should learn to button your lip."

Feeling that this, the second rebuke she had received that day, was unjust, Kate merely said, in a colourless tone: "Yes, ma'am: I will endeavour to do so."

"Foolish child!" said her ladyship, pinching her chin,

and laughing. "Pokering up because I venture to give you a hint! Must I apologize?"

"Oh, Aunt Minerva, *no*!" Kate exclaimed remorsefully. "It is rather for me to apologize!"

She felt even more remorseful when she later overheard Lady Broome asking Pennymore if Mr Torquil had not yet come in: and slipped out of the house to look for him. It seemed to be the least she could do to atone for having upset him. She caught a glimpse of Mr Philip Broome driving himself down the avenue in his natty curricle, and had just enough time to admire his forward-stepping pair before the trees hid him from her sight. She was conscious of envy, because he was escaping from Staplewood, but banished so impious a thought, and trod swiftly across the lawn, in the direction of the belvedere.

But when she reached it she found that it was empty. She went down on to the bridge and paused there, wondering whether to search through the woods, or to go back to the house. Instead of doing either, she called: "Torquil! Tor—quil!"

Before the last syllable had left her lips, she was frozen with dismay, because, from somewhere in the wood beyond the lake, she heard a scream of intolerable anguish. It sounded human, and for a moment she was paralysed. Then, acting on impulse, she picked up her skirts, and ran, not away from the sound but towards it, crying: "Torquil, where are you? *Torquil!*"

No voice answered her; there was no repetition of the dreadful scream she had heard. She stopped, listening with straining ears, and trying to recollect from which direction the scream had come. The silence closed in on her, with not even the twitter of a bird, or the rustle of some small creature in the undergrowth, to break it. She caught her breath on a scared sob, but steeled herself to go on, impelled by the fear that it had been Torquil who had screamed and who might now be lying insensible somewhere in the wood. She kept on calling to him, but still received no answer, and was just about to run back to the house, to summon help, when she almost stumbled over the mangled corpse of a rabbit. She started back, with an involuntary cry of revulsion, and stood staring down in horror. It was quite dead, but blood was still oozing from it, and she saw that it had been snared, for someone had wrenched the snare out of the ground, and cast it aside.

As she stood, fighting back nausea, she heard hasty footsteps approaching, and the next moment Dr Delabole came into sight round a thicket, gasping for breath, and uttering: "Miss Malvern, where are you? Miss—Oh, there you are! I—I thought I heard you call out for help!" He saw what was holding her gaze riveted, and said: "Oh, tut, tut! Very distressing! Quite horrible, indeed! But only a rabbit, you know! Don't look at it!"

She turned her eyes towards him, and fixed them on his face. "I heard a scream," she said, shuddering. "A *human* scream!"

"Yes, yes, they do sound human!" he agreed sympathetically, taking her arm, and gently leading her away. "No doubt a cat got at it, or a fox, or even a weasel!"

"Dr Delabole, it was caught in a snare! I—I *saw* the snare!"

"Oh, then, that accounts for it! I must own that I myself deprecate the use of snares, but one can't stop gamekeepers and gardeners from setting them! In nine cases out of ten the rabbits are killed outright—strangled, you know!—but every now and then they are not killed, and then they scream, and their screams attract some predator—"

"What cat, or fox, or weasel would remove it from the

snare, and—and tear its head off?'' she demanded, in a shaking voice.

"Why, none, to be sure, but a fox may well have *bitten* its head off while it was still in the snare!''

"The snare has been pulled out of the ground. I saw it.''

"Did you? I must confess I didn't notice it, but it's very likely! In trying to drag the poor creature away the fox— or even a dog, perhaps!—wrenched the stake up—''

"And then disentangled it from the wire? Dr Delabole, do you take me for a fool? No animal perpetrated that— that horror!''

"No, I fear you may be right,'' he said, grimacing. "I suspect you may have surprised some ruffianly louts from the village. Boys can be abominably cruel, you know. But what brought you into the wood, Miss Malvern?''

"I came in search of Torquil,'' she replied. "I thought he might be in the belvedere, and I was going to return to the house when I heard that scream.''

"Came in search of Torquil?'' he repeated. "My dear young lady, Torquil has been in his room for the past hour!''

"But I heard my aunt asking Pennymore if he had not yet come in!''

"Did you?'' He hesitated, glancing ruefully down at her. "Well,—er—she asked me that too, and I am afraid I—er—prevaricated! Between ourselves, Miss Malvern, her ladyship is inclined to *fret* Torquil! You know what he is!—down as a hammer, up like a watch-boy, as the saying is! He came in, riding grub, and shut himself up in his room, positively snarling at me that he didn't wish to talk to anyone! So I—er—fobbed her ladyship off! I trust you won't mention the matter to her! She would give me a fine scold!''

"You may rely on my discretion, sir."

"I was persuaded I could. And, if I were you, I would not mention to anyone the distressing incident that took place in the wood. Such things are best forgotten—though very regrettable, of course!"

"I don't think I could ever forget it, sir, but I certainly shan't talk about it! It turns me sick!"

"Most understandable! No sight for a delicately nurtured female's eyes!"

"No sight for *anyone's* eyes, sir!" she said fiercely.

"Very true! I was myself most profoundly affected! I can only be thankful that Torquil didn't see it: it would have quite overset him, for he is very squeamish, you know—very squeamish indeed!"

They had crossed the bridge by this time, and she felt she could well have dispensed with his company. He insisted on accompanying her to the house, however, and would have brought a dose of sal volatile to her room had she not been resolute in declining it. He recommended her to lie down on her bed before dinner, and promised to make her excuses if her aunt should ask where she was. She thanked him, and tried to feel grateful, but without much success.

Chapter Nine

Kate was so much shaken by her gruesome experience that it was some time before she could compose herself; but after half an hour her limbs ceased to tremble, and she was able to drag her mind from the slain rabbit. She had felt at first that she could not bear to go down to dinner, but a period of calm reflection restored her to her usual good sense. Whatever excuses Dr Delabole might make for her, her absence from the dinner-table must inevitably bring Lady Broome to her room, and Lady Broome, she knew, would ask shrewd questions. She had little appetite, but still less did she want to talk about what she had seen.

She was agreeably surprised when she entered the Long Drawing-room to find that Torquil had apparently recovered from his sulks, and was in high good humour, talking with remarkable affability to his mother. Kate had expected to be told that he was laid low with a headache, for this was in general the sequel to one of his bursts of temper; but in the event it was Sir Timothy who was the absentee. After slamming the door on Dr Delabole, it seemed that Torquil had cast himself on his bed, and had fallen into a deep, natural sleep, which had wonderfully refreshed him. His brow was unclouded; his eyes were neither over-bright, nor heavy with drowsiness; and there was a delicate colour in his cheeks. He looked to be in a state of purring content, and so well-disposed towards his fellow-men that instead of resenting the doctor's intrusions into his conversations with Lady Broome he invited them, calling upon Delabole to support him on a disputed point. He seemed to have banished from his mind his quarrel with Kate; and when Pennymore came to announce that dinner was served, and Lady Broome rose from her chair, he exclaimed: "But where is Philip? Shall we not wait for him?"

"No, we are a sadly diminished party tonight," responded Lady Broome, disposing her shawl about her shoulders. "Philip is dining at Freshford House."

"Oh, *no!*" protested Torquil. "Why didn't anyone tell me? I wanted to have my revenge on him!"

"As Philip didn't see fit to inform me of his intention until noon, and you have been sound asleep for hours, there was no opportunity to tell you of it," said Lady Broome composedly. "You will be obliged to revenge yourself on Kate instead."

"That would be no *revenge,* madam!" he objected. "I can give Kate thirty, and beat her every time!" He threw a challenging look at Kate, and laughed. "Can't I, coz?"

"At billiards you can," she agreed. "I notice, however, that you dare not challenge me to a rubber of piquet!"

"No, no, I hate cards! I'll tell you what, though! I'll challenge you to a game of Fox and Geese!"

"Why, what's that?" she asked.

"Oh, it's a famous game! Don't you know it? I was used to play it with Philip, when I was in the schoolroom, but from some cause or another I gave it up—I daresay it got to be a bore. You have a board, with seventeen geese and one fox, and the game is for the geese to entrap the fox, and for the fox to seize as many geese as he can, so that he can't be caught. Mama, where is the board? Don't tell me it was thrown away!''

"My dear, I don't know what became of it!''

Fortunately, since he showed signs of falling into a pet, Kate recollected that she had seen a board, marked in the shape of a cross, in the cabinet that contained the chess and the backgammon boards, and was able to unearth it. When she held it up for his inspection, enquiring: "Is this it?'' he exclaimed delightedly: "Yes, that's it! If you can't find the pieces, we can use draughts—though it would be a pity not to play with the set Philip made for one of my birthdays! He carved them out of wood, and painted them: white geese, and a red fox, carrying his brush high! One of the geese had the most comical expression, and two of them were shockingly lop-sided. Let me look!''

He fell on his knees in front of the cabinet, and began to pull out the various boxes it contained; but Lady Broome intervened, saying: "After dinner, my son!''

"Yes, very well! but I must find the pieces first!'' he said.

"No, you must *not!*'' said Kate firmly, pulling him to his feet. "I know how it would be, if you did find them! You would begin to teach me how to play, and the end of it would be that I shouldn't get any dinner at all! Come along!''

She smiled at him as she spoke and gave his hand a coaxing squeeze. This had the effect of banishing the mutinous look from his face. He smiled back at her, a brilliant light in his eyes, and raised her hand to his lips, holding it in an uncomfortably strong grip, and said: "To please you, coz, anything!''

"I'm much obliged to you, Torquil,'' she said, in a prosaic voice, and disengaging herself, "but there's no need for these heroics! You should rather please your mama, who is being kept waiting for her dinner!''

He flushed, and for a moment he looked as if he would fly into a miff; but after biting his lip, he cast her a side-long glance, and burst out laughing. He was still giggling when they reached the dining-room, in a childish way which Kate found exasperating, but he stopped when Lady Broome spoke to Kate, asking her if she had seen how well the roses had stood up against the storm, and said suddenly: ''I'm hungry! What's in that tureen, Mama?''

''Calves' feet and asparagus,'' she replied.

''Oh, good! I like that!'' he said.

Since it was seldom that he took any interest in what he ate, Kate was mildly surprised, and still more surprised when instead of eating a few mouthfuls, pushing the rest about on his plate, and complaining that it was unfit to eat, he ate his portion with avidity, and demanded some of the beef which Dr Delabole was carving. Kate, who was find-ing it difficult to swallow, and could only by the exercise of will-power subdue her nausea, was obliged to avert her eyes from the blood oozing from the sirloin; but Torquil pronounced it to be roasted to a turn, and—rather greedily, she thought—applied himself to it with zest.

''Your long sleep has given you an appetite!'' said the doctor playfully.

''Did I sleep for a long time? I don't remember.''

''Indeed you did! Badger was hard put to it to rouse you!''

''Oh, I remember *that!* I woke up to find him shaking me, and very nearly came to cuffs with him for interrupting my dream!''

''What were you dreaming about?'' asked Kate. ''It must have been something very agreeable! I find that whenever I have a very vivid dream I am only too thankful to wake up from it!''

"I don't know! The devil of it is that it slipped away! But I do know it was agreeable!'' There was a general laugh, which made him look round challengingly, a spark of anger in his eyes.

"How can you know that, if it slipped away from you, my son?'' asked his mother.

He considered this, and then laughed reluctantly. "Oh, it does seem absurd, doesn't it? But I do know, though I can't tell how. Kate! *You* understand, don't you?''

"Perfectly!'' she assured him. "I don't even remember my bad dreams, but I know when I've had one!''

"Do *you* have bad dreams?'' he said, turning his head to look searchingly at her.

"Uncomfortable ones, now and then,'' she acknowledged.

"But not shocking nightmares? Things which haunt you—make you wake in a sweat of terror?''

"No, thank God! Only very occasionally!''

"I do,'' he said earnestly. "Sometimes I dream that I'm running from a terrible monster. Running, running with weights on my feet—! It hasn't caught me yet, but I think that one day it will. And sometimes I dream that I've done something dreadful, and that's—''

"For heaven's sake, stop, Torquil!'' exclaimed Lady Broome. "You are making my blood run cold!'' She gave an exaggerated shudder, and added, in a tone of affectionate chiding: "Detestable boy! Next you will be telling us ghost stories, and we shall none of us dare to go upstairs to bed! You know, Kate, a ghost is the one thing we lack at Staplewood! It was a sad disappointment to me when Sir Timothy brought me here as a bride, for in those days I was a romantic; but I understand that the owners of haunted houses find it impossible to induce their servants to remain with them, so I've learnt to be thankful that no ghost wanders about Staplewood, and no invisible coach drives up to our door in the middle of the night, as a warning that the head of the house is about to die!''

"Yes, indeed, my lady, and so you may be!" said the doctor. "That puts me in mind of a strange occurrence which befell me many years ago, when I was sojourning in Derbyshire.''

Torquil muttered: "O God!" but Lady Broome invited the doctor to continue, and cast a quelling look at her son, which made him give a smothered giggle.

By the time the doctor had come to the end of his anecdote, the second course had been set on the table, and Torquil was pressing Kate, in dumb show, to eat a cheesecake. She shook her head, whereupon he exclaimed, interrupting the doctor, that she must be ill, since she had eaten almost nothing; and she said in a hurry that she would have a little of the jelly. "But *are* you ill?" he asked anxiously.

"No, no! Just—just not hungry!" she assured him, touched by his solicitude.

He smiled engagingly upon her. "Oh, I'm so happy to hear you say so! I was afraid you meant to cry off from our game!" he said ingenuously.

She choked, but managed to gasp: "Not at all!"

Lady Broome came to her rescue, reproving Torquil for breaking in so rudely on the doctor's story. "And let me tell you, my son, that to draw attention to Kate's loss of appetite is even more uncivil! She is feeling the heat, as I am myself—but I notice that you don't remark on *my* loss of appetite! Dear child, if you have finished, shall we go upstairs?''

Kate had not finished, but she thankfully abandoned the

jelly, and followed her ladyship from the room. On their way up the Grand Stair, Lady Broome said: "Dr Delabole informs me that you had an unpleasant experience this afternoon, in the wood. Very disagreeable, and it is no wonder that it made you feel squeamish, but it doesn't do to refine too much upon such things, my love. People who live in the country are for ever killing something! There is really very little difference between the unlettered yokel who sets snares for rabbits, and the gentleman who shoots pheasants, except that one is a poacher, of course. I must tell the head-keeper to be on the watch."

Kate returned no answer. She could only suppose that Dr Delabole had not revealed the gruesome details to her aunt; and, recalling his advice to her not to mention the episode, she thought that this was very probable: Lady Broome could scarcely have dismissed the matter so coolly had she known the full sum of it, nor could she have expected Kate to banish it from her mind. But when they reached the Long Drawing-room again, she recommended Kate to prosecute a search for the missing fox and geese, saying, with an expressive smile: "We shall have no peace unless they are found! The game might quite as well be played with draughts, but you know what Torquil is, once he takes an idea into his head!"

Fortunately, Kate discovered the pieces in a box at the back of the cabinet; and by the time Torquil and Dr Delabole came into the room, she had set the board out on a small table, and was arranging the geese on it. Torquil cried delightedly: "Oh, you've found them! Capital! But that's not the way to set them out, coz! I'll show you!"

She was very willing to learn the game, but had it not been for Dr Delabole, who drew up a chair at her elbow, and quietly instructed her, she must have been hopelessly bewildered by Torquil's exposition. The rules of the game were simple, but the play called for some skill. Having been beaten twice, in the least possible number of moves, she began to master the tactics, and was soon forcing Torquil to exercise his considerable ingenuity to win. When the tea-tray was brought in, and Lady Broome called a halt, she would have put the pieces away, but Torquil begged for just one more game, and she readily agreed—subject to Lady Broome's approval. It was the gayest evening of any she had yet spent at Staplewood.

Lady Broome said: "Very well, but come and drink your tea first, both of you! I am persuaded that you at least must be in need of it, Kate! Such squeaks of dismay as you've been uttering, and such crows of triumph!"

"Oh, I do beg your pardon, ma'am. Have we been very noisy?" Kate said penitently. "It is the most ridiculous game, but excessively exciting! When I find the fox about to pounce on one of my geese, I can't help but squeak! But as for crowing, that was Torquil, and very unhandsome it was of him! *I* had no occasion to crow!"

"Oh, what a bouncer!" mocked Torquil. "You cornered me once, and if that wasn't a crow that you gave I never heard one!"

"Well, it's my turn to be the fox this time," said Kate merrily. "And your turn to squeak! See if I don't snap up your geese!"

The final game was prolonged; Torquil won it, and said virtuously: "Observe that I'm not crowing, coz!"

She laughed. "That's worse! Gracious, how exhausted I am!"

Dr Delabole took her wrist, and shook his head solemnly: "A tumultuous pulse!" he pronounced. "I shall prescribe warm tar-water—excellent for a fever!"

"Ugh!" shuddered Kate. "It sounds horrid!"

"*All* medicines are horrid!" stated Torquil.

"Very true," agreed Lady Broome, casting a cloth over her embroidery frame, and rising to her feet. "However, I hardly think we shall have to dose Kate with tar-water, or anything else! My dear, if you are ready, shall we go up to bed? It is growing late."

"Of course I am ready, ma'am! I wish I may not have been keeping you up: you should have told us to stop playing! Goodnight, sir—goodnight, cousin! If you hear a shriek in the night, you will know that I have had *your* nightmare, and have wakened just as I was about to be caught!"

She waved her hand to him, and went away with Lady Broome. She said, halfway along the gallery: "How well Torquil looks tonight! I shouldn't wonder at it if that long, *natural* sleep did him all the good in the world. He had an appetite, too. Do you know, ma'am, it's the first time since I came here that he has *wanted* his dinner? What a pity it is that he suffers so often from insomnia, and has to be given composers! Surely they must be very bad for him? I mean," she added, remembering the snubs she had received, "that it is a pity he can't sleep without them!"

"A great pity," agreed her ladyship. "But I hope he may be in a way to be better." She paused outside the door of Kate's bedchamber, but instead of bidding her goodnight she said: "I shall come and tuck you up presently, so don't fall asleep! I want to talk to you."

She then went to her own room, leaving Kate considerably surprised, and quite at a loss to guess what they were going to talk about.

A very sleepy abigail was awaiting her. She had tried to dissuade Ellen from waiting to put her to bed, but without success. Ellen had looked shocked, and had said that she knew her duty. "It isn't your duty if I don't desire you to undress me," had argued Kate. But Ellen had said that it was her duty, and that her ladyship would be very angry if she failed in it.

"Well, her ladyship won't know!"

"Oh, yes, miss, she will—begging your pardon! Miss Sidlaw would tell her, and I'd be turned off! Oh, pray, miss, don't say I must go to bed before you do!"

Since Ellen was plainly on the verge of tears, Kate was obliged to give way. She reflected that although no great hardship was suffered by Ellen or Sidlaw at Staplewood, where early hours were the rule the life of a fashionable lady's dresser must be arduous indeed. Perhaps a governess's lot was preferable: she might have very much more to do during the day, but at least she was allowed to sleep at night.

She had just tied on her nightcap when Lady Broome tapped at the door. She jumped into bed, telling Ellen to admit her ladyship, and then go to bed, and sat up amongst the pillows, hugging her knees.

Lady Broome had taken off her dress, and was wearing an elegant dressing-gown of lavender satin, lavishly trimmed with lace and ribbons. Kate exclaimed involuntarily: "Oh, how pretty! How well it becomes you, ma'am! Ellen, set a chair for her ladyship before you go, if you please! I shan't want you again tonight."

"Yes, the purple shades do become me," said Lady Broome, sitting down beside the bed. "Very few women can wear them. Now, you look your best in blue, and orange-blush. I wonder how yellow would become you? Not amber, or lemon, but primrose. Have you ever worn it?"

"Now and then, ma'am," replied Kate.

"I must send for some patterns," said Lady Broome, and went on to talk about silks and muslins and modes, until Kate said firmly that she had so many dresses already that she had no need of any more. She did not think that her aunt had come to her room to discuss fashions, and waited for the real object of her visit to be disclosed.

She had to wait for several minutes, while Lady Broome continued to talk of furbelows, but at last Lady Broome said: "You looked particularly well in the dress you wore for our dinner-party; Torquil could scarcely take his eyes off you! My love, I must tell you that you have done Torquil a great deal of good! I am so grateful to you: you are precisely the kind of girl he needs!"

A little overcome, Kate stammered: "You are very good, aunt! I hope you may be right, because it has seemed to me that—that by trying to keep Torquil out of the sullens I could—in some sort—repay you for your—your kindness to me!"

"Dear child!" Lady Broome said, in a voice of velvet, and stretching out a hand to clasp one of Kate's. "If that was your aim, you have succeeded! He is in far better frame! Dr Delabole has been telling me that there has been a marked improvement since he had the benefit of your companionship."

Kate swallowed, and said rather faintly: "Has there, ma'am?"

"Yes, indeed there has been!" Lady Broome assured her. "There is a want of disposition in him, and he still has odd humours, but I now have every hope that he will drive a better trade—because his ardent desire is to please you!"

Kate could only stare at her. It did not seem to her that Torquil had any desire to please anyone but himself; and she was unable to repress the thought that if his mother thought him improved since her arrival at Staplewood his previous state must have been parlous indeed.

Lady Broome smiled at her, pressing her hand. "He has

a great regard for you, you know! I have come to believe that you would be just the wife for him!''

Kate gasped. "Are you joking me, ma'am?"

"No, indeed I am not! I should welcome such an alliance. Have you never thought of it?"

"Good God, no!"

"But why not?"

Utterly taken aback, Kate said, groping for words: "I'm too old—it would be quite unsuitable! Dear Aunt Minerva, forgive me, but—but you must be all about in your head!"

"Oh, no, I'm not, I promise you! I think it will be best for Torquil to marry a woman who is older than himself; and as for *unsuitable,* what, pray, do you mean, Kate?"

"I mean that I'm a penniless nobody!"

Lady Broome raised her brows. "You are certainly penniless, my dear, but scarcely a *nobody!* You are a Malvern, as I am myself, and if Sir Timothy thought me fit to be his wife you must surely be fit to become his son's wife!"

"Yes, if I were younger, or he older! If we loved one another!"

"Oh, love—!" said Lady Broome, shrugging her shoulders. "It isn't necessary for a successful marriage, my dear, but you may be sure that Torquil is in love with you!"

"Fudge!" exclaimed Kate wrathfully. "Oh, I beg your pardon, ma'am, but it *is* fudge! Why, he was fancying himself in love with Miss Templecombe when I first came here!"

"I am thankful that you drove her out of his head! She would not have done for him!"

"No, very likely not, but the thing is that he is by far too young to be fixing his interest! Good God, ma'am, he hasn't been granted the opportunity to meet any—any el-

igible girls! When he is older—when his health is established!—and you permit him to leave Staplewood—''

"I shall not do so." The words, granite-hard, fell
heavily, and all at once, seeing the grim set to her aunt's
mouth, and the stern resolution in her eyes, Kate was
afraid, and almost shrank from her. But the revealing moment was swiftly gone: Lady Broome laughed softly, and
said: "He is too handsome, and too big a matrimonial
prize! Every matchmaking mother in London would be on
the scramble for him, and he would fall a victim to the
first designing female who set her cap at him! No, no, I
mean to see him safely riveted before I set him loose upon
the town! Does that seem unfeeling? Believe me, I know
him too well to run any risks! His constitution will always
be delicate, I fear, and a few weeks racketing about London would knock him up, just as his father was knocked-
up. That is why I wish him to marry a woman of sense,
not a giddy girl.''

Kate said carefully: "Yes, ma'am, you must hope that
he will do so, but not for some years yet, surely! He is
only nineteen, and young for his years, I think. I have been
acquainted with many boys of his age, and although some
of them were what my father called callow halflings they
were none of them so—so *childish* as Torquil!''

"Exactly so!" said Lady Broome. "Other boys are sent
to school, and find their feet. It was not possible to expose
Torquil to the rigours of school-life. He was the sickliest
child, and at one time I despaired of rearing him. But I
did rear him, thanks to Dr Delabole's skill and understanding, and he is now going on prosperously. But he is excitable, and easily led. I don't scruple to tell you, my dear,
that I dread what might be the result if he were allowed
to run free. I believe, however, that if he were married, it

would give him the ballast he lacks. And that," she said, with a smile, "would be a weight off my mind, Kate!"

"Aunt Minerva!" said Kate, drawing a long breath, "I collect that you think *I* should be able to give him ballast, but I do beg you to believe that you are mistaken!"

"Oh, no!" replied her ladyship. "I'm not mistaken!"

"But I don't wish to marry him!" Kate blurted out. "Such a notion never entered my head!"

Lady Broome rose, and began to draw the curtains round the bed. "Well, dear child, now that I have put it into your head, consider it! You are four-and-twenty, and have no expectations. You may not be in love with Torquil—I do not require that you should be—but you don't dislike him, I trust, and if you marry him your future will be assured. More than that: you will be a woman of consequence, for it is not a small thing to be the wife of Broome of Staplewood. Think it over, Kate!"

She bent and kissed Kate's cheek, and then closed the curtains, blew out the candle, and went away, leaving Kate in a state of considerable perturbation.

She had never been more thunderstruck, for she knew how large were her aunt's ambitions, and had supposed that she had set her heart on Torquil's contracting a brilliant alliance. It was not impossible. He had position, wealth, and an extraordinarily beautiful face; and when he was in a complaisant mood he could be charming. It was unfortunate that he was put out of humour so easily, and was subject to fits of dejection, but these were faults which he could overcome, and no doubt would, as his health improved. Shrewdly assessing Lady Broome, she had supposed that a love of power, rather than of persons, was the motive behind her refusal to countenance his fleeting infatuation for Dolly Templecombe, and her determination to keep him at Staplewood for as long as she could. She

was far from being a doting parent: she showed her niece
more affection than she showed her son; and although she
took meticulous care of him there had been times when
Kate could have believed that she held him in aversion.
She certainly despised him. Perhaps that was to be expected in a woman who enjoyed excellent health, and had
hoped to provide Staplewood with a worthy heir. Kate,
herself warmhearted, could not enter into such feelings, but
she could dimly perceive that they might exist, just as she
could perceive that there might well be jealousy without
love. Lady Broome wanted to keep Torquil under her
thumb, and would strongly oppose the influence of a wife.
Kate could understand that, and had supposed that she
might expect to retain her influence for several years. Yet
here she was, proposing for him a most ineligible marriage
when he was no better than a schoolboy!

Then, as Kate lay cudgelling her brain to discover a
solution to the problem, it flashed suddenly into her head
that by marrying Torquil to her own niece she might hope
to keep him in subjection, and to continue to reign at Staplewood after Sir Timothy's death. It seemed fantastic, but
the more Kate thought about it the more possible it became, except that Lady Broome, who was no fool, could
hardly imagine that her niece was a bread-and-butter miss
with no mind of her own. It then occurred to her that she
was deeply indebted to her aunt, and she recalled that Mr
Philip Broome had spoken to her of obligations, and sacrifices, and had assured her of his support. She sat up with
a jerk, and sat frowning into the darkness. She wondered
if this was what he had meant. Recollecting his sardonic
manner, and the cold contempt in his eyes when he had
looked at her upon his first coming to Staplewood, she
realized that he must have assumed that she had lent herself to Lady Broome's dark schemes. Angry tears started

to her eyes, and she was shaken by a sob of sheer rage, and a strong desire to slap his face. How dared he suppose her to be such an abandoned, mercenary creature? Admittedly, he had very soon changed his mind, but he apparently thought she might yield to the temptation of a title, riches, and security. Well, Mr Philip Broome should shortly be made to repent of having so basely misjudged her; while as for needing his help in the matter, she was very well able to help herself. She gave her pillow a savage thump, and was just about to lie down again when another thought occurred to her: why, if he did not hope to succeed his uncle, was he opposed to Torquil's marriage? Sooner or later, Torquil was certain to marry, unless he died. He was unlikely to die of his various aches and ills, but he might meet with a fatal accident. Kate gave a shiver, and whispered fiercely: *"No!"* because the idea that Mr Philip Broome would do his young cousin a mischief was totally unacceptable to her. Torquil had talked in a very theatrical way about the fatal accidents which had so nearly befallen him, but it had not taken her long to realize that no reliance could be placed on what Torquil said. A very little reflection, moreover, had shown her how ridiculous his accusations were: even had Philip loosened a coping-stone, wired a fence, or sawn through the branch of a tree, it was improbable that any of these accidents would have killed him. He might have broken his neck at the wired fence, but, in fact, he had cleared it, and when he fell out of the elm-tree he had come off with a few bruises. As for the coping-stone, although he said it had fallen in front of him, missing him by inches, Kate thought it had probably fallen nowhere near him. She had a comical vision of Mr Philip Broome inexpertly setting booby-traps, and claiming as his victims some quite unoffending persons, and chuckled.

She became serious again as she recalled the mysterious

hints Lady Broome had several times dropped. She had not actually accused Philip of trying to kill his cousin, but she had said that he coveted Staplewood, and his uncle's title. The only real charge she had brought against him was that he had a bad influence over Torquil. Kate thought that if he exercised any influence at all—which was doubtful—it was a good one; and was intelligent enough to guess that Lady Broome would consider any other influence than her own a bad one. She lay down again, grimacing. Whoever Torquil's bride might be, she would find herself with the devil of a mother-in-law. "And it won't be me!" she said, snuggling her cheek into the pillow.

Chapter Ten

Kate found her aunt alone in the breakfast-parlour next morning, and seized the opportunity to ask her if she did not think that it was time to bring her visit to an end. Lady Broome seemed amused, and said: "No: why should I?"

"I don't believe it, but if Torquil is developing a tendre for me, ma'am, I feel I ought to remove myself."

"Why, if you don't believe it? Are you so anxious to leave us?"

"Oh, no, no, ma'am!"

"I'm glad of that. I have done my best to make you happy."

"Yes, and I have been happy!" Kate assured her. "You have been more than kind, and I shan't know how to be contented, away from you, and dear Sir Timothy! And Staplewood, of course. The thing is that I must not encourage Torquil to dangle after me, and I shall find it awkward to keep a proper distance, after the habits of easy intercourse we have acquired. If I treat him with the cool civility of a stranger he will demand to know what he has done to offend me, perhaps, and what could I say?"

"My dear child, what a great fuss about nothing! You will go on as before, and I am persuaded you will know how to depress any fit of gallantry. I expect you will do just as you ought: you have such superior sense!"

"But—"

"I should be very hurt if you were to leave Staplewood before the end of the summer," said Lady Broome. "It would be an unkindness which I cannot think I have deserved."

Aghast, Kate stammered: "No, no, dear aunt! But in the circumstances—after what you said to me last night—"

"My dear, I told you to think it over. You have had no time to do so as yet, have you?"

In the middle of trying to tell her aunt, with civility, that no stretch of time would cause her to alter her decision, Kate was interrupted by the tempestuous entrance of Torquil, closely followed by the doctor. "Mama!" said Torquil explosively. "I've seen a heron by the lake!"

"Good-morning, Torquil!" said his mother, in repressive accents.

"Oh, good-morning, ma'am—good-morning, Kate! Did you hear what I said to you, Mama?"

"Very clearly: you have seen a heron by the lake! Will you have coffee, or tea?"

"Tea—it don't signify! The thing is that the gun room is locked, and Pennymore says you have the key to it!"

"Yes?"

"Well, give it to me!" said Torquil. "I must shoot that heron!"

"Oh, *no!*" exclaimed Kate impulsively.

"Indeed no!" said Lady Broome. "My son, you know I have the greatest horror of guns! I do beg you won't start shooting things! What I endured when your father was used to have shooting-parties! I was for ever on the jump, because I *cannot* accustom myself to sudden bangs, and I have the greatest dread that there will be a fatal accident!"

"Oh, gammon!" said Torquil rudely. He turned his head, as his cousin came into the room, and demanded: "Philip! Is there any danger of a fatal accident, if one goes out shooting?"

Mr Philip Broome, after collectively greeting the assembled company, replied: "Danger to what?"

"People, of course!"

"Well, that depends on the man who is handling the gun. Coffee, if you please, Minerva!"

"Exactly so!" said the doctor. "None at all if that man were Sir Timothy, or yourself, but every danger if that man were a novice!"

Torquil reddened angrily. "Is that meant for me? Whose fault is it that I'm a novice?"

"Not mine, my dear boy!"

"No! My mother's!"

"I am afraid that is true," confessed Lady Broome. "By the time you were old enough for your father to teach you how to handle a gun, he had been obliged to abandon his shooting. I own I was thankful that I was spared any more shocks to my nerves!"

"That won't fadge! There was Philip, or any of the keepers!"

"But I don't recall that you ever, until today, expressed a wish to be taught how to shoot!" she said mildly.

"What if I didn't? I *ought* to have been taught!" He sat glowering, and suddenly said: "And, what's more, I ought to have the key to the gun room! I think Papa is a regular dog-in-the-manger! He can't shoot himself now, but—"

"You will be silent, Torquil!"

"I won't! Philip, will you teach me how to shoot?"

"No, certainly not! I once tried to teach you how to carry a gun, without waving it about, and pointing it at anything rather than the ground, and I failed miserably."

"That was when I was twelve!"

"You will have to hold me excused. Fight it out with your mother!"

"She says she can't bear the noise! Did you ever hear such balderdash? As though she would be startled by a shot fired down by the lake! I've seen a heron there!"

"Have you? What of it?"

"Good God, Philip, unless it's shot it will have every fish in the water!"

"It's welcome to them," said Philip, unmoved. "Nothing but roach and sticklebacks. Your father was never fond of fishing, so he didn't stock the lake. When I was a youngster I was used to waste hours hopefully casting a line on to it, until my uncle gently broke it to me that there were no trout in it. A severe blow!"

"Then I do trust that the heron's life may be spared!" said Kate. "I've never seen one—only pictures—and I would like to!"

"Well, you will have to get up very early in the morning," Philip warned her.

"If I can't shoot it, I can trap it!" said Torquil, his eyes brightening.

"No! Oh, no, no, no!" cried Kate sharply.

"You will do no such thing, Torquil," said Lady Broome. "I will have no trapping at Staplewood, and I wish to hear no more talk of killing. I trust, Philip, that you spent an agreeable evening, and had a tolerable dinner? You said that Mr Templecombe had invited you to take pot-luck with him, and in my experience that means cold mutton, or hash!"

"True, but I knew I was safe in Gurney's hands, ma'am. Most of the rooms were under holland covers, and I rather fancy we were waited on by the pantry-boy, but the dinner was excellent. Gurney allowed Lady Templecombe to take the upper servants to London, but when she tried to wrest his cook from him she drew blank.''

"How very selfish of him!''

"Not at all. He gave her leave to engage an expensive French chef for the Season, so she was well-satisfied.''

Torquil, who had been sitting in brooding silence, got up abruptly, and left the room. Kate saw her aunt look quickly at the doctor, who said: "I too must beg to be excused, my lady,'' and followed Torquil.

"May I know who holds the key to the gun room, Minerva?''

"I do.''

Philip nodded and began to carve some cold beef. When he had finished breakfast, he went away to visit Sir Timothy, and remained with him for an hour. Meanwhile, Kate tried to continue her discussion with Lady Broome, but found her evasive, and disinclined to take her seriously. When Kate said, in desperation, that under no circumstances would she marry Torquil, she laughed, and replied: "Well, you have told me that twice already, my love!''

"I think you don't believe me, ma'am. But I am perfectly sincere!''

"Oh, yes, I believe that! You may change your mind.''

"I promise you I shall not. I—I don't wish to leave you, but don't you think I had better do so, ma'am?''

"No, I don't, you foolish child! What a piece of work you do make of it! I begin to regret that I ever mentioned the matter to you: I did so only because I wished to assure you that I shouldn't oppose the match. Now I must go and talk to Chatburn: you haven't met him, have you? He is Sir Timothy's bailiff, and a very worthy man, but aptly named, so you must not be surprised if you don't see me again this morning!''

Kate was left feeling that she had been annihilated. Lady

Broome had made her realize that to flee from Staplewood would be as ungrateful as it would be theatrical, and she was passionately determined to show her aunt that she was neither. She would be obliged to remain at Staplewood until the end of the summer, but she was uneasy. She knew that Torquil liked her; she knew that he was beginning to fancy himself in love with her; but while she had no doubt that he would abandon his suit to her the instant more attractive metal came within his range she doubted her ability to cast a damper on his pretensions without exciting his precarious temper, or causing him to fall into one of his fits of dejection. It was only twenty-four hours since he had announced that he would like to marry her, and she had snubbed him. He had flung away in a fury, and, although no evil consequences seemed to have resulted, she knew that the effects of his rages on his constitution were dreaded by his mother, and his doctor. She foresaw that it would be difficult to hold him at arm's length without provoking or wounding him, and tried, quite unavailingly, to think how it could be done.

When Lady Broome had left her, she went out on to the terrace, but a gusty wind soon drove her to the shrubbery, where she walked up and down for some time, before sitting down on one of the benches which had been placed there for Sir Timothy's convenience. She sat there for twenty minutes, her brain occupied with the problems confronting her, and her fingers plaiting and unplaiting the fringe of her shawl. There was a furrow between her brows, and although her eyes were fixed on her busy hands it was plain that her thoughts were abstracted.

''What troubles you, Cousin Kate?''

She looked up quickly, startled, for she had not heard Mr Philip Broome's approach. He was standing a little way away, and she had the feeling that he had been there for several minutes, watching her. She exclaimed, with a tolerable assumption of liveliness: "Good God, sir, how you did make me jump! I didn't hear you."

He came forward unhurriedly, and sat down on the bench beside her. "I know you didn't: you were too intent on your work!"

"On my work?" she echoed, bewildered. Her eyes followed the direction of his levelled quizzing-glass, and she flushed, and said, in some confusion: "Oh, my fringe! How absurd! It is one of my bad habits to make plaits, or knots, or pleats when I'm—when my mind is otherwhere!"

"Yes?" he said. "And where was your mind?"

"Oh, in a dozen places at least!" she said lightly.

He was silent for a minute, and began to unplait her fringe. Since he was looking down at it, Kate had the opportunity to study his profile. He had regular features, and a well-shaped head, and was generally held to be passably good-looking. Kate decided that he was a very handsome man: not, of course, as handsome as Torquil, but far more virile. His was a strong face, and if his mouth was stern, and his eyes very keen and hard, she knew that his smile was unexpectedly attractive, warming his eyes, and softening the lines about his mouth. He might be inflexible, but it was impossible to suspect him of being unscrupulous.

He raised his head, turning it slightly to look at Kate. He was not smiling, but although his eyes were searching they were kind. He repeated: "What troubles you, Kate?"

"My dear sir, nothing!"

"No, don't try to hoax me! What has happened to put you in a worry?"

"Merely a small, private matter, sir."

"That's taught me to mind my own business," he observed.

She could not help laughing. "I wish it may have done so! The truth is that I'm confronted with a problem, and haven't made up my mind how to settle it."

"Perhaps I can help you."

"Thank you, I don't require help!"

He hesitated. "Or advice? Mine is that you should leave this place."

This made her remember that she had a crow to pluck with him. She stiffened, and her eyes flashed a challenge. "Why, sir?" she demanded.

Again he hesitated, before saying: "Do you recall that I warned you yesterday that you might be required to make what I believe would be a sacrifice, in return for the benefits bestowed on you?"

"Very clearly! And you meant, did you not, that my aunt might propose to me that I should marry Torquil?" She waited for his answer, and, when he nodded, swept on, in a voice vibrant with wrath: "And when you came here, and—and looked at me as if I were a—a designing *trollop,* you believed I was in a string with my aunt! *Didn't* you?"

He smiled ruefully. "Yes, I did. I beg your pardon! Does it mitigate the offence when I assure you that I very soon learned that I had misjudged you?"

It did, of course, but she saw no reason why she should forgive him so easily, or deny herself the satisfaction of raking him down, so she evaded this question, and gave him a rare trimming. He bore it meekly, but with such an appreciative twinkle in his eye that she was goaded into saying: "And if you had been within my reach, sir, when I realized what you thought of me, I would have boxed your ears!"

"Most understandable!" he said sympathetically. "But I *am* within your reach now, so if you would like to box my ears, pray do so! I won't attempt to defend myself."

"There is nothing I should like more," she assured him, "but I hope I have too much propriety of taste to allow myself to be carried away by indignation!"

"I was hoping that too. But don't you mean too much sense of justice? It was very bad of me, but you must remember that I'd never met you."

"Then you shouldn't have prejudged me!" she said severely.

"I know I shouldn't. I hope it may be a lesson to me."

"So do I, but I doubt it!" she retorted, trying not to laugh. However, having discharged her spleen, her natural good-humour reasserted itself, and she did laugh, and said candidly: "As a matter of fact, when I came to think it over, I did perceive that there was a good deal of excuse for you. It must have looked as if I were trying to lure Torquil into matrimony. The thing was that it never entered my head that I ought to hold him at a distance, because he is only a schoolboy, and I am *years* older than he is. And my aunt told me that he lacked young companionship, which indeed he does, poor boy! To own the truth, sir, I am excessively sorry for him."

He looked at her, an arrested expression in his eyes. "Are you?"

"Well, of course I am! Are not you?"

"I am very sorry for him," he agreed.

She thought he sounded indifferent, and suspected that he had no liking for Torquil. "I know you don't think so," she said, "but I believe he would be very much better if he were not cooped up here. It seems to me quite shocking!"

"Does it?"

"Yes, it does! My aunt believes that London would knock him up, and dreads his being ill. I fancy she is afraid he would go the pace too fast, and commit some extravagant folly, through being so excitable. I expect she is quite right, because he's green, and would be *bound* to hob-nob with the sort of young man who is always ripe for a spree: I daresay you know what I mean?"

"Choice spirits," he said, with the glimmer of a smile.

"Is that what they are called? Well, I do see that that might be dangerous, and I perfectly understand my aunt's anxiety. But what I do *not* understand is why he must be kept at Staplewood the whole time, and never permitted to go *anywhere*. One would have supposed that my aunt would have wished to try if one of the wateringplaces might not be of benefit to him, but—" She stopped, and said, in a conscience-stricken tone: "I didn't mean to say that. I know I should not."

"Are you afraid I might tell Minerva? I shan't."

"No, but I shouldn't criticize her."

"On the contrary! You should—and, in fact, you do!"

"Yes," she confessed. "I can't help doing so, but I feel it's ungrateful, because she has been so kind to me."

"Are you fond of her?" he asked abruptly.

She began to plait her fringe again, and did not answer immediately, but when he laid his hand over her unquiet ones, checking her, she looked up, and said, with an embarrassed flush: "Oh, dear! was I at that again? No, I'm afraid I'm not fond of her. Not *very* fond of her, that is! I don't know why, because she seems to be fond of me, and in general, you know—"

"Seems?" he interrupted, keeping his hand over hers.

She met his eyes, a little shyly, and found that they were smiling, inviting confidence. Without knowing why she did so, she said impulsively: "I don't think she's fond of anyone! It makes me far from easy. I can't explain!"

"You need not: I know what you mean. Minerva has overwhelmed you with gifts—you called her generosity *crushing,* but you wouldn't feel crushed if you believed she held you in affection, would you?"

"Ah, you do understand! I should be grateful, but not crushed!" She sighed, and said ruefully: "I thought there was nothing I wouldn't do to show my gratitude, but I can't marry Torquil! It is quite out of the question. When my aunt suggested it to me, I thought she must be out of her mind!"

It was a moment or two before he answered her. He began to speak, and then shut his mouth hard, as though he were exercising considerable restraint. Finally, he said, in a brusque voice: "No. Obsessed!"

She nodded. "I know that: Staplewood and the succession! But that's not it!"

"You are mistaken."

"No, I don't think I am. She seems to be determined to keep Torquil under her thumb: not just now, but always! And I fancy she believes that if he married me she could do it, that I shouldn't interfere, or try to take him away, or—or usurp her position."

"Undoubtedly."

"It is a shocking thing to think of anyone, but what else *can* I think?" said Kate. "You see, my father told me how very ambitious she is, so I supposed that she must be hoping that Torquil would make a splendid match. But, of course, if he married a girl of the first stare it is not to be expected that she could keep her here, in—subjection, is it? Well, even if the girl were willing to allow my aunt to rule the roast, she might not be willing to be buried here all the year round!"

"Most unlikely. But there is more to it than that, Kate: such a girl would not be, as you are, alone in the world. She would have parents, perhaps brothers and sisters, certainly more distant relations—uncles, aunts, cousins."

"If it comes to that," said Kate, "I have distant relations too! I am not acquainted with them, but—"

"Exactly so!" he said. "*But* they are not concerned with your welfare!"

"Oh, no! I daresay most of them don't know I exist!"

"It is precisely that circumstance which, in Minerva's eyes, makes you a desirable wife for Torquil."

He spoke with deliberation, and her eyes widened a little, searching his face. The vague uneasiness which troubled her deepened; she said carefully: "I collect that you think that my aunt might try to—to constrain me—to *force* me to marry Torquil, but I promise you it isn't so! It was only a *suggestion!* I have told her that I shall never do so, and, although she has begged me to think it over, I am persuaded she realizes that I shan't change my mind."

As though urged by some inner impulse, he grasped both her hands, and held them in a compelling grip, saying harshly: "Kate, go away from this place! On no account must you marry Torquil!"

"Well, of course I must not!" she returned, slightly amused. "Even if I weren't too old for him, he isn't *fit* to be married!"

"Why do you say that?" he asked quickly.

"Good God!" she exclaimed. "Surely you must be aware that he hasn't yet outgrown the schoolboy? He hasn't learnt to control his temper, for one thing! The least check makes him ride rusty. As for forming a lasting attachment, fiddle! I daresay it may be years before he does so. At the moment he is inclined to fancy himself in love with me, but he was fancying himself in love with Miss

Templecombe when I first came here, and it was only when he heard of her engagement that he transferred his affections to me. Would you care to lay odds against his transferring them yet again if some reasonably pretty girl were to appear in the neighbourhood? Of course you would not!''

He released her hands. "Of course I would not," he agreed, and sat heavily frowning at the ground between his forearms, which he had laid along his spread legs, his hands clasped between his knees.

In some perplexity Kate looked at his down-bent head, and said: "You don't wish Torquil to be married, do you, sir?" She waited for a reply, but he only shook his head. She continued: "Why not? I can readily understand that you would not wish him to marry an adventuress, but I have the oddest feeling that you would oppose his marriage to anyone. You have told me that you don't covet his inheritance, and I believe you don't indeed. But I cannot feel that you hold him dear, so—so *why,* Mr Broome?''

He glanced up at that, wryly smiling, and said, "Oh, no! I refuse to be *Mr Broome*—Cousin Kate!''

"You know very well that I am *not* your cousin!" she said.

"I know that you refused to acknowledge the relationship! What was it you said?—at the worst you could only be a connection of mine! Excessively rag-mannered I thought you!''

She gave a gurgle of laughter. "You must own that you earned it!''

"Oh, I do!" he answered.

"That is a great concession," she said. "I am very conscious of it—Cousin Philip! But I would have you know that I cut my wisdoms a long time ago, and I am well-aware that you are fobbing me off. You have not answered my question.''

''I can't answer it. If I were to disclose to you, or to anyone, my reason for opposing Torquil's marriage— No, I can't do it! I am not even perfectly sure that there *is* a reason.'' He rose jerkily. ''Come! We have sat here for long enough, Kate! Minerva will be wondering what can have become of you.''

She privately thought this unlikely, but when she encountered her aunt presently, Lady Broome said: ''Oh, there you are! Dear child, I have been looking for you all over!''

Surprised, Kate said: ''But you told me, ma'am, that you were going to be engaged with the bailiff! I've been in the shrubbery.''

''Yes, so Sidlaw informed me. With Mr Philip Broome!''

''Yes, certainly. Did Sidlaw inform you of that too, ma'am?'' asked Kate, a trifle ruffled.

''To be sure she did! Oh, don't take a pet, my love! She only told me because I asked her if she had seen you anywhere! Such a scold as she gave me for letting you wander about alone!''

''Good heavens! What harm did she imagine could befall me? Besides, I wasn't alone: Mr Broome was with me, and she knew that, didn't she?''

''Yes, dearest, and of course she didn't imagine any harm would befall you! But she is very prudish, and she thought it right to nudge me on to warn you not to permit Philip to sit with you in the shrubbery!''

''I should think she must be quite Gothic,'' said Kate, beginning to be very angry indeed.

Lady Broome laughed, and grimaced. ''Indeed she is! But she was right in this instance: it isn't the thing for a young female to jaunter about with a single gentleman, you know!''

"I am afraid I don't know it, Aunt Minerva," said Kate, in a dangerously quiet voice. "I have yet to learn that there is the smallest impropriety in walking, sitting, or even jauntering about with a single gentleman. And I cannot help wondering why, if you don't think it the thing, you encourage me to go out with Torquil.''

"That is a little different, my dear: Torquil is your cousin, and—as you have said!—only a boy. Philip is another matter, and is not, I fancy, to be trusted to keep the line.''

"Is it possible that you suspect me of flirting with Mr Broome?'' enquired Kate. "Let me assure you that I haven't the faintest wish to flirt with him!''

"Or with anyone, I hope!'' said Lady Broome playfully.

"Oh, as to that, there's no saying!'' replied Kate coolly.

"Naughty puss!'' said her ladyship, pinching her cheek. "I perceive that Sidlaw was right when she gave me a scold for not looking after you better!''

"Not at all!'' returned Kate. "I'm not a green girl, or a romp, and I am very well able to look after myself. And if she thought Mr Philip Broome was in the petticoat line she must be a great goosecap! Pray set her anxious mind at rest, dear ma'am! He shows no disposition to flirt with me!''

"Oh, tut-tut!'' said Lady Broome. "Don't pull caps with me, you foolish child! You are not so *very* old, you know, and even though you are neither a green girl nor a romp, you are not yet as much up to snuff as you think you are. A pretty thing it would be if I *didn't* look after you! There, give me a kiss to show me that I'm forgiven!''

Melting, Kate embraced her warmly. "As though there

were anything to forgive!'' she said, not without difficulty, for the words stuck in her throat.

The entrance into the hall of Pennymore, bearing the post-bag, relieved her embarrassment. Lady Broome took it from him; and, with a kindly smile, told Kate to run upstairs to put off her hat. A nuncheon, she said, had been set out in the Blue saloon; and, unless Kate wished to wound the cook's sensibilities, she would partake of it, because he had baked a Savoy Cake for her especial delectation.

Kate did go upstairs to remove her hat; but when she came out of her bedchamber she did not immediately go to the Blue saloon, but to her aunt's drawing-room instead, where she found Lady Broome at her writing-table, already busy with her correspondence. She said haltingly: ''I suppose there are no letters for me, ma'am?''

''No, my dear, none,'' replied Lady Broome, not raising her eyes from the letter she was reading.

Kate went quietly away, heavy-hearted.

Chapter Eleven

On the following afternoon, Lady Broome, in response to an urgent entreaty from Kate to set her some task to perform, sent her down to the lodge, with what Kate knew to be a frivolous message. She accepted it without comment, realizing that her aunt was a trifle out of sorts, and set off down the avenue reflecting that if ever she had yearned for a life of indolence the weeks she had spent at Staplewood had cured her. Her only duties were trivial, and occupied perhaps an hour in the day. For the rest of the time she was at liberty to amuse herself as best she might. She could read, write, walk, busy herself with stitchery, play at battledore and shuttlecock with Torquil, or loiter her time away. She had the run of the library, and, after skipping her way through a number of old novels, she embarked on the Decline and Fall of the Roman Empire, with the laudable object of widening her knowledge. She had just begun to read the second volume, but it could not have been said that she viewed the prospect of reading four more volumes with enthusiasm. Riding during the summer months was mere hacking along country lanes; she had exhausted all the possibilities of walks taken within the grounds of Staplewood; and when she

wished to go on an exploratory ramble beyond the grounds
she was frustrated by Lady Broome's insistence on her
being accompanied by one of the footmen on such expe-
ditions. As for stitchery, once she had mended a rent in
her dress, and darned her stockings, she was at a stand.
She could fashion a dress, but she had no turn for embroidery, which was the only kind of stitchery her aunt
recognized as a genteel occupation for ladies of mode.
Games of battledore and shuttlecock with Torquil were
more a penance than a pleasure, for not only was he an
indifferent player but an extremely bad-tempered one as
well, frequently hurling his battledore from him in disgust,
tearing the feathers from the shuttlecock, or walking off
the court in a fury.

The worst of it was, as she had speedily realized, that
there was nothing for her to do at Staplewood. Lady
Broome had told her that she would find a great deal to
do, but this was far from the truth: what there was to do
was done by the servants, and very well done. Lady
Broome had said that she relied upon Kate to overlook the
staff, and to see that nothing was neglected; but Kate had
been quick to realize that this was an improvised duty, and
one which her aunt had no intention of delegating.

To Kate, accustomed all her life to be busy, this lazy,
cushioned existence, at first delightful, soon became intolerable, but the mischief was that her aunt could not believe
that she really did yearn for employment. In bringing Kate
to Staplewood, and lapping her in expensive luxury, she
expected her to revel in it; and since Kate was too well-
mannered to betray her discontent and did indeed enjoy
the comfort of Staplewood—she continued in this misap-
prehension, and thought that Kate's entreaties to be given
work to do emanated from a very proper desire to requite
her generosity.

Having delivered the message at the lodge, Kate went back to the house, leaving the avenue, and making a detour through the park. It was wooded, and here and there Lady Broome had caused to be planted clumps of rhododendrons and azaleas, which were just now in bloom, lending splashes of brilliant colour to the landscape, and filling the air with their scent. There could be no doubt that she knew how to create beauty. Kate had at first supposed that a landscape gardener had been employed to lay out the gardens, and to open prospects in the most felicitous way imaginable, but Lady Broome, laughing such a notion to scorn, had assured her that she had planned the whole, and had seen it carried out under her direction. It was yet another example of her genius for organization; and when Kate was held spell-bound by one of the enchanting vistas she was easily able to understand her aunt's love of Staplewood, into which she had thrown so much inventiveness. Kate had been shown the original plans of the gardens, and she knew that until her aunt's reign the gardens had been formal, the park too thickly wooded, with too many bushes, and too few prospects. Lady Broome had improved these out of recognition. She had improved the house, too, changing it from an overcrowded store of furniture and pictures, good, bad, and indifferent, into a stately show-place where nothing offended the eye. But Kate could not feel that she had been as successful in the house as she had been in the gardens, for, in creating a show-place, she had destroyed a home.

She was thinking about this when her attention was caught by the sudden appearance on the scene of a dog, which appeared to be the result of a misalliance between a hound and a setter. He came bounding into view from behind a clump of azaleas but halted in his tracks at sight of her, and stood looking the picture of guilt, with one paw raised, and his tail clipped between his legs, posed for instant flight. He had barely outgrown his puppyhood, and when Kate laughed, and invited him to come to her, he obeyed with all the alacrity of a dog of exuberantly friendly disposition, and gambolled round her, uttering encouraging barks.

The sight of him brought it forcibly home to Kate that, with the exception of Sir Timothy's aged and obese spaniel bitch, which only left the East Wing when led out by Sir Timothy's valet for a circumscribed airing, he was the first dog she had seen at Staplewood. It had not previously occurred to her that this was a strange circumstance, but as she patted and stroked the trespasser it did occur to her.

Frustrating his attempts to lick her face, she said laughingly: "Well, sir, and what are you doing here, pray? It's my belief that you've been hunting! Oh, you bad dog!"

The stranger at once acknowledged the truth of this accusation, and deprecated its severity, by flattening his ears, and furiously wagging his lowered tail. Kate laughed again, and said: "What is more, you know very well you have no business here! Be off with you!"

He dashed off immediately, and she thought she was rid of him, until he reappeared, some minutes later, bringing her a peace-offering in the shape of a withered tree-branch, which he dragged along the ground, and proudly laid at her feet.

"If you imagine," Kate said, "that I am going to throw that for you to retrieve you very much mistake the matter! It's a game I should weary of long before you did! Besides, I know I ought not to encourage you. *No,* sir! Go home!"

After inviting her to relent, retreating a little way from the branch, and all the time watching it with cocked ears and wagging tail, making short dashes at it, and urging her to participate in his favourite sport by a few yelping barks, he seemed to realize that it was useless to persist, and once more bounded off.

Kate proceeded on her way, wishing that there were dogs at Staplewood which she could take for walks, and recalling, with a reminiscent smile, the three obstreperous dogs owned by the Astleys which had added so much excitement (and embarrassment) to the walks she had taken with the children. In the midst of these reflections she was startled by a gruff voice, which suddenly commanded her to stand and deliver. She looked quickly round, not so much alarmed as vexed, for she had no difficulty in recognizing Torquil's voice, disguised though it was. It was precisely the sort of schoolboy trick he was all too fond of playing, and she found it unamusing. "For heaven's sake, Torquil!" she exclaimed. "*Must* you be so childish?"

He emerged from behind a bush, brandishing a double-barrelled shotgun, and saying gleefully: "I frightened you, didn't I, coz?"

"No, but you are frightening me now!" Kate said, eyeing the shotgun with misgiving. "Don't point that thing at me! Is it loaded?"

"Of course it is! And I did frighten you. You jumped nearly out of your skin!"

He shouldered the gun as he spoke, which relieved Kate's more immediate apprehensions, but she demanded in a sharp voice how he had managed to come by it. "I broke in through the gunroom window when the servants were at dinner!" he replied triumphantly. "No one heard me! I stuffed my pockets with cartridges too. I'm up to everything, ain't I? If Mama won't let anyone teach me, I'll teach myself!"

"Torquil, indeed you must not!" she said. "Do, pray, put it back! If you are so set on learning to shoot I'm persuaded your mama will relent! I'll try what I can do to convince her that it is only right that you should be permitted to! *This* isn't the way to learn, I promise you! What you should do is to have a target set up, *well* out of range of the house and the gardens, so that Aunt Minerva need not be disturbed by the bangs."

"Not I!" he said, his eyes gleaming, and a rather unpleasant smile curling his beautiful lips. "I'm going to keep it, and I know where, too! Disturbed by the bangs, indeed! That's a loud one! Doing it rather too brown, my dear mama!"

"Torquil, you should not speak so of your mother!" Kate said earnestly. "It is most improper! Besides, how can you tell that she is not speaking the truth? Many people have the greatest dread of sudden noises, you know— and not hen-hearted people either!"

She was interrupted by her unknown acquaintance, who once more bounded up to her, this time with the desiccated remains of a very dead mole, which he spat at her feet, plainly feeling that it must be acceptable to her. "Ugh!" she exclaimed. "What a horrid animal you are! No, I don't want it!"

"Where did that dog come from?" asked Torquil shrilly.

"I haven't the least idea. I suspect him of playing truant. He has been trying to induce me to play with him!"

"I hate dogs! I'll shoot him!" said Torquil.

"*Shoot* him?" Kate cried. "You will do no such thing!"

"Oh, yes, I will! He's a savage dog, and a stray!"

"Don't be so absurd! He's not at all savage!" said Kate wrathfully. "Why, he—" She stopped, becoming aware suddenly that the dog was growling at Torquil, bristling, and backing away from him.

She moved forward to soothe him just as Torquil fired.

The shot missed both her and the dog by several inches, and its only effects were to send the dog off in a panic, and to shock her into frozen immobility. Torquil sent the second charge after the flying animal. It failed to hit its target, but peppered the trunk of the tree. "Hell and damnation!" swore Torquil furiously.

"How *dare* you?" demanded Kate, recovering her voice. "Do you realize that if you had shot wide to the left instead of to the right you might have killed me?"

"You shouldn't have moved," he said sulkily. "I wasn't trying to shoot *you!*"

"Oh, I *am* so much obliged to you!" Kate flashed.

He started to speak, but broke off as his valet came running up, out of breath, but managing to gasp: "No, no, sir! Now, Master Torquil, give over, do ! Let me have that gun!"

Torquil spun round, pointing the gun at him, and saying between his teeth: "Oh, no, you don't, Badger! Keep off!"

Badger halted abruptly. "Now, you know that's foolishness, Master Torquil!" he said, in fondly chiding accents. "Give it to me, like a good boy! Whatever must Miss be thinking of you? And whatever would her ladyship say, if she got to hear you'd stolen one of Sir Timothy's guns? Now, you give it to me quiet-like, and I'll put it back where it belongs, and no more said!"

"Come and take it from me—if you dare!" said Torquil tauntingly.

"Please to go away, miss!" begged Badger, keeping his eyes on the gun. "I won't be answerable for it if you was to get hurt! Master Torquil, you're scaring Miss, and that I'll be bound you don't want to do!"

"He is not scaring me at all!" declared Kate, in a cold rage. "He discharged both barrels, and the gun is unloaded!" She walked up to Torquil, and held out her hand.

"Give me that gun, if you please! Unless you mean to hit me over the head with it?"

The wicked glitter died out of his eyes, and he began to giggle. "Oh, coz, what a jokesmith you are. Always full of gig! I wouldn't beat your brains out on any account! You are too pretty!"

She removed the gun from his slackened grip, and handed it to Badger, who received it wordlessly, but with obvious relief. Torquil watched the transfer, and sighed. "I was trying to shoot a dog," he explained. "I missed him, but not by so *very* much, Badger! Oh, Kate, dearest Kate, don't be in a pelter! don't go away! I swear to you I didn't mean to shoot at you!"

"No, I don't suppose you did," she replied. "But until you have learnt to mend your temper you need not look to me to advance your cause! I am more likely to advise your mama to sweep the gunroom bare! You are not to be trusted with firearms, Torquil!"

She left him glowering, just as Dr Delabole came hurrying up. He looked to be very much alarmed, but when he saw that Badger was in possession of the gun some of the anxiety left his face, and he heaved a sigh of relief. He came from the direction of the house, and met Kate before he was within tongue-shot of Torquil. He stood in her path, making it necessary for her to stop, and asked, in an urgent undervoice: "What has happened, Miss Kate? I heard a couple of shots!"

"Torquil was firing at a dog," she replied reticently.

"Oh, if that was all—!"

"*All?*" she repeated, as though she could not believe her ears. "Upon my word, sir, you take it very calmly! For my part, I think it iniquitous! How *could* he have done such a thing?"

"Yes, yes, it was very bad—iniquitous indeed! But he

doesn't like dogs, you know. In fact he suffers from a positive antipathy!''

"The antipathy was shared by the dog!" snapped Kate. "Nothing could have been more friendly than the dog's attitude to me, but he bristled and growled at Torquil! No doubt his instinct warned him to beware!"

"Very true! The instinct that tells dogs that they stand in danger is most remarkable. The thing is that Torquil was once, when he was a child, severely bitten by a dog— a big retriever it was, belonging to Sir Timothy! The experience left an indelible impression on the poor boy's mind."

"It doesn't excuse his conduct in trying to shoot a dog that belongs to someone else!" retorted Kate.

"Of course not! Of course it does not! I daresay he felt that he had a right to shoot a stray dog that was, no doubt, hunting on his land—which, in point of fact, he had, you know. Not that I wish to say it was not very wrong of him! Very wrong indeed! But you must be aware, Miss Kate, how easily he flies up into the boughs! Quite loses control of himself! He suffers from irritation of the nerves, and if he was frightened, you know, his impulse would be to protect himself. I haven't the least doubt that he fired at the dog without pausing to think!"

"I haven't any doubt of that either," said Kate dryly. "He is not fit to be allowed to handle guns, and so I have told him!"

"Indeed no! Most certainly not!" he said. "But pray don't be afraid, Miss Kate! I can promise you that it won't happen again!"

She inclined her head, making it plain that she wished to proceed on her way, and he immediately stood aside, bowing very politely, and again reassuring her that she need not be anxious.

She went on towards the house, regaining the avenue, and walking slowly along it. She was not afraid, but she was a good deal disturbed, because it had seemed to her, for a few seconds, that the expression on Torquil's face had been almost fiendish. She shivered, and was forced to remind herself that as soon as the dog had vanished from sight so too had the fiendish look from Torquil's face, and so swiftly that she could not be sure that she had not imagined it. He had certainly levelled his gun at Badger, but Kate was much inclined to think that he had done so only to frighten the valet, and would not have fired it even if it had been loaded, which he must have known it was not. Remembering the wary look in Badger's eyes, and his urgent entreaty to her to go away, it occurred to her that he really was frightened, standing stock-still for fear that Torquil would pull the trigger. But Kate knew that he was devoted to Torquil, and had looked after him almost since he was first breeched, and it seemed incredible to her that he could have supposed himself to be in danger. It was as though Sarah had been terrified of herself when, in one of her childhood's rages, she had been crossed, and had threatened all sorts of revenges. A smile hovered at the corners of Kate's mouth as she thought of Sarah's responses to fits of temper in her nursling. "Throw that inkpot at me, Miss Kate, and you'll go supperless to bed!" Sarah would have said, wholly unimpressed by defiance.

Badger had said nothing like that. He had tried to coax Torquil, speaking to him in a soothing way, never taking his eyes from the gun. It was possible that he was naturally of a timid and a subservient disposition, but he had never given Kate that impression. It occurred to her, recalling her own experiences in Mrs Astley's household, that Lady Broome might resent any attempt on Badger's part to keep Torquil in order. She was herself so strict with Torquil that it seemed unlikely, but Kate knew that four out of five mothers could be counted upon to rush to the support of their children in any struggle with nurses or governesses. Such an attitude might well be part and parcel of Lady Broome's imperious character: she tolerated no rival authority at Staplewood; and it was probable that Badger dared not offend her for fear of being dismissed from her service.

Kate, giving herself a mental shake, decided that she was growing fanciful, and ought to put the unpleasant episode out of her mind. It refused to be banished, however, and, as she walked, various circumstances to which at the time she had attached no importance, obtruded themselves in her memory. Torquil was never allowed to ride out without his groom; and even when he strolled with her in the grounds either the doctor or Badger seemed always to be within earshot. Another recollection darted into her head: on the night of the storm she had been jerked out of her bed by a cry of terror, and had found that she could not open her door; and on the following morning Badger had worn all the signs of having been embroiled in a fight. Dr Delabole had said that he was inclined to be quarrelsome in his cups, and had broadly hinted that he had come by his injuries in a tavern brawl. But Mr Philip Broome had obviously disbelieved him, saying that he had never seen Badger above his bend. The doctor had parried the thrust, but he had been on the defensive, and had clearly been grateful for Lady Broome's intervention. Was it possible, Kate wondered, that Torquil, starting up from his nightmare in terror, had fought with Badger? If that were so, he must have been distraught, or still asleep. Kate remembered that the eldest Astley child had suffered from hideous nightmares which had made her quite unmanageable until someone had succeeded in waking her. She had supposed it to be a childish thing, which the little girl would outgrow: certainly the family doctor had said so. But Torquil, with his migraines, and his precarious temper, was just the sort of boy to have nightmares, and to be quite beside himself for several minutes, even to be violent. Mr Philip Broome had said: "He can be violent," and he had warned her to be careful. That was another of the things to which she had attached no importance, but it was beginning to assume significance. The dreadful suspicion that Torquil was not in his right mind could not but occur to her, and she was obliged to give herself another mental shake, and to tell herself that ungovernable rages were very much more likely to spring from ill-health and injudicious pampering than from a disorder of the brain. She knew an impulse to ask Philip what he had meant by his warning, but instantly repressed it. Her suspicion was altogether too lurid to be discussed, she decided.

She was roused from her meditations by the sound of horses approaching at a smart trot, and turned her head to see that she was being overtaken by Philip, driving his curricle and pair. At sight of him, her resolution wavered, but what he said, as he drew up beside her, put all thoughts of Torquil out of her head. "I was coming in search of you, Cousin Kate! There's a splendid old gentleman in Market Harborough, who wants very much to see you. Do you care to drive there with me?"

"An old gentleman to see *me?*" she said incredulously. "Surely you must be mistaken! I am not acquainted with any old gentlemen!"

"I fear, cousin, that you are getting to be above your company," he said, quizzing her. "Which is something I did not expect! In fact, I assured Mr Nidd that his apprehensions were quite groundless."

"Mr Nidd?" she cried joyfully. "Here? Come to visit me? Oh, how glad I am! Is Sarah with him?"

"No, he's alone. Are you coming?"

"Yes, yes, if you please! I wish you had brought him here!"

"I was very ready to do so, but I couldn't persuade him to come. He appears to think that you might not wish to see him."

"Not wish to see him!" exclaimed Kate. "How *could* he have thought so? When I have written again and again to Sarah, begging her to send me a reply!"

"And didn't she do so?"

"No, and although my aunt made nothing of it, it has had me in a dreadful worry! My aunt said that in expecting letters from what she calls 'persons of that order' I was asking rather too much, and that once Sarah knew I was happy here she would be thankful to be relieved of the expense and the responsibility of looking after me. But I cannot believe that my dear Sarah would—would abandon me in such a heartless way, and I have been wondering whether she is sick or even *dead!* For God's sake, Cousin Philip, Mr Nidd hasn't come to break *that* news to me, has he?"

"I shouldn't think so. According to what he said to me, he has come to discover whether it is *you* who are either sick or dead. I reassured him on both points, but I believe, Kate, that you should allow me to drive you to Market Harborough, to talk to him yourself."

"Indeed I will!" she said, with alacrity.

He stretched down his hand to her, and she laid her own in it, and was just about to get up beside him, when she hesitated, and asked, looking up at him: "Ought I not to tell my aunt? Ask her leave?"

"No, my child: that is precisely what you ought *not* to

do!'' he replied, tightening his hold on her hand, and compelling her to climb into the curricle. ''If I know her, Minerva would hit upon some way of preventing you from having a tête-à-tête with Mr Nidd.''

''She could not do so!'' declared Kate hotly, disposing herself beside him.

''Do you think she could not?'' he said, casting a light shawl across her knees, and turning his horses. ''You may, of course, be right, but *my* guess is that either she would escort you to Market Harborough herself, and remain with you throughout, or—which, now I come to think of it, is more likely—send a carriage to bring him to Staplewood, and trust to its splendour, and her own condescension, to abash him. But from what I have seen of Mr Nidd,'' he added reflectively, ''I shouldn't think he could be easily abashed.''

Kate could not help laughing a little at this. ''Very true, sir!'' she acknowledged. ''He is the most redoubtable old man! He was kindness itself to me, and I hold him in considerable affection!''

''That doesn't surprise me,'' he returned. ''I took a liking to him myself.''

She turned her head to study his profile. ''Did you? Yes, you would, of course! But how came you to meet him, sir?''

''Oh, by the merest chance! Whenever I have occasion to transact business in Market Harborough, I stable my cattle at the Angel. Today, when I walked into the yard to recover my curricle, Mr Nidd was there, hob-nobbing with one of the ostlers, with whom he appeared to be on excellent terms. I should suppose him to have been making enquiries about Staplewood and the Broomes, for as I emerged from the inn I heard the ostler say that here was

Mr Philip Broome, and why did not Mr Nidd ask questions of me.''

''And did he?''

''No, but as I apprehend that he was bent on discovering information about my uncle and Minerva that was hardly to be expected. He told me that he was your Sarah's father-in-law, and that she was very anxious to know that you were well, and happy.''

''What did you tell him?'' she asked breathlessly.

''I told him that, to the best of my belief, you were in high force. As to your being happy, I could not take it upon myself to say, but I suggested to him that he should judge for himself, and offered to drive him back to Staplewood with me. Which he declined, saying that he didn't wish to intrude upon you uninvited. On reflection, I came to the conclusion that he had the key to the cupboard in his pocket and I promised to convey to you the intelligence that he was putting up at the Cock, in Market Harborough—and see how you received the news! Not that I had the least doubt, but it was plain that he had.''

She digested this in silence, until some time after he had negotiated the awkward turn out of the main-gates, and was driving his forward-stepping pair along the lane which wound its way to Market Harborough. She sat beside him, staring frowningly ahead, only now and then mechanically putting up a hand to straighten her bonnet, which the wind, in spite of the ribbons that were tied under her chin, was making spasmodic attempts to lift from her head. At last she asked, in a voice she tried to render casual: ''Did he say—you told me, but I might not have understood you!—that Sarah had received none of my letters to her, sir?''

''None since the first, which you seem to have written on your arrival at Staplewood.''

''I remember.'' She relapsed again into silence, but

broke it after another pause. "Cousin Philip—*do* letters go astray, or—or get lost in the post?"

"Rarely, unless they are wrongly directed."

"I thought not. That forces me to believe that they were never posted. My aunt instructed me to lay them on the table in the hall for Pennymore to collect, and I did so, never dreaming—" She stopped, and after a moment said: "Cousin, do you think it possible that my aunt can have taken my letters, and—and destroyed them?"

Her tone implored him to reassure her, but he replied coolly: "I not only think it possible, but very probable."

"But *why?*"

He glanced down at her. "I told you this morning, Kate that the circumstance of your being alone in the world makes you valuable to Minerva. I collect that Mrs Nidd is devoted to you, and I'll hazard a guess that if she knew that you were unhappy, or being constrained to do something against your will, she would fly to your rescue, even braving Minerva's quelling top-loftiness."

"Dear Sarah!" sighed Kate, smiling faintly. "Of course she would!"

"Depend upon it, Minerva is well aware of that."

"Oh, no, no! Why, she told Sarah that she might be sure of a welcome at Staplewood, if she chose to visit me!"

"I can almost hear her saying it. Knowing that there was very little likelihood of Sarah's undertaking such a journey uninvited, and none at all, if communication between you could be severed!"

Kate wrung her hands. "You mustn't say such things! I can't and I won't believe them! It would be too shocking—too dreadful!"

"Very well, Kate: I won't say them."

"But you have said them, and I shan't be able to forget them, because—because—"

Her voice failed, and he said: "Because you know, in your heart, that they are true?"

"No, no, I don't know that, but I can't help wondering if there might be *some* truth in them! If my aunt didn't intercept my letters to Sarah, *who did?* And—and who but she could have stolen Sarah's letters to me? Pennymore takes the post-bag to her, and it is she who opens it, and sorts the letters. Only this morning I asked her if there were no letters for me, and she said there were not. Surely, knowing how anxious I was, she would not be so cruel as to lie to me? Every feeling revolts! You, I know, dislike and despise her, but—"

"You're mistaken!" he interrupted. "I certainly dislike her, but I am far from despising her! She is not only a woman of iron determination, but a very clever woman as well. I am persuaded she would stop at nothing to gain her ends. It will be well for you, my poor child, if you face that disagreeable truth."

She made a gesture, imploring him to say no more, and for quite some time he drove on in silence. When he did speak again, it was on an indifferent subject, and in a cheerful tone which did much to restore her composure. She managed to answer him in kind, but she was a prey to agitating reflections, and knew that these would recur. A period of quiet thought, in the solitude of her bedchamber, would be necessary to enable her to consider dispassionately all that he had said, and all that she knew about Lady Broome. Meanwhile, the most sensible thing to do was to put the matter aside for the time being, and to respond to the unexceptional remarks he was making with at least the assumption of calm interest. It was not so very difficult, for he made her laugh when he described Mr

Nidd as being as spruce as an onion, and after that she became much more at her ease. "If that was so," she said sapiently, "he must be wearing his bettermost clothes! I'm glad you like him—and you do, don't you?"

"Oh, to the top of the glass! A capital old gentleman—with salt under his tongue!"

"He has plenty of that!" admitted Kate. "Sometimes he offends people by being so outspoken, and using cant terms, which shock Sarah! She was on tenterhooks, when I stayed with her, in case he should say something improper to me. But he never said anything to make me blush, though I must own that I learned a great many words from him which Sarah says are excessively vulgar! I collect he wasn't uncivil to you?"

"Not at all. On the other hand, he didn't truckle to me, and I liked that. I know he regarded me with a critical eye, and I suspect that he thinks me a mere stripling. Promising, but immature!"

"I perceive that he must have been *very* civil to you!" said Kate, with a twinkle. "You should hear what he says to his grandsons! And he even calls Joe—that's his only son—a chawbacon! Which," she added, after a moment's consideration, "is perfectly true, of course! But so kind, and *good!*"

"I should dearly love to hear what he calls his grandsons, and look forward to meeting them, and Joe, and Sarah," he replied.

"But you aren't at all likely to, are you?" Kate pointed out.

"Oh, I wouldn't say that! It depends on circumstances!" he responded.

Chapter Twelve

On arrival at Market Harborough, Mr Philip Broome drove to the Angel, and left Kate in a private parlour there while he went off to the Cock, to fetch Mr Nidd. She would have gone with him, but he told her that Mr Nidd had forbidden him to bring her to what he had described as a mere sluicery. "He says it wouldn't be fitting, and I daresay he's right—even if he wrongs it in calling it a mere sluicery! As I recall, it is a respectable inn, situated not far from the postroad. However, it doesn't cater for the gentry, so I think you will be more comfortable here."

She agreed to it, and sat down by the window to wait his return. Twenty minutes later, she saw him crossing the street, with Mr Nidd trotting along beside him, and realized, with deep appreciation, that Mr Nidd was indeed looking as spruce as an onion, in his Sunday coat and smalls, a natty waistcoat, and a rigidly starched collar, whose points, she guessed were causing him considerable discomfort. She wished Sarah might have been present to have been gratified by the sight of him, for not all her efforts had hitherto prevailed upon him to wear a collar, except for Church-going, and great occasions. His favourite form of neckwear was a large, spotted silk handkerchief, which he knotted round his throat with great taste and artistry.

In another few minutes, she was welcoming him with outstretched hands, and exclaiming: "Oh, Mr Nidd, how happy it makes me to see you again!"

Much gratified, he said: "That makes a pair of us, miss! And very kind I take it that you should say so! Now, wait a bit while I put me hat down careful somewhere! It's a new 'un, and I don't want it spoiled!"

Philip took it out of his hand, and set it down with meticulous care upon a side-table. Mr Nidd, watching this with a jealous eye, was pleased to approve, and said he was much obliged. He then received Kate's hands in a reverent clasp, but reproved her for demeaning herself. "Because there ain't no call for you to treat me as if I was a lord, missy, and, what's more, you didn't ought to!"

"I'm not acquainted with a lord," countered Kate, "and I shouldn't hold out my hands to him if I were! Dear Mr Nidd, if you *knew* how much I have yearned for news of you all—! How is Sarah? Could you not have brought her with you?"

"No, and nor I wasn't wishful to, miss!" said Mr Nidd, with sudden malevolence. "Sarey's cut her stick!"

"Cut her stick?" repeated Kate uncomprehendingly.

"Loped off!" pronounced Mr Nidd, in bitter accents. "Ah! For all she cares, I could be living on pig-swill! Which I pretty well was!" he added, with a darkling look.

"Properly speaking, it was him as left her," replied Mr Nidd, in a reluctantly fair-minded way. "Not but what it was only in the way of business, mind! Joe's gone off with Young Ted to Swansea, with a wagon-load of furniture, which a gentleman as is moving house hired him to convey, being as a friend of his had highly recommended Josiah Nidd & Son, Carriers, to him."

"What a stroke of good fortune!" said Kate. "Except, of course, that it means, I suppose, that he will be absent for several weeks. But I can't believe that Sarah wished him to refuse such an advantageous engagement!"

"No," admitted Mr Nidd. "All Sarey wished was for Joe to drive a harder bargain, which I'm bound to say he did do—though not as hard a one as I'd have driven, mind! So off he went, leaving Sarey to keep house for me and Will, which would have been all right and tight if she'd done it, but she didn't, Miss Kate! What I say is, she ain't got no call to go trapesing off to nurse them dratted brats of Polly's!"

"Oh, dear! Are they ill, then? But you know you shouldn't call your grandchildren dratted brats, Mr Nidd!"

"Nor I wouldn't, if it wasn't true!" he replied, with spirit. "I speaks of people as I find 'em, miss, and why the good Lord see fit to saddle me with a set of grandchildren that ain't worth two rows of gingerbread I don't know, and never will! They've got the measles, Miss Kate—all six of 'em! And what must Polly do, clumsy fussock that she is, but tumble down the stairs with a tray of chiney, and break four plates, two bowls, and her leg! I got no patience with it!"

Kate could not help laughing, but she said: "What a disaster! No wonder Sarah went to the rescue! And you know very well you wouldn't have wished her *not* to have done so! What's more, you won't make me believe she didn't make provision for you and Will!"

"If you call it making provision for me to hire Old Tom's rib to cook me dinner for me, Miss Kate, all I've got to say is that you can't have eaten anything that rabbit-pole woman ever spoiled! Which, of course, you haven't. Meself, I'd as *lief* sit down to a dish of pig-swill!"

At this point, Mr Philip Broome, who had been silently

enjoying Mr Nidd's embittered discourse, intervened with an offer of refreshment. "Forgive me, but before I leave you to be private with Miss Malvern, what would you wish me to order for you, Mr Nidd? Sherry, or beer? I've never sampled the sherry here, but I can vouch for the beer!"

"Thanking you kindly, sir, beer's me tipple. Not that I ain't partial to a glass of sherry in season," he added grandly, if a trifle obscurely.

Philip lifted an eyebrow at Kate. "And you, cousin?"

"I should like some lemonade, if it might be had."

He nodded, and left the room. "I've took a fancy to that young fellow," said Mr Nidd decidedly. "He ain't a buck of the first head, nor he ain't as fine as a star, but to my way of thinking, Miss Kate, he's true blue! *He'll* never stain!"

To her annoyance, Kate felt herself blushing, and knew that Mr Nidd was watching her closely out of his aged but remarkably sharp eyes. With as much nonchalance as she could assume, she replied: "Yes, indeed: Mr Philip Broome is most truly the gentleman! But tell me, Mr Nidd—"

"Now, hold hard, miss!" begged Mr Nidd. "I'm one as likes to have everything made clear, and what I don't know, and didn't care to take the liberty of asking him, is what relation he is to the Bart? He ain't the Bart's son, that's sure, because, according to what you wrote to Sarey, the Bart's son has got an outlandish name, which I don't hold with. And what's more, Miss Kate, you said the Bart's son was the most beautiful young man you'd ever clapped eyes on, and if you was meaning this young fellow, it don't fit! Not but what he's as good-looking as any man need to be—ah, and would strip to advantage, too!"

"He is Sir Timothy's nephew," answered Kate briefly.

"It is my turn to ask questions now, Mr Nidd! Is it true that Sarah has received only one of my letters to her?"

"Gospel true, miss!" asseverated Mr Nidd. "That was the scratch of a note you wrote to her when you first arrived at this Staplewood, and it relieved Sarey's mind considerable, because you told her how kind your aunt was, *and* the Bart, and what a beautiful place it was, and how happy you was to be here, which got up her spirits wonderful. Properly hipped she was, after you'd gone off! She took an unaccountable dislike to her ladyship, but I'm blessed if I know why! Happy as a grig she was when she read your letter, until she got into the dumps again because she never had no answer to the letter *she* wrote *you,* nor so much as a line from you from that day to this."

"Mr Nidd," said Kate, in a rigidly controlled voice, "I have never had a letter from Sarah. I have written to her repeatedly, begging her to reply, but never has she done so. When Mr Broome told me that you had come to Market Harborough the most terrible apprehension seized me that you had come to tell me Sarah was ill, or—or *dead!*"

The effect of this disclosure on the patriarch was profound. After hearing Kate out in great astonishment, he wrapped himself in a cloak of silence, and, when she started to speak again, raised a forbidding hand, and said: "I got to think!"

In the middle of his ruminations, the waiter came in with a tray, which he set down on the table. Having offered Kate, with a low bow, a glass of lemonade, he carried a tankard over to Mr Nidd, and gave it to him with a much lower bow, intended to convey condescension, contempt, and derision. Fully alive to the implications of this covert insolence, Mr Nidd, taking the tankard with a brief thank'ee, recommended him to wipe his nose on a handkerchief instead of on the knees of his smalls, and told him to take himself off. After thus routing the adversary, he refreshed himself with a copious draught from the tankard, wiped his mouth on the back of his hand, and said portentously: "It's a good thing I've come, Miss Kate, that's what it is! Yes, and so Sarey will have to own! If I've told her once she ought to come herself to see how you was going on, I've told her a dozen times! But would she do it? *Oh,* no! She took a maggot into her head that you wouldn't want her to come here, poking her nose in, now that you was living with your grand relations, and nothing me nor Joe said made her think different!"

"Oh, no, no!" Kate cried distressfully. "How *could* she have thought such a thing of me?"

"It's no manner of use asking me that, miss, because there's no saying what notions a nidgetty female will take into her head—even the best of 'em! 'Well,' I says to her, 'it ain't like Miss Kate to act bumptious, and more shame to you, Sarey, for thinking it!' Then she started napping her bib, and saying that she didn't think no such thing, and nobody could wonder at you being so took up with your relations that you was forgetful of your old nurse. 'Well,' I says, sharp-like, '*I* don't wonder at it, because I ain't bottleheaded enough to believe it!' Then she sobs fit to bust her laces, and says as how I don't understand! Which was true enough! 'I can't explain!' she says. 'That's easy seen!' I told her . But argufying with a ticklish female don't do a bit of good, so I gave over. But the more I thought about it, the more I didn't like it, nor think it was natural. 'Something havey-cavey about this,' I says to myself: so when Sarey took herself off to Polly's house I bought a new hat, and a shirt with winkers, packed up me traps, and came to Market Harborough on the stagecoach."

"But—do you mean that Sarah doesn't know?" asked

Kate, dismayed. "Mr Nidd, you shouldn't have come here without telling her! Only think how anxious she must be!"

He looked a little guilty, but replied in a very lofty way that he had left a message with Tom's wife that if anyone were to enquire for him she was to say that he had gone into the country to visit a friend. "Which ain't gammon," he assured Kate, "because the buffer at the Cock is an old friend of mine. Regular bosom-birds we was used to be, afore I retired. Many's the time I've fetched up at the Cock with a wagon-load of goods, and greased the tapster's boy in the fist to make up his bed in the wagon, in case there might happen to be a prig, sneaking on the lurk. So don't you worry your pretty head about that, Miss Kate! You got troubles of your own!"

"Indeed I haven't!" said Kate quickly. "My aunt is kindness itself, I assure you!"

"It's my belief," said Mr Nidd, eyeing her narrowly, "that you're being put upon, miss!"

"No, no, I promise you that isn't true! Aunt Minerva treats me as if I were her daughter—only I hope she would allow a daughter to be more useful to her than I am! Whenever I beg her to give me some task to perform, the best she can think of is to ask me to cut and arrange flowers!"

Mr Nidd looked to be unconvinced. "Well, I got a notion you're moped, miss!" he said. "I *may* be wrong, but I disremember when I last had the wrong sow by the ear. I daresay I never did, because I've got a deal of rum-gumption, and always did have—whatever Sarey may tell you to the contrary!"

"I know you have, Mr Nidd, but if you think I look moped you've made a mistake this time! To own the truth, I'm bored! From not having enough to do! And the worst of it is that I can't persuade my aunt that I am yearning for occupation. You know, I have never been used to lead a life of indolence.''

''No, and nor you ain't been used to enjoying yourself neither!'' he retorted. ''Many's the time Sarey has got to fretting and fuming because you don't go to balls, and routs, and such-like as a young lady should, and the only thing which plucked her up when you didn't write was thinking as you was probably too taken up with parties to have a minute to spare! Now, you don't mean to tell me that you're bored with parties already, Miss Kate!''

''No, but I haven't been to many parties, Mr Nidd!'' she replied ruefully.

''You're bamming me!'' he exclaimed.

''I'm not, I promise you! The thing is, you see, that Sir Timothy's health does not permit him to go to parties, or—or even to entertain people at Staplewood. My aunt gave a dinner-party for his particular friends, when I first came here, but it wasn't very amusing. You mustn't suppose me to be complaining, but when Sarah pictures me in a whirl of gaiety she is fair and far out!''

''You don't say, miss! Well, I'm bound to say that's got me properly pitch-kettled, that has! No pleasuring at all! You'd have thought that it wouldn't disturb the Bart if she was to invite a few young people to supper, and one of them small balls, got up sudden! By what I'm told, the Bart's got his own rooms, and commonly shuts hisself up in them for the best part of the day, so I don't see how a snug party of that nature need worrit him! No, and I don't see neither why her ladyship don't make it her business to arrange it! How old is this son of hers?''

''Torquil is nineteen, but he—''

''So that's what his name is, is it? Unnatural, I call it, and it's to be hoped he *don't* talk ill!'' interrupted Mr Nidd, cackling at his own wit.

Kate, according it a dutiful smile, said: "Unfortunately, Torquil suffers from a—a delicate constitution, and the least excitement brings on one of his terrible headaches. It is an object with my aunt to keep him as quiet as possible."

"What, him too?" said Mr Nidd incredulously. "Seems to me, miss, that we'd ha' done as well, me and Sarey, to have sent you to a pest-house! I never did, not in all my puff!"

She laughed. "Neither Sir Timothy nor Torquil suffers from an *infectious* complaint, Mr Nidd!"

"Dutch comfort, Miss Kate! Next you'll be telling me that the nevvy's in queer stirrups!"

"Indeed I shan't tell you anything of the sort!" said Kate indignantly.

"Nor I wouldn't credit it if you did! I can see with my own ogles that he's in prime twig! But, lordy, this'll make Sarey look blue! You know what she is, miss: no sooner did she read your letter, saying as how your cousin was the most beautiful young man you'd ever beheld, than she got to thinking what a good thing it would be if you and he was to make a match of it. Which there's no denying it would be, if he was quite stout. But if he's ticklish in the wind it won't do, Miss Kate!"

She said earnestly: "Mr Nidd, pray don't encourage Sarah to think there is the least possibility of my marrying Torquil! It is too absurd! Sarah must have forgotten that I am four-and-twenty! There are five years between Torquil and me—and I haven't the smallest inclination to set my cap at him! He is certainly beautiful, but I can conceive of few worse fates than to be married to him! He is nothing more than a spoiled schoolboy, and his temper is shocking! Pray let us be done with that nonsense!"

"I'm agreeable, miss," said Mr Nidd affably. "Not but

what it'll come as a disappointment to Sarey, because
there's no denying that it would have been a spanking
thing for you. However, what can't be cured must be endured, and it's as plain as a pack-saddle that the nevvy's
nutty on you! Now, if he was to offer for you—''

"I should be very much surprised!" Kate interrupted.
"I'm not on the catch for a husband, Mr Nidd, and I shall
be much obliged to you if you won't make plans for me!
Let us rather talk about your own affairs! I do, most solemnly, beg that you will go back to London! I don't mean
that I'm not deeply grateful to you for having come to
Market Harborough, for I am—more grateful than I can
tell you!—but Sarah must by this time be in a perfect stew!
And if I were to dash off a note to her, you could take it
to her, couldn't you?"

"Yes, Miss Kate, and I could take it to the Post Office
too. I got a notion I won't go back yet, because I ain't
easy in my mind, and I'm not wishful to leave you here!
It sticks in my gullet that you ain't had any of Sarey's
letters, nor she any of yours, barring the first of 'em. It
don't smell right to me, missy, and that's the truth!"

"It—it doesn't smell right to me either," confessed
Kate. "But until I have spoken to my aunt about it, I—I
would liefer not discuss it! If it was she who was responsible, she *must* have had some good reason, even—even if
I can't think what it can have been."

"No, nor me neither!" said Mr Nidd acidly. "And, if
you ask me, she'll find herself in a proper hank, when she
starts to explain what her reason was! Don't you try to sell
yourself a bargain, miss, because you ain't a paperskull,
no more than what I am, and you know well she can't
have a good reason! Mark me if she ain't playing an un-
dergame!"

Kate got up, and went to the window, and began to twist the blind-cord around her finger. "I know, but—"

"The best thing you can do, miss, is to come back to Sarah!" said Mr Nidd. "Lor', wouldn't she jump out of her skin with joy! Yes, and what's more, if she knew you was with us again she'd come home herself, ah, and in an ant's foot, too! Then p'raps we'd get some wittles fit to eat! All you got to do, miss, is to pack your traps, and leave it to me to settle the rest. You wouldn't object to travelling on the stage, would you? I'd take good care of you."

Kate turned her head to bestow upon him a warm, smiling look. "I know you would, Mr Nidd—bless you! But I couldn't, after all her kindness, leave my aunt in such a way! It would be beyond everything! I think I know why she—why she tried to stop me corresponding with Sarah. You see, she doesn't want me to leave Staplewood, and I expect she must know that I *couldn't* do so if I became estranged from Sarah. I've said from the start that I *should* leave, after the summer, and I've remained firm in that resolve. It was very wrong, of course, to tamper with my correspondence, but—but she is a woman who has been used to have her own way in everything, and—and once I've—well, brought her to book!—I'm persuaded she won't do so any more. Now that I've seen you, and know that Sarah hasn't given me up, I can be easy again, and be sure that if I found myself obliged to leave Staplewood, I shouldn't find that Sarah had closed your doors against me! Dear Mr Nidd, your visit has been the greatest comfort to me, but I do, most earnestly, beg that you will go back to London!"

As she spoke, the door opened, and she looked quickly over her shoulder, to see that Mr Philip Broome had entered the room. He said: "I'm sorry to interrupt you,

Cousin Kate, but we stand in imminent danger of being scandalously late for dinner! Unless we set forward immediately, we shall fall under Minerva's displeasure.''

"Oh, good God, that would never do!'' she exclaimed, with would-be lightness. "Have I enough time to scribble a note to Mrs Nidd? I have been asking Mr Nidd if he will be so good as to take it to her, and I *promise* I won't keep you waiting above ten minutes!''

"By all means,'' he said, casting a glance round the room, and discovering a writing-table. He strode over to it, and pulled open two of its drawers. "Wonderful! Not only paper, but wafers as well, and a pen! And even ink in the standish! In general, when one wishes to write a letter in a posting-house, one finds that there is only a kind of mud at the bottom of the standishes. If you care to sit down here, Kate, I'll take Mr Nidd down to inspect my horses. You will join us in the yard at your convenience.''

She agreed gratefully to this suggestion; and although it was evident that Mr Nidd was much inclined to dig his heels in, he yielded, after staring pugnaciously at him, to the unmistakeable message in Mr Philip Broome's eyes, accompanied as it was by the flicker of the smile of a conspirator.

But as soon as Philip had closed the door, he said that he had told Miss Kate that he would be happy to take her letter to the Post Office, but he hadn't made up his mind to go home, not by a long chalk he hadn't.

Leading the way down the stairs, Philip said, over his shoulder: "Does she wish you to do so?''

"Yes, she does, sir, and it goes against the pluck with me to do it!'' said Mr Nidd, in a brooding tone. "I wouldn't wish to offend you, Mr Broome, sir, but I been telling Miss Kate that the thing for her to do is to come back with me to London!''

"I shouldn't think she agreed to that," Philip commented.

"No, sir, she didn't," said Mr Nidd, nipping ahead to hold open the door into the yard. "After you, sir, *if* you please!— No, she said that she couldn't leave her aunt in a bang, as you might say, being as how her ladyship had been so kind to her. Which, begging your pardon, I take leave to doubt!"

"True enough. Her ladyship has been more than kind to her."

"Well, if you say so, sir—!" replied Mr Nidd dubiously. "I didn't cut my eye-teeth yesterday, nor yet the day before, and you don't have to tell me you don't cut no shams, because I knew from the moment I clapped my ogles on you that it was pound-dealing with you, or nothing! *But,* Mr Broome, sir, I'll take the liberty of telling you to your head that I ain't easy in my mind! It don't *smell* right to me, somehow!"

Philip did not immediately answer, but after a short pause he said: "Does it make you easier when I tell you that if any danger were to threaten Miss Malvern—which I don't anticipate!—I should instantly bundle her into a chaise, and restore her to her nurse?"

"You would?" Mr Nidd said, regarding him with obvious approval.

"Most certainly!"

"Well, that's different, of course!" said Mr Nidd graciously. "If *you* mean to look after Miss Kate, there's no call for *me* to kick my heels here!"

"Thank you!" said Philip, holding out his hand, and smiling. "We'll shake hands on that, Mr Nidd!"

"Thanking *you,* sir!" said Mr Nidd ineffably.

Kate, emerging from the house several minutes later, was relieved to find that her aged well-wisher had apparently formed the intention of departing for London on the following morning. He received from her a hastily written note to Sarah, and stowed it away in his pocket, promising to deliver it as soon as he reached the Metropolis. It was plain that he had been making shrewd, but, on the whole, appreciative comments on the well-matched bays which had just been harnessed to Mr Philip Broome's curricle; and, on bidding Kate a fond farewell, he was moved to say that he knew he was leaving her in good hands. She hardly knew what to reply to this, but murmured something unintelligible, her colour much heightened, and could only be grateful to Philip for not prolonging the embarrassing moment. As he swept from the yard into the main street, he said conversationally: ''A truly estimable old gentleman! A downy one, too! He says it don't smell right to him. Precisely my own opinion!''

''You did not tell him so?'' she asked anxiously.

''Oh, no! All I did was to assure him that you were in no danger, and that if it became imperative on you to leave Staplewood I would convey you to London, and hand you over to Mrs Nidd. Why, by the way, did you refuse to go with him?''

''How could I do so?'' she demanded. ''Whatever my aunt has done, she doesn't deserve to be treated so shabbily! Good God, Cousin Philip, the clothes I am wearing at this moment I owe to her generosity! Besides,—''

''Yes?'' he said, as she broke off. ''That isn't all your reason, is it?''

''No,'' she admitted. ''Not quite all. You see, before my aunt took me away from Sarah, I had been staying with her for far too long a time—much longer than I had anticipated. I know what a charge I must have been, though she was very angry when I ventured to say so, and told me that if I dared to offer her money for my board she would never forgive me. So I can't go back to her until I've secured a post. When I left Wisbech I thought I should have been able to do so immediately, but—but it turned out otherwise. None of the ladies who were advertising for governesses hired me. Either they wanted an accomplished female, able to instruct her pupils in the harp, and the piano, and the Italian tongue, or they said I was too young. It was the most mortifying experience! I became utterly despondent, and began to wonder whether I might not be able to turn the only talent I possess to good account.''

"And what is your only talent?" he asked.

"Oh, dressmaking! I *did* think of seeking a post as abigail to a lady of fashion, but Sarah wouldn't hear of it. She said it wouldn't do for me—"

"She was right!"

"Yes, I think perhaps she was: I can't imagine when a modish abigail finds the time to go to bed! So then I hit upon the idea of seeking employment in a dressmaker's establishment, but Mr Nidd was strongly opposed to it.''

"I said he was a downy one," observed Philip.

"Yes, but I still think I might try my hand at it, if all else fails. He says that unless one can afford to set up for oneself, or at least to buy a share in a flourishing business, there is no possibility of making one's fortune in the dressmaking line.''

"None at all, I imagine."

"You can't tell that!" she objected. 'For my part, I shouldn't wonder at it if you are both wrong. Consider! even if I had to serve an apprenticeship in the workroom, and subsist for a time on a pittance, I should be *bound* to rise rapidly to a more elevated position, because I can do more than sew: I can *design!* I truly can, sir! I have been used to make all my own dresses, and no one has yet called me a dowd! On the contrary! Mrs Astley's odious mother said that she marvelled at my extravagance, and would like to know where I found the money to purchase such expensive gowns!'' She chuckled. ''And the joke was that when she said that, I was wearing a coloured muslin dress which cost exactly eighteen shillings! It was perfectly plain except for a knot of ribbons at the waist, but of excellent cut and style, which, of course, was what misled her. I don't mean to boast, but doesn't that *show* you?''

''I should have to see the garment before I ventured to give my opinion,'' he said, his countenance grave, but his voice a trifle unsteady.

She burst out laughing. ''What a shocking Banbury man you are, sir! How dare you poke fun at me? Did I sound like a bounce?''

He shook his head gloomily. ''Every feeling was offended!'' he assured her.

She laughed more than ever, but said: ''Seriously, sir—''

''Seriously, Kate, Mr Nidd is right: it won't fadge!''

She sighed. ''Perhaps it might not. Lately I have been wondering if I could not obtain a situation with an old lady. I daresay you know the sort of thing I mean: as companion, or housekeeper, or even the two combined. It would be dreadfully dull, I expect, but at least Sarah wouldn't kick up a dust, and say it wasn't a genteel occupation.''

''I suppose you wouldn't consider being a companion-housekeeper to a gentleman?'' he suggested.

''I shouldn't think so. Sarah would think it most improper, and it would be, you know. Unless he was a *very* old gentleman. Why, do you know of a gentleman who wants a companion-housekeeper?''

''As it chances, I do. But not a *very* old one, I'm afraid!

I mean he isn't bedridden, or queer in his attic, or anything of that nature. Not a *dotard!*''

"I certainly shouldn't consider such a post in a dotard's house!" she said, amused. "In fact, unless I were offered a handsome wage, which, I own, would tempt me, I don't mean to consider it at all! An old lady is the thing for me!"

"You cannot have given enough thought to it, Kate! Old ladies are always as cross as crabs!"

"What nonsense!" she said scornfully. "I have known *several* who were most amiable! And no female is commonly afflicted with gout, which most old gentlemen are, I find. It makes them insupportably cross!"

"The gentleman I have in mind is not afflicted with gout, and I am persuaded you would find him amiable, and—and compliant.''

"Indeed?" said Kate, stiffening. "And how old *is* this gentleman, sir?"

"Nine-and-twenty. But very nearly thirty!" he replied.

Since she knew this to be his own age, she could not doubt that he meant himself, and was making her an offer. But what kind of an offer it was remained a matter of painful doubt. He knew her to be friendless and penniless, and it was possible that he was offering her a *carte blanche,* meaning to set her up as his mistress; it seemed very unlikely that he wished to marry her, for (as she dismally reminded herself) she had nothing but a pretty face to recommend her. She felt suddenly that if that was what he meant it would be more than she could bear; and realized that it would be one more illusion shattered. She had not allowed herself to hope that he would offer marriage, for she knew herself to be ineligible; she was not even sure that he loved her. He had certainly revised his first, unfavourable estimate of her character; and when he looked at her she could fancy that there was a warm, appreciative light in his eyes. But he was not a man who wore his heart on his sleeve: indeed, if it was possible to detect a fault in him, thought Kate, sternly resolved to do so, he had too much reserve. Not, of course, a stupid sort of indifference, but a coolness of manner, which made it hard to know what he was thinking.

Doggedly determined not to betray herself, she said, in a light voice, which she hoped expressed contemptuous amusement: "I won't pretend to play the dunce, sir. I assume that you are talking about yourself. I don't find it diverting!"

"I was talking about myself, and I am extremely glad you don't find it diverting!" he said, with some asperity.

Her heart began to beat uncomfortably fast, and she could feel the colour mounting into her cheeks. She turned her face away, saying: "This is quite improper, sir! I told my aunt that you showed no disposition to flirt with me, and I *believed* it!"

"So I should hope! For God's sake, Kate—! I'm not flirting with you! I'm trying to tell you that I love you!"

"Oh!" uttered Kate faintly.

Mr Philip Broome, indignant at being given so little encouragement, said in a goaded voice: "Now say you're much obliged to me!"

"I don't know that I am," responded Kate, almost inaudibly. "I—I don't know what you mean!"

With all the air of a deeply reticent man forced to declare his sentiments, he said: "Exactly what I said! I LOVE YOU!"

"You needn't shout! I'm not deaf!" retorted Kate, with spirit.

"I was afraid you might be! I could hardly have put it more plainly! And all you can say is *Oh!* As though it was a matter of no consequence to you! If you feel that you can't return my—my regard, tell me so! I've dared to hope, but I was prepared to have my offer rejected, and although it would be a severe blow, I trust I have enough conduct not to embarrass you by persisting!''

''You—you haven't made me an offer!'' said Kate. She added hurriedly, and in considerable confusion: ''I don't in the least wish you to! I mean, I would far, far liefer you didn't if you are trying to— Oh, dear, how very awkward this is! Mr Broome, *pray* don't offer me a *carte blanche!*''

''A *carte blanche?*'' he exclaimed, apparently stunned. By this time she was crimson-cheeked. She stammered: ''Is—isn't that the right term?''

''No, it is *not* the right term!'' he said savagely, drawing his horses in to the side of the lane, and pulling them to a halt. ''What kind of a loose-screw do you take me for? Offer a *carte blanche* to a delicately bred girl in your circumstances? You must think I'm an ugly customer!''

''Oh, no, no! *Indeed* I don't!''

He possessed himself of her hands, and held them in a hard grip. ''I am proposing to you, Kate! Will you marry me?''

Her hands instinctively clung to his; a happiness she had never known before flooded her being; but she said foolishly: ''Oh, no! Don't! You can't have considered—Oh, dear, how improper this is!''

Mr Philip Broome, after one swift glance round, dragged her roughly into his arms and kissed her. For a delirious moment Kate yielded, but every precept that Sarah had drummed into her head shrieked to her that she was violating every canon of propriety, and behaving without delicacy or conduct. She made a desperate attempt to thrust him away, uttering an inarticulate protest. He released her with unexpected alacrity, ejaculating: ''I might have

known it!'' and set his horses in motion again. ''That's
what comes of proposing in a curricle! Straighten your
bonnet, Kate, for the lord's sake!''

She had suffered a severe shock at being so brusquely
repulsed, but she now saw that Mr Philip Broome had not
experienced a change of heart. A couple of people had
come round a sharp bend in the lane, and were advancing
slowly towards them. From their attire, Kate judged them
to be members of the farming fraternity; and from the circumstances of the young man's arm being round the girl's
waist, and his head bent fondly over hers, it seemed safe
to assume that they were a courting couple. They were
wholly absorbed in each other, and cast no more than cursory, incurious glances at the curricle.

''Phew!'' whistled Philip, as soon as the curricle was
out of earshot. ''It's to be hoped they didn't see!''

''Yes, it is!'' Kate agreed warmly. ''And if they did, it
serves me right for behaving like a—like a *straw-
damsel!*''

Chapter Thirteen

Mr Philip Broome burst out laughing. "Oh, Kate, you enchanting rogue! Where did you learn that? Not from Mr Nidd, I'll swear!"

In consternation she said: "No, no! It was *very* bad of me to have said it! The thing is I couldn't think of a more genteel way of putting it, and for some reason or other the expression stuck in my memory, and—and sprang to my tongue! I heard one of Papa's men say it—oh, years ago, and asked Papa what it meant. He burst out laughing too. But he did tell me, and warn me not to say it, so I have no excuse, and I beg your pardon."

"You may say anything you please to me, my love. I hope you will."

She had been smiling, but these words brought her back to earth, and she said, in a troubled voice: "I don't think—I don't think you ought to make me an offer!"

"No, it's quite improper, of course," he said cheerfully. "Before addressing myself to you, I *ought* to ask permission of your father, or your mother, or your guardian; but as you haven't a father, or a mother, or a guardian, I do trust you'll overlook the irregularity! Something seems to tell me that if I were to apply to Minerva she would send me to the rightabout! Do you feel you could, without sinking yourself beneath reproach, tell me if you could bring yourself to marry me?''

"Not—not without sinking myself beneath reproach!" she answered sadly.

Taken aback, he demanded: "Now, what the devil—?"

She resolutely raised her eyes to his face, and managed to say: "I believe you haven't understood my circumstances. You shouldn't be proposing to a female of no fortune, or to one whose relations don't own her! *Your* family must surely oppose such an unequal match! You see, I haven't sixpence to scratch with. I am a *pauper!*"

"I call that a very grandiloquent way of putting it!" he objected. "As for saying you haven't sixpence to scratch with—! Well, that's the outside of enough! A shockingly ungenteel expression, let me tell you, my little love, and one that I never thought to hear on your lips!"

Kate was betrayed into retorting: "Considering you have just heard a *much* more shocking expression on my lips, you can't have felt surprised! What a complete hand you are, Cousin Philip!"

"And what an abominable little gypsy *you* are, Cousin Kate!" he said affably. "Let us be serious for a minute! You're talking the most outrageous fustian I ever listened to in my life, you know—and that *does* surprise me, because you're not at all addlebrained! If your relations don't own you, so much the better! They sound to me a very disagreeable set of persons. As to mine, I have no closer relations than my uncle Timothy, and you can't suppose that he would oppose the match! I almost wish he would, if it were within his power to cut me out of the succession. I daresay my more remote relations don't care a pin what I do: I know *I* don't give a pin for *their* opinions! Finally, my little pea-goose, I understand your circumstances a great deal better than you seem to understand mine! I'm not a rich man, Kate. I can't offer you the consequence of a large country estate, a mansion in Berkeley Square, and a handsome fortune. I am possessed of what I have been used to consider a comfortable independence. My wife will be able to command the elegancies of life, but not its extravagances. Broome Hall doesn't compare with Staplewood, you know. I should describe it as commodious rather than stately, and my fortune won't run to a town-house—at least, not a permanent one."

He spoke apologetically, and was obviously sincere. Kate's ever-lively sense of humour got the better of her, and she said, in the voice of one suffering a severe disappointment: "Not?"

"Not!" said Philip firmly. "You would have to be content with a furnished house for a few weeks during the Season!"

Kate sighed audibly. "Well," she said, making a reluctant concession, "as long as it is in the best part of town—!"

"I thought," said Philip, glancing appreciatively down into her dancing eyes, "that we were going to be serious, my sweet witcracker?"

"Yes, so did I, and so I would have been, if *you* hadn't talked such fustian! Dear sir, when my father was serving, we lived for the most part in billets, which ranged from a very dirty, draughty cottage on the Spanish and Portuguese border, to rooms in a palatial, and even more draughty, château, north of Toulouse. When Papa sold out, and we settled in London, we lived in lodgings which varied with Papa's fortunes. To be sure, at the outset, when it was high tide with him, we had an elegant set of rooms in Clarges Street; but we ended in far from elegant rooms in Thames Street. Poor Papa could never manage to be beforehand with the world for more than a few weeks at a stretch. You see, he was a gamester, and whenever he had a run of luck nothing would do for him but to—er—waste the ready as fast as he could! I can't tell you how many times he has come home, and emptied guineas into my lap, or how many expensive trinkets he has given me! He had a great many faults, but no one could accuse him of being clutch-fisted. He was the most generous man imaginable, and a great dear, but not—not at all reliable!''

''Something of this I have learnt from Minerva. Did he leave you in debt, my poor child?''

''Oh, yes, but nothing to signify!'' said Kate sunnily. ''Not gaming debts! He was very punctilious in all matters of play and pay. I sold my trinkets, and one or two other things, to pay the tradesmen's bills, and came off all right.''

''But without sixpence to scratch with?'' he suggested.

She smiled. ''True! But I had the good fortune to please Mrs Astley, and she hired me to be governess to her children. And Sarah was there, in the background, ready to shelter me at a moment's notice. I wish you might see the house she persuaded Mr Nidd to buy for his wagons, and horses, and stable-hands! It is close to the Bull and Mouth, in the city, and was used to be an inn. It is the quaintest, most delightful place imaginable! It had fallen into a shocking state of disrepair, but Mr Nidd and Joe furbished it up, and turned one side of the yard into a snug home for the family. When I left Mrs Astley, I lived with the Nidds until my aunt came to sweep me off to Staplewood. They were so *kind* to me, Joe, and his father, and the grandsons!'' Her eyes filled, and she was obliged to flick away the sudden tears. She continued hurriedly: ''I was spoiled to death there, and enjoyed myself excessively! I know my aunt finds it impossible to believe that I *could* have enjoyed it, but—but she wasn't reared as I was, and I must own that she is very high in the instep!''

''What you mean is, insufferably top-lofty!'' interpolated Philip ruthlessly.

She was obliged to acknowledge the truth of this stricture, and could not resist confiding to him, with her infectious chuckle: ''When she found me in a chat with the coachman here, she said she hoped I hadn't a taste for low company! But I'm afraid I have, though I didn't dare to tell her so!''

''So have I!'' he said, hugely entertained. ''I see that we were made for one another! How soon will you marry me?''

''I don't know! I haven't had time to think! And should you not *consider* before you make me an offer?''

''I did consider, very profoundly, and I have already made you an offer.''

''Yes, but you haven't been acquainted with me for very long, and I don't think you did consider profoundly.''

''Well, you're beside the hedge, my sweet! You don't suppose that a man of my years, and settled habits, proposes marriage without consideration, do you?''

She answered seriously, wrinkling her brow: ''Yes, I think I do. There have been many cases of gentlemen, much older than you, proposing on the spur of the moment. And afterwards regretting it.''

''Very true!'' he said, rather grimly. ''I know of one such case myself. But you are the only woman I've known with whom I wish to spend the rest of my life, Kate. I could never regret it, and I mean to see to it that you don't regret it either! When will you marry me?''

Before she could answer him, they were both startled by a stentorian shout behind them. Kate turned quickly, but Philip had no difficulty in recognizing Mr Templecombe's voice. "The devil fly away with Gurney!" he said wrathfully. "Am I never to enjoy a moment's privacy with you?"

"Well, you can't expect to be private with me in a curricle!" Kate pointed out.

"No, and I can't expect to be private with you at Staplewood either!" he said, checking his horses. "Minerva takes good care of that!"

"There's always the shrubbery," she reminded him demurely.

"Oh, no, there is not! Expecting every minute to see Minerva coming in search of you, and with two gardeners liable to look over the hedge at any minute!— Well, Gurney, what do you want?"

Mr Templecombe, who was riding a good-looking covert-hack, reined in alongside the curricle, pulled off his hat, and bowed to Kate. "How do you do, ma'am? Happy to renew my acquaintance with you! Hoped I might have the pleasure of meeting you again, but you haven't been out riding lately, have you?"

"No, it has been rather too hot," she explained, smiling at him. "How is your sister? I hope you, and Lady Templecombe, are pleased with her engagement? I wished to send her my felicitations, but thought our acquaintance too slight to warrant my doing so."

"I don't know that—never much of a one for the conventions, y'know!—but she'll be very much obliged to you, that I *can* vouch for! Took a great fancy to you! As for Amesbury, I should rather think I am pleased! He's a great gun: known him all my life! Wouldn't you agree that he's a great gun, Philip?"

"Yes, an excellent fellow," said Philip. "What do you want to say to me, Gurney? I can't stay: we are going to be late for dinner as it is!"

"I'll go along with you as far as to your gates," said Mr Templecombe obligingly. "Only wished to warn you that I'm going on a bolt to the Metropolis tomorrow, and don't know when I shall be back. So you can't come to stay with me, dear boy! A curst bore, but there's no getting out of it! M'mother's beginning to cut up a trifle stiff: says it's my duty to show my front! Says I ought to bear in mind that I'm the head of the family. Says it presents a very off appearance when I don't show. I daresay she's right. She's holding a dress-party, and says I positively must be there."

"Undoubtedly you must!" said Philip. "If only to see to it that the butler doesn't water the wine, or the cook spoil the ham!"

"Exactly so! Not that there's much fear of old Burley's watering the wine: he's a strict abstainer! Still, I do see that it wouldn't be the thing for me to stay away from m'mother's dress-party."

"No," agreed Kate. "How uncomfortable it would be for her not to have you there to be the host!"

"Just what she says, ma'am! But the deuce of it is that once she gets me to London it's all Lombard Street to an egg-shell I shall find myself regularly in for it! I can tell you this: I'm fond of Dolly, but I shall be glad when we've got her safely buckled!"

All this time he had been riding beside the curricle, but a cart was seen approaching, and he was forced to fall back. As he continued to rattle on, in his insouciant style, and Philip's eyes had naturally to be fixed on the road ahead, the burden of maintaining conversation fell on Kate, who slewed round into a most uncomfortable position, and was heartily glad when it was again possible for him to ride alongside the curricle. "I say, dear boy, what's happened to that groom of yours?'' he asked, suddenly struck by the groom's absence.

''He—er—is suffering from an indisposition,'' replied Philip, directing a quelling look at his tactless friend.

''Suffering from a— Oh—ah! Just so!'' said Mr Templecombe hastily. ''What I wanted to say to you is that I'd be glad of a word with you before I go. Tell you what! You take Miss Malvern back to Staplewood, and come and eat your mutton with me! No need to change your dress! I want to ask your advice.''

''I'm sorry, Gurney: I believe I must not,'' said Philip, looking anything but pleased.

''Humbug, dear boy! Her ladyship don't want you, and *you'll* excuse him, won't you, Miss Malvern?''

''Of course I will,'' replied Kate, with a cordiality that earned her a fiery, sideways glance from Philip. She said, in a lowered voice: ''Please go! I must have time to think, and—and you must know there will be no opportunity for you to be private with me this evening!''

Apparently he did know this, for after hesitating for a moment he said curtly: ''Very well, Gurney: I'll come.''

''Capital!'' said Mr Templecombe, undismayed by this ungracious acceptance. ''I'll be off then: must warn my people to lay an extra cover! 'Servant, Miss Malvern! Shall hope to see you again when I come back!''

The gates of Staplewood were within sight; Mr Templecombe waved his hat in farewell, and cantered off. Kate said reproachfully: ''How could you be so uncivil?''

''Easily! I felt uncivil!''

''But you can't be uncivil to people only because you *feel* uncivil!'' Kate said austerely.

''I can, if it's to Gurney. He don't give a button! We've been friends all our lives—even went to school together!''

Since Kate knew, from her military experience, that

young gentlemen who were fast friends greeted one another in general by opprobrious names, and never seemed to think it necessary to waste civility on a chosen intimate, she had long since abandoned any attempt to fathom masculine peculiarities, and now said no more, merely smiling to herself as she tried to picture the inevitable results, if any two females behaved to each other in a similar style.

Mr Philip Broome, having negotiated the entrance to Staplewood in impeccable style, glanced down at her, and instantly demanded: "What makes you smile, Kate?"

"Oh, merely that gentlemen are always uncivil to their friends, and polite to those whom they dislike!"

"Well, naturally!" he said, making her giggle.

"I won't ask you to explain," she said. "Even if you could do so—which I take leave to doubt!—I shouldn't understand!"

"I should have thought it must be obvious! However, I don't mean to waste the few minutes left to us in trying to explain what is quite unimportant, Kate, my darling, will you marry me?"

"I—rather think I will," she replied, "but you must give me time to consider! I know it sounds missish to say so, but you *have* taken me by surprise, and—and though I would try to be a good wife to you I can't feel that I *ought* to accept your offer!"

"One thing at least you can tell me!" he said forcefully. "Do you feel you could love me? I mean—oh, deuce take it!—*do* you love me? I don't wish to sound like a coxcomb, but—"

"Oh, Philip, how *can* you be so absurd?" said Kate, stung into betraying herself. "Of course I love you!"

"That," he said, whipping up his horses, "is all I want to know! Tomorrow, my darling, when you have considered, we will discuss when it will be most convenient for

us to settle on a suitable date for the wedding! Yes, I know
you are wondering how to break the news to Minerva, but
you need not: I'll do that—and instantly remove you from
her sphere of influence! O my God! there's the stable-clock
striking six already! Why did you urge me to dine with
Gurney? Shall I come in with you? Minerva is likely to
be out of reason cross, you know!''

''Perhaps she will be, but not nearly as cross as she
would be if you were to accompany me!'' replied Kate,
preparing to alight from the curricle. ''She dislikes you
quite as much as you dislike her, Philip! I mean to come
to points with her, and nothing could more surely bring us
to dagger-drawing than *your* presence, believe me!''

''You are full of pluck, Kate!'' he said admiringly. ''But
if your courage fails you at the last moment, don't hesitate
to tell me! I shall fully sympathize!''

She smiled, and took the hand he was holding out to
her, to facilitate her descent from the curricle. Once on the
ground, she looked up at him, with shyly twinkling eyes.
''I promise you it won't. I don't mean to tell her that you
have been so obliging as to make me an offer, of course!''
She pulled her hand out of his tightening clasp as she
spoke, and went swiftly up the steps to the principal entrance to the house.

It stood open, as it always did in summer-time, during
the daylight hours, and the inner door, leading from the
lobby into the hall, was on the latch. She let herself softly
in, without, however, much hope of being able to run upstairs unobserved. Lady Broome insisted that one or other
of the footmen should keep a watch on the door, and be
at hand to bow her, or any visitor, in, and to relieve the
gentlemen of their hats and coats. But on this occasion no
one came into the hall, and Kate, who had more than half
expected Pennymore to meet her, charged with a reproach-

ful message from her aunt, thankfully darted up the stairs, to fling off her crumpled walking-dress, and to hurry into the evening-gown she trusted Ellen would have laid out in readiness. She thought, fleetingly, that it was odd that neither of the footmen had been lying in wait for her; but she was not prepared to be greeted by the news, conveyed to her by Ellen, in awe-stricken accents, that the household was in an uproar, because my lady had fainted clean-away an hour after Miss had left the house, and had been carried up to her bed in a state of total collapse.

"And they say, miss—Mrs Thorne, and Betty, and Martha—that her ladyship had never fainted in her life before, and Betty says as her aunt was just the same, never having a day's illness until she was struck down with a palsy-stroke, and never rose from her bed again!"

Without attaching much weight to this story, Kate was surprised, for it had not seemed to her that Lady Broome was on the brink of a palsy-stroke, although, looking back, she remembered thinking that her aunt was out of sorts when she had sent her on a useless errand. She said, in a disappointingly matter-of-fact way: "Nonsense, Ellen! I expect she has contracted this horrid influenza, which is rife in the village. Quickly, now! Help me into my dress! I'm shockingly late already!"

Ellen obeyed this behest, but said that everything was at sixes and sevens, on account of her ladyship's being very ill, and Mrs Thorne's having given it as her opinion that it was a Warning: a pronouncement which had operated so powerfully on the cook's sensibilities that he had ruined the cutlets of sweetbread ordered for the Master's dinner, and had been forced to boil a fowl, which he proposed to serve with bechermell sauce, being as the Master couldn't seem to stomach rich meats.

While privately thinking that the chef had seized on

Lady Broome's sudden indisposition as an excuse for having over-cooked the cutlets, Kate realized that it must be a very rare occurrence, for it had clearly disorganized the establishment.

She discouraged Ellen's ghoulish desire to cite all the examples of fatal collapse which had, apparently, carried off half her aunts and uncles and cousins, and repeated her belief that Lady Broome's disorder was merely a severe attack of influenza.

In the event, she was justified, greatly to Ellen's disappointment. Just as she was about to leave her room, and to go in search of Sidlaw, a perfunctory knock on the door was instantly succeeded by Sidlaw's entrance. She said immediately: "Come in! I was just going to see if I could find you. What's this I'm hearing about her ladyship? Has she caught this horrid influenza that is going so much about?"

She was well aware that the dresser regarded her with mixed feelings, being torn between jealousy and a reluctant admiration of her sartorial taste; and had long since come to the conclusion that she owed the grudging civility paid to her by Sidlaw to her aunt, who must, she guessed, have laid stringent orders on her devoted attendant to treat her niece with respect. She was not, therefore, surprised when Sidlaw sniffed, and said she was sure she was thankful Miss had come home at last.

"Yes, I'm late," agreed Kate. "I'm sorry for it, since I apprehend her ladyship was taken ill suddenly."

"There was nothing you could have done, miss!" said Sidlaw, instantly showing hackle. "Not but what—"

"I don't suppose there was, with you and the doctor to attend to her," interrupted Kate. "What's the matter? Is it the influenza?"

"Well, that's what the doctor says, miss," Sidlaw replied, with another sniff which indicated her opinion of the doctor. "What *I* say is that she carried a bowl of broth to that hurly-burly creature—for Female I will not call her —that lives in the cottage all covered over with ivy, not two days ago, and, say what I would, I couldn't hinder her! She only laughed, and said that I should know she never caught infectious complaints."

"Yes," interpolated Ellen, unable to restrain herself. "And Miss Kate was with her, Miss Sidlaw, and *she* hasn't caught the influenza as you may see for yourself!"

"That's nothing!" said Kate hastily, to save Ellen from annihilation. "I am not prone to succumb to infectious diseases! And it must be remembered that I didn't enter the cottage! You may go now!"

"*She'll* never be worth a candle-end!" said Sidlaw, with gloomy satisfaction, as the hapless Ellen withdrew. "I told my lady how it would be if she took a village scrub into the house!"

Kate thought it prudent to ignore this, and asked instead if she might visit her aunt. To this, Sidlaw replied with a flat veto, saying that the doctor had given a dose of laudanum to my lady, to send her to sleep. "She told me, miss, that she felt as though she'd been stretched on the rack, and had all her joints wrenched, and she isn't one to complain! As for her head, she'd no need to tell me that was aching fit to burst, because I could see that from the way she kept turning it from side to side on the pillow! And nothing I could do eased it: not even a cataplasm to her feet! So I was obliged to send for Dr Delabole, for all she kept on telling me she'd be better presently! *I* knew she was in a high fever!"

A second knock fell on the door; Sidlaw, ignoring Kate, opened it, and said sharply: "Well, what do *you* want?"

Kate, having caught a glimpse of Pennymore, said coldly: "That will do, Sidlaw: you may go!"

Sidlaw turned white with anger, and shut her mouth like a trap. Paying no further heed to her, Kate smiled kindly at the butler, and said: "What is it, Pennymore?"

It was beneath Pennymore's dignity to betray even a flicker of triumph. To all appearances he neither saw nor heard Sidlaw as she stalked, snorting, out of the room. He said, with undisturbed calm: "Sir Timothy sent me to enquire, miss, if you would do him the honour of dining with him. In his own room, miss."

"How very kind of him!" said Kate. She had not been looking forward with much pleasure to an evening spent in Torquil's and the doctor's company, and she spoke with real gratitude. "Pray tell Sir Timothy that I am very much obliged to him, and will join him directly."

Pennymore bowed, and said: "Sir Timothy's dinner will be served immediately, miss. We are a little behindhand this evening. Her ladyship's sudden indisposition has, I regret to say, quite upset certain members of the staff."

"So I've been given to understand!" said Kate, twinkling.

An almost imperceptible quiver of revulsion crossed Pennymore's face. He said: "Yes, miss. It is unfortunate that Mrs Thorne's nerves are so easily irritated. The maids naturally take their tone from her, and if the housekeeper falls into a fit of the vapours one can scarcely blame her underlings for behaving in a deplorably theatrical way. And the cook, of course, is a foreigner," he added, not contemptuously, but indulgently. He then bowed slightly, and withdrew.

It had not taken Kate many days to realize that the senior members of the staff were split into two factions: those who owed allegiance to Sir Timothy, and those who were

Lady Broome's supporters. Pennymore, and Tenby, Sir Timothy's valet, were at the head of the first faction, and were followed by the two footmen, the coachman, and the head groom; while Sidlaw and Mrs Thorne, both of whom had come to Staplewood with their mistress, were Lady Broome's worshippers. Whalley, Kate thought, was certainly one of Lady Broome's chosen servants, and possibly Badger as well. The leaders of each faction lived in a state of constant warfare, which was not the less bitter for being concealed, in general, by a cloak of exquisite civility. Kate, nettled by Sidlaw's insolence, could not help chuckling inwardly at what she knew would be Sidlaw's rage at having been betrayed into speaking so roughly to Pennymore. Then she scolded herself for being uncharitable, knowing that Sidlaw, who really did love her mistress, was overset by anxiety.

When she left her room, Sidlaw was hovering in the gallery, and moved a few steps towards her, holding herself very stiffly. She said, in a wooden voice: "I am afraid, Miss Kate, I took a liberty which you did not like in opening the door to Pennymore without your leave. I hope you will be so kind as to overlook it."

"Why, of course!" said Kate, with her swift smile. "You are in a great worry about her ladyship, aren't you? I shan't think of it again! But pray don't let yourself be thrown into gloom! Depend on it, my aunt will feel very much more the thing tomorrow. I have only once in my life had influenza, when I was ten years old, but I recall that for the first twenty-four hours I felt so ill that I told my nurse I was dying!"

Sidlaw showed some signs of relaxation, and even tittered, but Kate's next words, caused her to become rigid again. Kate said: "I hope you won't hesitate to tell me, when you wish to be relieved for a little while: I should like very much to be of use to my aunt, and can very well sit with her while you rest.''

''Thank you, miss,'' said Sidlaw, in arctic accents, ''I do not anticipate the need to ask for assistance.''

Kate had expected to be snubbed, so she did not press the matter, merely nodding, and going down the stairs.

Chapter Fourteen

Kate had not previously penetrated to the East Wing, but when she passed through the door which shut it off from the Great Hall, and was met by Tenby, who conducted her to the saloon that was known as the Master's Room, she knew, after a quick glance round, that Sir Timothy, allowing his wife a free hand in the rest of the house, must have prohibited her from laying a finger on his own apartments. The room was not shabby, but it was rather overfurnished, as though Sir Timothy had crammed into it all the pieces for which he had a fondness, and cared nothing for the formal arrangements dear to Lady Broome's heart. He was seated in an oldfashioned wing-chair when Tenby ushered Kate into the room, talking to Dr Delabole, but he rose, and came forward, murmuring, as he saw the appreciative look in her eyes: "More homelike, Kate?"

She laughed. "Yes, indeed, sir! Good-evening, Dr Delabole! I learn from Sidlaw that my aunt has contracted the influenza which is running so much about, and is feeling very poorly. I hope you don't expect any prolonged indisposition?"

"Oh, no, no!" he replied reassuringly. "It is a severe attack, you know: very severe, and we must expect her to be pulled by it, and must endeavour to persuade her not to exert herself prematurely: she must resign herself to being in a tender state for at least a sennight. We shall be hard put to it to do it, if I know her ladyship!'' He laughed gently. ''I daresay you won't credit it, but when I revived her from her faint, she tried to struggle to her feet, and insisted that there was nothing amiss! And when our good Sidlaw told her that she had fainted she snapped her nose off, saying: 'Nonsense! I never faint!' However, she soon found that she couldn't stand without support, so we were able to carry her up to her bed, and mighty glad she was to be there, for all she wouldn't own it! I have just been telling Sir Timothy that I have given her a soothing draught, and that she is now asleep. I shall visit with her during the night, but I fancy she won't wake for some hours. And Sidlaw will be with her, you know: she has had a truckle-bed set up in the dressing-room, and is entirely to be relied on.''

''Oh, yes! There can be no doubt of that,'' said Kate. ''She has been giving me a sharp set-down for offering to lend her my assistance! I knew she would: so would my own old nurse if anyone offered to help her in the same situation!''

''Oh, I shouldn't go into her room, if I were you, Miss Kate. It is a very infectious complaint, and it would never do if *you* were to be ill!''

''I don't think it at all likely that I shall be,'' answered Kate. ''I know it's fatal to say that, but I was lately in a house positively *stricken* with influenza, and between us the cook, and the second housemaid, and I nursed the mistress of the house, her three children, and two other servants, and the cook and I were the only ones who didn't take the infection! I'm not afraid.''

He laughed heartily at that, and said that he now expected to be summoned to her bedside; advised her not to go to her aunt for a day or two; and archly warned Sir Timothy that he should warn my lady that she must not take ill again, if she did not want her lord to console himself by flirting with a pretty young lady.

Sir Timothy accorded this witticism a faint, cold smile, and inclined his head courteously. Daunted, the doctor laughed again, not so heartily, and said that he must hurry away to seek his own dinner, or Torquil would be growing impatient.

Sir Timothy smiled again, very sweetly, and the doctor bowed himself out of the room. Sir Timothy's eyes travelled to Kate's face of ill-concealed disgust, and amusement crept into them. "Just so, my dear! An intolerable mushroom! Or do I mean barnacle? He keeps me alive, for which I must be grateful—or ought to be! Will you drink a glass of sherry with me?"

"Yes, if you please, sir. But if you mean to talk in that style you will be sorry you invited me to dine with you, because I shall sink into the dismals, and become a dead bore!"

"Impossible!" he said, with his soft laugh. "You have a merry heart, my child, and I don't think you could ever be a dead bore." He poured out two glasses of sherry as he spoke, and came back to his chair, handing her one of them with a slight, courtly bow.

"I don't know that, sir: I do try not to be a bore, at all events! As for a merry heart—well, yes! I think I have a cheerful disposition, and—and I own I delight in absurdities! But that's not at all to my credit! I always laugh at the wrong moment!"

The door opened just then to admit Pennymore, followed by the first footman, carrying a tray of dishes. When these had been set out, Pennymore informed Sir Timothy

that he was served, and Sir Timothy formally handed Kate
to the table, saying, as he did so: "I had meant to invite
Philip, to make it more amusing for you, but the silly
cawker has gone off to dine with young Templecombe. He
sent up a message from the stables. You must accept my
apologies for him!"

"Not at all, sir! Isn't there a proverb that says one's too
few, and three's too many?"

"Very prettily said!" he approved. "You've a quick
tongue and a ready wit: that's what I like in you, Kate. If
I had a daughter, I should wish her to be of your cut. But
I daresay she would have been a simpering miss, so perhaps it's as well I have no daughter. What are you offering
me, Pennymore?"

"Compôte of pigeons, sir, with mushroom sauce. Or
there is a breast of fowl, if you would prefer it."

"With a béchamel sauce!" said Kate. "I know all about
that! It *ought* to have been sweetbreads, but I am very glad
it's not, because I don't like them!"

"Why isn't it sweetbreads?" he asked, rousing himself
from the melancholy which had descended on him with
the thought of the daughters who had died in early childhood.

Very willing to divert him, she gave him a lively description of the effect Lady Broome's fainting fit had had
upon Mrs Thorne's sensibilities, and the chef's excitable
temperament; and of the analogy Ellen had discovered in
an attack of influenza, and the palsy-stroke which had laid
one of her aunts low. He was a good deal amused, and the
rest of dinner passed happily enough. When the covers
were removed, and Pennymore set the port and brandy
decanters before his master, he was moved to bestow an
approving glance upon Kate, and, later, to inform Tenby
that he hadn't seen Sir Timothy so cheerful this many-a-

day. To which Tenby replied: "He hasn't much to make him cheerful, Mr Pennymore: as we know!"

Pennymore shook his head sadly, and sighed, looking in a very speaking way at the valet, but not giving utterance to his thoughts. Tenby echoed the sigh, but maintained a similar silence.

Left alone with his guest, Sir Timothy offered her a glass of port, which she declined, saying, however, that she was very content to nibble a fondant while he lingered over his wine. "Unless you would prefer me to withdraw, sir?" she said, her fingers poised over the silver dish in front of her. "Pray don't say I must! It is so cosy here—quite the cosiest evening I've spent at Staplewood!"

"You haven't much taste for formal pomp, have you, Kate?"

"No," she said frankly. "Not every day of the week, at all events!"

"Nor have I, which is why I prefer to dine in my own room. But I don't permit Pennymore to wait on me in the general way. Only when Minerva is away from home, or indisposed. To deprive her of the butler would be rather too much!"

She ventured to say: "I fancy Pennymore would prefer to wait on you, sir."

"Yes, he is very much attached to me. You see, we were boys together. He has been with me through some dark times: a true friend! He's fond of Philip, too, and so am I. It's a pity Philip and Minerva dislike one another, but I suppose it was bound to be so: Minerva doesn't care for children, you know. And I'm bound to own that when they first met he wasn't at all a taking boy! He was a sturdy little ruffian, tumbling in and out of mischief, and impatient of females." He stared down into his wineglass, a reminiscent smile playing round his mouth. "Disobedient

too. I never found him so, but I'm afraid he was very
troublesome to Minerva. She resented my affection for
him—very naturally, I daresay; and he resented her being
in his aunt's place. He was very fond of my first wife: the
only woman he *was* fond of in those days, for he was
barely acquainted with his mother. Anne was very fond of
him, too, and never jealous, as God knows she might have
been, when she saw him so stout and vigorous, and had
the anguish of watching her own son die. We lost all our
children; two were still-born; and only Julian lived to stagger about in leading-strings. Both my little girls died in
their infancy—faded away! They were all so sickly—all
of them, even Julian! But nothing ever ailed Philip! Some
women might have hated him, but not Anne! She thought
of him as a comfort to us." He looked up at the portrait
which hung above the fireplace. "That was my first wife,"
he said. "You never knew her, of course."

Kate, who had already stolen several glances at the portrait, answered: "I wondered if it was. I wish I had known
her."

"She was an angel," he said simply.

Knowing that his mind had drifted back into the past,
Kate remained sympathetically silent. His eyes were still
fixed on the portrait, fondly smiling; and Kate, also looking at it, thought that no greater contrast to the first Lady
Broome than the second could have been found. Anne had
been as fair as Minerva was dark, and nothing in her face,
or her languid pose, suggested the vitality which characterized the second Lady Broome. It might have been the
fault of the artist, but, although she had a sweet face it
lacked decision. She was reasonably pretty, but not beautiful: the sort of woman, Kate thought, one might easily
fail to recognize, unless one had been particularly well-

acquainted with her. No one who had once met the second Lady Broome could fail to recognize her again.

She was still gazing at the portrait when she discovered, to her discomfiture, that Sir Timothy had withdrawn his eyes from it, and was watching her instead. "No," he said, as though he had read her thought, "she wasn't like your aunt."

"No, sir," agreed Kate, unable to think of anything else to say.

He stretched out a frail hand to pick up the decanter, and refilled his glass. "Your aunt has many good qualities, Kate," he said, with deliberation, "but you must not allow her to bullock you."

"No, I d-don't mean to!" Kate replied, stammering a little. "But she hasn't tried to—to bullock me, sir! She has been only too kind to me—far, far too kind!"

"She is a woman of great determination," continued Sir Timothy, as though Kate had not spoken. "Also, she is ruled, mistakenly, I think, by what she conceives to be her duty. I don't know why she brought you here, or why she treats you with kindness, but I do know that it was not out of compassion. Some end she has in view. I don't know what it may be: I have not cared enough to discover what it is." He raised his eyes from their contemplation of the wine in his glass, and turned them towards Kate. She saw that they smiled in self-derision, and was shocked. He returned his gaze to his wineglass, and said cynically: "You will find, my child, that as you approach the end of your life you will no longer care greatly for anything, and will be too tired to take up arms against a superior force. One becomes detached."

"You still care for Staplewood!" Kate said, in an effort to raise his spirits.

"Do I? I did once, but of late years I have grown aloof

from it. I am beginning to realize that when I am dead it won't matter to me any longer, for I shall know nothing about it.'' He raised his glass to his lips, and sipped delicately. ''Oh, don't look so distressed! If I cared—'' He stopped, and stared ahead into the shadows beyond the table, as though he were trying to see something hidden in them, and yet was afraid to see it. His lips twisted into a wry smile, and he brought his eyes slowly back to Kate's face. ''Perhaps it's as well we can't see into the future!'' he said lightly. ''I didn't think I cared for the present either, or for people, but I found myself fond of you, Kate— as if you were my daughter!—which is why I've roused myself from my deplorable lethargy to warn you not to let yourself be bullied or coaxed into doing anything your heart, and your good sense, tell you not to do.''

Kate began to speak, but he checked her, with a thin hand upraised, and a shrinking expression in his eyes. ''I don't know what it is that Minerva has in mind, and I don't wish to know,'' he said, on a querulous note of old age. ''I'm too old and too tired! I only want to be left in peace!''

Kate said calmly: ''Yes, sir. I shan't do anything to disturb your peace. You may be sure of that!''

He drank a little more wine, and seemed to regain his customary detachment, and, with it, his tranquillity. He sat in silence for a minute or two, watching the play of the candlelight on the wine still remaining in his glass, but presently he sighed, and said: ''Poor Minerva! She should have married a public man, not a man who had never an ambition to figure in the world, and was worn-out besides. She has many faults, but I cannot forget that when my health broke down she abandoned the life she loved without one word of complaint, and brought me home—for I was too ill then to decide anything for myself—and would never afterwards own that she wished to return to London. She has a strong—compelling—sense of duty, as I've told you: it is a virtue which she sometimes carries to excess. She has also unbounded energy, which I have not, I am ashamed to say. She's ambitious, too: she wanted me to enter politics: couldn't understand that I'd no interest—no wish to shine in that world! Or in any other,'' he added reflectively. ''It was my brother Julian who was ambitious—Philip's father, you know. I never had but one ambition: to hand my inheritance on to my son! It seemed to me to be of the first importance that the line should not be broken. Well, no matter for that! When the doctors told Minerva that London-life wouldn't do for me, and she came to live with me here, from year's end to year's end, she knew she must find another interest, or mope herself to death. That was admirable: another woman, of less strength of character, would have repined, and dwindled into a decline!''

''But instead,'' Kate reminded him, ''she interested herself in what she knew to be dear to you: Staplewood!''

He was shaken by soft laughter. ''Ironical, isn't it? I taught her to love Staplewood; I taught her to be proud of the Broome tradition; I encouraged her to squander a fortune transforming the gardens, and replacing all the furniture in the house, which she declared to be too modern, with furniture of an antique date. I daresay she was right. Perhaps the mahogany chairs and tables which my father bought, and the carpets he laid down, were out of harmony with the house: I never thought so, but I grew up with them, and accepted them without thinking much about them. But I think I haven't much taste. I recall that Julian, when he came here once on a visit, said that Minerva had improved the place out of recognition. That was high praise, for he had excellent taste himself. But as Minerva's interest in Staplewood grew, mine diminished. Unreasonable, wasn't it?"

"Perhaps," said Kate diffidently, "you felt it had become more hers than yours, sir."

He considered this, slightly frowning. "No, I don't think so. I don't feel that to this day. I've always known that it was within my power to call a halt, but I've never done so. At first because I was glad that she was so eager to enter into my own feeling for Staplewood; and later—oh, later, because, in part, I knew I was to blame: it was I who had encouraged her to devote herself to the place, and how, when she had learnt to love it, could I *dis*courage her? And, in part, because I felt myself to be unequal to a struggle with her." The derisive smile touched his lips again. "I like to blame my declining health for that, but the truth is that Minerva has a stronger character than mine. She doesn't shrink from battle as I do, and she is by far more ingenious than I am. All I wish for is peace! Very ignoble! Dear me, how I've rambled on! One of the infirmities of old age, my dear! But I have begun to be uneasy about you, and I know your aunt as you do not. I've told you what are her good qualities, so you won't think I don't recognize them when I tell you that you are deceiving yourself if you believe that her kindness and her caresses spring from affection. Poor Minerva! She is a stranger to the tender feelings which elevate your sex, and make us coarser creatures adore you!"

She smiled at this, but said: "I am not deceived, sir. I must be grateful to my aunt for her exceeding kindness, but I know that she brought me here to serve—oh, a foolish end! I have told her that I shan't do so, and I can assure you that I shan't let myself be coaxed, or bullied. So pray don't tease yourself any more! I am very well able to care for myself."

He looked relieved, and proposed a rubber of piquet. It was plain that whatever he might guess he shrank from having his suspicions confirmed, and would not willingly intervene in his wife's schemes. Kate liked him too well to despise him, but she was forced to realize that there was a milkiness in his character which did indeed make him appear ignoble. It was possible that his health was responsible for his reluctance to face a difficult situation, but she could not help feeling that he had probably chosen, all his life, to look the other way when in danger of being faced with anything unpleasant. She made no attempt to embroil him with his wife, but received his invitation to play cards with every appearance of cordiality. In fact, she had hoped to have escaped one of these sessions, and to have had an opportunity to retire early to her bedchamber, not because she wished to go to bed, but because she had as yet had no opportunity to think over all that had occurred during the most eventful day of those she had spent at Staplewood. The extraordinary happenings had begun with Torquil's disquieting behaviour in the park; this had been followed by the astonishing news that Mr Nidd was in Market Harborough; and the climax had been reached when she had received an offer of marriage from Mr Philip Broome. This, not unnaturally, had cast everything else into the background; and she was honest enough to admit to herself that very little of the period of reflection which she so earnestly desired would be wasted in consideration of any other problem. She felt that her mind was in turmoil, making it impossible for her to concentrate on the play of her cards. And, strangely enough, it was not the chief problem which teased her: whether or not to accept Philip's offer: but a host of minor difficulties, which her experience of the male sex led her to think that Philip would dismiss as frivolities. But they were not frivolous, nor would the

Broomes think them so. When she left Staplewood, she would leave also everything that Lady Broome had given her, and how, with barely enough in her purse to enable her to bestow vails on Ellen, and on Pennymore, was she to purchase her bride-clothes? And from whose house was she to be married? And who would give her away, in her father's place? These details might seem unimportant to Philip, but they would not seem unimportant to his relations; and although he might say that he didn't care a pin for their opinions he would be a very odd man if he did not wish his bride to present a creditable appearance. A bride who was unattended by relations of her own, and came to Church from a carrier's yard, would inevitably earn the contempt, and perhaps the pity, of the Broomes, and that would gall Philip past endurance.

She wondered if this had occurred to him, and whether he might already be regretting his rash proposal; and, if so, whether he would find an excuse to cry off, or put a brave face on it. She felt that she could bear it best if he were to cry off, but she also felt that he was not the kind of man to play the jilt, and became so lost in these melancholy reflections that Sir Timothy asked her if she was tired.

Could she but have known it, Philip was not regretting it in the least; and none of the difficulties which she perceived had occurred to him. Nor would they have dismayed him had they done so. On the contrary, he would have welcomed them as heaven-sent excuses to escape from the fashionable wedding so much more desirable to women than to men. Had he been asked what kind of a wedding he would like to have, he would have replied without an instant's hesitation that he would much prefer a private ceremony, with no guests invited, except a groomsman to act as his best man, and Sarah Nidd to give Kate away.

In point of fact, he was not, at that moment, thinking about weddings. On arrival at Freshford House he had driven his curricle to the stables, and had handed his horses over to Mr Templecombe's head groom. Halfway to the house, he was met by his host, who greeted him by demanding, in incredulous accents, if her ladyship was trying to discourage his visits to Staplewood by refusing to house his groom.

"That's it," replied Philip cheerfully.

"Well, I thought that must be the reason why you tipped me the office to bite my tongue! Coming it strong, ain't she? I've heard of hosts who make it a rule not to house their guests' postilions or cattle—some of 'em stipulate that only one servant is allowed!—but I call it the outside of enough to tell you she won't have your groom! Next she'll be asking you not to bring your valet!"

"Oh, she didn't say she wouldn't have my groom! She merely suggested that his presence added unnecessarily to the expenses of maintaining the establishment, and hinted that some unlucky investments had made it imperative for my uncle to retrench. As for Knowle, she had no need to ask me not to bring him! From the moment that the servants at Staplewood discovered that he was not so much a gentleman's gentleman as a general factotum they treated him—even Pennymore!—with an hauteur which made him so uncomfortable that he begged me not to bring him here again! Tenby looks after me—and, since I don't belong to the dandy-set, and am perfectly able to dress myself without assistance, that doesn't impose a very arduous task upon him!"

"I wonder that Sir Timothy should permit such a thing!" Mr Templecombe blurted out.

"He doesn't know," said Philip curtly. "And he won't know of it from me! He is far from well—seems to have aged overnight! He lives in his own wing of the house for the most part of the day. When I remember—" He broke off, clipping his lips together.

"Very distressing," agreed Mr Templecomb sympathetically. "Haven't seen him riding out this age. I know he don't hunt nowadays, but he was used to hack round his estates until he had that nasty attack last year. Didn't seem to pluck up after it. Think he's had notice to quit, dear boy?"

"I don't know. He is so much changed! He seems to be content to let all go as it will—wishes only to be left in peace! I suppose, looking back, he always had too gentle a disposition—no stomach for a fight! But in those days, while my aunt lived, he was not put to the test: they were in perfect accord!"

Mr Templecombe tactfully refrained from any other comment than an inarticulate murmur of assent; but after a decent interval had elapsed, he coughed, and ventured to ask: "What does that oily scoundrel say of him?"

Philip had no difficulty in recognizing Dr Delabole in this description. "What you might expect! He sees no cause for immediate alarm—must remind me that my uncle is an old man, and has a weak heart! He impresses upon me that he must not be agitated, and hedges me round with a host of medical terms, when I ask for a more precise diagnosis. He is Minerva's creature, but—" He paused, his brows drawing together as he considered the matter. A wry smile twisted his mouth; he said: "I must do him the justice to own that he is very attentive to my uncle, and very quick to apply restoratives when my uncle suffers one of his spasms."

"Ever thought of consulting one of the medical nobs?

Croft, or Holford, or—or—well, I don't know much about any of 'em, but it stands to reason a fellow who sets up his plate in London must be top-of-the-trees.''

"Yes, I have frequently thought of it, but have been foiled, not by Delabole or by Minerva, but my uncle himself! He has accepted what he feels to be the inevitable, and has begged me not to ask him to submit himself to the ordeal of being catechised and physicked by some stranger. So what can I do? The devil of it is that I fear he may be right!''

They had by this time reached the house, and Mr Templecombe, with an understanding nod, pushed him into the hall, saying: "Shouldn't wonder at it if he was. Very painful for you, but no sense in letting yourself be thrown into gloom by what you can't mend. Come and eat your dinner—such as it is! The merest picnic! You know how it is with me now that m'mother has taken Dolly off to London, and left the house in holland covers!''

Having had previous experience of Mr Templecombe's mere picnics, Philip was unalarmed. Dinner might be set out in the breakfast-parlour, and served by the pantry-boy, but Mr Templecombe's notion of a picnic included plovers' eggs, some fillets of salmon, with a caper sauce, a blanquette of fowl, and a raised pie. There were no kick-shaws, by which term Mr Templecombe scornfully described fondues and trifles and jellies, opining sagely that Philip had no greater liking for them than he had himself. "Females like 'em, but for my part I think 'em only fit for routs and drums and balls! Well, I put it to you, Philip! How many evening parties have you been to where you wanted to *eat* the refreshments?''

"True!'' agreed Philip. "They look pretty, but, myself, I make a bee-line for the ham!''

"Exactly so! And that reminds me!'' said Mr Templecombe, looking round the table. "There ought to be a ham now! A devilish good one, too, of our own curing! Here, Tom, where's the ham?"

The pantry-boy said apologetically that it was all ate up, barring a bit near the knuckle; and upon Mr Templecombe's demanding indignantly who had eaten it all up, grinned, and said simply: "You did, sir!"

"It must have been a good ham!" remarked Philip, helping himself generously to a dish of salmon. "All the same, I don't want any, you know. By the by, what was it you wanted to consult me about?"

"Tell you after dinner! Know whom I ran into t'other day in Bond Street? Old Prudhoe! Never more surprised in my life! Haven't seen him in years!"

"No, nor have I. Was he on the toddle?" asked Philip, mildly interested. "I suppose you haven't heard anything of poor old Treen, have you? I met Minstead when I was last in London, and he told me that it was bellows to mend with Treen: said he was about to wind up his accounts, but I haven't seen any notice in the papers."

Since both gentlemen shared a large circle of acquaintances, they fell easily into reminiscence; and, one thing leading to another, and both being landowners and agriculturists, they slid from reminiscence into such fruitful topics as the delinquencies of tenants, and the pigheadedness of farmers; and it was not until they had retired to the library that Philip repeated his question, by which time Mr Templecombe had been able to think of some detail of winter sowing on which he might conceivably have wanted advice—if he had not known quite as much about the most modern methods of farming as his friend. Philip very obligingly gave him the benefit of his own experience, but he was not deceived, and when Mr Templecombe opened his mouth to argue, and then shut it again, he grinned sardonically, and said: "That wasn't what you wanted to ask me, was it? Empty the bag, Gurney!"

"Well, no!" confessed Mr Templecombe. "Fact is, I don't want to ask you anything! Dashed delicate, and I wouldn't mention it if you wasn't a friend of mine! Or if you was still visiting Staplewood as often as you used to do. Can't get it out of my head that you may not know, and that it ain't the part of a friend to keep mum!"

"May not know what?" asked Philip levelly.

Mr Templecombe picked up the brandy decanter, and replenished both glasses. Having taken a fortifying drink, he said: "No use beating about the bush. It's Torquil. People are beginning to talk, Philip."

"What do they say?" Philip still spoke in a level voice, but a grim note had crept into it, and his eyes were suddenly uncomfortably searching.

"Why, that there's something devilish odd about him! They don't understand why he should be kept so close, for one thing. You know, dear boy, you can't expect people to believe he's still invalidish when they see him careering all over the countryside on that nervous chestnut of his! Don't believe it myself! Well, you gave me a pretty broad hint when you told me not to let him dangle after Dolly, didn't you?"

"With extreme reluctance! I could not let— But I might have spared myself the pains! I found that Minerva was as anxious as I was to prevent such a marriage. That confirmed me in my suspicion! Under ordinary circumstances, one would have supposed it to be a very eligible match, but I fear that the circumstances are not ordinary. Your sister has too many relatives, and this place is too near Staplewood. I collect, by the way, that she didn't break her heart over Torquil?"

"Oh, lord, no! I don't say she wasn't a trifle dazzled—

well, he's a dashed handsome boy, ain't he?—but Amesbury no sooner showed his front than she tumbled into love with him, and never gave Torquil another thought. Was he badly hit?''

''I don't think so. Understand me, Gurney, this mustn't be talked of! It is all conjecture—I can prove nothing!''

''Well, it's a good thing you've warned me!'' said Mr Templecombe, wagging his head. ''Otherwise I might have gone on the gab all over the county, mightn't I?''

''No, of course you wouldn't!'' said Philip contritely. ''Forgive me! The truth is that I never come to Staplewood in these days without being blue-devilled by fears which I can't prove, and therefore dare not utter. The less I say the better, Gurney! You'll have to bear with me!'' He added, with a flash of humour: ''That ought not to be difficult; you've been doing it any time these dozen years!''

''Oh, longer than that! Twenty at least!'' retorted Mr Templecombe. ''Rising thirty, ain't you? Well, I know you are, because there's only a couple of months between us. By Jove, it's more than twenty years! You were eight when you first came to live with your uncle, weren't you?''

''You didn't have to *bear with me* in those days!'' protested Philip.

''Oh, didn't I just? Did *I* ever come off the best from a set-to? Did *I* have a natural right? Did *I*—''

''No, Gurney, honesty compels me to admit you didn't! They were good days, weren't they?''

''Depends on which way you looked at 'em,'' said Mr Templecombe caustically. ''Not being as strong as you, I looked at 'em, in general, from underneath!'' He tossed off the brandy in his glass, set the glass down, and said, in quite a different voice: ''Is Torquil queer in his attic, Philip?''

''Is that what people are saying?''

"Whispering. It's what *I'm* saying."

"I can only give you one answer: I don't know."

"You suspect it, don't you?"

"I've suspected it for years. At first, it was merely a thought that flashes into one's head, and then is banished. He was a sickly child, and it was reasonable to suppose that his bodily ills should have an effect upon his nerves. I can recall his falling into strong convulsions, when he was a baby; and if ever there was an infectious complaint going about, as sure as a gun he would catch it! He was used to suffer from sick headaches too, so everyone cosseted and indulged him till he became abominably spoilt. If he was crossed, he threw himself into an ungovernable rage, which in general ended in a fit of the vapours. The only person who could control him was Minerva. She established a complete mastery: he was afraid of her, and still is."

"Well, that don't surprise me!" said Mr Templecombe, with feeling. "So am I! Most awe-inspiring female!"

"I suppose she is. At all events, she inspires Torquil with awe. As he grew older, he became much improved in health, thanks, I believe, to Delabole, but it was not thought advisable to send him to school. It was hoped that by the time he reached manhood he would be well. And physically I think he is well. Mentally—I think he's worse. Lately, I've noticed a disquieting change. This must go no further, Gurney!"

"Yes, it's likely I'd go buzzing it about, ain't it?" said Mr Templecombe, incensed.

"No, of course it isn't! But I have to be so careful to guard my own tongue— If I'm wrong—if Torquil isn't mad—what a shocking thing it would be in me even to hint at such a thing!"

Mr Templecombe nodded. "So it would. Not sure you

couldn't be summonsed for libel, or slander, or something. What's this disquieting change you've noticed? He seemed all right and regular when I last saw him.''

"Except at certain times, he *is* all right and regular. But he is growing to be suspicious, to fancy everyone his enemy—particularly me.''

"You don't mean it! Why, he was used to follow you about like a tantony-pig! A curst nuisance he was, too!''

Philip smiled. "He was, wasn't he? Well, it was only to be expected that he would want to follow me about: for one thing, he was lonely, poor little fellow; and for another, I am ten years older than he is, and became a hero in his eyes. Of course, that didn't last, but until a year or two ago he continued to be very fond of me. In his sane moments, he still is, but he is convinced that I am his chief enemy and would be happy to see him underground.''

Mr Templecombe sat up with a jerk. "Then I'll tell you what, Philip! Lady Broome put that notion into his head! Jealous of your influence over the boy!''

"I think she did put it into his head, but not for that reason. She was afraid that if I saw too much of him I should learn the truth—if it is the truth. But it wouldn't have taken root in a sane mind! It may have been there already. I've been informed, on good authority, that a feeling of persecution, suspicion of everyone, sudden hatred of one's nearest and dearest, are among the better known symptoms of madness.''

"But— Good God, does your uncle know of this?''

Philip was silent for a moment, heavily frowning. "I don't know,'' he replied at last. "Minerva has seen to it that he and Torquil should live at opposite ends of the house, and he rarely comes out of his wing until dinnertime. Sometimes I think he doesn't know, but it is as I told you: he shrinks from facing what is unpleasant.''

''No wish to shove my oar in,'' said Mr Templecombe, with a deprecatory cough, ''but should you not tell him, dear boy?''

''No. Good God, no! What have I to tell him but my suspicions? If he shares them and shuts his eyes to them, God forbid that I should force him to look them in the face! If he is in ignorance, long may he remain so! He is too old, too worn down by trouble, to be made to suffer such a blow! I'll have no hand in blackening his last days! All his hopes are centred in Torquil: the son who is to carry on the succession!''

''Shouldn't have thought, myself, that he cared as much for the succession as Lady Broome does,'' suggested Mr Templecombe.

''Oh, with her it's an obsession!'' said Philip impatiently. ''But he does care for it: make no mistake about that! I hope with all my heart that it may please Providence to carry him off before it becomes necessary to confine Torquil!''

''As bad as that?'' exclaimed Mr Templecombe, startled.

''I fear it. He is becoming violent,'' said Philip brusquely. ''Unless I am much mistaken, he severely mauled his valet, on the night of the storm. I saw Badger on the following morning, and he was in bad shape, I can assure you—and mighty anxious to escape questioning. Delabole told me a lying tale about his being quarrelsome in his cups, forgetting that I knew Badger well!''

''Yes, but—here, I say! If Torquil's violent, why doesn't Badger cut his stick?''

''He's devoted to him. No doubt, too, Minerva makes it well worth his while to remain—and to keep his tongue between his teeth!''

Mr Templecombe, his brow furrowed, considered the

matter, and presently entered another caveat. "That's all very well, but what about the rest of 'em? Don't any of 'em suspect?"

"I don't know, but I think not yet. Whalley is in Minerva's pay; Pennymore and Tenby may suspect, but they are deeply attached to my uncle, and wouldn't for the world say a word to upset him. As for the footmen and the maids, I fancy they look upon Torquil's migraines as commonplaces. They know that he is subject to them, and they are quite accustomed to being kept away from his room when he is laid-up. Whether he really is still subject to them I don't know, but strongly doubt. They afford Delabole an excuse for drugging him, and as Torquil doesn't seem to remember anything that happened during one of his attacks, I daresay it is not too difficult to persuade him that he has been prostrated by migraine. But if his fits of mania become more frequent, as I fear they may, it won't be possible to conceal from the servants that the balance of his mind is disturbed. Nor will it be possible to allow him as much freedom as he now enjoys."

"Poor little devil!" said Mr Templecombe. "No wonder he's dicked in the nob!"

"That's what I thought, until I realized that Minerva wouldn't insist on Whalley's accompanying him whenever he rides out unless she had good reason. She's no fool! He is never allowed to go beyond the gates without Whalley."

"Nevertheless he does go beyond them," said Mr Templecombe dryly. "At least he did once, to my certain knowledge, and for anything I know he may have escaped more than once."

"When was this?"

"Oh, about six months ago! I heard of it from my people. Mind you, I didn't make much of it, and nor did anyone else, except that he was thought to be uncommonly wild. He bounded into the Red Lion, in the village, late one evening, boasting about having given 'em all the slip, at Staplewood, and calling for brandy. Well, Cadnam— you know: the landlord!—well, he thought he was half-sprung already, but when he tried to fob him off with a glass of port Torquil flew into a passion, and hurled the glass at his head. Seems he had a notion of milling Cadnam down: according to the tale I heard—but I only got it third hand, and I daresay it was pretty garbled!—it took a couple of fellows to hold him back. Then Delabole walked in, and they say Torquil quietened down at once, and looked devilish scared. Well, the doctor ain't popular in the village, and as soon as he'd led the boy off, those who were in the tap enjoyed a good laugh, and said that it served my lady right for keeping the poor lad in leading-strings, and she'd only herself to thank that he'd got into such prime and plummy order the instant the doctor's eye was off him. As far as I could discover, none of 'em thought any more about it until Badger came into the Red Lion the next evening, and said that that was just how it was. He spun a yarn about Torquil's having been in a quarrel with his mother, and being ordered up to bed by her and so—and so—and so! If only he'd had enough rum-gumption to have buttoned his lip, it's my belief the affair would have been forgotten in a sennight, but when he went to such pains to assure Cadnam that Torquil was shot in the neck, and to beg him not to mention the matter, for fear of its getting to my lady's ears—well, that made Cadnam, and a couple of others who were in the tap at the time, think there was something dashed smokey about it, and—oh, you know how fast a rumour spreads in a place like this, Philip!''

"Oh, my God, what a muttonhead! what a damned, well-meaning clunch!" exclaimed Philip bitterly.

"Yes, but there's nothing to say the boy *wasn't* shot in the neck," said Mr Templecombe. "And if it weren't for the doctor's continued presence at Staplewood, there'd be a good deal less scandal-broth brewed! Lady Broome says he's there on Sir Timothy's account, but that won't fit! We all know he was sent for when Torquil took the small-pox, and dashed nearly slipped his wind, and that was *before* Sir Timothy got to be so feeble! Well, there's a nasty on-dit being whispered over the tea-cups: daresay you know what it is!"

"I can guess! That Delabole is Minerva's lover? I don't think it's true, but true or not it was bound to be said," replied Philip indifferently.

"Yes," agreed Mr Templecombe. "The thing is she ain't over and above popular, dear boy! And another thing that has people in a puzzle—well, it has me in a puzzle too!—is why the devil she brought Miss Malvern to Staplewood. Seems an odd start!" Receiving no answer to this, he said, with a shrewd glance at Philip: "Very agreeable girl, ain't she?"

"Very," agreed Philip.

"Got a great deal of countenance," persevered Mr Templecombe.

"Yes."

"Oh, very well!" said Templecombe, incensed. "If you don't choose to tell me you're tail over top in love with her, it's all one to me! I may not be one of the tightish clever 'uns, but I've got eyes in my head, and I know what's o'clock!"

Chapter Fifteen

Kate lay awake for a long time after she had blown out her candle that night, trying to think what she ought to do; but although she had longed all the evening for the opportunity to consider her problems in the seclusion of her own room, she found herself quite unable to pursue any very consecutive or useful line of thought. When she tried to think dispassionately about Philip's proposal, and to weigh in the balance the possible advantages to him of the marriage against the certain disadvantages, her mind refused to remain fixed, but strayed into foolish recollections: how he had looked when he had first met her; how his smile transformed his face; what he had said to her in the rose-garden; what he had said in the shrubbery; what he had said in his curricle; and what he had looked like on all these occasions. The mischief was that no sooner had his image imposed itself on her mind's eye than she was wholly unable to banish it, which was not at all conducive to impartial consideration. She came to the conclusion that she was too tired to think rationally, and tried to go to sleep. When she had tossed and turned for half an hour, she told herself that it was the moonlight, which was keeping her awake, and she slid out of bed to draw the blinds across the unshrouded windows. Every night Ellen shut the windows, and drew the blinds; every night, when Ellen had left her, she flung up the windows, and swept back the blinds; and every morning Ellen, who had a deeply inculcated belief in the baneful influence of the night air, and seemed to be incapable of understanding that her young mistress had become inured to it during the years she had spent in the Peninsula, remonstrated with her, and prophesied all manner of ills which were bound to spring from admitting into the room the noxious night airs. Failing to convince Ellen that she could not sleep in a stuffy room, Kate had adopted the practice of opening her windows when Ellen had carefully closed the curtains round the bed, and withdrawn to her own airless and tiny bedchamber.

The wind had died with the sun, and it was a hot, June night, so still that Kate could almost have supposed that a storm was brewing. But the sky was cloudless, with the moon, approaching the full, sailing serenely in a sky of dark sapphire. Nothing seemed to be stirring abroad: not even an owl hooted; and the nightingales, which had enchanted Kate when she had first come to Staplewood, had been silent for several weeks. Kate stayed for a moment by one of the windows, gazing out upon the moonlit gardens, wondering if Philip had yet returned from Freshford House, and listening for the sound of horses trotting up the avenue. Ghostly in the distance, the stable-clock struck the hour. She listened to it, counting the strokes, and could hardly believe it when it stopped at the eleventh, for it seemed to her that she had been lying awake for hours. She had never felt less like sleeping; and, after one look at the crumpled bedclothes, drew a chair to the window, and sat down, wishing that a breeze would get up to relieve the oppressiveness of the atmosphere. The house was wrapped in silence, as though everyone in it but herself was asleep. She concluded that Lady Broome must be better, until her ears caught the sound of someone coming on tiptoe along the gallery, and guessed that the doctor was on his way to take a last look at his patient. Or had he done so, and was he creeping back to his quarters in the West Wing? It had seemed to her that the footsteps were coming from the direction of her aunt's bedchamber. A board creaked outside her door, and the footsteps stopped. She waited, her eyes widening, and her breathing quickened. Someone was listening, no doubt for some sound to betray that she was still awake. There was a nerve-racking pause, and then she heard a faint grating noise, as of someone cautiously inserting a key into the lock of her door. She was out of her chair in a flash, and had reached the door and wrenched it open before Sidlaw, wearing a drab dressing-gown, and a night-cap which imperfectly concealed the curl-papers with which she had screwed up her sparse gray locks, could turn the key in the wards. For a moment they confronted each other, Kate's eyes flashing with wrath, and Sidlaw obviously discomposed. The key had been jerked out of her hand, and lay on the floor. She stooped to pick it up, and Kate said, in a dangerously calm voice: "Thank you! I'll take that!"

"Well, I'm sure, miss—!" said Sidlaw, bridling. "If I'd known you was awake, I would have brought it in to you, but not hearing a sound, and not wishing to wake you out of your first sleep, I thought it best to slip it into the lock on the outside."

"Indeed?" said Kate, still standing with her hand imperatively outstretched.

Sidlaw reluctantly surrendered the key, plunging at the same time into an unconvincing account of having found it earlier in the day, but having forgotten to restore it to

Kate's door until this very moment, when she had suddenly remembered it. "I've been so taken-up with her ladyship, miss, that I'm sure it's no wonder the key slipped my memory!"

"And I expect you found it in a most unexpected place, having hunted for it for weeks!" said Kate, with false affability, and a glittering smile. "I won't embarrass you by asking where it was. Goodnight!"

She shut the door, not waiting for a response, and audibly locked it, resolving to afford no one the chance of abstracting the key again, but to keep it in her pocket all day.

However, it was a large, oldfashioned key, and when, next morning, she put it into the pocket which hung round her waist, and was reached through a slit in her petticoat, it knocked uncomfortably against her leg whenever she moved, so she was obliged to put it in her reticule instead, until she could find a safe hiding-place for it.

She found only Torquil in the breakfast-parlour, and he seemed to have finished eating, and to be waiting for her to appear, for he had no sooner responded to her cheerful greeting than he said impulsively: "You *aren't* angry with me, coz, are you?"

More important considerations had thrust so far to the back of her mind the recollection of his conduct on the previous day that she had almost forgotten it, and replied, in surprise: "Angry with you? No—why would I be? Oh—! You mean because you fired at that poor, friendly dog, and missed hitting me by inches? No, I'm not angry, though I own that I was vexed to death at the time. Goodmorning, Pennymore!"

"I knew you wouldn't be!" said Torquil, ignoring the butler, who was setting a tea-pot down before Kate, and a dish of the hot scones she liked. "Matthew said you were all on end, and ready to come to dagger-drawing with me, but I knew *that* was a clanker!''

''Dr Delabole exaggerates, but I was certainly very much shocked,'' she replied, with reserve. ''The dog was not a stray, but a truant, and hardly more than a puppy: you had no business to be firing at him, you know!''

''He had no business to be in the park! Besides, I don't like dogs! And I didn't miss you by inches! You shouldn't have moved!''

''Well, never mind!'' she said placably. ''Have you heard how your mother does this morning?''

''No, and I don't— Oh, yes! Matthew said she had had a restless night, I think: I wasn't attending particularly! He's with her now. But that's not important! I didn't mean to frighten you yesterday, Kate! And if you were frightened I'm sorry for it! There!''

He uttered this apology with the air of one putting considerable force upon himself, and she was obliged to laugh, which made him look black. However, his brow cleared, and his eyes lost their dangerous sparkle, when she begged him not to ring a peal over her before she had finished her breakfast, and he said with a little giggle: ''You are such a funny one, coz! I wish you will marry me! Why won't you? Don't you like me?''

''Not enough to marry you,'' she answered calmly. ''And, let me tell you, Torquil, if there is one thing I dislike more than quarrelling over the breakfast-cups, it is having offers of marriage made to me over them! You should remember that if I *did* marry you you would find yourself leg-shackled to a haggish old woman while you were still in your prime!''

''Yes,'' he said naïvely, ''but Mama says that if I'm married to you she'll let me go to London!''

Her eyes danced appreciatively. "That is certainly an object," she agreed.

"And you would be Lady Broome, you know, because when my father dies Staplewood will be mine, and the title, too, of course. I shouldn't think it will be long before he pops off the hooks, either, because he's pretty well burnt to the socket now."

She felt no desire to laugh at this speech, which was uttered in a voice of total unconcern; and replied coldly: "It so happens that I have no wish to be Lady Broome. Pray don't say any more on this head! Believe me, you don't appear to advantage when you speak of your father in that callous style!"

"Oh, pooh! Why shouldn't I? I don't care a rush for him, or he for me!"

The entrance of the doctor put an end to any further remarks of this nature. Pointedly turning her shoulder on Torquil, Kate enquired after her aunt's condition. Dr Delabole said that he had hoped that her fever might have abated itself by today, but that it had been a particularly violent catching, aggravated by colic. She had suffered a disturbed night, and was still a little feverish, and disinclined to talk. "So I think you should not visit her until she feels rather more the thing," he said. "I have great hope that a change of medicine will put her in better cue. Torquil, my dear boy, do you care to drive with me into Market Harborough to procure it?"

"Not if *you* mean to handle the reins!" said Torquil rudely.

"No, no!" said the doctor, laughing indulgently. "I shall be happy to sit at my ease while you do the work. I know you are a better whip than I am—almost as good a fiddler as Mr Philip Broome! And where, by the way, *is*

Mr Broome? I didn't hear him come in last night, so no doubt he has overslept this morning!''

"Lord, no! he never does so!" said Torquil. "He was getting up from the table when I came into the room! I daresay he's with my father.''

He then began to argue with the doctor about which horse should be harnessed to which vehicle; and Kate got up, and left the parlour while the respective merits of the whisky and the more fashionable tilbury were still being discussed.

There was no sign of Philip in any of the rooms on the entrance-floor, so that unless he had retired upstairs to the library, he had either gone out, or was indeed sitting with his uncle. Kate, who had been longing to see him ever since she had awakened from an uneasy sleep, felt just a little ill-used. If he was anxious to see her, as surely he should have been, if he was really in love with her, he need not have come down to breakfast at an hour when he must have known she would not be present, she thought, forgetting that it was just possible that he might have wished to avoid meeting her in the presence of Torquil and the doctor. If he had gone out, or was visiting his uncle, it looked very much as if he were avoiding her; which must surely mean that he was trying to find a way of escaping his engagement. Kate, whose overnight lucubrations had led to an uneasy sleep, infested with worrying dreams, was hoping, without realizing it, for reassurance. She did not find it in the library, which was as empty as the saloons; and it was in a despairing mood that she came slowly down the stairs again, trying to persuade herself that it behoved her to make everything easy for Philip by telling him that, after thinking the matter over, she had come to the conclusion that she did not love him enough to marry him.

This melancholy resolve brought tears to her eyes, and although she resolutely wiped them away, she was obliged to keep one hand on the baluster-rail, because her vision was still blurred. It cleared miraculously when she heard herself hailed by Philip Broome, who appeared (as it seemed to her) from nowhere, and came up the stairs two at a time, exclaiming: "Kate! I was coming in search of you! What's this Pennymore has been telling me? No, don't answer me! We can't talk on the stairs! Come down to the Red saloon, where we can be private!"

There was nothing at all lover-like, either in this imperious command, or in the ungentle grasp round her wrist; but the depression lifted from Kate's heart. As he almost dragged her down the stairs, she uttered a protest, which he most uncivilly disregarded, pulling her into the saloon, and shutting the door firmly. He then said, searching her face with hard, penetrating eyes: "When I stepped out on the terrace before breakfast, I found the carpenter mending one of the gunroom windows! Is it true that it was Torquil who broke in, yesterday, and stole one of my uncle's shotguns?"

"Why, yes!" she replied, tenderly massaging her wrist. "I shall be excessively obliged to you—Cousin Philip!— if you will have the goodness to inform me of your intention when next you mean to manhandle me! You have bruised me to the bone!"

Swift amusement suddenly softened his eyes; he exclaimed: "Oh, Kate, you dear rogue! *What* a plumper! Show me this bruise!"

"Very likely it won't be visible until tomorrow," she said, with a dignity that admirably concealed the intense pleasure she felt at being called a dear rogue.

"And still more likely that it will never become visible!" he retorted, advancing upon her, and possessing himself of both her hands, and holding them in a strong clasp. "Stop bantering me, and tell me the truth! Did Torquil, in fact, try to shoot you?"

"Good God, no! Of course he didn't!" she replied. "He tried to shoot a dog, and missed both the dog and me, for which I am heartily thankful! He's not fit to be trusted with guns, as I told him! I was in such a rage! But how did Pennymore know of it? He wasn't there! No one was there, except Badger, and, later, Dr Delabole!"

"One of the stable-hands saw you from the avenue, and was trying to summon up the pluck to dash to your help— or so he says!—when the appearance of Badger on the scene relieved him of the necessity to show his mettle. The story had reached Pennymore's ears by the time you went to bed."

"Grossly exaggerated, I make no doubt!"

"Very likely. Is it true that Torquil threatened to shoot Badger?"

"With an empty gun! He was only trying to frighten Badger! He gave the gun up to me the instant I told him to do so, and I promise you there is no need for you to be cast into high fidgets!"

"On the contrary, there is a very urgent need!" he said. "Kate, let me take you away from this place!" His clasp tightened on her hands. "It isn't safe for you to remain here, believe me!" He looked down into her upturned face, and deep into her eyes, his own glowing with a light which made her pulses jump. "You *pretty* innocent!" he said, in a thickened voice, snatching her into his arms, and roughly kissing her. Then, as she burst into tears of relief, he slackened his embrace, and demanded: "Why, Kate! Kate, my darling, what's the matter?"

"Oh, nothing, nothing!" she sobbed. "Only I thought— I was afraid—that you might be regretting it! And although

I think you *ought* to, I couldn't bear it if you did! And I *know* you haven't thought how you would like to be married to a female who has only her nurse to support her at the altar!''

His eyes laughed, but his voice was perfectly grave as he replied: "You are very right! I *hadn't* thought of it. You wouldn't care, I suppose, to depend on *my* support, if your nurse should be unequal to the task?''

She gave a rather watery giggle, and subsided again on to his chest. "Don't make game of me! You know very well what I mean! What would all your relations think?''

"Of course! That is a serious consideration. I wonder why it should not have occurred to me?" he said, apparently much struck. "Could it have been because what they think doesn't seem to me to be of consequence?''

"It is of consequence to me," she said, into his coat.

"Is it? Then there's only one thing for it! We must be married privately, by special licence!''

"Oh, Philip, as though that would make it any better! Do, do be serious!''

"I am being serious, little wet-goose. I am determined to remove you from Staplewood as soon as may be possible; and since neither of us, I hope, is so lost to all sense of propriety as to consider a flight to the Border to be pardonable in any but extremely ramshackle persons— what one might call the baggagery, you know!—I believe my best course will be to convey you to London, to the protection of your nurse, for just so long as it will take me to procure the special licence, and to send an express to my steward, telling him to make all ready for our homecoming. After which, I mean to carry you off to Broome Hall immediately. Oh, Kate, my dear love, you don't know how much I long to see you there! Oh how much I hope that you will like it!''

"I am very sure I shall," she replied, with simple conviction. "But it would be quite as ramshackle for me to run away to London with you immediately as to fly with you to the border, my dear! Consider! Surely you could not wish me to behave with such a want of conduct—so ungratefully? Every feeling must be offended!"

"You have no cause to be grateful to Minerva!"

"Oh, yes, I have!" she said, smiling mischievously up at him. "If she hadn't brought me here I should never have met you, my dear one!"

His arms tightened round her until she felt her ribs to be in danger of cracking, but he said unsteadily: "That was not her object, you artful little Sophist!"

"No, far from it! What was that you called me?"

"A sophist, my love—an artful one!"

"What does it mean?" she asked suspiciously.

"One who reasons in a specious way!" he answered, laughing at her.

"Oh, I don't!" she said indignantly. "How can you be so uncivil?"

"I am not on ceremony with you!" he retorted.

"No, so I collect!" she said, gently disengaging herself. "We must discuss this, you know—and without prejudice, if you please! Come and sit down! We shan't be disturbed: Torquil and Dr Delabole are going to Market Harborough, and you know my aunt is unwell, don't you? Which is one of my reasons for not dashing away to London in such an unseemly fashion—as though she had been ill-using me, and I had seized the chance offered by her illness to escape! You should know what sort of gossip that would give rise to! Could anything be more unjust? Whatever her motive was in inviting me here, I have received nothing but kindness from her, and I will not leave Staplewood in such haste as must astonish all those who know that I had the intention of remaining here until the end of the summer, and lead to conjectures, which might reflect on me, you know, and that you wouldn't like!"

It was evident, from the arrested expression on his face, that this possibility had not occurred to him. He said emphatically: "No!"

"Of course you wouldn't! As a matter of fact, I shouldn't like it myself. I wish you will not stand there frowning down at me! It puts me in a terrible quake!"

He smiled, and came to sit beside her on the sofa, saying: "Fibster!"

"Not at all! You wouldn't believe how pudding-hearted I can be!"

"No, that's true: I wouldn't! If you were pudding-hearted you wouldn't remain here!"

"I'm not afraid of Torquil," she said quietly, "but I promise you I dread telling my aunt that I am going to marry you, Philip. I must do so: to go away without telling her would be very much too shabby, don't you agree?"

"You may leave it to me to tell her!"

"On no account! That would not only be rag-mannered, but it would make it seem as if my conscience was shockingly guilty. It will be your task to break the news to Sir Timothy."

"That's easy! I mean to do so at once, and I have a strong notion that he will be pleased."

"I hope he will be. He invited me to dine with him yesterday, and—and he did me the honour to say that he liked me, and would have wished a daughter to have grown up to resemble me. And I think he was perfectly sincere, because he warned me not to let myself be bullied or cajoled into doing what my heart, and what he called my good sense, told me was wrong. I believe that he did so out of affection, and I know that he shrank from the task. Well, he warned me that I was deceiving myself if I supposed that my aunt had brought me to live with her out of compassion. He said that although he didn't know what it might be he did know that she must have had a motive—and to say that of her must have been excessively distasteful to him.''

He had listened intently to her, an expression of gathering surprise in his face, and he exclaimed: ''Then he must indeed hold you in affection! I believed I enjoyed as much of his confidence as anyone, but he wouldn't have been so frank in talking to me. I have sometimes wondered whether he is frank with himself—allows himself to take notice of what is unpleasant. It is painful to see how much he shrinks from facing anything that—oh, that must disturb his peace! He was not always so, Kate! If you had known him when my Aunt Anne was alive—in the days of his happiness—! I suppose his can never have been a strong character, but—but even though I can't now *respect* him, I can never forget how much I owe to him, or cease to love him! I wish I could explain to you—make you understand—''

She was a good deal moved, and checked him, laying a hand over his hard-clenched ones, and saying gently: ''I do understand. I have seen what you describe: his character is not strong, but he is very lovable. *I* have loved him almost from the moment of first seeing him, and I can readily understand what *your* feelings must be, and—and why you hold my aunt in such dislike and your own aunt in such veneration. He told me how it had been: he said she was an angel.''

He nodded, biting his lip. ''She wasn't a beauty, or a clever woman, but so *good!* In those days, Staplewood was my home, not a—a show-place! And my uncle cared for it as he no longer does! I daresay Minerva improved the gardens, but what *he* cared for, before his health broke down, was his *land!* I have been riding about the estate lately, and I can tell you this, Kate: my own land is in better heart! Minerva talks glibly enough, but she knows nothing about agriculture, and thinks, because the fellow that became bailiff when old Whatley was pensioned off flatters her, that he's first-rate. Well, he ain't! My uncle must know it, for it's only a few months since he gave up hacking round the estate, but he seems not to care!''

''No,'' agreed Kate. ''He told me that I should find when I approached the end of my life that I should no longer care very much for anything. I thought it was the saddest thing I had ever heard said.''

He did not answer for a moment or two, and when he did speak it was sombrely. ''It may be best for him.''

She hesitated before saying: ''You think there is trouble coming to Staplewood, don't you? Is it Torquil?''

''I fear it.''

''Philip, is—is Torquil *deranged?*'' she asked, horror in her eyes. ''Oh, I can't think it!''

''I tried for years not to think it, but lately I have realized that instead of outgrowing his strange humours he has become worse. I think him dangerous, Kate; and I know that he can be violent. If he is excited, or thwarted, it is as though his rage overpowers his brain, and he lets his instinct govern him. And his instinct is to kill. That is why—''

''You are thinking of his having shot at that dog!'' she interrupted. ''I too suspected for a dreadful moment that he was mad, but I promise you that he didn't mean to shoot *me!* Even when I ripped up at him, which you may suppose I did—I was never more angry!—I *know* he had no thought of injuring me! He was—oh, like a sulky schoolboy! Saying that if I hadn't moved I shouldn't have been in danger, and that he wasn't aiming his piece at me. It's true that he threatened to shoot Badger, but, you know, Philip, he cannot have meant to do so, because he must have known he had fired both barrels! And, if you bear in mind that he *is* only a schoolboy, you will own—or you would, if you had been there!—that the temptation to hold Badger at bay must have been irresistible! He came running up in *such* a stew! And stood positively transfixed when Torquil pointed the gun at him, and warned him to keep off, in the most dramatic style! I must say, it put me quite out of patience with him, for nothing could encourage Torquil more than to stand trembling with fright! A man who has known Torquil since his childhood, and is, I fancy, devoted to him! How *could* he suppose that Torquil would shoot him?''

Philip replied, with a curling lip: "He could not—if he believed Torquil to be sane! Or if, unless I am very much mistaken, Torquil had not tried to kill him on the night of the storm!''

"Oh, no! Oh, no!'' she whispered, recoiling. "The scream I heard— Are you telling me it was *Badger* who screamed?'' He shrugged, and suddenly she remembered that she had not recognized the voice, and that Badger had been seen on the following morning with sticking-plaster on his face, and a bandage round his neck; and she buried her face in her hands, with an inarticulate moan of protest. "You must be mistaken! you *must!*'' she uttered, when she could command her voice. When he did not answer, she said urgently: "He must have woken up in a night-terror: my aunt told me that he is subject to them! And as for the dog, Dr Delabole told me that he was once, as a child, badly bitten by a retriever, and it left him with a dread of dogs!''

He frowned. "Yes, it's true that my uncle's Nell did

turn on him. Minerva insisted on having her shot, but from
what I knew of Torquil it was my belief that he came by
his deserts. He had a pet rabbit once, and strangled it.
You've probably heard of brats who pull the legs off flies?
Well, that wasn't enough for Torquil! When he was nine
he tried to wrench a kitten's tail off. Have you forgotten
that when I arrived here, and walked in on you, he had his
hands about your neck?''

She had turned very pale, and her eyes dilated in a look
of sick dismay. She was obliged to swallow once or twice
before she could speak, for her throat was suddenly dry.
Shuddering convulsively, she at last managed to say, in a
sort of croak: ''Then—was it Torquil—? That rabbit I
found in the wood! But Dr Delabole said it was boys from
the village—that Torquil had been in his room for an hour!
Oh, no! Oh, no! it is too terrible, too appalling! Oh, poor
boy—poor, unhappy boy!''

She broke into tears, again covering her face with her
shaking hands. Philip drew her gently to rest against his
shoulders, patting her, and stroking the nape of her neck
in a way that conveyed comfort and reassurance. He said
when she had mastered her emotion: ''What rabbit was
this, Kate?''

A quiver of revulsion ran through her, and it was in a
halting, scarcely audible voice that she recounted the episode. He listened to her in silence, but when she ended,
asked her, rather sharply, if the doctor had been searching
for Torquil.

''I don't know. I thought so, because I heard my aunt
ask Pennymore if Torquil had not come in yet. That was
why *I* was searching for him. He had left me in a rage,
and I felt that the least I could do, having upset him, was
to find him, and bring him back to the house. But when I
told Dr Delabole that I was looking for Torquil he said

that Torquil had been in his room for an hour past. I quite thought that he would be laid low by one of his migraines, for that is in general what happens after one of his fits of passion, but it seems that he fell asleep, and woke so much refreshed— Oh, no, Philip, he could not have done that dreadful thing! Why, he was in his most amiable mood! Indeed, he was *gay,* and he looked so much better, so much happier! I had expected him to be at outs with me, because I had lost my temper with him, and said some pretty cutting things to him, which made him dash off in a fury. He seemed to have forgotten about that, and you may be sure that I didn't remind him that we had quarrelled!'' She broke off abruptly, as he interjected: ''O God!'' as though the words had been wrenched out of him, and demanded, in bewilderment: ''What do you mean? Why do you look like that?''

He replied with deliberate calm: ''I think that the whole affair was wiped from his mind as soon as he had satisfied his instinct to kill. I don't pretend to understand the minds of madmen, but it has seemed to me on several occasions that he has no recollection of what he has done when temporarily out of his senses. I even think that to kill, in an inhuman, bestial way, that rabbit, or a bird caught in a net, or some other helpless creature, satisfies some terrible instinct in himself, and acts on him like a powerful narcotic. More than that! As a tonic! If he had the smallest remembrance of what he has done when possessed by his fiendish *other* self I daresay he would be as horrified as you are.''

''He knew that he had tried to shoot that dog!'' she said swiftly. ''He has just begged my pardon!''

He said, his frown deepening: ''I fancy his behaviour was due more to fright than to madness.''

''But it was only a playful young dog—hardly more than a puppy!'' she protested. ''Even a person who was afraid of dogs must have seen how friendly it was! Why, it—'' She stopped suddenly, remembering that the dog had bristled and growled and backed away from Torquil.

"Friendly to Torquil?"

"No. It—it seemed to fear him!" she blurted out.

"Animals do fear him," he replied. "That's why there are no dogs at Staplewood, other than my uncle's old spaniel bitch, who is too old and lazy to stray from his side. They say that animals know when one is afraid of them: it is certainly true of horses. Is it fantastic to suppose that instinct warns them to beware of madmen? Gurney spoke last night to me about what he called the 'nervous chestnut' Torquil rides. I let it pass, but I've ridden that horse, Kate, and he went as sweetly as you please for me. Torquil has only to take the bridle in his hand to set him sidling, and bucking, and no sooner is Torquil in the saddle than he begins to sweat. And, make no mistake, Torquil isn't afraid of any horse that was ever foaled! I don't say I've never see him unseated—the best of us take tosses!—but I have never seen him unseated by the efforts of his mount to get rid of him, or fail to win the mastery over the most headstrong brute in the stables! But horses don't show their fear of one by growling, and bristling, and they rarely savage one. Certainly Torquil has never been savaged by a horse, but a dog did once turn on him, and that experience left him with a dread of dogs. I think he acted of impulse when he tried to shoot your friendly stray. He may have been hovering on the brink of one of his crazy fits, but you were not afraid of him, and you recalled him to his senses, probably by speaking sharply to him—as I did, when I found him with his hands round your throat, and as Minerva has the power to do. He stands in great awe of Minerva, and in a little awe of me. It seems that he is also in awe of you. But the day is coming—and soon, I fear—when even Minerva won't be able to control him. That is why, my darling, I can't feel easy while you remain at Staplewood.''

"But my aunt doesn't know—*cannot* know—!'' Kate stammered. "She believes that it is merely irritation of the nerves—that he is much better—!''

"In fact, he is much worse!'' he interrupted. "Until now, although I have suspected that he suffered from some intermittent mental disorder, I could never be perfectly sure of it. I have frequently driven over from Broome Hall to visit my uncle, but of late years I've only stayed for one night.'' He smiled wryly. "Minerva has not encouraged me to prolong my visits! Indeed, she has been most ingenious in finding reasons why I shouldn't do so. But this time I've been deaf to all her hints, and I've seen much that it wasn't difficult to conceal from me for a few hours. I tell you frankly, Kate, I have been shocked by the deterioration in Torquil! Irritation of the nerves? Is that what Minerva calls it? Irritation of the brain would be nearer the mark, and well she knows it! Why do you imagine that she still keeps him in the nursery-wing?''

"She told me—so that he may be quiet!'' Kate faltered.

"So that he may be kept safe!'' he said grimly. "Why do Delabole and Badger both have their quarters in that wing? Why is he never permitted to ride out alone? To find his level amongst youngsters of his own age?''

"Because—oh, Philip, pray don't say any more! You dislike my aunt too bitterly to do her justice! If she is deceiving herself—or, which I think very likely, is being deceived by Dr Delabole, can you wonder at it that she should cling to the belief that his rages spring from ill-health, and will vanish when he grows stronger? Or even that she should shrink from facing a terrible truth?'' She sprang up, and took a hasty turn about the room. "You have pity for your uncle! *He* shrinks from facing it! If Torquil is indeed mad, how can it be possible that he shouldn't know it?''

He was prevented from replying by the entrance of Pennymore, wearing the look of one whose sense of propriety had been outraged. He addressed himself to Kate, saying, in his stateliest manner: "I beg your pardon, miss, but since her ladyship is unwell I feel it my duty to inform you that Mrs Thorne has seen fit to Prophesy!''

Chapter Sixteen

Philip gave a shout of laughter: conduct which Pennymore considered to be so unseemly that he ignored it, keeping his eyes fixed on Kate. He said in a perfectly expressionless voice: "In consequence of which, miss, the chef, so far as I am able to understand him—but he has relapsed into the French tongue, which he is regrettably prone to do when excited—has formed the intention of leaving Staplewood tomorrow."

Philip's shoulders shook, but Kate was not amused. "Good God!" she exclaimed.

"Yes, miss," agreed Pennymore, according this very proper way of receiving the tidings the tribute of a slight bow. "Furthermore, one of the kitchen-maids has so far forgotten her position as to fall into the vapours."

"But this is a Greek tragedy, with Pennymore the Chorus!" said Philip.

Pennymore said arctically: "If you will permit me to say so, Master Philip, it is hardly a laughing matter!"

Recognizing that by using this form of address Pennymore was trying to reduce him to school status, Mr Philip Broome grinned, but obligingly begged pardon.

"But—but why does the chef wish to leave?" asked Kate.

"On account of the Prophecy, miss. I'm sure Mrs Thorne has a perfect right to dream of Horrors, if she so wishes, but I do not consider it advisable to describe her dreams to the household. In fact, far otherwise, for it has a very upsetting effect on the female staff, not to mention the chef—but that was to be expected, him being a Foreigner. Mrs Thorne, miss, makes quite a habit of dreaming of Disaster. The first time she did so, the second footman tripped on the back stairs the very next day, and fell to the bottom."

"Good gracious!" said Kate. "Was he badly injured? You don't mean, surely, that he broke his neck?"

"Oh, no, miss! It was worse than that," said Pennymore. "He broke three of the Sèvres cups, thus ruining the Set."

"Not *worse,* Pennymore!" protested Kate.

"He could have been better spared, miss, I assure you," replied Pennymore darkly. "A very unsatisfactory young man, and easily replaceable, which the Sèvres china was not. However, what with that and Mrs Thorne's dreaming she saw Staplewood being burnt to the ground a couple of nights before the kitchen-chimney caught fire, so that rock-salt had to be thrown on the range, which set dinner back an hour, she's only got to dream she saw lions and tigers in the garden for none of the young maids to stir out of the house for a sennight."

"What's her latest dream?" asked Philip.

"Well, sir, it is Extremely Unpleasant, and not at all the sort of thing one would expect of a respectable female, however given to what I will call Odd Humours. She says that she dreamed there was a coffin in the Blue saloon, with blood streaming from it. Yes, miss, most distasteful, and, I venture to say, highly unlikely. Unfortunately, one of the maids informed Miss Sidlaw, and she was so much provoked that she took it upon herself to give Mrs Thorne a scold, quite as if she thought she was standing in my lady's shoes.''

"Oh, that will never do!" Kate said quickly.

"No, miss, nor it hasn't. There has been a Quarrel between them," replied Pennymore. "And," he said, coming to his grand climax, "Mrs Thorne is now laid down upon her bed with Spasms. I thought you would wish to know, miss."

This rider incensed Mr Philip Broome into saying acidly: "Oh, indeed? And what made you think so?"

Kate, more accustomed than her betrothed to this time-honoured phrase, intervened hastily. "You did very right to tell me, Pennymore. I'll try what I can do to reconcile Sidlaw and Mrs Thorne."

"I'll deal with the chef," offered Philip. "You needn't look at me so despitefully, Pennymore. Do you think I can't do it?"

"I was merely thinking, Master Philip, that being as Miss Kate has lived in Foreign Parts, it might be better if *she* was to speak to the chef—in his own tongue," said Pennymore coldly.

"No doubt it would be, if he were a Spaniard, but I daresay I am quite as fluent in French as she is, even though I haven't lived in foreign parts! And don't imagine you can come it over me by calling me Master Philip, you old bangster, because you can't!"

"Now you've offended him!" said Kate reproachfully, when Pennymore had bowed himself out of the room.

"Not I! Didn't you see his mouth twitching? Pennymore and I are old friends—which won't deter him from combing my hair presently for using cant terms in front of a lady! Kate, you don't mean to embroil yourself in this cat-fight, do you?''

"Yes, of course I do! That is to say, I hope I may be able to smooth things over: it's the least I can do for my aunt! I must go: where is my reticule?''

"It's here," he said, picking it up from the table. "Good God, what do you carry in it? It weighs a ton!"

"Oh, it's my door-key! I put it in my reticule because I couldn't think of a secure hiding-place for it. I can't stay to explain it to you now, but I will presently!''

He was obliged to be satisfied, for she hurried away on the words, and was no more seen until she put in a belated appearance at the table on which a cold nuncheon had been set out. Mr Philip Broome, who was moodily eating cheese, rose at her entrance, and ejaculated: "At last! I thought you were never coming back! What the deuce kept you so long?''

"I collect, from that question, that you had no difficulty in persuading the chef to remain at his post!" Kate said, with asperity.

"Very little. I take it your task was not an easy one?''

"No, dear sir, it was not at all easy! It was singularly exhausting, in fact!''

"You don't look exhausted," he said, smiling at her. "You look to be in high beauty! Did you succeed in reconciling the warring cats?''

"Oh, no, only time will do that!" she said cheerfully. "The best I could achieve was to flatter each into believing that *her* behaviour was in the nature of a triumph for the other, and that if either of them failed in this hour of trouble the house would fall to pieces, and my aunt suffer a relapse. So now they are not speaking to one another, and I can see that I shall have to be a go-between until they make up their quarrel, or until my aunt is well enough to leave her room."

He picked up the carving knife, but at this he put it down again, and demanded to be told for how many more days she meant to remain at Staplewood.

"Well, until I know how my aunt goes on, I can't tell that," she responded. "Not many, I hope. But you cannot, in all seriousness, expect me to run away at this moment, when at last I have the opportunity to be of real use to my aunt! You may think it a paltry service—indeed, if you found it easy to pacify the chef, I daresay you do!—but I promise you it was not at all easy to soothe and remonstrate with two angry women, one of whom thinks herself first in consequence, and the other of whom, though amiable, suffers from every imaginable disorder, and has so much sensibility that the least unpleasantness brings on all her most distressing symptoms. What is in this pie?"

"Venison. I never heard such—"

"How good! I wish you will give me some: I am perfectly ravenous!"

"Kate, how *can* you let that fat, lazy creature bamboozle you?" he expostulated. "You don't mean to tell me that you swallowed all those plumpers?"

"Every one!" she assured him, with a chuckle. "I admired her fortitude, too, for keeping up so bravely, when she has had the influenza, *and* a severe colic, just like my aunt—only worse! It seems to be one of her peculiarities that whenever anyone in the house is indisposed she becomes indisposed in exactly the same way. Only *she* never says a word about it."

"I wish you had allowed me to deal with her!"

"That wouldn't have answered the purpose at all: she would very likely have gone into convulsions! What she needed was sympathy, not a jobation! She had enough of *that* from Sidlaw! Of course, they are both shockingly jealous, which makes it difficult to bring them about.''

"I thought they were bosom-bows!"

"Yes, so did I, when I first came here, but I soon found it was no such thing. They are in—in defensive alliance against Pennymore and Tenby." She looked up, no longer funning, and said: "This is a very unhappy house, isn't it? Not in the least what I had supposed an English home would be like. It is more like three houses, with no love between any of them. Sir Timothy and my aunt are always very civil to each other, but they seem to live as strangers. And Torquil lives apart from either of them. And, although my aunt and Sir Timothy don't quarrel, their servants do! Which makes it uncomfortable—don't you think?"

"It was not always so," he replied. "And our home won't be!"

"Oh, no!" she agreed, smiling warmly at him.

He stretched out his hand to her across the table. "Can't I persuade you to let me take you away tomorrow, Kate?"

She laid her own hand in his, but shook her head. "Not while my aunt is unwell, and I can be of use here. You could not wish me to do what my conscience tells me is wrong!"

"I wish to have you in safety."

"I don't think I am in danger. Even when I've put him in a flame, Torquil hasn't offered me any hurt, and he doesn't think I'm one of his enemies."

"At least promise me one thing!" he said urgently.

She looked speculatively at him, the mischief back in her eyes. "Are you trying to sell me a bargain?" she enquired.

"No, you suspicious little wretch! I want you only to promise me that you won't go alone with Torquil beyond sight of the house. I think you may be right that *at the moment* he regards you as his friend, but there is no depending on people whose minds are unhinged. Anything might happen to make him turn on you, without warning! A sudden fright, a rash word from you—even an attempt on his part to embrace you! If you were to struggle, I have the greatest fear that he would be unable to resist the temptation to strangle you. I tell you in all seriousness that you owe it to yourself, far more than to my intervention, which might have come too late, that he didn't strangle you on that day when he had his hands about your throat. You stood perfectly still, and although his—how shall I put it?—his *demon* stirred, it didn't fully wake. What would have happened if I had not come in, I don't know, but I believe you are safe enough as long as there is someone within sight: Torquil is still sane enough to know that the atrocious things he does are wrong, and to fear discovery—to be detected in the act!''

"But he forgets! Does he only pretend to have forgotten?''

"No, I think not,'' he said decidedly. "It may be fanciful, but I have sometimes wondered if he forgets because his mind *refuses* to remember what he has done in one of his mad fits. Do you understand at all?''

She nodded. "Yes—I think I do. I'll take care. And you will be here, won't you?''

"You may be sure of that. I suspect that Delabole locks the door into the West Wing when he goes to bed, but it's easy enough for an active boy to climb out through any of the windows: I did so, several times, when shut up as a punishment! So I think you should lock your door, just to be on the safe side. And that reminds me! Why, my love, do you carry the key in your ridicule?''

She told him how, on the night of the storm, she had been unable to open her door, and had discovered next morning, when she had opened it without the smallest difficulty, that the key was missing from the lock; how her aunt had suggested, in gentle amusement, that when she had leapt out of bed she had been half-asleep; and how she had said that the key should be found.

"But it never was, and it's my belief it was never lost, but in Sidlaw's possession all the time!" Kate said, her eyes kindling. "I was only just in time, last night, to stop her from locking me in again! She thought I was asleep, of course, but was made to look nohow! Oh, how much I dislike that woman! But why should she do such a thing? Did my aunt order her to? And *still* why? To keep Torquil out? I can't believe it! Even you think it unlikely that he would kill me without provocation, and how much less likely must my aunt think it!"

He had listened to her in attentive silence, a slight frown between his brows, and he now said slowly: "I think it more probable that it has been done to keep you in than to keep Torquil out. Has your door been locked every night?"

"I don't know! I've never tried it since that night!" she said. "I supposed that no one had been able to find it, and I forgot about it."

"Had you left your room *before* that night?"

"Yes, once, before you came. It was after the dinner-party—oh, weeks ago! I wasn't sleepy, and I sat sewing in my room till my candle began to gutter. I still wasn't sleepy, and I drew back the blinds to look out, wishing that I could take a walk in the garden. Then I saw a man, by the yew hedge, but only for an instant: I think he must have caught sight of me for he drew back immediately, and he might well have done so, you know, for although the moonlight was faint, it was shining into my window. I thought, of course, that it was a burglar, and ran along

the gallery to my aunt's room. She wasn't there, but she
came up the stairs at the end of the gallery, just as I was
wondering what I should do. She was looking very tired
and it was the first time she ever spoke crossly to me. She
told me to go back to bed. She said the figure I had seen
was one of the servants. And then Torquil came into the
gallery from the West Wing, and I thought he was drunk.''
She paused, considering it. "And I still think he was
drunk! He said that he had been in the woods, and that the
doctor and Badger were still hunting for him. He was giggling, too, and—oh, chirping merry! He drank a great deal
at dinner, and afterwards slipped away. It was uncivil, but
one couldn't really blame him: it was *such* an insipid
party! Sir Timothy enjoyed it, but my aunt said it was an
intolerable bore, and I must own I think it was very silly
of her to have included Torquil, particularly when he
didn't at all wish to be included.''

"Was he amiable?''

"Well, he started in the sulks, but he behaved perfectly
properly at dinner.''

"Then I should suppose that he was included in that
party to silence the on-dits.''

She looked startled. "Are there any?''

"According to Gurney, people have begun to whisper
that there's something odd about him. It isn't surprising.''

"No—I suppose it isn't,'' she said sadly. "But how
dreadful if it came to his ears!''

"It isn't likely to. Don't look so harassed, love! Would
you care to take a walk with me through the park, or shall
I have my horses put to, and tool you round the countryside?''

"Good God, no!'' she exclaimed. "That would give the
tattleboxes something to talk about indeed!''

"What of it?''

"Philip, it would be all over the house in a twinkling of a bedpost. Sidlaw would tell my aunt, making it appear that I was behaving in a—in a clandestine way! No, don't laugh! She's an archintelligencer, you know: that's why the other servants hate her. She watched me go into the shrubbery, the day you came and sat beside me there; and she told my aunt, and my aunt spoke to me about the *impropriety* of it. I was never nearer to pulling caps with her! No, and never so thankful, when you set me down yesterday, that no one saw me enter the house! It is bad enough that we are *secretly* betrothed: it is not at all the thing! I couldn't bear it to come to my aunt's ears before I've told her myself that you've offered for me! She would think me so sly!" She saw that his brows had drawn together, and said imploringly: "Oh, Philip, don't look angry! Pray *try* to understand!"

"I am angry!" he responded harshly, adding, as her eyes widened in dismay: "Oh, not with you! Never with you, Kate! Only with circumstance! I think it intolerable that we should be obliged to hide our teeth—play the concave-suit!—because of Minerva's illness! But I do understand your scruples. You are very right: neither of us could bear the sort of backstairs gossip, and speculation, which would be provoked by any indiscretion. I must still wish that you would let me remove you from Staplewood—but I'll say no more on that head!" He took her hand, and kissed it. "Don't be troubled, my sweet! God forbid I should try to persuade you to do anything against your conscience!"

"It would weigh on me all my life if I left my aunt *now!*" she said, searching his face with anxious eyes.

"Very well," he replied. He hesitated for a moment, and then, as she looked enquiringly at him, shook his head, crookedly smiling. "No. There's a great deal I could say to you, but it would only set you at outs with me so I'll keep my tongue. Must I conceal the news from my uncle? I should wish to tell him—and at once.''

Her face brightened. ''Oh, yes, pray do tell him! Then, if he gives his consent, it will make everything right, won't it?''

''His consent, my little love, is not necessary!''

''His approval, then,'' she said docilely.

''That's not necessary either, though I should wish him to approve.''

''It is necessary to me,'' she said. ''It would be very hard, but I hope I should have the resolution not to marry you, if he should dislike it very much.''

''In that case,'' he retorted, walking to the door, ''there will be nothing for it but to abduct you!''

He left her laughing. She went upstairs to find Sidlaw lying in wait for her. Hostility flickered in Sidlaw's eyes, but she spoke with meticulous civility. ''If you please, Miss Kate, may I have a word with you?''

''Certainly! What is it?'' Kate said, forcing herself to speak pleasantly.

''I did not venture to intrude on you, miss, when you and Mr Broome were eating a nuncheon, but I should be glad if you would speak to Mrs Thorne, which I do not care to do myself, under the circumstances.''

Repressing an exasperated sigh, Kate asked what she was to speak about, and thereby unleashed a spate of complaints, most of which she judged to be groundless. However, she promised to adjust them; and even to order the chef to make some tapioca jelly, which her ladyship thought she could fancy. She then went to the housekeeper's room, where she was relieved to find that Mrs Thorne was so far restored to health as to have been able to consume a sustaining meal, the remains of which were to be seen on a tray. She said that she had been trying to keep up her strength.

It was nearly half an hour later when Kate escaped from her garrulity, and Torquil and the doctor had returned from their expedition. She heard Torquil's voice in the hall, demanding to be told where she was, and slipped away to her room. It had occurred to her that if she wrote to Sarah, explaining her circumstances, and warning her that she might shortly be arriving in London, Mr Philip Broome would see her letter safely posted.

Her room contained an elegant little writing-table, furnished (ironically, Kate thought remembering the fate of her previous letters) with writing-paper, ink, wafers, a selection of pens, and a knife with which to sharpen them. Kate sat down to write to Sarah. She had meant to have given a full account of the situation at Staplewood, but the ink dried on her pen as she realized that, whatever she might confide to Sarah by word of mouth, it would be injudicious—even dangerous—to set the whole story down on paper. So it was quite a short letter that was written, but it contained one piece of news which, Kate guessed, would delight Sarah.

She had been vaguely aware, while she tried to compose her letter, of voices in the garden, and as she wrote the superscription someone ran up the terrace-steps, immediately below her window, and Torquil shouted: "Kate! Are you there? Do come down!"

She rose, and went to the window, leaning out to look down into his upturned face. He was smiling, and his eyes sparkled; as soon as he saw her, he said again coaxingly: "*Do* come out, coz! See what I've brought from Market Harborough!" He held up a circular metal plate, with a hole in the centre.

"But what is it?"

"Why, a quoit, of course! Matthew has been showing me how to throw it, and I can tell you it requires a great deal of skill! We've paced out the ground, and driven in the iron stakes at either end—" He looked over his shoulder to shout to the doctor: "What did you tell me the stakes are called, Matthew?"

"Take care!" Kate said warningly. "Don't disturb your mother!"

He looked rather impatient, but said nothing. Dr Delabole, who had come across the lawn to the foot of the steps, said: "Hobs, my boy, hobs! Do you care to try your skill, Miss Kate? It is quite a diverting pastime!"

She agreed to go down, wondering if Philip had emerged from the East Wing, and hoping that she might be able to snatch a word with him on her way out into the garden. However, there was no sign of him downstairs so she was obliged to go out with the anxious question in her head unanswered.

The rules of the game were quite simple, the players standing facing one another, by one of the hobs, and being provided with an equal number of quoits, which they cast, in turn, at the opposite hob, the object being to throw the quoits as near as possible to the hob.

The doctor offered himself as scorer, but had first to combine this role with that of instructor, Kate never having played the game before, and making a number of wild casts. Torquil, on the other hand, seemed to have a natural aptitude for it, getting the range immediately, and sending his quoits spinning towards the hob with an expert flick of his wrist. He was obviously enjoying himself, intent on improving his skill, and flushing with gratification when the doctor said jovially that he would have to be handicapped.

"I wish he might be!" said Kate fervently.

"Nothing easier!" declared the doctor. "We can extend the range, you know: there is no limit! You shall be allowed to stand halfway, and he shall throw from—what do you say, Torquil? Twenty yards?"

"What is it now?' asked Kate. "It seems more than that to me already!"

"Eighteen," replied Torquil. He watched her throw the quoit she was holding, and exclaimed: "No, no, don't *hurl* it! Use your wrist! Here, let me show you!" He came running up to her, looking just like an eager schoolboy, for he had thrown off his coat, and his neckcloth, and his hair was dishevelled. He grasped her hand, with his strong fingers, and forced her to bend her wrist over. "There! Do you see what I mean?"

She said meekly that she did see what he meant, but doubted her ability to carry out his instructions, adding that she had never before suspected that her wrists were made of tallow. She then caught sight of Philip, who was leaning his arms on the stone parapet of the terrace, watching them, and hailed him with relief, inviting him to take her place.

The instant the words were out of her mouth she knew that the suggestion was unwelcome to Torquil, and realized that he was afraid his cousin would outshine him. Half his pleasure in the sport arose from the applause which greeted his best shots. It was regrettable, but understandable: even pathetic, Kate thought; and wished she had held her tongue.

But Mr Philip Broome said hastily: "No, no, I'm no match for Torquil! I haven't played quoits for years!"

The cloud vanished from Torquil's brow. He laughed, and said boastfully: "I have *never* played before!"

"Doing it too brown, you young gull-catcher!"

"I swear it's true!" Torquil said, his eyes alight with glee. "Matthew, isn't it true?"

"I'm afraid it is," said the doctor, with a lugubrious shake of his head. "There's no beating you at it!"

"Oh, isn't there, by Jove?" said Philip. "That puts me on my mettle! Have at you, Jack-sauce! Cousin, if you mean to sit on the steps, sit on my coat!"

He stripped it off, and handed it to her, murmuring, with a reassuring smile: "I shan't have to abduct you after all!"

She gave him a look of heartfelt relief, but no further words passed between them. He walked away to bargain for a few practice-throws, and she carefully folded his coat of Bath superfine, and sat down to watch the contest, at first thinking that Torquil was by far the better player, and then, as Philip's casts began to improve, coming to the conclusion that he meant Torquil to win, but not easily enough to make him suspicious. Now and again his cast beat Torquil's, but more often his quoit was found to lie an inch further from the hob. At the end of the match, Torquil was flushed, and triumphant, very hot, and beginning to be very much excited. He promptly challenged Philip to a return game, and snapped the doctor's nose off, when that well-meaning but tactless gentleman advised him against over-exertion, repeating the challenge, the sparkle in his eyes hardening to a glitter.

"Tomorrow," Philip replied.

"I tell you, I'm not tired!"

"You may not be tired, but I am! What's the time, doctor?"

The doctor, pulling out his watch, announced that it was nearly half-past five, at which Kate sprang up, exclaiming: "As late as that? We shall be late for dinner! For heaven's sake, don't start another game!"

"Oh, what the devil does it signify? Mama ain't coming down!''

"No, but your father means to dine with us, and it won't do to keep him waiting," said Philip imperturbably. "Furthermore, I have already had one brush with Gaston, and, I warn you, Torquil, if his sensibilities are wounded again, *you* shall have the task of applying balm!''

"Gaston? What are you talking about?" asked Torquil impatiently.

"It's my belief," said Philip, eyeing him severely, "that you knew all about it, and took care to be well out of the way! See if I don't give you your own again, that's all!''

"But I didn't!" protested Torquil, diverted. "I swear I don't know what you're talking about! I believe you're hoaxing me!''

He was still hovering on the brink of fury, but his curiosity had been roused, and by the time Philip had regaled him with a highly coloured description of his encounter with the chef, he was laughing again, and had forgotten his determination to play another game of quoits.

He was strumming on the pianoforte at the far end of the Long Drawing-room when Kate next saw him, twenty minutes later, and paid no heed to her. She thought he looked tired, and dispirited, and so, apparently, did Dr Delabole, who was watching him covertly when Kate came into the room, an anxious frown on his forehead. It vanished when he became aware of her entrance, and he got up bowing, and smiling, and handing her to a chair, with the slightly overdone civility which characterized him. Torquil stumbled over a passage, and brought his hands down in a crashing discord, ejaculating savagely: "Fool, fool, cowhanded fool! I shall never be first-rate, never!''

He jumped up from the pianoforte, slamming down the lid, and coming with hasty, impetuous strides down the room, just as Sir Timothy entered, leaning on Philip's arm. For a nerve-racking moment Kate feared that he was going to brush past his father, and fling himself out of the room, but either his cousin's presence, or Sir Timothy's gentle voice, bidding him good-evening, made him stop in his tracks. He responded awkwardly: "Oh—good-evening, sir!" and, after standing undecidedly beside a chair in the middle of the room, sat down, but took no part in the general conversation. This did not augur well for the comfort of the evening, but his temper gradually improved, and he ate what was, for him, a very good dinner. By the time Kate left the dining-room, he had made three spontaneous remarks, and had allowed himself to be drawn into a sporting discussion.

As she walked up the Grand Staircase, Kate wondered how to keep him diverted, and decided that the best plan might be to set out the Fox and Geese. This had amused him on a previous occasion, and might do so again. On the other hand, he might despise it as a child's game: one never knew with him how long a craze would last. Everything depended on his mood, and tonight this seemed to be uncertain.

But when he came in he was smiling at something Philip seemed to have said to him, and as soon as he saw the Fox and Geese board, exclaimed: "Oh, I'd forgotten that! Look, Philip, do you remember?"

Philip waited until Sir Timothy had lowered himself into his accustomed chair before turning his head towards Torquil. "Look at what?— Good God! You don't mean to tell me those are the pieces I once made?" he exclaimed incredulously. He walked over to the table, and laughed, picking up one of the lop-sided geese. "Ham handed, wasn't I? How in the world have they survived? Do you still play?"

"Oh, no, not for years, until I played with Kate, three or four evenings ago! I thought they had been lost, but she found them at the back of the cabinet over there, and we had a famous battle! I beat her all hollow, and she swore revenge on me. Are you ready to begin, coz?"

"Do say you don't wish to play, Kate!" begged Philip. "I am persuaded you would liefer talk to my uncle! I shall then offer, very good-naturedly, to play as your deputy. Lord, how it takes me back! I wonder if I remember the rules?"

He sat down as he spoke, and began to set out the seventeen geese. Torquil, who had been inclined to resent his intervention, at once became enthusiastic, and Sir Timothy made an inviting gesture towards a chair near his own.

She had purposely set out the fox and geese on a table towards the other end of the room, and although it was not out of tongue-shot, a low-voiced conversation could be maintained which would neither disturb the players nor be overheard by them. Nevertheless, Kate moved her chair rather closer to Sir Timothy's, saying, as she sat down: "Philip was right, sir: I have been anxious to talk to you ever since—ever since I knew that he does *indeed* wish to marry me!"

"But you were in doubt? He must have expressed himself very badly!" said Sir Timothy.

She laughed, blushing a little. "No, but—I wasn't expecting him to make me an offer, and I was afraid he might regret it. After all, it is only a week since we first met!"

"Are you afraid *you* might regret it?" he asked, still amused.

"Oh, no, no!"

"Then why should he? He is not at all volatile, you know!" He held out his thin hand, and as she shyly laid her own in it, said softly: "I think you will suit very well, my dear. I'm glad to know that you are going to be happy. I feel sure you will be, both of you.''

"Thank you, sir!" she whispered, fervently squeezing his hand. "As long as you don't dislike it—!''

"There's only one thing I dislike about it, and that is that I must lose you. You brought the sunshine to Staplewood, my child! And I fear that when you leave I shan't see you again. Your aunt won't make you welcome. It is not I, but she, who will dislike your marriage to Philip. You know that, don't you?" She nodded, and he continued, sighing faintly: "Philip tells me that you mean to break the news to her yourself. You would oblige me very much, Kate, if you won't do so while she is still so unwell. She is all unused to having her will crossed, and I am afraid it will upset her very much.''

She replied immediately: "You may be easy on that head, sir: I will do nothing to upset her until she is better. What does Dr Delabole say of her?''

"He went up to see her when we left the dining-room, and has promised to report to me how she goes on. I daresay he will soon be with us, so I will say only one thing more to you, my dear! Whatever your aunt may say to you, let Philip be the judge of what is best for you to do— and be sure that you both take my blessing with you!''

Chapter Seventeen

Kate had no opportunity that evening to exchange more than a few whispered words with Philip as she slid her letter to Sarah into his hand, for although Sir Timothy went away to bed, escorted by Dr Delabole, before the tea-tray was brought in, Torquil remained, and it was not many minutes before the doctor returned. This had the effect of making Torquil invite Kate to walk down to the bridge with him, to see the moonlight on the lake. The arrival of the first footman, carrying in the tea-tray, provided her with an excuse; she added that she was rather tired, trusting to Philip to divert his wayward mind. This he did by proposing a game of billiards, but not before Torquil had announced his intention of going down to the lake by himself.

Kate was thus left to sustain the burden of Dr Delabole's conversation, which was largely concerned with Lady Broome's state of health, but interspersed with anecdotes, of which he seemed to have an inexhaustible fund. It struck her that under his cheerful manner he was concealing anxiety, but when she asked him if he thought Lady Broome's condition more serious than he had divulged to Sir Timothy, he quickly denied it, assuring her that her aunt was on the mend. "It was a severe attack, though soon over, and it has pulled her—there's no denying that, as I told her, when she was determined to get up. She bit my nose off, but that's a sign of convalescence, you know!" He chuckled reminiscently. "How it did take me back! I daresay you would find it hard to believe that she could ever have had a temper, but I promise you she had! Oh, dear me, yes! Quite a violent one! I have been acquainted with her since she was twelve years old—watched her grow up, you might say. Ay, and watched her bridle her temper, until she had it under such strict control that I had almost forgotten how passionate she was used to be until she flew at me for saying she must remain in bed! That brought the old days back to me! Not that I mean to say that it was more than a spurt of temper, but it put me on my guard!"

"But didn't you say that it was a sign she was on the mend?" asked Kate, raising her brows.

"Oh, yes, and so it is! Yesterday, when the fever was so high, she felt too ill to be cross, or obstinate: *that* caused me to feel considerable anxiety!" He cast an arch look at Kate. "I fancy I have no need to tell you, Miss Malvern, that she is very, very strong-willed! Once she is determined on a course, it is a hard task to turn her from it! I should have preferred her to remain in bed for another day, but if she is of the same mind tomorrow I shan't attempt to argue with her, for I know it would do more harm than good. She is suffering from considerable irritation of the nerves, and must be kept as calm as possible, if she is not to have a relapse into another attack of colic. That might indeed be serious!"

He went on talking in this strain until the tea-tray was removed, and Kate felt she could excuse herself without incivility.

She passed a peaceful night, and woke with a sensation

of well-being. Only one fence remained to be jumped, and
although it was likely to be a rasper she had no doubt of
clearing it: Sir Timothy's blessing had removed her scruples, and beyond that last obstacle a happy future awaited
her.

But she did wish that Lady Broome had not fallen ill at
just this moment. To remain at Staplewood while her aunt
was ignorant of her engagement to Mr Philip Broome did
not suit her sense of propriety. She felt it to be double
dealing, and was too honest to offer her conscience the sop
of Sir Timothy's request to her not to divulge her engagement until Lady Broome was sufficiently recovered to
withstand what he plainly felt would be an unpleasant
shock. Nor could she persuade herself that Lady Broome
might not be so very angry after all: for the niece whom
she had so generously befriended to fall in love with the
man she most hated and mistrusted would be seen by her
as an unpardonable piece of disloyalty—if she did not see
it as treachery, which she was very likely to do, thought
Kate ruefully, wishing that the ordeal were behind her. It
had not needed Dr Delabole's reference to Lady Broome's
girlish furies to convince her that under her iron calm Lady
Broome concealed a temper, and she wondered, quaking a
little, just how violent it would be if her aunt allowed it
to overcome her, and what effect it might have upon her
health. It would be a shocking thing to make her seriously
ill: infinitely worse than to keep from her, when she was
barely convalescent, news that would certainly upset her.
Philip had said that she owed her aunt nothing, because it
had been to serve her own ends that Lady Broome had
been kind to her; but however selfish her motive had been,
the fact remained that she *had* been kind, and had continued to be kind when Kate had told her that under no circumstances would she marry Torquil. She had certainly

hoped that Kate would change her mind, but she had put no pressure on her. Her only unkindness had been to try to sever the link that tied her niece to Sarah Nidd. That had been unscrupulous, but Kate was inclined to believe that she had not supposed herself to be inflicting more than a passing sadness. It would be incomprehensible to Lady Broome, whose exaggerated notion of her own consequence Kate had long thought to be one of her least amiable faults, that her niece could hold her nurse in more than mild affection. If she had known that Kate actually loved Sarah, she would have deplored such a sad want of particularity, and might even have considered it a kindness to wean her from her predilection for what she herself called Low Company.

Philip, of course, would say that she did not care a straw how much pain she inflicted when scheming to achieve her own ends; but Philip disliked her too much to do her justice. It was strange that so level-headed a man could be so deeply prejudiced. Kate could understand dislike, but not a prejudice so bitter that it led him to believe that her aunt, knowing Torquil to be mentally deranged, meant to entrap her into marrying him. That shocked her, for it seemed to be a discordant note in his nature, making him, for a disquieting moment, almost a stranger to her, an intolerant man, without pity or understanding. But she knew that he had both. His affection for his uncle had not blinded him to the weakness in Sir Timothy's character, but he understood, far better than she did, the circumstances which had worn his uncle down, and would never, she knew, abate one jot of his sympathetic tenderness. He had said that though he could no longer respect Sir Timothy he could never cease to love him, and these were not the words of an intolerant man. The thought that he was kind only to those whom he held in affection occurred only

to be dismissed. He did not hold Torquil in affection, but
that he pitied him was shown in his treatment of him. A
man who could let his prejudice govern him might have
been expected to have extended his hatred of Lady Broome
to her son, but this, plainly, Philip had never done. He
must always, Kate thought, remembering Torquil's joyful
greeting when he had arrived at Staplewood a week ago,
have been kind to Torquil, even when he was a schoolboy,
and had probably wished a tiresome small boy at Jericho.
Torquil had told her, in one of his melodramatic moods,
that Philip had made three attempts to murder him. How
much of that lurid tale had been due to a fantasy in his
brain, and how much to his undeniable love of play-acting,
she could not know, but she suspected that someone had
put the idea into his head that his cousin was his enemy.
It was not difficult to guess who had done it, for only one
person at Staplewood had a motive for attempting to turn
Torquil against Philip: Lady Broome, who hated Philip as
much as he hated her, and made no secret of the fact that
his visits were unwelcome. Philip believed that she was
trying to keep him away because she feared that if he saw
too much of Torquil he would discover what she knew to
be the truth about him; to Kate's mind, it went to prove
that she did not know the truth. For Lady Broome to have
sown poison in what she believed to be a sane mind was
bad enough; to have done so, knowing that Torquil's hold
on sanity was precarious, and that when in the grip of
mania he was homicidal, would have been unpardonable.

It seemed to Kate, bearing in mind her aunt's domi-
neering disposition, that Lady Broome saw in Philip a
threat to her absolute authority over Torquil; perhaps
feared that he would support Torquil in his burning wish
to break away from her rule. That he had given her no
reason to suspect him of any such subversive ambition

probably weighed with her not at all: he could not do right in her eyes.

She said that she deprecated his influence: the truth was, Kate thought, that she was jealous of Torquil's affection for his cousin, for what little influence Philip possessed over him was good; and bitterly resented Philip's tacit refusal to allow her to reduce him to the position of a mere guest at Staplewood, dependent on formal invitations for his visits. He came when he chose: it could never be too often for Sir Timothy. Pennymore had told Kate that Sir Timothy became quite like his old self when Mr Philip was at Staplewood; and this, she guessed, was another cause of Lady Broome's resentment. She could perceive how galling it must be for her aunt to see Sir Timothy's eyes brighten when Philip came into the room; to know, as she surely must, that Philip was much dearer to him than was his son; and to be powerless to bring about an alienation between them. That, Kate thought, was at the root of the trouble: Lady Broome wanted always to be in command of every person at Staplewood, and of every situation that might arise; but she had not been able to command that situation. Nor had she been able to kill Torquil's affection for Philip: he had only to come face to face with him to see in him, not an enemy, but the indulgent big cousin of his childhood. And Philip she could not command at all, having neither power nor influence over him. He was quite civil to her, never seeking to interfere with her arrangements, but he went his own way, perfectly at home at Staplewood. This might have been expected to have made his visits more acceptable to her, for she was not obliged to entertain him, and he made no demands on her. In fact, it was an added offence: she called it "behaving as though Staplewood belonged to him". Really, Kate thought, when it came to imputing evil there wasn't a penny to choose between them: neither could see good in the other.

Her reflections were interrupted at this point by the timid tap on the door which heralded Ellen's entrance, and they were not resumed, Ellen bringing messages which banished all but domestic matters from her mind. The chef wished to know when it would be convenient to her to issue her orders for the day; and Mrs Thorne would be glad if she could spare a moment to have a word with her.

Entering the breakfast-parlour half an hour later, she was surprised to find only Philip there, lingering over his coffee, and reading an article in the Monthly Magazine. He cast this aside when she came in, and got up, advancing towards her with his hands held out. "Good-morning, my sweet!" he said lovingly. "I've been waiting for you." He possessed himself of her hands, and kissed them. "I wish you will tell me how you contrive to look more beautiful every time I see you?"

She blushed, raising shyly smiling eyes to his face. "Oh, Philip, you—you palaverer! I don't!"

"But you do! I think myself pretty ill-used, I can tell you: very unkind of you, when you know I daren't kiss you!" He moved to the table, to pull her chair out. "Come and sit down!" He pushed the chair in again as she did so, and dropped a kiss on the top of her head, at which precise moment Pennymore came in, bearing a teapot, and a dish of hot scones.

Not by so much as a blink of the eyelids did he betray that he had observed Mr Philip Broome's improper conduct, but Kate was almost overcome by confusion, and, as soon as Pennymore had withdrawn, took her betrothed severely to task.

He had gone back to his own seat, on the other side of the table, but he was quite impenitent. "Bless you, my

pretty widgeon, we've nothing to fear from old Pennymore!'' he said.

"What if it hadn't been Pennymore, but James, or William?" she demanded. "Or the doctor? Or Torquil? A
pretty scrape we should have been in!"

"Stop scolding, archwife! Delabole was finishing his
breakfast when I started to eat mine; and Torquil—having,
according to Delabole's account, passed a disturbed night
finds himself very languid this morning. I imagine that
Delabole laced his lemonade, last night, with what drug it
is that he uses to keep him quiet. He became drowsy, after
drinking it; yawning, and complaining that he couldn't
keep his eyes open—for which, I assure you, I was profoundly thankful! I had the devil of a time with him, you
know. I think the full moon excites him: he was quite
determined to go down to the lake. The only thing to do
was to try whether I could tire him out.''

She asked in quick alarm: "Was he violent? I thought
he was in—in one of his distempered freaks, before he
went down to dinner, but then he seemed to recover, and
I did hope— But when Dr Delabole came into the drawing-room, I saw his eyes change—you know how they
do?"

He nodded. "Yes, I know. He wasn't violent, but within
ames-ace of flying into a passion when Delabole tried, in
his hamhanded way, to coax him up to bed. When he got
to threatening to climb out of his window, and boasting of
the number of times he'd done so in the past, I thought it
was time to intervene—before Delabole became sick with
apprehension!"

"Intervene? You don't mean you *compelled* him to go
to bed, do you? I don't doubt you *could,* just as my aunt
does, but I hope you did not, because it would set him

against you. It even sets him against my aunt, when she makes him knuckle down to her, and she is his mother!''

"No, of course I didn't! Much heed would he have paid! I accused him of trying to play nipshot, to escape having to own he couldn't beat me twice. That was quite enough for him! He forgot everything else in a burning desire to prove me wrong.''

She smiled. "If he won the first game, you must have been playing very skilfully, I think! You are a far better player than he is!''

"I *was* playing skilfully,'' he said, with a rather rueful laugh. "It takes a deal of skill to miss one's shots by a hair's breadth! And even more *just* to win against a suspicious youngster, let me tell you! All the urging he needed to challenge me to a third game was supplied by Delabole, who again tried—or seemed to try—to induce him to go to bed.'' He drew his snuff-box from his pocket, flicked it open, and took a meditative pinch. "Everything he said might have been expressly designed to set up Torquil's bristles. That was either another example of his hamhandedness, or a very shrewd piece of work. I added my mite by showing reluctance to go on playing, which made young Torquil all the more determined to embark on a third game. He was still full of vigour: the only things he complained of were the heat, and thirst. That was Delabole's chance to drug him, I fancy. At all events, he soon became sleepy, began to play badly, and ended by flinging his cue down in a rage, and staggering up to bed. Delabole then entertained me with a glib explanation of his behaviour. He would have done better to have kept his tongue! Said he was afraid Torquil had a touch of the sun, if you please! He embroidered the story this morning. I don't pretend to understand the jargon of his trade—he didn't intend that I should—but the gist of it was that Torquil's constitution is still so sickly that the least excitement, or over-exertion, makes him feverish.'' He shut his snuff-box with a snap, and restored it to his pocket, saying, as he flicked away a grain from his coat: ''He was also at pains to tell me that his extreme reluctance to allow Torquil to go out last night arose *not* from the fear that the boy would escape from the grounds, but from the fear that he would take cold, if he went from a hot room into the night air.''

''Well, I suppose that *is* possible,'' said Kate reasonably. ''People in England seem to dread the night air, and, if Torquil has a weakly constitution, no doubt the doctor is afraid a cold might turn to an inflammation of the lungs, or even a consumptive habit.''

''I should rather say that he has a remarkably strong constitution, to have survived all the illnesses which have attacked him.''

''Had he had a great many illnesses?''

''Oh, everything you can think of, including small-pox!''

''Small-pox! But he's not marked! He must have had it very slightly!''

''He did, but I don't advise you to say that to Minerva. She and Sidlaw nursed him, and she made what she said to be his critical condition her excuse for calling in Delabole—and putting an end to Dr Ogbourne's attendance on the family.''

''Oh, Philip, *Philip!*'' Kate protested. ''How can you say such things? If Torquil is prone to catch diseases, no wonder she keeps Dr Delabole at Staplewood! Sir Timothy, too! Oh, it is too unjust—I won't listen to you!'' She glanced at the clock on the mantelpiece, and jumped up. ''Good God, it is nearly eleven, and I said I would see the chef at half-past ten! He wishes to know what are my orders for the day! If I thought this meant anything more than casting an eye over his bill of fare, and approving it, I should develop a headache, and send a message that I was too unwell to see him.''

She went to the door, but he reached it ahead of her, and barred her passage, laying a detaining hand on her arms. ''Wait!'' he said. ''You think me unjust! But at least believe that what I have said to you doesn't spring from *prejudice!* If I could be proved to be mistaken, I would own to it *gladly*— not reluctantly!''

She smiled tremulously, and said simply: ''Of course you would. Let me go now! If I keep him waiting any longer, I shall wound Gaston's sensibilities, and find him once more bent on leaving Staplewood immediately!''

He released her, and opened the door. His countenance was set in stern lines, but there was a look of deep concern in his eyes. Seeing it, she was impelled to kiss her fingers and to lay them fleetingly on his cheek as she passed him. The sternness vanished; he even smiled; but the concern in his eyes remained.

Chapter Eighteen

By the time Kate had had a lengthy session with the chef, a lengthier one with the housekeeper, and had been forced to endure the slow garrulity of the head-gardener, it was past noon, and she was feeling very ready for a nuncheon. Few things, she ruefully decided, were more exhausting than being obliged to listen to what amounted to monologues, delivered in a rambling style, and almost wholly devoid of interest. The chef, not content with having his suggested bill of fare for dinner approved, laid several alternatives before her, and enthusiastically described his method of dressing various dishes, even going to the length of disclosing the particular herb he used to give its subtle flavour to a sauce of his own devising. Mrs Thorne, with equal enthusiasm, described, in revolting detail, the various ailments to which she was subject; and Risby, seeing her go into the rose-garden with a basket on her arm, joined her there, watching her proceedings with a jaundiced eye, and prefixing his subsequent remarks with the information that she shouldn't ought to cut flowers in the heat of the day. He then followed her round, discoursing in a very boring way on the proper care of gardens, with digressions into the different treatment demanded by what appeared, from his discourse, to be plants of extreme delicacy and sensibility. Escaping from him at last, Kate realized that she had been subjected to those floods of eloquence because Lady Broome never encouraged her servants to talk to her of anything beyond the sphere of their duties, not even Mrs Thorne, who had come to Staplewood from the Malvern household, and was slavishly devoted to her. They all stood in awe of her, the only one amongst them to whom she unbent being Sidlaw.

Pennymore met Kate, when she entered the house, with the intelligence that Mr Philip had taken Sir Timothy out in the tilbury. He was beaming with satisfaction, and when she said: "Oh, I'm glad! It will do Sir Timothy good!" he replied: "Yes, miss, it *will* do him good, as I said to Tenby, when he was misdoubting that it might be too much for his strength. 'What Sir Timothy *wants* to do,' I said, 'won't harm him!' Which he was bound to agree to, seeing that he knows as well as I do that Mr Philip will have an eye to him, and turn for home the instant he thinks Sir Timothy is growing tired. Wonderful, it is, the way he perks up when Mr Philip comes to stay! It seems to put new heart into him, as one might say. Now if you will give me your basket, I will myself put the roses into a jug of water, Miss Kate, until you have eaten a nuncheon. You will find it waiting for you in the Red saloon."

She also found Dr Delabole waiting for her. He was eating strawberries with evident relish, and he instantly recommended them to her, saying that they had been picked that morning, and were still warm from the sun. As the sun was streaming in through the window, this was hardly surprising, but he rattled on, extolling the superiority of strawberries plucked and eaten hot from their bed over those bought in London; and drawing her attention to the particular excellence of the strawberries grown at Staplewood. "I have never tasted better!" he said earnestly. "But everything grown at Staplewood is so good! Her ladyship's genius for providing food to delight the eye in her arrangement of the flower-gardens does not lead her to neglect the inner-man! She is a remarkable woman, as I am persuaded you must agree! Truly remarkable! *All* is done under her supervision! She even orders what vegetables are to be grown; and the fruit trees, you know, are of the choicest varieties!"

"How is my aunt today?" Kate asked, hesitating between a ham, and some cold beef.

"Not as stout as I could wish," he replied, "but better! decidedly better! As I foretold, nothing would do for her this morning but to leave her bed. And now she is determined to see you! Had she wished to see anyone else I must have withheld my permission, but *you,* I know, can be trusted not to chafe her nerves. I daresay you may think I am making a great fuss about nothing: *she* certainly thinks so! But the truth is—though she would rip me up for daring to say so!—that she is *not* quite herself yet! These stomach disorders are not to be trifled with. And her attack was a particularly violent one: indeed, at one moment I was really alarmed!"

It struck Kate that he was more uneasy than the occasion seemed to warrant, but before she could do more than assure him that she would try not to chafe her aunt's nerves Pennymore came in, carrying a covered dish, which he set down before her, saying that he had ventured to suggest to the chef that a baked egg might be welcome to her. "Which, miss, he was very glad to cook for you, knowing, as he does, that you never partake of anything at breakfast but a scone, and a cup of tea."

"Why, how kind of you both!" said Kate. "Pray tell Gaston that it is precisely what I was wishing for!"

"And precisely what I should have recommended, had I been applied to!" said the doctor, in a hearty tone. "But we can always rely on our good Pennymore!"

Pennymore was so much revolted by this playful remark that he became suddenly afflicted by deafness, and left the room without betraying by so much as the flicker of an eyelid that he had heard it.

Undismayed, the doctor said archly: "You are to be congratulated, Miss Kate! You have made yourself beloved of us all, from Sir Timothy down to the kitchen-maids! One would say you had been managing large households all your life!"

"I afraid you are offering me Spanish coin, sir," she replied coolly. "I have never met the kitchen-maids, and have had very little to do with managing the house." She saw that he was about to utter another of his fulsome compliments, and said, before he could do so: "How does Torquil go on today? I am sorry he should be laid up again."

"Oh, it was nothing more than a touch of the sun, and becoming overtired! He was a little feverish last night, to be sure, but he is a great deal better today, and will come down to dinner, I hope. I could have wished that Mr Philip Broome had not come out on to the terrace yesterday— and that *you*, Miss Kate, had not called to him to take your place at quoit-throwing! Not that I blame you! You cannot be expected to understand the effect Mr Broome's visits have upon Torquil! It is sad that it should be so, but Torquil is never so well when his cousin is at Staplewood." He sighed, shaking his head. "He is so excitable, and so anxious to vie with Mr Broome! It is very natural, and very natural that Mr Broome should encourage him. Most good-natured of him indeed! But he does not appreciate how necessary it is that Torquil should not be allowed to exert himself beyond his strength. It would be wonderful if he did! Young men of vigorous constitution seldom realize how easily such frail boys as Torquil can be knocked-up.''

She returned no answer to this, and, after a moment, he said, with a little laugh: ''And now I learn that he has taken Sir Timothy out in the tilbury! No doubt with the kindest of intentions, but imprudent—very imprudent! I wish I may not have Sir Timothy on my hands, as well as her ladyship!''

Kate had meant to have preserved a strict silence, but this was too much for her resolution. She raised her eyes from her plate, and stared at the doctor, saying, with an air of astonishment: ''But surely, sir, I have heard you trying to persuade Sir Timothy to go out for drives?''

''Ah, yes, but in the barouche, not in a tilbury! It is an effort for an old man to climb up into any of these sporting carriages, you know.''

She rose, pushing back her chair, and said: ''I expect he had as much assistance as was needed. Excuse me, if you please! I have been cutting fresh roses for my aunt's room, and must now go to arrange them in a bowl. Do you permit me to take them to her myself, or is she, perhaps, resting?''

''Oh, certainly, certainly!'' he said, hurrying to open the door for her.

She went out, and, some twenty minutes later, mounted the Grand Stairway, carefully carrying the glass bowl in which she had arranged a dozen half-opened roses. At the head of the stairs she encountered Sidlaw, who had been lying in wait for her in the upper hall. She said pleasantly: ''Is her ladyship ready to receive visitors? Dr Delabole tells me that at last it is safe for me to see her. I am so glad she is better.''

Sidlaw's sniff expressed her opinion of the doctor. She said grudgingly: "She is *in a way* to be better, miss, but further than that I will not go. I thought I would drop a word of warning in your ear, which is why I've taken the liberty of intercepting you."

"No need," Kate said lightly. "The doctor has already warned me not to chafe her nerves."

"Him!" Sidlaw ejaculated. Her face worked; she spoke with suppressed passion, twisting her bony fingers together. "*He* doesn't know—nobody knows except me! It was worry that wore her down, till she was in a state to take any infection. She's never given way, never once let a living soul suspect what a struggle it has been to her to support her spirits. She's had nothing but trouble—she that I thought to see become a leader of fashion! Such style as she had! Everything prime about her! And so beautiful!"

"She is still very handsome," offered Kate, hoping to check the flow of this unaccustomed eloquence.

But Sidlaw was obviously suffering from pent-up emotion, and she swept on, unheeding. "She ought to have married a nobleman—one of those who were the sprigs of fashion, twenty years ago! There was several dangling after her, for she was very much admired, I promise you! She was born to be a duchess, as over and over again I told her! And what must she do but throw herself away on Sir Timothy, a man old enough to have been her father!" She gave a gasp, and made an effort to control herself. Darting a rancorous look at Kate, she said: "I shouldn't have said so much. I'm sure I don't know what came over me, miss."

"I don't regard it," Kate replied. "I know how anxious you have been since my aunt took ill, and how devotedly you've nursed her. You're tired—overwatched! Will you take these fresh roses in to her, and see if I may go in? I don't wish to disturb her if she's sleeping."

"Sleeping!" Sidlaw said scornfully. "It's little enough sleep she's had for weeks past!" She took the bowl from Kate, muttering that it was to be hoped Kate would do more for her aunt than cut roses, and walked off down the gallery to Lady Broome's bedroom.

She reappeared a minute later, carrying a vase of wilted flowers, and told Kate, ungraciously, that she might go in to sit with my lady. "And you'll please to remember, miss, that she's in a poor state!"

"I'll remember," promised Kate.

Sidlaw dumped the vase down, and went before her to open Lady Broome's door. "Miss Kate, my lady!"

"Come in, Kate!" said Lady Broome. "That will do, Sidlaw!... Dear child, come and sit down where I can see you!"

She held out her hands, and, when Kate took them in hers, pulled her down to kiss her cheek.

She was reclining on a Carolinian day-bed, drawn across the foot of the great four-poster, and wearing one of her elegant dressing-gowns. At first glance, Kate did not think that she looked ill, but when she studied her more closely she saw that the lines on her face were accentuated, and her eyes rather strained. She said, with a smile, and a gesture towards the fresh roses, which had been placed on a small table beside her: "There has been no need for Sidlaw to tell me who has kept my room supplied with flowers every day! Thank you, my love! Such a refreshment, their scent! So tastefully arranged too!"

"I think roses arrange themselves," said Kate, sitting down on the low chair by the day-bed. "Are you feeling better, ma'am? After such a violent catching, I expect you are sadly pulled."

"A little," Lady Broome acknowledged. "It is a judgment on me for boasting that I am never ill! I am keeping my room today, but I shall leave it tomorrow. What a shockingly bad chaperon I've been to have left you alone! I am afraid it must have been awkward for you, my poor child."

Kate stared at her in patent surprise. "Good God, ma'am, how should it have been?"

"One young female in a household composed of gentlemen? Fie on you!" said Lady Broome playfully.

"But one of the gentlemen was Sir Timothy," Kate reminded her.

Lady Broome laughed. "To be sure! I wish he may have known that he was a deputy-chaperon, but I doubt it! One would have supposed that Philip would have seen the propriety of removing himself when his hostess was taken ill—though why I should have supposed it I don't know! He has never yet shown the smallest consideration for anyone but himself. When does he mean to take himself off? Has he said anything about it?"

"Not to my knowledge, ma'am." Kate rose as she spoke, and went to draw one of the heavy brocade curtains a little way across the window. She looked over her shoulder, and asked: "Is that better, ma'am?"

"Dear Kate!" sighed her ladyship. "Always so thoughtful, so quick to perceive a need! The sun *was* dazzling me a trifle. Do you know, ever since you came to Staplewood, you have made me forget that I have no daughter? You are so exactly what I should have wished my daughter to be like! Indeed, I find myself thinking that you *are* my daughter—and so, I know well, does Sir Timothy! You have even been managing all the household affairs, *to the manner born*, Delabole tells me!"

Considerably embarrassed, Kate stammered: "There has

been very little to manage, ma'am! I only wish there had been more! I am conscious—deeply conscious!—of—of how much I owe to your kindness!''

"Yet you will not do the only thing I have ever asked of you!" said Lady Broome, with a melancholy smile.

Kate had been about to return to her chair, but at these words she checked, and stiffened. She said, in a constrained voice: "If you mean, ma'am, as I believe you do, that I won't marry Torquil, I beg you will say no more! It is too much to ask of me!"

"Is it? I told you to think it over, Kate, but I'm afraid you haven't done so. You have only perceived the evils of such a marriage: not its advantages. Believe me, these are very real! You are no longer a girl, dreaming of romance: you must surely be considering your future, for you don't want for sense. Sit down!"

"Aunt Minerva, *pray* say no more!" Kate begged.

"Don't argue with me, girl!" Lady Broome said, with a flash of temper. "Sit down!" She controlled herself with a visible effort, and forced up a smile. "Come! I have something to tell you—something I have never told anyone, not even Delabole!" She waited until Kate had reluctantly resumed her seat, and then held out a coaxing hand. "Don't hold off from me!" she said caressingly. "That would quite break my heart, for I have come to love you dearly, you know." Her fingers closed round Kate's hand, and held it. "There! That's better! You are the only comfort left to me, child—the only hope! Do you think me a happy woman? I'm not. Life has used me harshly, I think: everything I most wanted has been denied me! I wonder what sins I can have committed to have made fate punish me so cruelly?"

"Oh, don't say so, dear ma'am!" Kate interrupted. "You are not yourself! This is nothing but a sick fancy!"

Lady Broome sighed, and shook her head. "No, alas, it is the truth. I have put a brave face on it, but I've failed in everything I set out to do. I hope you will never know how bitter a thing that is."

"Now, how can I tell you civilly that you are talking nonsense?" said Kate, in a rallying tone. "If the effect of my visit is to cast you into dejection I shall be in hot water with Dr Delabole, and Sidlaw too, and very likely I shall be forbidden to come near you again! Tell me, if you please, if you failed when you set out to make Staplewood beautiful!"

"Ah, you don't understand!" said Lady Broome. "I only did so because I realized, when I was obliged to give up all that I most enjoyed, that unless I could discover *something* of interest to keep me occupied I should mope myself to death. You must remember that I was still a young woman when I knew that I must bring Sir Timothy here, not for a visit merely, but for the rest of his life. That was a severe blow. I have grown accustomed, but in those days I detested the country. Your father told you how ambitious I was, but I don't think he knew that my most passionate ambition was not to marry a Duke, but to escape from the intolerable boredom of my home! My father—your grandfather, my love—was not of a sociable disposition. In fact, he was excessively untoward, and he had my unfortunate mother quite under his thumb. Had it not been for his sister, I should have found myself buckled to the Squire's son before I had been allowed even a glimpse of London! She, however, offered to bring me out, and to frank me for one Season. She was married to a man of birth and property, and moved in the first circles. She had married her daughters to men of fortune and consideration, and said she would do the same by me. But she reckoned without my lack of dowry."

Kate blinked. "But surely, ma'am—! I mean, when my grandfather cut Papa out of his Will, you must have been heiress to all his property!"

"I was, but he was never wealthy, and he suffered some bad reverses on 'Change. I was used to think him a shocking pinch-penny, until my mother explained matters to me. Well, that's past history: I've told you only that you may understand why I married Sir Timothy. I had many admirers, but the only offers I received were from men I could not like well enough to marry. My aunt said I was a great deal too nice, and I knew she wouldn't invite me to spend a second Season in Mount Street: indeed, she told me that if I threw away my chances she would wash her hands of me. And I knew that if I went back to my home at the end of the Season I should never see London again. I can tell you, I was in such despair that I could almost have brought myself to marry *any* man who could give me position, and the means to live up to it! But then Sir Timothy proposed to me, and I became engaged to him." She saw that this story was winning no response, and pressed Kate's hand, saying with a faint smile: "Ah, you are thinking that I was very mercenary, are you not? I wish you had known Sir Timothy twenty years ago: one of the most charming men imaginable! So handsome, too! He fell in love with me as soon as he saw me. It was at the Opera. He came up to my aunt's box, and begged for an introduction."

"And you, ma'am? Did you fall in love with him?"

"No, no! I liked him very well, but I had no notion then that he would one day propose to me. He is twenty years older than I am, you know, and in those days that seemed very old indeed to me. I respected him, however, and gladly accepted his offer. My aunt told me that it was indelicate of me to show joy at my engagement, but Sir

Timothy didn't think so: it made him very happy, for he was afraid that he might be too old to make *me* happy. The Broomes said he was *infatuated*. His sister Maria— an odious woman!—told him that he would soon become a cuckold if he married a girl young enough to have been his daughter. So vulgar! I have always been glad that she didn't die until she had been forced to acknowledge that she had wickedly misjudged me. But they all disliked me, and Philip, of course, positively hated me! He was the most disagreeable boy: as self-important then as he is to-day! But we were married in spite of them, and I became most sincerely attached to Sir Timothy. He wanted an heir, and when Torquil was born he thought nothing too good for me. His first wife had not cared for London, so the Broome town-house had been disposed of, but because I loved London he bought a house in Berkeley Square for me. Oh, how happy I was—for just three years! London, for the Season; then Brighton, then back to London again, for a few weeks; then visits to our particular friends—large house-parties, you understand! Theatricals were all the rage: I recall going to the Priory, at Stanmore, when Lady Cahir took the chief part in *Who's the Dupe,* a most diverting farce, and very well played. Then we had parties here, always during the hunting-season. I once held one over Christmas: *that* was a triumph indeed! And—''

"But where was Torquil?" Kate interrupted. "Did you take him with you?"

"Good God, no! I did keep him in London for a time, but it did not agree with him: he was always ailing, and Sir Timothy became so nervous that he would lose him— the children of his first marriage all died, as I daresay you've been told—that I sent him here, with his nurse.''

"I wonder you could bear to part with him!" Kate said, before she could stop herself.

"My dear child, I make no secret of the fact that I am not one of those women who dote on infants! To own the truth, I find them repulsive! They are for ever screaming, or dribbling, or being sick! Besides, his nurse managed him far better than I could—even had I not been much too busy to make the attempt. To be a successful hostess takes up one's time and energy, I promise you. And I was successful. And then it ended."

She stopped, leaving Kate at a loss for something sympathetic to say. Having no social ambition herself, and with the unfading memory of her mother, who could never bear to be parted from either her husband or her child, it was difficult for her to appreciate what her enforced abandonment of a life of high fashion had meant to her aunt. That it had meant a great deal to her was patent in her face. Lady Broome was looking into the past with fixed, embittered eyes, and her mouth set rigidly. In desperation, Kate faltered: "It must have been very hard for you, ma'am."

Her words recalled Lady Broome from her abstraction. She brought her eyes around to Kate's face, and said "Hard...!" A contemptuous little laugh shook her. "No, you don't understand, do you?"

"You see, I don't think I should enjoy the sort of life you've described," Kate excused herself. "So I can't enter into your feelings. But I do understand that—that coming here to live—giving up all that you liked so much—must have been a sacrifice."

"No one has ever known what it cost me, not even Sidlaw! Whatever my faults, I've never been one of those women who weep and whine, and fall into lethargies, throwing everyone into gloom with their die-away airs! And no one—not even Maria!—could accuse me of failing in my duty to my sick husband! I sold the town-house; I took on my shoulders all the business which Sir Timothy was too enfeebled to attend to; and devoted myself to Staplewood, knowing how much he loved it! I hadn't cared, until then, to acquaint myself with its history, but to please him I began to study the Broome records, and to bring them into order. I had supposed that it would be a drudgery, but I became fascinated. I believe I know more about the Broomes than Sir Timothy does—and I sometimes think I care more! But there was one thing he cared for, and had never disclosed to me. It wasn't until I found the genealogical tree—at the bottom of a chest, full of old letters, and accounts, and forgotten deeds!—that I realized that for two hundreds years Staplewood, and the title, had descended from father to son in unbroken sequence. How many families can boast of that? I understood then why Sir Timothy was so anxious every time Torquil contracted some childish ailment, and I became determined—*determined!*—that it should be no fault of mine if he descended, like the children of Sir Timothy's first marriage, into an early grave.''

Kate, who had listened to this speech in gathering dismay, began to feel sick, but clutched at the straw offered by the rapt, almost fanatical, light that shone in Lady Broome's eyes, and the little triumphant smile which curled her lips. The doctor, she thought, had been right when he had warned her that her aunt was by no means restored to health: she was obviously feverish. She said: ''Well, he hasn't done so, has he? So that is another object you haven't failed to achieve! Dear aunt, you have let yourself be blue-devilled by nothing more than the dejection which—so I am told!—is the aftermath of a fever! I think I should leave you now: Dr Delabole warned me that you are not as well as you think, and I see that he was right! The thoughts are tangled in your head: what a shocking thing it would be if I believed some of the things you've said! I don't, of course: I haven't much experience of illness, but I do know that people who are recovering from a severe bout of fever are not to be held accountable for anything they may say when they are feeling low, and oppressed.''

She would have risen, as she spoke, but Lady Broome startled her by jerking herself upright on the day-bed, and saying, in a voice of barely repressed exasperation: "Oh, don't talk as if you were the ninnyhammer I know you're not! Sit still!'' She cast aside the light shawl which covered her legs, and got up, and began to pace the room with a nervous energy that seriously alarmed Kate. After a pause, during which she managed to bring her sudden spurt of temper under control, she said, with what Kate felt to be determined calm: "I had not meant to come to a point with you so soon, but what happened on the day that I was taken ill has forced it on me. Kate, if you feel that you owe me anything—if you feel a particle of affection for me!—marry Torquil, before it becomes known all over the county that he's insane! Staplewood must—*shall!*—have an heir in the direct line!'' Her eyes, unnaturally burning, perceived the sudden blanching of Kate's countenance, her widening stare of horror. Misreading these signs, she exclaimed: "What, have you lived at Staplewood for so many weeks and remained blind to the truth? You're not a green girl! You're not a fool! Don't tell me you have never suspected that Torquil is mad!''

Deathly pale, Kate flinched, and threw up a hand, as though to ward off a blow. She said numbly: "I thought— oh, I was *certain!*—that you didn't know!''

"*I?*" said Lady Broome incredulously. "Good God, Kate, why do you suppose that I brought Delabole to live here? Why have I kept Torquil in the old nursery wing? Why have I never allowed him to go beyond the gates without his groom, or to consort with any of the boys and girls of his own age? Why do you imagine that Badger was at hand when he tried to shoot you?''

Kate shook her bowed head, and uttered, almost inaudibly: ''He didn't try to shoot me. It was the dog. Torquil gave the gun to me as soon as I told him to.''

This seemed to give Lady Broome pause. The angry lights died out of her eyes; she said, after a moment's cold consideration: ''If you say so, I believe it. It proves how right I was when I judged you to be a suitable wife for him. I have observed you closely, and I've seen how good your influence has been. He likes you, and you've made him respect you: it may be that marriage might arrest the progress of his insanity; it may even be that you are the cause—oh, quite unwittingly!—of its increase during the past weeks. Delabole is of the opinion that his—how shall I put it?—his *manhood,* first roused by the Templecombe child's empty prettiness, grew stronger when I brought you to live at Staplewood, and has excited his brain. You've held him at a distance, and he has found relief in—committing certain acts of violence.''

Kate looked up quickly, an appalled question in her eyes. Lady Broome smiled with a sort of indulgent contempt. ''Oh, yes!'' she said, faintly amused. ''I know about the rabbit you found. I know everything that Torquil does. I have known for years—ever since I first realized that there was more to his fits of ungovernable rage than mere childish naughtiness. What I suffered—the despair!—the chagrin—when the knowledge was forced on me that the taint had reappeared in my son—my only son!—I can't describe to you! He inherited his sickly constitution from Sir Timothy, but his madness came to him through me! Oh, don't look so alarmed! it didn't come through the Malverns, but through my mother! One of her great-uncles had to be confined: it was kept so secret that very few people knew about it, and it didn't appear either in my grandfather's or my father's generation. Or in mine! I had never dreamed that it would visit my son! It was only when Torquil's nurse spoke to me—told me that she was puzzled by him—that I began to suspect the truth. I dismissed her at the earliest opportunity that offered, as you may suppose! I said that he was too old for a nurse, and appointed Badger to attend to him. He had previously been employed to wait on my predecessor's nursery, and had been dreading dismissal from the moment Sir Timothy married me. Fortunately, as it chanced, Sir Timothy's rather exaggerated notions of his obligations to his dependants made him insist on Badger's continuing at Staplewood; and, still more fortunately, Badger became deeply attached to Torquil. I daresay he was sincere, since Torquil, when he grew out of infancy, was an amazingly pretty little boy, you know! Of course, I've been obliged to pay both him and Whalley to keep their lips buttoned, but I never grudge the price of faithful service. Delabole, too! I knew *he* could be bought! I sent for him when Torquil had the small-pox. Dr Ogbourne had previously attended the family, but I knew that he was beginning to be suspicious, and I seized that chance to be rid of him. I hoped, at that time, that I might be mistaken, and that Torquil's disturbing fits of violence did indeed arise from ill-health, but as time went on I knew that his brain was sick, as well as his body. That was the most crushing blow of all I had suffered. I felt at first, that my one remaining ambition had been shattered. But I don't readily despair, and I thought that if he survived, if I could keep him quietly at Staplewood, guard against any excitement, never let him go beyond the gates alone, and, above all, establish my mastery of him, his malady might be cured, or, at the worst, remain in abeyance. I saw that it would be necessary to maintain a constant watch over him, for although there were periods—sometimes lasting for weeks—when he was perfectly docile, one never knew when something would upset him, and bring on one of his attacks of mania. I soon learned, however, that these almost always occurred at the time of the full moon: they still do, but there have lately been signs that this can no longer be depended on. And it is becoming increasingly difficult to control him. *I* can do so, and perhaps you can; but the day is coming when it will be necessary to confine him more closely. It will be too late then to give him a wife, and all my care, all the sacrifices I have made, all the stratagems I've been forced to employ to hide his lunacy from everyone but those few I can trust, will have been wasted! That, Kate, *is* why I depend on you to fulfil the only hope I have left!''

Kate had sunk her head in her hands, and she did not raise it. She said, in a voice of suppressed anguish: ''But what of him? What of him, ma'am? Haven't you *one* thought to spare for him?''

Lady Broome frowned down at her in utter incomprehension. ''I don't understand you,'' she said coldly. ''I must, surely, have told you enough to make you realize that he is never out of my thoughts? I have watched over him, nursed him through all his illnesses, supplied his every want, cosseted him, borne with his odd humours—and you can ask me that! Do you think it has been an easy task? Let me tell you that it is so long since I enjoyed peace of mind that I have forgotten what it was like to go care-free to bed, and to wake in the morning without feeling that there was a heavy cloud hanging over me! My greatest anxiety now is that I may not be able for much longer to hide the truth about him. It was easy enough when he was a child, but he has grown too strong for

Badger to overpower. Delabole can do it, but Torquil has become very cunning, and has several times given them both the slip. Neither of them can control him as I can, with no more than a word! When I set out to master him it was with the future in mind: it was imperative that he should stand in awe of me, acquire the habit of obeying me. Childhood's habits are not easy to shake off, you know. If I could have induced Delabole to be sterner—but he has always been too easy-going, and Badger, of course, merely dotes on Torquil. He's not afraid of either of them: indeed, he holds them in contempt!''

Kate said faintly: ''Does Sir Timothy know the truth?''

''Good God, no!'' Lady Broome exclaimed. ''I've kept them apart as much as I could, so that he shouldn't guess. I think the shock would kill him! No one knows, except Sidlaw. It was a fortunate circumstance that until about three years ago Torquil was hardly ever out of flannel. He caused me many anxious moments, but Sir Timothy got into the way of thinking of him as invalidish. So did everyone else, and so they might well! What I went through with him—! I can't remember any epidemic that passed him by—he even had typhus, and but for me would have died of it! As for the number of times he was laid up with a putrid sore throat, or a heavy cold in the head, to say nothing of his sick headaches, they are past counting! I think only one person is suspicious, and that, I need hardly say, is Sir Timothy's dear nephew. But he can't *know* that Torquil isn't sane, and although I don't doubt he would be happy to make mischief I do him the justice to believe that he wouldn't run the risk of causing his uncle to suffer what might well be a fatal heart-attack unless there was an end to be served. But there is none! While Torquil lives, sane or mad, Philip cannot become Broome of Staplewood. And

if Torquil were to father a son Philip would never succeed
Sir Timothy!"

It was several moments before Kate could trust herself
to speak. Hot words rose in her throat, but she choked them
back. Digging her nails into the palms of her hands, she
at last said, with no more than a tremor of indignation
shaking her voice: "So it was to entrap me into marrying
Torquil, whom you knew to be insane, that you invited me
to come to Staplewood! And I thought it was so kind of
you, ma'am!"

Lady Broome lifted her eyebrows quizzically. "Well,
and have I not been kind to you, Kate? Over and over
again you've said that you wished there was something
you could do to repay me, but when I tell you the only
thing I want from you, you give back. I hadn't thought
you would offer me nothing but lip-service. As for entrap-
ping you—what moonshine! Pray, how did I do so? I had
no power to *force* you to come to Staplewood, and I have
no power to keep you here. You are free to go whenever
you wish."

Kate got up. "I will go tomorrow, ma'am," she said
quietly.

Lady Broome smiled. "Certainly—if you have the
money to pay the coach-fare! Or do you expect me to frank
you?"

"No, ma'am."

"No? I hope you don't mean to sell the pearls I gave
you!"

Kate instantly unclasped the necklet, and held it out.
"Please to take it, ma'am!"

Lady Broome laughed indulgently, and went to sit down
again on the day-bed. She patted it invitingly, and said:
"Come, dear child! I was only making game of you! If
you still wish to go back to London when you've heard

what I have to say to you, I'll send you in my own chaise—only not, I think, tomorrow. Such a sudden departure would present a very odd appearance, and give rise to the sort of gossip neither you nor I should like. What, can't you bring yourself to sit down beside me?''

''I think it is time I left you, ma'am. Pray don't say any more! It is quite useless to try to persuade me to do what you wish. Indeed, it is worse than useless, for I might be led into saying what would be grossly uncivil, and that I am determined not to do.''

''Well, if you choose to stand—!'' said Lady Broome, shrugging her shoulders. ''I am not going to try to persuade you; I am merely going to ask you to look at two pictures. The first is what your life will be if you go back to London. You may find another situation—though you weren't being very successful when I came to offer you a home, were you? What can you earn, as a governess fit only to teach young children the alphabet? Twenty pounds a year? You won't be able to save much out of that paltry wage to provide for your old age. And when the children grow old enough to be taught accomplishments you will be dismissed, and it will be all to do again—with the little money in your purse dwindling until you are ready to scrub doorsteps only to earn a few shillings to pay your landlady. Do you hope for marriage? Believe me, my dear, men may make up to you, while you keep your looks, but even a tradesman thinks twice before he offers for a penniless woman no longer in the first blush of youth. Yes, it's an ugly picture, isn't it?''

''Very ugly, ma'am.''

''Now contrast it with my second picture!'' invited her aunt. ''It is what life would be like if you married Torquil. You would be rich enough to be able to indulge your whims; you would become, in due course, Lady Broome—"

"Unless Torquil murdered me in one of his rages!"

"I have no fear of that. I should not permit him to be alone with you during the periods when he is liable to take leave of his senses. At all other times he is perfectly tractable. It may well be that if you make him happy he will grow calmer. If not, and he has to be confined, you will be free to amuse yourself as you please. You won't find me a strict mother-in- law! I shall present you at the outset, of course—"

"And will you present Torquil too, ma'am? Wouldn't it be rather too exciting for him?" Kate interrupted sweetly.

"Much too exciting," replied Lady Broome. "Torquil will be kept at home by a sudden indisposition. In any event, it would not be for me to present him, but for his father to take him to a levée. While it is safe for him to remain at large, you would have to content yourself with no more than brief visits to London with a female companion: that can easily be arranged. If he gets beyond control either the West Wing can be made secure, or—and this is something I have had in mind for some time—it might be preferable to acquire a house in one of the quieter watering-places, and send him there, in Delabole's charge. Delabole will know how to set about hiring suitable attendants: men who have had experience of looking after mad persons."

"Oh, stop, ma'am! For God's sake, stop!" begged Kate, pressing her hands over her ears. "You are talking about your *son!*"

"My dear child, do you imagine that I mean to send him to Bedlam? He will be perfectly kindly treated, and no money will be spared to make him comfortable. As for you, once you have given Staplewood an heir—why, provided you are discreet, which I don't doubt you would be, I shall turn a blind eye on any little *affaires* which you may have!''

Feeling that if she did not escape she would become hysterical, Kate went hurriedly to the door. Her aunt's voice followed her. ''Think carefully before you give me an answer!'' she said.

Chapter Nineteen

Kate left the room feeling stunned. Listening to the incredible things her aunt had said, a ghastly suspicion had crossed her mind that Lady Broome was as mad as her son, but although Lady Broome's eyes had flashed once or twice in anger there had been no such glitter in them as Kate had learnt to recognize in Torquil's eyes; and when she had spoken of Torquil's childhood, and of her fantastic scheme for his future, she had done so without a trace of feeling. Only when she described her own emotions had she shown any feeling: she had not uttered a word of pity for her unhappy son; it had not seemed to occur to her that it was far more his tragedy than hers. To Kate, this, if not madness, was an egoism so monstrous as to be unbelievable.

She caught her breath on a dry sob, and went rather blindly along the gallery to her own room. But just as she opened her door she was arrested by Mr Philip Broome's voice, reaching her from the Great Hall. It was unusually sharp; he demanded imperatively: "What the devil has been happening?"

"Well, sir, that's more than I can tell you," replied a voice Kate knew well. "All I know is that this young gentleman seems to have come to grief, jumping over the wall alongside your lodge-gates, but there was no making sense out of what any of the folks dithering round him tried to tell me, for they were all too scared to do more than say that the young gentleman had broken his neck. Which he hasn't, nor anything else, so far as I can discover. He just stunned himself. So I had them lift him into the chaise and I brought him up to the house."

"*Sarah!*" Kate shrieked, racing to the head of the stairs, and almost tumbling down them in her haste. "Oh, Sarah! Oh, Sarah!"

She flung herself into Mrs Nidd's arms, her overwrought nerves finding relief in a burst of hysterical sobs. Mrs Nidd gave her a hearty kiss, but spoke bracing words. "Now, that's quite enough, Miss Kate! There's no need for you to fall into the vapours just because I've come to see you. You should know better than to create such a humdurgeon!"

"Take me away, Sarah! Oh, take me away!" Kate gasped imploringly.

"Yes, lovey, but all in good time. You sit down there, like a good girl, or I shall have to be cross with you!"

She thrust Kate into a chair, and turned back to the group gathered about the settle, on which Torquil's inanimate form had been laid. One of the footmen was standing with a bottle of smelling-salts in his hand, and looking singularly helpless; Pennymore was anxiously watching Mr Philip Broome; and Philip himself was on one knee beside the settle, feeling Torquil's pulse. "Here, you silly creature!" said Sarah, addressing herself to the footman, and wresting the smelling-bottle away from him. "What do you think I gave you that for?" She pushed him aside, and began to wave the salts under Torquil's nose. "Nothing broken, is there, sir?"

"I don't think so," Philip answered curtly. "His doctor

will know. Pennymore, have you sent to fetch Dr Delabole?''

''Yes, sir: James has gone to find him. Mr Philip, it would be as well to move him out of the hall: we don't want to disturb Sir Timothy!''

''He's out of earshot: I left him in his bedroom, going to rest before dinner.'' He glanced up at Sarah. ''The pulse is quite strong: he'll do! You are Mrs Nidd, aren't you?''

''Yes, sir, I am. Ah, he's coming round! That makes the second time, and it's to be hoped he don't swoon off again, like he did before. Nothing would do for him but to get on his feet, and it's my belief he was just giddy, and shook up, whatever the lodge-keeper may say to the contrary! Not that I paid the least heed to him, for a bigger jolterhead I never did see!— *That's* better, sir! You take it easy over the stones, and you'll soon be as right as a trivet!''

Torquil who had opened his eyes, lay blinking hazily for a few moments, but his clouded gaze gradually cleared, and he said thickly: ''Oh, it's you, Philip! I took a toss.''

''So I've been informed,'' responded his cousin unemotionally. ''Keep still!''

''Oh, to hell with you!'' Torquil said angrily, struggling up. ''I'm in a capital way! Did you think I'd broken my neck? Diddled again, coz!'' He pushed Philip roughly aside, and swung his feet to the floor, and looked round the hall. He stared blankly at Sarah, and demanded: ''Who the devil are you?''

''I'm Miss Kate's nurse, Master Torquil, and that's no way for a young gentleman to talk!'' replied Sarah, apparently regarding him as one of her nurslings.

''Oh!'' said Torquil doubtfully. A sudden smile swept over his face. ''*I* know! You are *Sarah!*'' he said ingenuously. ''Kate's Sarah! But how the devil—no, how the *deuce!*—do you come to be here?''

''There's no need for you to worrit yourself over that,

sir. I came to Market Harborough on the night-coach, and hired a chaise to drive me here—and just as well for you I did!'' Sarah said severely. ''Now you stay quiet, like a good boy, till the doctor comes!''

''I don't want him!'' Torquil declared, his smile vanishing. ''Prosy bag-pudding!'' His eyes travelled to his cousin's face, and gleamed defiance. ''*This* will teach them not to keep the gates shut when I tell them to open them!''

''Is there any hope that it may teach you not to overface your horses?'' asked Philip. He added softly, with a smile that took the sting out of his words: ''Top-lofty young cawker!''

''Oh, damn you, Philip, I'm *not!*'' protested Torquil. ''You know I'm not! The clumsy brute must have jumped off his fore! Serve him right if he broke his legs! I hope he did: he's a commoner! Oh, my God, *no!*''

This venomous ejaculation was provoked by the sight of Dr Delabole, descending the wide stairway with unusual haste. The doctor said, with fond joviality, as he crossed the hall. ''Ah, there was no need for me to be alarmed, I see! I haven't been summoned to attend a corpse! My dear boy, how came you to do anything so imprudent? I thought you were sleeping, when I myself retired to seek repose!''

''Tipped you the double didn't I, Matthew?'' mocked Torquil unpleasantly.

''You did indeed!'' acknowledged the doctor, with unabated amiability. ''And very naughty of you it was! However, I shan't scold you! I fancy you punished yourself!'' He was flexing one of Torquil's legs as he spoke and said laughingly, as he frustrated an attempt to kick him off his balance: ''Well, that's not broken, at all events! Let me see if you are able to stand on your feet!— Capital! Unless you have fractured a rib or two, which I can't tell until I have you stripped, there's nothing amiss with you but a

shaking, and a few bruises. I shall ask our good James to
carry you up to your room—''

''The devil fly away with you!'' interrupted Torquil,
taking instant umbrage. ''I'm damned if I'll be carried!
Here, James, give me your arm up the stairs!'' His eyes
alighted on Kate, who had recovered her composure but
was still sitting, rather limply, on a very uncomfortable
chair placed with its high carved back against the wall.
''Lord, coz, are you here?'' he said. ''I didn't see you!
You're looking as blue as megrim! Did you think I was
dead? No such thing! I'm as right as a ram's horn!''

She straightened her sagging shoulders, and got up.
''Well, I'm glad of that, even if you don't deserve to be!''
she said.

At this inopportune moment, a hot and agitated groom
burst unceremoniously into the house, pulled up short as
soon as he saw Torquil, and uttered devoutly: ''Thank
Gawd!''

''Oh, it's you, is it?'' said Torquil, his wrath springing
up. He shook James off, and advanced, rather shakily, towards the groom. ''You insolent hound, how dared you
get in my way?''

He found his passage barred by his cousin, and glared
up at him, his chest heaving. Philip said sternly: ''Go upstairs, Torquil! I'll deal with Scholes.'' He paused, watching Torquil's long fingers curl, like a hawk's talons, and
dropped his hand on the boy's shoulder, giving him a
friendly shake. ''Go on, you gudgeon! Making a show of
yourself!''

Torquil's angry eyes held his for a dangerous moment;
then they sank, and he muttered something inaudible, before flinging round on his heel. He staggered, and would
have fallen but for Delabole, who caught him as he
lurched, and signed to James to carry him up the stairs.
Philip turned towards Pennymore, saying calmly: ''Well,

there doesn't seem to be much wrong! I fancy the only damage he suffered is to his pride, which is why he's in such a pelter. You needn't wait: the doctor will know what to do for him. Or you, William! Scholes, I want a word with you: don't go!'' He held out his hand to Sarah, saying, with a smile: ''My uncle having retired to rest, Lady Broome being laid up with influenza, and my young cousin being as graceless as he is foolhardy, it's left to me to welcome you, Mrs Nidd! Which, believe me, I do! But ought you to have left your excellent father-in-law to the mercies of Old Tom's Rib?''

''Oh, I never did!'' said Sarah, dropping an instinctive curtsy. ''If it isn't like Father to spread it about that I deserted him! I'll have you know it was his own daughter I went to, sir, and for all he's a grumble-gizzard he wouldn't have had me do other!'' She perceived that Philip's hand was still outstretched, and blushed, saying in a flustered way, as she put her own hand into it: ''Well, I'm sure, sir—!''

''I'm glad you've come,'' he said. ''Kate—er, Miss Malvern!—has been longing to see you. What *did* happen this afternoon?''

''It's just as I told you, sir: I was coming out here in a chaise, when all of a sudden the postboy had to pull up, because there was half-a-dozen people in the way, *in*cluding a silly widgeon with a baby, who kept on screaming that the horse had come down on top of her, which, of course, it hadn't. You don't have to worry about her, sir, because I gave her a good scold, and told her to be off home. Well, as soon as Mr Torquil came round, I had him lifted into the chaise, for I've never had a bit of patience with people who can't think of anything better to do in a situation like that than to stand about gabbing, and wringing their hands, and I never will have! So then the lodge-keeper opened the gates, and we drove up to the house.

That's when this young fellow—'' she nodded at the groom—''came galloping up. But there was nothing for him to do for Mr Torquil, so I told him to see what he could do for the horse. It looked to me as if he'd broken one of his forelegs. Had he?''

Scholes, his stricken gaze imploring Mr Philip Broome's clemency, said miserably: ''It's true, Mr Philip, but as God's my judge it ain't my fault! Nor it ain't Fleet's fault neither, though he says if he'd have known what Mr Torquil was going to do he'd have opened the gates, no matter what her ladyship's orders was! If Whalley had of been there, it wouldn't have happened, but knowing as how Mr Torquil was in bed with a touch of the sun, he'd taken my lady's mare to the village, to be reshod. There was only me and young Ned in the yard, sir, and I was busy grooming your bays, and never dreamed Mr Torquil had come down to the stables, and had ordered Ned to saddle up for him. And, although I fetched the lad a clout, I don't see as how you can blame him, for, let alone he's a gormless chawbacon, you couldn't hardly expect him to start argufying with Mr Torquil. The first I knew of it was when I see Mr Torquil leading his chestnut out. I ran, quick as I could, but he was in the saddle by the time I got to him, and listen to me he would not. He was in one of his hey-go-mad moods, Mr Philip, and maybe I done wrong to catch hold of his bridle, because it made him fly up into the boughs, the way he does when he's crossed, and he slashed his whip at me. And then the chestnut reared, and the next thing I knew was that I was on the flat of my back, and Mr Torquil going off at full gallop, and young Ned standing there with his mouth halfcocked, and his eyes fairly popping out of his head. So I rode Sir Timothy's old gray down the avenue, on his halter—and—and the rest is like this lady says, sir! And what her ladyship will say I dursn't think on!''

"She won't blame you," Philip said. "What have you done about the chestnut?"

"I've left him with Fleet, but he'll have to be shot, Mr Philip, no question! Only I dursn't do it without I'm ordered to!"

"You may say that I ordered you to shoot the poor brute."

"Yes, sir. Thank'ee, sir. But it'll go to my heart to do it!" said Scholes. "Such a prime bit of blood and bone as he is! What can have come over Mr Torquil to cram him at the wall, like he must have done, I'll never know!"

He then withdrew, sadly shaking his head, and Philip, looking at Kate, said grimly: "This I fancy, is where we kick the beam. It will be all over the county by tomorrow." He glanced at Mrs Nidd, saying, with a wry smile: "What a moment for your arrival! I feel I ought to beg your pardon!"

"Well, I hope you won't, sir. It's for me to beg yours, if my lady is laid up, which I didn't know, or I wouldn't have come—not until she was in better cue, that is!"

"But I *told* you, Sarah, in the letter which I gave to *you*, Phil—Cousin Philip!—asking you to make sure it was taken to the Post Office!" Kate exclaimed.

He regarded her in some amusement. "Yes, but, although the posts are much improved, I hardly think Mrs Nidd could have received a letter sent off yesterday in time to have caught the nightcoach to Market Harborough!"

"Good God, was it only two days ago I wrote it?" said Kate, pressing her hands to her temples. "It seems an age!"

"The only letter I've had from you, Miss Kate, barring the first one you wrote, was the scratch of a note Mr Nidd brought me," said Sarah. "And, to give credit where it's due, he brought it to Polly's house as soon as he got off the coach! What's more, I didn't hear a word out of him

about being fed on *pig-swill!* Pig-swill indeed! I don't say
Tom's wife has got my hand with pastry, but I hope you
know me better, Miss Kate, than to suppose I'd leave Father to someone who doesn't dress meat any better than—
than—''

"Than I do!" supplied Kate, with the glimmer of a
smile. "But if you haven't read the letter I wrote two days
ago, you can't know that—that I have become engaged to
Mr Philip Broome!''

"I've got eyes in my head!" retorted Mrs Nidd, with
asperity. "Not but what it was Father nudged me on! You
may say what you like, Miss Kate, but Father's got a deal
of rumgumption—for all his twittiness!''

"But I never said that he hadn't! I have the greatest
respect for Mr Nidd!" said Kate demurely.

"So have I," said Mr Philip Broome. "I thought him a
truly estimable old gentleman! What did he tell you, Mrs
Nidd?''

"Well, sir, if you'll pardon the expression, he said the
pair of you was smelling of April and May!" replied Sarah
apologetically. "He took a great fancy to you, sir—which
is a thing he don't often do!—and I'd like to wish you
both very happy, for I can see you're just the man for Miss
Kate! Which I never thought to see, and which makes *me*
as happy as a grig!''

In proof of this statement, she dissolved into tears; but
soon recovered, and went upstairs with Kate to make the
acquaintance of Mrs Thorne. On the way, Kate hurriedly
put her in possession of such facts as it was desirable she
should know, to all of which Sarah responded calmly that
there was no need for her to trouble herself.

So, indeed, it proved. After a ceremonious beginning,
which made Kate quake, perceptible signs of thaw set in:
a circumstance attributable on the one hand to Mrs
Thorne's warm praise of Miss Kate; and on the other to

the keen, if spurious, interest Mrs Nidd showed in the delicacy of Mrs Thorne's constitution. When Kate wondered (audibly) whether, perhaps, she ought to inform Sidlaw of Mrs Nidd's arrival, Mrs Thorne not only said that Miss Sidlaw (for all the airs she gave herself) had nothing to do with any of the household arrangements, but offered to have the bed made up in the small room adjoining Kate's. She then made Sarah free of her little parlour, and said that it would be quite like old times to entertain a visitor to dinner in the Room. "Before Sir Timothy took ill," she said impressively, "there was often above twenty visiting dressers and valets to be catered for. Oh, dear me, yes! But her ladyship has given up entertaining, so you'll find us a small company, ma'am. There's only me, and Mr Pennymore, and Tenby. And Miss Sidlaw, of course. But Miss Sidlaw and me are not speaking."

After this awful pronouncement, she led the way to the little room beside Kate's, and said she would have Mrs Nidd's baggage sent up immediately. Then she withdrew, whereupon Kate hugged Sarah convulsively, saying: "Oh, Sarah, I'm so *glad* you've come! You don't know how glad I am!"

"Well, if I don't it's no fault of yours, dearie!" said Sarah, patting her soothingly. "The idea of you coming hurtling down the stairs, screeching 'Sarah!' like a regular romp! Whatever must they all have thought of you? A pretty way to behave, Miss Kate! As though I'd never taught you better! Now, just you give over, and tell Sarah what's the matter!"

Thus adjured, Kate gave a shaky laugh, and took her to her own room where they would be safe from interruption until Ellen came up to dress her for dinner. "Which won't be nearly long enough for me to tell you the things I tried to write, in the letter Mr Philip Broome despatched for me, and found I couldn't. Sarah, my aunt intercepted my letters to you!''

''Yes,'' said Mrs Nidd grimly. ''So Father told me! That's why I came! That, and him saying that things didn't smell right to him. But what I *don't* know is why she should have done so, and Father, for all he thinks himself so long-headed, don't know either! So what with that, and me being uneasy in my mind ever since her ladyship took you away, Miss Kate, I thought that the sooner I came to see for myself the better!''

''I think it was to make a breach between us. I haven't asked her: after what passed between us today, it isn't—it doesn't seem to me to be important any longer. She—she brought me here to—to marry me to my cousin Torquil, Sarah!''

''Well,'' said Sarah, ''I won't deny that when you wrote that he was the most beautiful young man you'd ever seen I *did* hope you and he would make a match of it, but now that *I've* seen him I do hope you won't marry him, love— which it stands to reason you can't, being as how you've accepted Mr Philip Broome's offer—for a more whisky-frisky, nasty-tempered young gentleman I trust I'll never meet!''

''Oh, Sarah!'' Kate whispered, covering her face with her hands. ''It's worse than that! Far, far worse! He—he isn't in his right mind! And my aunt knows it—has known it for years! She told me so today: that's why I put you to the blush when I *hurtled* down the stairs! I was feeling quite overpowered—my mind wholly overset! Philip told me, but I didn't believe him—I *couldn't* believe it possible that my aunt *knew!* But she did—she did! And the only thing she cares for is that he shall provide Staplewood with an heir! Before he has to be confined! She doesn't care for poor Torquil—only for Staplewood! Sarah, she is a *terrible* woman, and I must get away from her! I *must!*''

"And so you shall, Miss Kate, never fear! It sounds to me as if she's as queer in her attic as that son of hers is. Well, I didn't like her, though I'd have been hard put to it to say why, for I'm sure she was very agreeable and condescending. And when I think that it was me writing to her which brought her down on you—which, mind you, I never would have done if Father hadn't nudged me on!— I'm that sorry and mortified, love, that I don't know how to ask you to forgive me!"

Kate raised her face, mistily smiling. "There's nothing to forgive. If you hadn't written to her, I might never have met Philip, and that would have been more dreadful than all the rest!" She heard the stable-clock striking the hour, and exclaimed: "Good God, it's five o'clock already! We dine at six, and I must speak to Philip before we're beset by Delabole! To tell him—ask him— You see, he doesn't know that I've changed my mind—wish to leave Staplewood tomorrow! He has been urging me to let him take me to you at once, but I wouldn't go while my aunt was unwell, and I thought I could be useful to her! For she had been very kind to me, Sarah! Whatever her motive was, I can't forget that! But she won't wish me to remain another day under this roof when she knows that Philip has made me an offer, and I've accepted it, and I can't and I won't go on deceiving her!"

"Well, if ever I saw you in such a fuss!" ejaculated Sarah. "Give over, Miss Kate, do! She can't eat you! Not while I'm here she can't! And from what I've seen of him I shouldn't wonder at it if Mr Philip was very well able to protect you!"

"She hates him," Kate said, pulling one of her evening-dresses out of the wardrobe, and casting it on the bed. "She will think me a traitress, and when I remember all the things she has given me—all her kindness!—I *feel* like one! Sarah, I *dread* telling her!"

"Now, that's not like you, Miss Kate!" responded Sarah. "No, and it isn't like you to put off doing what's unpleasant! You may depend upon it, dearie that the longer you do that the worse it will be. Besides, it's not right you should be getting yourself engaged in a havey-cavey way! You should have told her ladyship straight-off!"

"I *couldn't* tell her!" Kate said hotly. "She was in a high fever! I wasn't even permitted to enter her room until today, and I promised Sir Timothy I wouldn't break it to her until she was well!"

"Oh, so he knows, does he?" said Sarah, pushing her round so that she could unbutton her poplin dress. "Stand still, for goodness' sake! how am I to undo your dress if you keep twisting and turning?— By what Father heard in Market Harborough, it seems he's not in very good point?"

"No, indeed he's not! And that's another thing that makes me think I ought not to have accepted Philip's offer! He's so very much attached to him, and I have the greatest fear that if I marry Philip my aunt won't permit him to come to Staplewood again. And that would break poor Sir Timothy's heart, I think."

"You'll just have to decide whether to break his heart, or Mr Philip's, won't you?" said Sarah.

This eminently practical point of view struck Kate forcibly. She said quickly: "Oh, there can be no question!"

She would have said more, but was interrupted by the arrival of Ellen, almost bursting with curiosity. When Kate made her known to Sarah, she dropped a curtsy, slopping some of the hot water in the can she was carrying. "Oh, yes, miss, Mrs Thorne told me! And, if you please, ma'am, Mrs Thorne said to tell you that your bedchamber is quite ready, and your bag carried up, and all. And Miss Sidlaw says as how you're to go to her ladyship's room, please, ma'am!''

Taking the can away from her, Sarah admonished her, though kindly, not to be so clumsy. "And that wasn't the message you were given, was it?" she said. "I'll be bound her ladyship never said anything so rough!''

"No, ma'am! I mean, it was Miss Sidlaw! Ever so cross she is! Betty says it's because Mrs Thorne didn't tell her you was come, ma'am, nor ask my lady's leave to make up the bed in the next room, nor anything!''

"Well, never you mind about that!" said Sarah. "I shall go pay my respects to her ladyship when Miss Kate is dressed.''

She then handed the can of hot water to Ellen, recommending her not to waste time prattling, but to pour the water out for Miss Kate to wash her hands, and to take care she didn't spill any more of it, and turned away to pick up the dress of pale orange Italian crape, and to shake out its folds. Trying in vain to catch her eye, Kate submitted to the ministrations of her youthful abigail, which, owing to the terror into which Sarah's critical eye cast her, were more than usually clumsy. When it came to combing out Kate's soft curls, Sarah took the comb firmly away from her, and set about the task of arranging them becomingly herself, bidding Ellen watch closely how she did it. To which Ellen responded slavishly, and dropped another curtsy.

Meeting Kate's anxious gaze in the looking-glass, Sarah favoured her with a small smile of reassurance, and said, as she adjusted a ringlet: "That's more the thing! The way you were doing it, my girl, it looked like a birch-broom in a fit!''

"Yes, ma'am!" said Ellen, giggling. "She *does* look a picture! If you please, will I take you to her ladyship's room now?''

"No, Miss Kate will show me where it is," Sarah replied, gently pushing Kate towards the door. "You can stay here, and make everything tidy. And mind you give that poplin dress a good shake before you hang it up! I'll put Miss Kate to bed, so you needn't wait up for her!"

"Sarah, you will take care, won't you?" Kate said urgently, as soon as the door was shut behind them. "I am *sick* with apprehension! Sidlaw must have told her—" She broke off, and lowered her voice. "Here she is! Don't tell her anything, Sarah! Don't trust her!"

"Anyone would think your senses was disordered, Miss Kate!" replied Mrs Nidd. "For goodness' sake, stop behaving like a wetgoose, and be off to your dinner!"

Kate threw her a speaking glance, but spoke with commendable calm to Sidlaw, who had by this time reached them, and come to a halt, standing with her hands primly clasped before her, and looking Sarah over with sour disparagement. "Sidlaw, this is my nurse, Mrs Nidd," said Kate. "Will you have the goodness to conduct her to her ladyship's room?"

"I was coming to do so, miss," Sidlaw replied, dropping a stiff curtsy. "I'm sure, Mrs Nidd, if Miss had seen fit to tell me she was expecting a visit from you, I should have seen to it myself that a bedchamber was prepared for you."

"Well, it would have puzzled her to do that, seeing that she didn't know I was coming to visit her," said Mrs Nidd cheerfully. "Not that I would have come, if I'd known her ladyship was poorly, but what's done can't be mended, and you won't find me any trouble! Now, you run along, Miss Kate! I shall be coming to put you to bed later on, so I won't say goodnight to you."

There was nothing for Kate to do but to make her way to the Long Drawing-room, which she did, feeling that Sidlaw at least had met her match in Mrs Nidd.

She had hoped to have found Mr Philip Broome waiting for her there, but the room was empty, a circumstance which, in the exacerbated state of her nerves, she was much inclined to think betrayed a lamentable unconcern with what he must surely have known was her anxiety to exchange a few words with him in private. She fidgeted about the room for what seemed to her an interminable time, and was just wondering whether the pre-prandial gathering was taking place in one of the saloons on the entrance floor when she heard his voice in the ante-room. A moment later, he came in, escorting Sir Timothy. At sight of him, her annoyance evaporated; and when his eyes smiled at her across the room her heart melted. She moved forward to greet Sir Timothy, and was adjusting a cushion behind his back when Pennymore came in, carrying a massive silver tray which bore two decanters and five sherry glasses. He set this down on a table by one of the windows and disclosed fell tidings. Her ladyship had sent a message to him that she was coming down to dinner.

None of the three persons present evinced any very noticeable sign of delight. Kate, in fact, looked aghast; Philip, inscrutable; and Sir Timothy merely said, in his gentle way: "Ah, I am glad she is so much better! Thank you, Pennymore: you needn't wait."

Kate seated herself beside him, and enquired whether he had enjoyed his drive that afternoon. His face lit up, and his eyes travelled fondly to his nephew. "Very much indeed," he answered. "It is a long time since I've driven round my lands. A barouche, you know, doesn't enable one to see over the hedges, which makes travelling in one very dull work. But Philip took me in the tilbury—and was obliged to own that I haven't quite lost my old driving skill! Eh, Philip?"

"Well, sir, I don't know about *owning* it!" replied Philip. "I never supposed that you had!"

"Then the next time you invite me to drive out with you, let it be in your curricle! I'm told you have a sweet-stepping pair of bays, and I should like to try their paces!"

"Willingly, sir. Do you mean to take the shine out of me?"

"Ah, who knows? I could have done so in my day, but I fear that's long past. As one grows older, one begins to lose the precision of eye which all first-rate fiddlers have." He turned to Kate, saying fondly: "And how have you passed the day, my pretty? Pleasantly, I trust? I hear your old nurse has come to visit you: that must have been an agreeable surprise, I daresay. I shall hope to make her acquaintance. Does she mean to make a long stay?"

"No, sir: she is married, you know, and cannot do so," Kate said. She hesitated, and then said, raising her eyes to his: "She is going to take me back to London—tomorrow, I hope."

It cost her a pang to see the cheerfulness fade from his face. He seemed to age under her eyes, but, after a moment, he smiled, though mournfully, and said: "I see. I shan't seek to dissuade you, my dear, but I shall miss you more than I can say."

She put out her hand, in one of her impulsive gestures, and laid it over one of his thin, fragile ones, clasping it warmly, and saying in an unsteady voice: "And I shall miss you, sir—much more than I can say! If I don't see you again—thank you a thousand, thousand times for your kindness to me! I shall never forget it—or that you bestowed your blessing on me."

Philip's voice cut in on this, sharpened by surprise. "What's this, Kate? *Tomorrow?*"

He had walked over to the window, and was standing with one of the decanters in his hand. She turned her head, encountered his searching look, but said only: "If it might be contrived! I think—I think it would be best. Sarah can escort me, you see, so I need not be a charge on you!''

''A *charge* on me? Moonshine! You may rest assured I shall go with you!''

He would have said more, but was interrupted by the entrance of Dr Delabole, who came in, exuding an odd mixture of goodfellowship and dismay, and shook a finger at Sir Timothy, saying: ''Now, you deserve that I should give you a scold, sir, for driving out with Mr Philip without a word to me! In the tilbury, too! Most imprudent of you— but I can see that you are none the worse for it, so I won't scold you!''

''On the contrary, I am very much better for it,'' replied Sir Timothy, with his faint, aloof smile. ''Thank you, Philip, yes! A glass of sherry!''

''Nevertheless,'' said the doctor, ''you must allow me to count your pulse, Sir Timothy! That I must insist on! Just to reassure myself!''

It seemed for a moment as though Sir Timothy was on the point of repulsing him, but as Kate rose to make way for Delabole, he said, in a bored voice: ''Certainly—if it affords you amusement!''

Kate, as Delabole bent over Sir Timothy, seized the opportunity to cross the room to Philip's side, and to whisper: ''I must speak to you! But how? where? Can you arrange for me to leave tomorrow?''

''Yes, I'll drive to Market Harborough, and hire a chaise in the morning. It can hardly be here before noon, however, which means you must spend a night somewhere along the road—Woburn, probably. What has happened? Have you seen Minerva?''

She nodded, unable to repress a shudder. ''Yes. I can't tell you now!''

''Did you tell *her?*''

"Not yet. I *could* not, Philip! Oh, when can I speak to you alone?"

"Come down early to breakfast and walk out to take the air: I shall be on the terrace. Minerva will see to it that we get no opportunity to be private this evening—did you know that she is joining us?" He glanced over her shoulder, towards the archway which led to the ante-room, and said, under his breath: "Take care! Here she is! Carry this to my uncle!" As she took the glass from him, he added, in quite another voice: "Sherry for you, doctor? Cousin Kate, I am going to pour you out a glass of Madeira!— Good-evening, Minerva! I am happy to see you restored to health! What may I offer you? Sherry, or Madeira?"

"A little Madeira, thank you, Philip. Sir Timothy!"

He rose, and came forward to meet her, punctiliously kissing first her outstretched hand, and then her cheek. "Welcome, my dear!" he said. "I hope you are feeling more the thing? You have been in a very poor way, have you not? Such a fright as you gave us all! Pray don't do it again!"

"You may be sure I shall try not to do so!" she returned, moving to a chair, and sinking down upon it.

"I wonder if a doctor ever had two such obstreperous patients!" said Delabole, solicitously placing a stool before her. "First there is Sir Timothy, playing truant when my back was turned, and now it is you, my lady, leaving your bedchamber in defiance of my orders! I don't know what is to be done with you, upon my word, I don't! And you did not even summon me to lend you the support of my arm! Now, how am I to take that?"

Lady Broome, receiving a glass of Madeira from Kate, and bestowing a smile upon her, replied: "Not amiss, I trust. Mrs Nidd most kindly lent the support of *her* arm— my niece's nurse, you know, who has come to visit her: a most respectable woman! Kate, dear child, I do hope my people have made her comfortable!''

"Perfectly comfortable, ma'am, thank you," Kate said, in a colourless tone.

"Ah, good! I told her Thorne would look after her. What a fortunate thing it was that she arrived in time to bring Torquil up to the house in her chaise! She has a great deal of commonsense, and I am vastly indebted to her, as, you may be sure, I told her.''

"Bring Torquil up to the house? Why should she have done so?" asked Sir Timothy, his voice sharpened by anxiety.

"Oh, he took a toss, and was momentarily stunned!'' she answered with an indulgent laugh. "Overfacing his horse, of course! So stupid of him! Fleet—you know what these people are, my love!—believed him to be dead, but, in point of fact, he is very little the worse for his tumble!''

"Not a penny the worse!" corroborated the doctor. "Merely bruised, shaken, chastened, and reeking of arnica! So he is dining in his own room this evening—feeling thoroughly shamefaced, I daresay! But no cause for anxiety, Sir Timothy! It may be regarded in the light of a salutary lesson!''

"We must hope so!" said Lady Broome, getting up. "Shall we go down to dinner now? Dr Delabole, will you give me your arm? Philip, you may give yours to your uncle! Which leaves poor Kate without a gentleman to escort her, but she is so much a part of the family that I shan't apologize to her!''

Dinner pursued what Kate had long since come to regard as its tedious course. Lady Broome maintained a light flow of everyday chit-chat, in which she was ably seconded by the doctor. She was looking a trifle haggard, but she held herself as upright as ever, and when she rose from the table she declined the doctor's offered assistance.

"Let James give you his arm, my lady!" said Sir Timothy, seeing her stagger and put out a hand to grasp a chair-back.

She gave a breathless laugh. "Very well—if you insist! How stupid to be so invalidish! It is only my knees, you know! They need exercise!"

But when she reached the head of the Grand Stairway she looked so pale that Kate was alarmed, and begged her to retire to bed. She refused to do this, but after pausing for a few moments, leaning heavily on the footman's arm, she recovered, and resolutely straightened herself, desiring Kate to summon Sidlaw, and to tell her to bring the cordial Dr Delabole had prescribed to the Long Drawing-room.

It took time to perform this errand, for Sidlaw was not immediately available. A young housemaid came in answer to the bell, and told Kate that Sidlaw was at supper, in the Housekeeper's Room; and, although she made haste to deliver my lady's command to her, the servants' quarters were so inconveniently remote that it was several minutes before Sidlaw came hurrying in. Upon being told that my lady wanted a cordial, she said that she knew how it would be, and had warned her ladyship what would be the outcome of going down to dinner before she was fit to stand on her feet. When she had measured out a dose of the restorative medicine, and Kate would have taken it from her, she said sharply: "Thank, you, miss! I prefer to take it to her ladyship myself!" and sailed off, full of zeal and fury.

Not at all sorry that, for the moment at least, she would be spared a tête-à-tête with her aunt, Kate followed her. By the time Lady Broome had swallowed the cordial, and Sidlaw, disregarding her impatience, had fussed over her, drawing a heavy screen behind her chair to protect her from an imaginary draught, placing a cushion behind her head, begging to be allowed to fetch a warmer shawl, and placing her vinaigrette on a small table drawn up beside her chair, the gentlemen, not lingering over their port, had come in. Sidlaw then withdrew, with obvious reluctance, and while the doctor bent solicitously over Lady Broome, Sir Timothy, smiling a little sadly at Kate, murmured: "A last game of backgammon, my child?"

She agreed to it; Philip got the board out of the cabinet, and sat down to watch the game; Lady Broome leaned back in her chair, closing her eyes; and the doctor went away to see how Torquil was going on. He came back in the wake of the tea-tray, with a comfortable account of Torquil, who had eaten a very good dinner, he said, and was now gone to bed. Lady Broome then put an end to the backgammon session by calling Kate to dispense the tea. She seemed to have recovered both her complexion and her strength, but as soon as the footman came to remove the tray she got up, saying that it was time she retired, and adding: "Come, Kate!"

Philip looked quickly at Kate, a question in his eyes. She very slightly shook her head, and, seeing Sir Timothy's hand stretched out to her, went to him, bending over him, with her free hand on his shoulder, preventing his attempt to rise from his chair. "Pray don't get up, sir!" she said, smiling wistfully.

He drew her down to kiss her cheek, whispering in her ear: "Come and see me before you go tomorrow, to say goodbye to me!"

"I will," she promised, under her breath.

"Goodnight, my pretty! Bless you!" he said, releasing her.

Lady Broome, waiting in the archway, watched this scene with placid complaisance, and said, as soon as she had passed through the ante-room: "I believe Sir Timothy does indeed look upon you as the daughter of his old age! He is so fond of you, dear child!"

"I am very fond of him, ma'am," Kate replied, walking slowly down the broad gallery, with Lady Broome's hand resting on her arm.

"Are you? I wonder! I am beginning to think, Kate, that for all your engaging manners, you are not very fond of anyone. Certainly not of me!"

Innate honesty forbade Kate to deny this; she could only say: "You are feeling low, and oppressed, ma'am: don't let us brangle!"

"I am feeling very low, and more oppressed than ever before in my life—almost at the end of my rope! You will own that I have enough to sink me in despair, even though you refuse to help me! Do you know, I have never asked for help before?"

"Aunt Minerva, I can't give it to you!" Kate said bluntly. "I thought there was nothing I wouldn't do to repay your kindness, but when you ask me to marry Torquil you are asking too much! I *beg* of you, don't try to persuade me to do so! It is useless—you will only agitate yourself to no purpose!"

They had reached the upper hall; Lady Broome paused there, her light clasp on Kate's arm tightening into a grip. "Think!" she commanded, a harsh note creeping into her voice. "If the advantages of such a marriage don't weigh with you, does it weigh with you that by persisting in your refusal you will have condemned Torquil to spend the rest of his life in strict incarceration?" She observed the whitening of Kate's cheeks, the look of horror in her eyes, and smiled. "Oh, yes!" she said, a purring triumph in her voice. "After today's exploit, there is left to me only one hope of guarding the secret of his madness. Do you realize that he might have brought his horse down on top of the woman who was leading her child by the hand? Do you know that he rode Scholes down in the stableyard? What, you little ninnyhammer, do you suppose that Scholes, and

Fleet, and whoever they were who were passing along the lane at that disastrous moment, are now thinking—and discussing, if I know them? Dr Delabole has done what he could to convince Scholes and Fleet that for Torquil to have spurred his horse into the wall was nothing but the act of a headstrong boy, but he might as well have hung up his axe! Only one thing can now silence the gabble-mongers, and that's the news that Torquil is about to be married to a girl of birth and character! That must give them pause! In any event, only one thing signifies: that there shall be an heir to Staplewood!"

"Oh!" cried Kate, losing control of herself. "Can you think of nothing but Staplewood? *The only thing that signifies!* Good God, what does Staplewood matter beside the dreadful fate that hangs over poor Torquil?"

"If Torquil could have been cured by the abandonment of my hopes of seeing my descendants at Staplewood, I suppose I must have abandoned them," said Lady Broome coldly. "It would have been my duty, and I've never failed in *that!* But it can make no difference to him. If I seem unfeeling, you must remember that I have had time to grow accustomed. Nor am I one to grieve endlessly over what can't be helped. I prefer to make the best I can out of what befalls me."

"It hasn't befallen you, ma'am!"

"No: not yet! Perhaps, if I can provide him with a wife, it never will. He may grow calmer when his passions find a natural outlet: Delabole considers it to be possible."

"Does he consider it beyond possibility that a child of Torquil's should inherit his malady?" Kate asked, unable to repress the bitter indignation which swelled in her breast.

"It is a risk I must take," said Lady Broome, sublimely unaware of the effect these words had upon her niece.

Kate managed to pull her arm free; she stepped back a

pace, and said, with a tiny contemptuous laugh: "There's another risk you would have to take, ma'am! Hasn't it occurred to you that Torquil's child might be a daughter?"

It was evident that this thought had never disturbed Lady Broome's incredible dreams. She stared at Kate, as though stunned, and when she spoke it was scarcely above a whisper. "God *couldn't* be so cruel!" she uttered.

Kate made a hopeless gesture. "Let me take you to your room, ma'am! It is of no use to continue arguing: it is as though we weren't speaking the same language! I am leaving you tomorrow, and—and I wish very much to do so without a quarrel with you!" She drew a resolute breath, and braced herself, and found the courage to keep her eyes steady on her aunt's face. "There is something else I must tell you, ma'am. I would have told you when—when it happened, but you were too ill to be troubled with what I know you will dislike—I fear, excessively! I can only beg you to believe that I haven't *wished* to deceive you, and that I can't and won't leave Staplewood without telling you that Mr Philip Broome proposed to me on the very day you took ill, and that I accepted his offer!"

Lady Broome received this disclosure in a silence more terrible, Kate thought, than any outburst of wrath would have been. She stood motionless, only her eyes alive in her rigid countenance. Between narrowed lids, they stared at Kate with such implacable fury that it was only by supreme effort of will power that she stood her ground, and continued to look her aunt boldly in the face. "So Sidlaw was right!" Lady Broome said, quite softly. "You little *slut!*" She watched the colour rush up into Kate's cheeks. "You can blush, can you? That certainly surprises me! I wouldn't believe Sidlaw—I *couldn't* believe that a girl who owed the very clothes on her back to me could be so ungrateful—so treacherous—as to encourage the advances of a man whom she knew to be my greatest enemy! He has proposed to you, has he? Are you so sure that he proposed *marriage?* I fancy he is not so blind to his interest as you imagine! Philip marry a penniless young woman whom neither her family nor his acknowledge? I won't say that I wish you may not have a rude wakening from this mawkish dream of yours, for I hope with all my heart that when he grows tired of you, and casts you off, you will remember to your dying day what I offered you, and you were fool enough to refuse!" She paused, but Kate did not speak. Scanning the girl's white face, an unpleasant smile curled her lips, and she said: "That gives you to think, does it not? I advise you to think more carefully still! Perhaps it didn't occur to you that he was trying to give you a slip on the shoulder?"

Kate's lips quivered into an answering smile; she replied: "It did occur to me, ma'am, but I was wrong. All you have said about my circumstances occurred to me, too. I daresay you won't believe me, but I tried to make him see how unequal such a match would be—how much his family must deplore it! But he said that that was a matter of indifference to him. You see—we *love* each other!"

"Love?" ejaculated Lady Broome scornfully. "Don't, I beg of you, nauseate me by talking sickly balderdash! Love has nothing to do with marriage, and I promise you it doesn't endure! No, and it won't make up to you for losing Staplewood, and the position that could be yours as Lady Broome! Or are you indulging the fancy that Torquil will die young, and that Philip will step into his shoes? Torquil will hold a long trig: I'll take care of that! He shall have no more opportunities to break his neck! Until I can instal him in an establishment of his own, I mean to see to it that he is never left for one moment alone, or allowed to go near the stables! My great-uncle lived to extreme old age, you know. I believe he was very troublesome at first, but when he became imbecile, which he very shortly did,

he was as easy to control as a child. Even his fits of violence abated! I remember my mother telling me that he
could be diverted merely by being given some new, foolish
plaything! You may rest assured that Torquil shall be provided with a thousand playthings, indulged, cosseted,
guarded from every infectious disease—''

''*Pleased with a rattle, tickled with a straw!*'' Kate
broke in, her voice anguished. ''For God's sake, ma'am,
stop! You cannot know what you are saying!''

''I know very well what I am saying. I have something
more to say to you, Kate! If you marry Philip, he will
never again, while I live, set foot inside this house! Don't
think I can't keep him away! I can, and will! If you are
as fond of Sir Timothy as you pretend to be, you won't
separate him from his beloved nephew! That is something
I have never done! Remember that!''

She cast a final, scorching glance at Kate, and swept
across the hall to the gallery that led to her bedchamber
with a firmness of step which belied her previous assumption of debility.

Kate, almost fainting with horror, managed to reach her
own room before her knees sank under her, and she collapsed into Mrs Nidd's arms, gasping: ''I must get away!
I *must.* She is so terrible, Sarah! I can't tell you what she
has said to me!''

''Well,'' said Mrs Nidd, dealing with this crisis after her
own fashion, ''as I don't want to know what she said,
that's no matter! And, as you won't be troubled with her
again after tomorrow, there's no call for you to be thrown
into affliction, Miss Kate! You give over fretting and fuming, and let me undress you, like a good girl!''

Chapter Twenty

A night spent in tossing from side to side, with brief intervals of sleep rendered hideous by menacing dreams, did little to restore Kate; and when she slipped out of the house to join Mr Philip Broome on the terrace next morning, she looked so wan and heavy-eyed that he said savagely, as he caught her into his arms: "I ought not to have let you face her alone! Oh, my poor darling, *why* did you shake your head at me? What did she say to upset you so much?"

She clung to him, trying to overcome her agitation, and said, in a strangled voice: "You were *right,* Philip, and I wouldn't believe the things you said of her! I thought it was prejudice! But you were *right!*"

He had to bend his head to catch her words, for they were uttered into his shoulder, but he did catch them, and, although his face darkened wrathfully, his voice was quite calm when he said: "Yes: I know. You shall tell me all about it, but not here! It is rather too public a place. Shall we go to the shrubbery, dear love?"

He did not wait for an answer, but drew her hand through his arm, and led her down the terrace-steps. She went without demur, too shaken to consider, or to care, who might be watching them. His coolness, the strong clasp of his hand on hers, steadied her, and by the time they had reached the rustic bench where they had sat together so short a time before, she had managed to regain her composure, and was even able to conjure up a wavering smile as she said, rather huskily: "I beg your pardon! Sarah warned me that there is no more certain way of making a gentleman cry off than to treat him to a fit of the vapours—and particularly before breakfast! I didn't mean to do it, and indeed it isn't a habit of mine, Philip!"

"In that case, I won't cry off!" he said. "Don't sit down! The dew hasn't dried yet!" As he spoke, he stripped off his well-fitting coat, and folded it, and placed it on the bench for her to sit upon. In reply to her expostulation that he would take cold, and her efforts to spread the coat that they might both sit on it, he thrust her down on to the bench, and seated himself beside her, putting a sustaining arm round her, and informing her that no one could possibly take cold on such a hot morning, and that he defied any amount of dew to penetrate his buckskins. After that, he kissed her, long and lovingly, told her not to be a goose, and gently pressed her head down on his shoulder. "Tell me!" he said.

So Kate, nestling gratefully within his embrace, her cheek against his waistcoat of striped toilinette, told him, rather haltingly, but quite calmly, all that Lady Broome had said in each of the painful sessions she had endured with her. His brow blackened as he listened, but he heard her in silence, until she disclosed that her aunt meant to incarcerate Torquil in a house remote from Staplewood, when his hard-held control broke, and he exclaimed: "Oh, my God, *no!* She couldn't do such a thing! It would be enough to send him completely out of his mind! What, banish him from the only home he has ever known, place Delabole, whom he detests, in charge of him, appoint strangers to take care of him——? No, no, Kate! She would never do so! Even I can't believe her capable of such inhumanity! I agree that he mustn't be allowed to roam at large; I know that it may become necessary to confine him, but that day hasn't come yet! If I had my way, I'd send Delabole packing, and engage a man, not only experienced in the care of those whose minds are unbalanced, but one able to endear himself to the poor lad——divert him——God knows it's not difficult!''

"Such a man wouldn't lend himself to the deception my aunt demands,'' Kate said sadly. "Nothing signifies to her but to keep it secret that Torquil has fits of insanity. That's what overset me. Suddenly I saw that she was monstrous. Sarah thinks her as mad as Torquil, but it came to me, as I listened to the appalling things she said, that she has never, in all her life, considered anyone but herself, or doubted that everything she does is good, and wise——beyond criticism! Sir Timothy said to me that she has many good qualities, but is a stranger to the tender emotions. It is most terribly true, Philip! She did not utter one word of pity for Torquil; it is *her* tragedy, not his! He has destroyed her last ambition, and that puts him beyond pardon. She doesn't love him, you see. I don't think she loves anyone but herself. She *will* send him away——and tell Sir Timothy that a change of air has been recommended for him!''

"Oh, no, she will not!'' Phil said, at his grimmest. "If she does indeed mean to do anything so cruel, she'll find she has reckoned without me! I've never spoken of Torquil's state to my uncle, but much as I love him I won't see Torquil sacrificed to spare him pain!''

"Philip, Philip, you won't be able to tell him! That is almost the worst of all! My aunt has told me that if you marry me you will never come to Staplewood again, while she is alive to prevent you! And she *will* prevent you! She——she is ruthless!''

"So am I ruthless!" he said, his eyes very bright and hard. "By God, I should be *glad* to cross swords with her! Don't look so troubled, my precious! That, at least, was an empty threat! Minerva has no power to keep me away from Staplewood. My uncle may be weak, but he won't support her on that issue! And when he dies she will discover that her despotic rule is at an end. She doesn't know it—I daresay the thought has never so much as crossed her mind!—but although my uncle has provided for a handsome jointure, his will strips her of power. It makes me, not her, Torquil's guardian, and his principal trustee—and you may be sure, Kate, that I shan't allow her to send him away from Staplewood—or to bully and browbeat him!" He got up. "I must go now, if I am to have a chaise here by noon. You won't see Minerva: she's not coming down to breakfast. Go up to your room as soon as you have eaten your own breakfast: I fancy Mrs Nidd can be relied upon to keep Minerva at bay!" He shrugged himself into his coat, and took her hands, and kissed them. "Keep up your heart, my darling! When we sit down to dinner, we shall be forty or fifty miles from Staplewood. Remember that, if you find yourself sinking into dejection! But you won't: you're too much of a right one!"

"No, no, I won't!" she promised. Her fingers clung to his, detaining him. "But I have been thinking, Philip! If you were to drive Sarah and me to Market Harborough, we could travel on the stage, and—and not be such a shocking charge on you! It is such an unnecessary expense! I know that the rates for a post-chaise are *wickedly* high, and—"

She was silenced by having a kiss planted firmly on her mouth. Mr Philip Broome said, with menacing severity, that if she had any more bird-witted suggestions to make, he advised her to keep them under her tongue; and, when she showed a disposition to argue with him, added, in a very ineffable way, that it did not suit his consequence to permit his promised wife to travel on the common stage.

That made her laugh; and when he left her, striding off in the direction of the stables, she walked back to the house in much improved spirits, and was able to greet Pennymore, whom she encountered in the Great Hall, with something very like her customary cheerfulness; and even to say in an airy voice that she had been lured into the garden because it was such a beautiful day. To which he responded: "Yes, miss! Very understandable!" with such a twinkle in his eye that unruly colour surged into her cheeks. He then said that as Mr Philip had done him the honour to admit him into his confidence he would like to take the liberty of wishing her happiness. "In which, miss," he informed her, with a fatherly smile, "Tenby desires to be included, Sir Timothy having told him last night of your Approaching Nuptials. Not that it came as a surprise to either of us! You will find only Mr Torquil and the doctor in the breakfast-parlour, Miss Kate, and I shall bring your tea to you directly."

Waiting only until the tell-tale blush had faded, Kate proceeded to the breakfast-parlour. The doctor rose at her entrance, and came forward to hand her to a seat at the table, full of forced joviality, but looking as though he too had passed a sleepless night. Torquil, who had apparently recovered from his fall, was in a boastful, defiant mood, ready to come to cuffs with anyone unwise enough to criticize his horsemanship. He instantly challenged Kate to do so, demanding belligerently if she had anything to say on the subject. When she answered calmly: "Oh, no! How should I?" he uttered a crack of laughter, and said: "Just as well!"

"Torquil, Torquil!" said the doctor reprovingly.

"Oh, stop gabbing!" snapped Torquil, casting at him a look of venomous dislike. "I'll tell you what, coz! We'll have a game of quoits after breakfast before it gets too hot!''

"I'm sorry, Torquil: I'm afraid I can't," she replied. "I am leaving Staplewood today, and I must pack my trunk."

"Leaving?" he ejaculated. "But you can't leave! I won't let you! I'll tell Mama— Kate, *why?"*

"But, Torquil, I didn't come here to *live,* you know!" she said, smiling at him. "Indeed, I think I have remained for an unconscionable time! It's very kind of you to wish me to stay, but I have been thinking for some weeks that it is high time I left Staplewood—only it has had me in a puzzle how to do so without putting your mama to the expense and inconvenience of providing me with an escort to London, which isn't at all needful, but which I know she would insist on doing. But now that my nurse has come to visit me the difficulty is solved. I shall go back to London with her. I wasn't expecting her, so have been as much taken by surprise as you are."

He startled her by thrusting his chair back, and almost flinging himself on his knees beside her, grasping her hands, and saying in an anguished voice: "Oh, Kate, don't go! Don't go! You're the only friend I've ever had, and if you leave me I shall have no one!"

The doctor rose rather quickly, but, encountering a fiery look from Kate, remained by his chair. Torquil, his head bowed over Kate's hands, had burst into sobs. She glanced pitifully down at him, but spoke to Delabole. "Please go away, sir!" she said quietly. "You are quite crushing my hands, Torquil: pray don't hold them so tightly!"

He released them immediately, saying between his sobs: "I'm sorry! I didn't mean to hurt you! Kate, you *know* I wouldn't hurt you! I *like* you! You're so *kind!"*

He sank his head into her lap, hysterically weeping; and the doctor, sighing deeply, but apparently satisfied that his mood was not violent, unobtrusively withdrew from the room. Kate laid a hand on Torquil's gleaming gold locks, gently stroking them. Her heart was wrung, but she said soothingly: "Of course I know you wouldn't hurt me! Don't cry! You will make me cry too if you don't stop, and you wouldn't wish that, would you?"

He raised his head, staring wildly up at her. "You are going because you think I tried to shoot you! But I *didn't*, Kate, I swear to you I didn't!"

"No, I know you didn't," she said, patting his hand. "To be sure, I was very cross with you at the time for being so careless, but that's all forgotten!"

"It's Mama!" he said suddenly. "*She* is sending you away! Because you won't marry me! O God, how I hate her!"

His voice shook with passion, and she sent a swift glance towards the door, guessing that the doctor's ear was glued to it, and afraid that he might precipitate a crisis by coming back into the room. He did not, however, and she said, preserving her calm: "You mustn't say that, Torquil. Moreover, your mama is quite as anxious for me to remain at Staplewood as you are. Get up, my dear, and sit here, beside me! That's better! Now own that you don't in the very least wish to be married to me!" Her smiling eyes quizzed him, and drew an answering gleam from his. Encouraged, she began to talk to him about things which were of interest to him. He seemed to be listening to her, but plunged her back into despondency by interrupting suddenly with the announcement that he wished he were dead. She tried to divert his thoughts, but unavailingly; a cloud had descended on his brow, his eyes brooded sombrely, and his beautiful mouth took on a tragic droop.

She left him presently, knowing that, however much he might like her, she had no power to raise his spirits. She had not dared to disclose to him that she was about to be married to his cousin, for she feared that this might fan into a flame the embers of his inculcated hatred of Philip, always smouldering beneath the surface of his affection. His mood was one of profound melancholy, but she thought that it needed only a touch to send him into one of his fits of ungovernable rage.

She was looking deeply troubled when she entered her bedchamber, a circumstance that prompted Sarah, expertly folding one of the evening-dresses Lady Broome had bestowed on her niece, to say briskly: "If Father was to see you, Miss Kate, he'd say you was looking like a strained hair in a can! You've got no call to be so down pin, love— not unless you've been breaking straws with Mr Philip, which I *don't* think!"

"No, indeed!" Kate answered. "I don't think I could!"

"Ah!" said Sarah darkly. "Time will show! Where has he gone off to?"

"Market Harborough, to hire a chaise to carry us to London. Don't put that dress in my trunk! I am not taking it. Only the dresses I brought with me!"

"Well, Miss Kate, you know best, but it does seem a shame to let a beautiful silk like this go begging!" said Sarah, sighing regretfully. "It isn't as if it could be of any use to her ladyship. Still, I daresay Mr Philip will purchase another for you, because the way he's wasting the ready is downright sinful! Not but what I'm looking forward to travelling in a post-chaise, and I don't deny it! It's something I've never done before, though we did come up to London in the Mail coach when we landed at Portsmouth—and a rare set-out *that* was!"

Kate laughed. "When Papa sent the baggage by carrier, and it was a week before it reached us? What a long time ago it seems!"

"Well, it is a long time. And if my Joe had brought the baggage it wouldn't have taken him a week! Where shall I put these dresses, Miss Kate? It won't do to leave them hanging in the wardrobe, where, as like as not, they'll be pulled out by one of the housemaids. I wouldn't put it past that saucy little minx, Phoebe, or whatever she calls herself, to try them on!''

After a little discussion, it was decided to pack them carefully in the chest of drawers, which was done, not without argument, Kate being determined to do her share of the work, and Sarah being equally determined that she should sit in a chair, and direct operations. But, as she paid no attention to anything Kate said, Kate soon abandoned the chair, and began to fold the dresses herself. This earned her a scold, Sarah exclaiming: "Good gracious, Miss Kate! That's no way to pack muslin! Just look how you've creased it!''

She plucked the garment out of Kate's hands as she spoke and was shaking it vigorously when a piercing scream almost caused her to drop it. She and Kate stood staring at one another for a startled moment. The scream was not repeated, but just as Sarah began to say: "Well whatever next!'' an even more unnerving sound reached them: someone downstairs was uttering wail upon wail of despair.

Deathly pale, in the grip of fear, Kate tore open the door, and ran out into the gallery, listening, with dilating eyes and thudding heart. She gasped: "It's Sidlaw! Oh, what can have happened? What can have happened?''

She picked up her skirts, and raced down the broad stairs, almost colliding in the hall with Pennymore, also hurrying to discover what had happened, and looking quite as pale as she was. The door into Lady Broome's drawing-room stood open. Within the room, an appalling sight met Kate's shrinking gaze. Lady Broome was lying on the floor, her face strangely blue, her tongue protruding, and her eyes, starting from their sockets, fixed in a stare of fury. Beside her, Sidlaw was kneeling, rocking herself to and fro, and sobbing over and over again between her wails: "I warned her! I warned her! Oh, my beautiful! Oh, my dear lady!"

Sarah, thrusting her way through the servants who had begun to congregate in the hall, some frightened, some in the expectation of excitement, shut the door in their faces, pushed Kate aside, and knelt down beside Lady Broome, while Sidlaw continued to wail and sob. Seeing that Pennymore was trembling so much that he was obliged to cling to a chair-back for support, Kate slipped out of the room, and, singling the second footman out from the small crowd of servants, quietly told him to find Dr Delabole, and to inform him that he was wanted immediately in my lady's drawing-room. She then dismissed the other servants, saying that my lady had had a seizure, and went back into the drawing-room to find that Sarah had risen from her knees, and was trying to induce Sidlaw to abate her lamentations.

Pennymore, who was looking as if he might faint, said hoarsely: "Stop her, Mrs Nidd, stop her! The master will hear her! Oh, my God, what are we going to do?"

Kate, feeling that if she allowed herself to look at Lady Broome's distorted countenance she too would faint, kept her eyes resolutely averted, and her voice under strict control. "I have sent William to fetch the doctor. I think you should find Tenby, and—and tell him that her ladyship has had a—a seizure. That is what I have said to the others. Tenby will know what to do if Sir Timothy should be upset."

"Yes, miss. I'll go at once," Pennymore replied mechanically, and went shakily out of the room.

Sidlaw's wails had changed to wild laughter. Sarah looked quickly round the room, saw a vase of roses standing on the desk, snatched it up, pulled the flowers out of it, and dashed the water into Sidlaw's face.

"Sarah, is she—is she *dead?*" Kate whispered, as Sidlaw's hysteria ceased into a gasp of shock.

Sarah nodded, and said authoritatively: "Help me to get this demented creature into a chair, miss! Come now, Miss Sidlaw, don't start screeching again, there's a dear! You sit down here, and pull yourself together!"

Huddled in the chair, Sidlaw said: "He's killed her! I knew it would happen! I *knew* it! She wouldn't listen, she wouldn't ever listen to me!" Her distraught gaze fell on Kate; she pointed a shaking finger at her, and said shrilly: "It lies at *your* door! You wicked, ungrateful hussy, *you* murdered her!"

A ringing slap from Sarah made her utter a whimper, and cower away. "That's enough!" said Sarah sternly. "One more word out of you and that's only a taste of what you'll get from me! You should be ashamed of yourself! A woman of your age behaving like a totty-headed chit of a girl with more hair than wit!"

Sidlaw said fiercely, glaring up at her: "I know what I know!"

"Yes!" retorted Sarah. "And *I* know what I know, you spiteful toad! And, what's more, I'll tell you I know, if you dare to say another word against Miss Kate! Don't you heed her, Miss Kate! She's clean out of her senses!"

Kate, who had fallen back, and was standing by the window, grasping a fold of the heavy curtain for support, shuddered, and said, in an anguished voice: "Don't, Sarah! don't!"

An interruption was created by the doctor, who came into the room, breathing hard and fast, as though he had been running. There was fear in his eyes, and when they alighted on Lady Broome's body a green tinge came into his face, and he uttered a groan. Only a perfunctory examination was needed to convince him that she had gone beyond his aid. As he drew down the lids over Lady Broome's dreadfully staring eyes, the fear in his own grew, and he was obliged to swallow convulsively, and to moisten his lips before he managed to say: ''There's nothing I can do. She's dead. I wanted to remain with her, but she wouldn't permit me to do so! She could always control him! I have never known her to fail! She did so this morning! I assure you, she checked his—his fury immediately! When I left this room, he was sitting in that chair, just as she had commanded him to do! I never dreamed—oh, dear, oh, dear, she must have told him—! I warned her to take care— I have frequently warned her that he was growing beyond her control! What a tragedy! What a terrible tragedy!''

He fell to wringing his white hands, whereupon Sarah, who had been regarding him with disfavour, said: ''If I may take the liberty of suggesting it, sir, I'll be obliged to you if you'd raise her so that I can pull the shawl from underneath her, and cover her with it!''

''Yes, yes! You are very right!'' he said distractedly. ''I am so much shocked I can't collect my wits! So many years I've known her! It is enough to unman anyone! Ah, poor lady! If only you hadn't sent me away!''

He tenderly lifted the dead woman's shoulders, and Sarah swiftly pulled the shawl of rose-coloured Norwich silk from under her, and would have spread it over the body had not Sidlaw darted out of her chair and snatched it from her hands, declaring that no one but herself should touch her dear mistress. She then burst into a flood of tears, casting herself over the body in an abandonment of hysterical grief.

The doctor implored her to be calm, but she was beyond listening to anything he said, and he was obliged to lift her forcibly to her feet, and to keep his arms round her to prevent her from collapsing. "What's to be done? I must give this poor woman a composer—she cannot be permitted to disturb Sir Timothy! I ought to go to him—prepare his mind to withstand this great shock! But her ladyship can't be left here, on the floor! I declare, I don't know which way to turn!"

"Well, sir," said Sarah, always practical, "seeing that you can't help her ladyship, and no one's come to fetch you to Sir Timothy, the best thing you can do is to get Miss Sidlaw up to her own bedchamber, and give her a dose of something to quieten her down. I'll undress her, and put her to bed, don't you worry!"

He agreed to this, and half led, half carried the weeping Sidlaw out of the room. Sarah, pausing only to beg Kate to go and sit in one of the adjoining saloons until she could come back to her, followed him, and Kate found herself alone.

The appalling implications of Lady Broome's violent death had at one moment almost overpowered her, but her fainting spirit revived when she was confronted with the need to exert herself. She glanced at the still form, lying under a silken shawl of incongruously cheerful colour, her face very set, and then went out into the hall. Pennymore was awaiting her there, and straightened himself, looking at her in a dazed way. "Her ladyship is dead," Kate said gently. "I expect you know that. Does Sir Timothy know?"

"No, miss. I couldn't take it upon myself to tell him, and no more could Tenby. Tenby told him what you said, and that the doctor was with her ladyship. Tenby says he's anxious, but quite calm. It's for Mr Philip to break it to him, Miss Kate. He'll know best how to do it, and—how much to tell him," he added, in a lowered tone.

"Yes," Kate said. "I think—I hope he will soon be

home again. Meanwhile, we can't leave her ladyship lying on the floor, can we?''

''No, miss, it's not seemly. Where were you wishing to lay her?''

''In her own room, I think. If you agree, will you send James and William to carry her body upstairs? I'll go up now to prepare the bed.''

''Yes, miss. I'll fetch them to you at once. I ought to have thought of it myself, but I'm not as young as I was, Miss Kate, and the shock seems to have chased the wits out of my head. I hope you'll excuse it!''

He hurried away, and Kate went up the stairs. She found a knot of housemaids in the upper hall, discussing the event in excited whispers, and by the time she had succeeded in dissuading the head-housemaid from calling the attention of her subordinates to the accuracy of Mrs Thorne's prophetic dream; checked, with a few well-chosen words, the gusty sobs of a stout damsel who seemed to believe that to refrain from bursting into tears at the death of a mistress with whom she had rarely come into contact would be a social solecism; and dispersed them all about their various businesses, there was barely enough time left to her to strip Lady Broome's great four-poster bed of its flaring patchwork quilt, its blankets, and all but one of its pillows, before slow and heavy footsteps approaching along the gallery made her bundle Ellen, who, scared but mercifully dry-eyed, had volunteered her assistance, into the adjoining dressing-room, and to shut the door on her, and to lock it.

The two footmen came in, bearing Lady Broome's corpse. They were both quite young men, but while James was evidently a good deal shaken, William, a more stolid character, wore an expressionless mask; and, when Kate said in a low voice: ''Lay her on the bed!'' he nodded adjuring his trembling colleague to go easy.

The body was still covered by the silk shawl, and when Kate had dismissed the footmen it was a few moments before she could bring herself to remove it and to spread a sheet in its place. She tried not to look at her aunt's unrecognizable countenance, or at the livid bruises on her throat, but when she had shrouded the body from head to foot, she was obliged to sit down for a few moments to recover her composure; and when she left the room she was very pale, and her hands were trembling slightly. She removed the key from inside the door, and inserted it on the outside, and turned it. After a moment's hesitation she removed it from the lock, for fear that some member of the household, impelled by morbid curiosity, might creep in, and draw back the sheet from that ghastly face.

She was about to go downstairs again when sounds of lamentation reached her. She had no difficulty in recognizing Mrs Thorne's voice, and she had never been closer to turning tail. Mrs Thorne had succumbed to the vapours, and that seemed to add the final touch to the nightmare. Gathering her resolution, she went quietly to the housekeeper's small parlour, where she found Mrs Thorne lying back in a chair, as rigid as a wooden doll, and two of the maids, one waving burnt feathers under her nose, and the other fanning her zealously but ineffectively with a tambour-frame. Restraining an impulse to box this foolish damsel's ears, and to shake the housekeeper till the teeth rattled in her head, Kate set about the wearing task of restoring Mrs Thorne to some semblance of calm. This she did by first getting rid of the maids, and next by agreeing that Mrs Thorne undoubtedly possessed the gift of second sight, and expressing awe, admiration, and wonder. This had a beneficial effect; Mrs Thorne forgot to maintain her rigid pose, and recounted for Kate's edification, and with a wealth of irrelevant detail, the various occasions when she had prophesied disaster. By the time she had reduced

Kate almost to screaming-point, she was herself, so much
recovered that it needed only a judicious amount of flattery, and the intelligence that Sidlaw had collapsed, and
had had to be carried to bed in raging hysterics, to bring
her to her feet, saying that she was sure she was very sorry
for Miss Sidlaw, but would have supposed she might have
thought of something better to do than to add to all the
commotion by kicking up such a dust. She herself, she
said, for all she hadn't been my lady's nurse, was just as
much attached to her, poor soul, and had much more sensibility than Miss Sidlaw, but would scorn to give way to
her feelings in such a nasty, vulgar way, but would continue to perform her duties, even though it killed her. Kate
thanked her, said she didn't know what any of them would
do without her, and escaped. And just as she was thinking
that at least she had managed to avert the danger of Mrs
Thorne's taking to her bed, with an attack of her celebrated
Spasms, she remembered another of the household whose
sensibilities were even more exquisite than Mrs Thorne's.
She felt a strong inclination to sit down on the nearest
chair, and to relieve her overcharged emotions by bursting
into tears; but instead of this, she turned towards the backstairs, and went resolutely to brave Gaston in his strong-
hold.

The big kitchen seemed to her to be crowded with persons whom she had never set eyes on before, all talking
at once; but her unprecedented arrival on the scene struck
even Gaston dumb with amazement. The menials who
waited on him might stand open-mouthed and goggling,
but Gallic address soon rescued him from his own astonishment, and he came forward, bowing deeply, and commanding the kitchen porter, whom he referred to in a very
lofty style as a *marmiton,* to set a chair for mademoiselle.
He begged her to inform him in what way he could serve
her, for to serve her, he said gallantly, would be

for him the greatest pleasure imaginable. So Kate, assuming the mien of a helpless innocent, said that she knew she could depend upon him to support her through this dreadful *brouhaha,* and what, she demanded of him, could he suggest in the guise of a dinner to set before a bereaved family, none of whose members, he would understand, would be able to support the sight of roast joints, or the raised pies which he cooked to such perfection. Gaston, even more susceptible than Mrs Thorne to flattery, rose magnificently to the challenge, bidding her to rest tranquil, and leave all to him: he would prepare a dinner—very small, but very choice—that would animate even the capricious appetite of Monsieur Torquil.

Kate got up rather quickly, managed to smile, and to thank Gaston, and hurried away, down the stone-paved passage to the Great Hall. In the need to prevent the disintegration of the household she had not had time to think of Torquil, but the chef's words brought home to her the full horror of her aunt's death, and filled her with icy dread. She went through the gothic door into the Great Hall, and found Mrs Nidd there, about to mount the stairs.

Mrs Nidd exclaimed: "There you are, Miss Kate! I've been looking for you all over! Wherever have you been hiding yourself, dearie?"

"I've been in the kitchen. Sarah, *where is Torquil?*"

"Well, that's more than I can tell you," said Sarah. "It seems that man of his—Badger, is it?—is searching for him in the woods. By what Mr Pennymore tells me, one of the footmen caught sight of him, making for the woods like one demented—which, of course, the poor lad is! Now, don't get into a fret! you've kept up wonderful till now, love, and acted just as you should, and like I knew you would, and you've got to remember that he won't go to the gallows for strangling his ma, like he would if he was sane, but only be shut up safe somewhere, where he can't harm himself, or anyone else. And it's my belief, Miss Kate, that if ever a woman deserved to be strangled, she did! Now, you come into this room, which they call the Blue saloon, though why they do I'm sure I don't know, for the only bit of blue in it is the curtains, and not so very much of it there either! Mr Pennymore has this instant brought in a tea-tray, and a dish of little cakes so light you'll never know you're eating them. No, I know you don't think you could swallow anything, dearie, but you'll find you can, and you've got to keep up your strength, you know!''

Having propelled Kate gently but inexorably into the Blue saloon, she pushed her into a chair, and began to pour out the tea. Kate sank her head into her hands, and Mrs Nidd, observing how her fingers writhed amongst her soft curls, went on talking, in a comfortable way which Kate found vaguely soothing. She was able presently to drink a little tea, and even to nibble a small cake, but that her mind was preoccupied she showed by breaking into Sarah's description of the fecklessness of Joe's sister Polly, saying abruptly: "Sarah, why did he do it? *Why?* I know he hated her, but he was so much in awe of her that she had only to *look* at him to bring him into submission! Sarah, what did she say to him to goad him into strangling her? She can't—oh, she *can't* have told him that he was mad, and must be shut up.''

"It's no use asking me what she said to him, Miss Kate, because I wasn't there, but after what you told me last night I wouldn't wonder at it if that's what she did tell him. I got into a chat with Mrs Thorne when you was at dinner, and from the things she said—not that she meant to cry her ladyship down, mind!—it was as plain as a pack-saddle that her ladyship was so full of her own conse-quence, and so set on getting her own way, no matter what it cost her, that when she found she couldn't, for all her plots and coaxings—like she did when you told her you wouldn't marry Mr Torquil!—there wasn't anything she wouldn't do, just for sheer, wicked spite! I can tell you this, love!—she was a regular bad one, and you don't need to waste a crumb of sympathy on her! If you ask me, this precious Staplewood of hers will be a happier place now she's dead! And don't tell me she was kind to you! She wasn't so very kind when she knew she couldn't make you marry Mr Torquil! No, and it wasn't kind of her to try to trap an innocent girl like you are into marrying a poor, mad boy that would strangle you as soon as look at you! Whenever I think of that it makes me fairly boil! Oh, well! They say you shouldn't speak ill of the dead— though why you shouldn't I'm sure I don't know!—so I'd best keep my lips buttoned, for speak good of her I could not! Drink up your tea, dearie!''

"Why did he go to her drawing-room?" Kate said, unheeding. "He never does so! Did she send for him? To scold him for trying to jump that wall yesterday? But she doesn't scold him for the—the crazy things he does!"

"Well, according to what the doctor said, Mr Torquil found the carpenter nailing bars across the window of his bedchamber, which her ladyship had given him orders to do, without a word to anyone," replied Sarah bluntly. "So Mr Torquil flew right up into the boughs, and rushed off in such a bang that the doctor couldn't stop him, to ask his ma what she meant by it. It seems the doctor went after him, and he *says* he wouldn't have left her ladyship alone with Mr Torquil if she hadn't ordered him to do so, and if he hadn't thought that she could handle Mr Torquil, like she always had done. He says that she told Mr Torquil to sit down, and that Mr Torquil obeyed her, so that he never thought she was in the least danger. He doesn't know what happened after that, no more than anyone else does, but he *did* say, if you remember, Miss Kate, that *she must have told him,* but *what* she must have told him he did *not* say!''

Kate, who had been listening to this speech with a puzzled frown knitting her brows, said incredulously: ''Good God! Did Dr Delabole tell you all this, Sarah?''

''Oh, no, he didn't tell it to *me!*'' said Sarah, refilling her cup. ''He told it to Mr Philip, in this very room, but I was here, you see—just downstairs after getting that archwife into her bed, and seeing her drop off to sleep! Well, I've got no sort of fancy for the doctor, but I'm bound to own I couldn't help compassionating him! Very rough Mr Philip was with him, raking him down till it was no wonder he had him quaking like a blancmange!''

Kate started up. ''Is Philip here?'' she cried eagerly. ''Oh, Sarah, why didn't you tell me?''

''You sit down, Miss Kate, and finish your tea!'' said Sarah severely. ''He *is* back, but he's gone out to search for Mr Torquil, and it won't do anyone a mite of good for you to run out searching for *him!* Don't you fret! He'll be here soon enough!''

As though in corroboration of this statement, he came into the room at that moment. He was looking pale, and his face was set grimly, his eyes very hard, and two deep clefts between his bows. In a shaking voice, Kate said: ''Have you found him? Have you found him, Philip?''

''Badger found him,'' he replied, and lifted a hand that was not quite steady to cover his eyes for a brief moment. He let it fall again, and said harshly: ''We were too late— both of us—''

''Dead?'' she whispered.

''Yes, dead,'' he answered.

Chapter Twenty-One

MRS NIDD, nearly dropping her cup, gasped: "Oh, my goodness gracious me!" but Kate said, as though she had been expecting it: "Did he drown himself, Philip?"

He nodded. "Badger saw him. I think he knew that it was too late to save him, but he plunged in off the bridge, and got his body to the shore. When I reached the lake he was holding him in his arms, and— Well, never mind! The poor old chap is all to pieces: said he was the only person who had ever loved Torquil, which is true, I suppose, though why he should have loved him God only knows! Torquil treated him like a dog." He paused, regarding Kate with sudden intensity. "Why did you say that? Did you know he had drowned himself?"

She made a helpless gesture. "No. I don't know, but when Sarah told me that Badger was searching the woods for him—it flashed across my mind that he once told me— oh, on my very first day here, when he took me down to the bridge!—that he often thought how pleasant it would be to drown. I didn't think he meant it, but he did, poor Torquil, he did!"

Her voice broke, and she turned away, battling with her tears. Philip said slowly: "I believe he did think it pleasant. There's no sign that he struggled to save himself: I don't think I've ever seen him look more peaceful. If I had been here—if I had known what he meant to do—I must have stopped him, but—I say this in all seriousness, Kate—I'm thankful that I was not here. For him, this is a most merciful end. When you've seen him—oh, no, don't shudder! There's nothing to distress you!—I believe you won't feel his death a tragedy.''

She blew her nose, and said, trying to speak cheerfully: ''No, I know it isn't a tragedy. Not his death! But I can't help thinking of his life, Philip! How lonely he was, and how unhappy!''

''He wasn't always unhappy, my darling. When he was a little chap he was the most engaging scamp—tumbling in and out of mischief. I was used to think that he must be lonely, but I've come to realize that perhaps it was only when he grew older that he felt the want of companionship.''

''And truer words than that, sir, you'll never speak!'' said Sarah. ''Children don't miss what they've never had, so you don't want to grieve over what's past, Miss Kate! You think of what the poor boy's future would have been, and thank God he's been saved from it! Where have you laid him, Mr Philip?''

''On his own bed. I carried him in through the West Wing entrance, and helped Badger to strip him, and put him into his nightshirt.'' A twisted smile just touched his stern mouth. He looked at Kate, and said: ''You might suppose him to be peacefully sleeping: no more than that.''

She wiped away her tears, and went to him, saying simply: ''Take me to see him, Philip. I—I should like to see him once more.''

He caught her hand, and kissed it. ''I will take you, but first I must have a word with Mrs Nidd about your journey. My darling, I had meant to have gone with you, but I can't leave my uncle at this present. I believe you wouldn't wish me to. After the inquests, and the funerals, I shall come to you, and with a special licence in my pocket, I warn you! Mrs Nidd, will you take these bills? There should be enough to pay all the expense of the journey. You will be later in starting than I had planned, but you should be able to reach Woburn tonight. Direct the post-boys to set you down at the George, and mention my name: I have frequently stayed there. Be sure to engage a private parlour! If anything should happen to delay you on the road, break the journey at Newport-Pagnell: there are two very tolerable houses there, the Swan and the Sergeant. I fancy—''

He was interrupted. Kate, who had been listening to these instructions with a blank look of incomprehension on her face, said, in bewilderment: ''But what are you talking about, Philip? There can be no question of my going to London! How could you think I would leave Staplewood at such a moment?''

He kissed her hand again, and held it in a strong clasp. ''Bless you, my little love!'' he said, in a much moved voice. ''But I wish you to go. I know how hateful Staplewood must have become to you, and I know, too, just how unpleasant—how harrowing—it is going to be, until this appalling business is over. I want to get you safely away before we are plunged into all the degrading consequences of two such deaths. Mrs Nidd, I know you will support me!''

''Well, no, Mr Philip!'' responded Sarah apologetically. ''In fact, if Miss Kate had said other than what she has said I'd have given her a thundering scold! She'll be marrying you for better or worse, sir, and if she has the worse *before* she's riveted to you, she'll be luckier than most! A pretty thing it would be if she was to sherry off with me when you've got a peck of troubles hung round your neck! Yes, and if that's the sort of hen-hearted girl you think she

is it has me in a puzzle to know why you offered for her!
A rare pickle you'd find yourself in if she was to scour
off!''

He looked to be very much taken aback, but the ready
laughter sprang to Kate's eyes, and she said: ''That's very
true! You may be able to deal with Gaston, but not with
Mrs Thorne, believe me! You would be excessively uncomfortable if you had no one here to keep house for
you—and, which is much more important, so would Sir
Timothy be! So you may put those bills back in your
pocket, sir—and stop insulting me!'' She lifted his hand,
which was still clasping hers, and laid her cheek against
it. ''Poor Philip!'' she said softly. ''I know, my dear, I
know! Pray don't ask me to go away!''

His hand tightened round hers; Mrs Nidd said: ''If you'll
pardon the liberty, sir, the person *I'd* be glad to see the
back of is the doctor, for I can't abide him, and nor can't
Miss Kate! A regular Captain Sharp, that's what he is, and
the way you rattled him off was a pleasure to listen to!
Let alone he's been living as high as a coachhorse here,
shot-free, if he hasn't been feathering his nest you may
call me a widgeon!''

That drew a smile from him. He said: ''I shouldn't
dare!''

''Are you going to send him away, Philip?''

''Not immediately. He is quite as anxious to make himself scarce as you are to see his back, Mrs Nidd, but I've
made it plain to him that I've no intention of permitting
him to leave Staplewood until after the inquests! His evi-
dence—if he says what he has himself suggested he should
say!—will be of the first importance. My uncle is not a
religious man, but I don't think he could bear it if the
verdict at the inquest made it impossible for us to bury
Torquil in the Churchyard, amongst his ancestors. Delabole has it in his power to convince the jury that when

Torquil took his own life he was not in the possession of his senses. He can do that, and will do it." He paused, and after hesitating for a moment, said, with the glimmer of a smile: "He is a rogue, and a toadeater—everything that is most contemptible! But he was never unkind to Torquil! Oh, he infuriated him with his tactlessness—and got Turkish treatment for it!—but he might, without hindrance, have subjected Torquil to the sort of harsh usage which must have made the unfortunate boy fear him. That he didn't do so—and God knows Torquil gave him cause enough!—must stand to his credit. I think he was genuinely fond of Torquil, and I am pretty certain that Minerva's charming scheme to marry the boy to you, Kate, frightened him. But once having fallen under her domination he lacked the courage to break free from her shackles. He has no more pluck than a dunghill cock, but—" He paused, and said ruefully: "He took good care of my uncle. I've no doubt Minerva paid him handsomely to do so, for it was all to her advantage to keep Sir Timothy alive, but—well, I must be grateful to him for that at least! That my uncle's health is so much improved—there was a time, you know, when I lived in hourly dread of hearing that he was dead—stands very much to his credit—and I find I can't forget that."

It was Kate who broke the silence that succeeded these words. She said quietly: "Have you told Sir Timothy, Philip?"

He shook his head. "Tenby says he is resting: asleep, he thinks. I shall tell him when he wakes. If I can't persuade you to leave Staplewood, Kate, I must pay off the post-boys: the chaise has been standing in the yard ever since my return. Wait for me: I shan't be many minutes."

He went away; and Kate, glancing at the bowl of pink roses on the table by the window, went to it, and drew out one half-opened bloom, and wiped its stalk with her handkerchief. It was in her hand when he came back, and she was holding it when she stood beside him, looking down at Torquil's still form. Her other hand was clasping Philip's, but as she gazed at that beautiful face, from which every trace of peevishness had vanished, she drew it out of his slackened hold, and brushed it across her brimming eyes, and said, under her breath: "Yes. He is just asleep, and dreaming so happily! So peacefully! Thank you for bringing me to see him: this is how I shall always remember him."

She bent over the dead boy, and slid the stem of the rose under his folded hands, and gently kissed his cold brow. Then she turned back to Philip, and he took her out of the room, his arm round her waist.

Neither spoke, until they had left the West Wing, and were walking down the gallery that led from it, past Lady Broome's bedchamber, past Kate's to the upper hall, when Kate said sadly: "No one could grieve over his death, but, oh, Philip, that is how he *might* have looked when he was alive, if his brain hadn't been so dreadfully afflicted!"

He answered only by the tightening of his arm around her waist; but when they reached the head of one of the wings of the Great Staircase, he paused, and kissed her, and said: "I must go down to my uncle. My poor darling, you're looking so tired! Will you rest on your bed before dinner? I wish you will!"

She smiled, but with an effort. "You do think me a poor honey, don't you? I'll go to my room, but I don't promise to rest on my bed: there's too much to think of, and I don't seem to have had time yet to—to regulate my mind. Philip, shall we be obliged to live here?"

"I don't know," he answered heavily. "Perhaps I shall be able to make some arrangement. If either of his sisters were alive—but they are both dead! Or if the mutton-head

Minerva engaged as bailiff could be trusted to manage the estate—"

"But he can't, can he? And—and even if he were the best bailiff imaginable he couldn't bear Sir Timothy company, could he? Philip, if your uncle wishes you to remain here, don't let the thought of me weigh with you! Do as you think you must! I don't doubt I shall accustom myself!" She summoned up a gallant smile, and added: "I *must* accustom myself, for now that Torquil is dead Staplewood will one day belong to you, won't it? I know you never wanted it, and I don't mean to try to hoax you into thinking that I do: it has never been a home to me, and—and just at the moment it is horrible to me! But if you took me to your own home, leaving your uncle in this huge, *awful* house with only servants to take care of him, I don't think I should ever be happy. I should be thinking all the time that I had failed quite miserably in my duty, and picturing Sir Timothy here, quite alone, with only his memories—and so many of them unhappy memories! And you would too, Philip! You might even regret that you had married me!"

"Never that!" he said. "I always hoped—but even if Torquil were alive, soon or late I must, I suppose, have been confronted with the same problem. O God, what a nightmare it is!"

She drew his head down, and tenderly kissed his cheek. "Yes, it *is* a nightmare, but Sarah says things are never quite as bad as one thinks they will be. And also she says it is a great mistake to cross bridges until one reaches them, so—so don't let us look beyond tomorrow! Go down now to Sir Timothy, my dear one! I'd come with you if I didn't know that he would liefer by far learn what has happened from you alone. I hope—oh, I *pray* that the shock may not cause him to suffer another, and fatal heart attack!"

Not daring to trust herself to say more, she went quickly to her room, and entered it without looking back.

She found Sarah there, unpacking her portmanteau. After one shrewd glance at her, Sarah pushed her into a chair by the window, saying: "Now, you sit there, like a good girl, Miss Kate! I don't want you under my feet!"

Kate smiled rather wanly, but attempted no argument. She was thankful to sink into the chair, and to lean back, closing her eyes. Sarah continued to bustle about, casting one or two measuring glances at Kate, but saying nothing until Kate presently opened her eyes, and straightened herself, sighing deeply. She then adjured her not to let herself fall into the doldrums. "For if you don't show Mr Philip a cheerful face, Miss Kate, you'd have done as well, and better, to have left this place, like he wished you to do." She went to Kate, and began to chafe one of her hands. "You want to look on the bright side, love!" she said. "I don't say it's easy, nor that it's very bright, but things could have been worse! The poor young gentleman won't ever be shut up now, and if the doctor can be trusted to tell the coroner, frank and open, that he wasn't in his right mind when he choked his mother to death, and flung himself into the lake—"

"Oh, if only I could be *sure* he wasn't in his right mind!" Kate cried. "But I think he was, Sarah! That's what has upset me so much. Oh, Delabole will say he wasn't: I'm not afraid of that! Perhaps—if my aunt had told him he was mad, he lost his senses, but when he saw that he had killed her—they came back to him. He wasn't out of his mind when he drowned himself. Whether he was afraid of the consequences, or—or afraid that he was mad, I don't know. But I can't help remembering that he said once, when we were discussing dreams, that sometimes he dreamed he was being chased by a monster, and sometimes that he had done something dreadful. My aunt interrupted him, and I thought no more about it until today. And then I remembered it, and the look on his face—an uneasy, scared look, Sarah! Do you think—do you think he was secretly afraid that he *had* done something dreadful? When he saw the carpenter nailing bars across his window, did it confirm his fear? If that was so—oh, poor Torquil, poor Torquil, what agony of mind he must have suffered!''

"Now, that's quite enough!" said Sarah, in a scolding tone. "You can't know what he thought, nor what her ladyship said to him, and you never will, so there's not a bit of good to be gained by dwelling on it! If he suffered, it wasn't for very long—not if Mr Philip was speaking the truth when he said that he looked happy. Didn't you think he looked happy, Miss Kate?''

Kate nodded, wiping her eyes. "Yes. He's smiling—as though he had at last found something he had been trying to find for a long, long time.''

"Well, that's all you've got to remember, love. There, you stay quiet till it's time I made you tidy for dinner! You're worn out, and no wonder.''

Kate sighed, and closed her eyes again. But presently she opened them, and said, rather drearily: "We shall have to live here, you know. We can't leave Sir Timothy alone in this dreadful house. And when he dies, it will be Philip's, and he doesn't want it, Sarah! And I don't want it either! It has never been *home* to me, and now it has become horrible! And everyone will think I married Philip because I was determined to become Lady Broome!''

"I shouldn't wonder at it if you find you're wrong,'' said Sarah. "I was talking to Mr Pennymore last night and by what he said it seems her ladyship wasn't at all well-liked by Sir Timothy's old friends. Well, it stands to reason they wouldn't like her, when she kept them away from him! *She* said it was on account of his always being so poorly, but Mr Pennymore says that it's his belief—and Tenby's too!—that it would do Sir Timothy good to see a few people. Just dropping in to have a crack with him, not waiting to be invited to a party! And what's more he told me that Staplewood hasn't been a home to him ever since her ladyship made it into a show-place. It'll be your task, Miss Kate, to make it a home again, and to make visitors welcome, what's more! As for its being horrible to you, it's only to be expected you should think so at first, but you can take it from me, dearie, that you'll get over that. Well, goodness, if everyone felt they couldn't bear to live in their houses, because something tragic had happened in them, half the big houses in the country would be standing empty!''

Kate smiled, and got up. "What *should* I do without you, Sarah?" she said. "You have so much *sense!* I beg your pardon for flying into alt: I'll try not to be so stupid again. I think the—the things that have happened today have been rather too much for me. I shall be better to-morrow!''

Sarah gave her a resounding kiss. "That's my good girl!" she said. She was interrupted by a knock at the door, and said: "If that's Ellen, I'll send her away!" She went to the door and opened it, saying as she did so: "I'll attend to Miss— Oh, it's you, sir! Yes, you can come in!''

"Philip?" Kate cried eagerly. "Come in, come in! How is Sir Timothy? Did you tell him what had happened?''

"I wasn't obliged to tell him that Minerva was dead. He had guessed it. As soon as I went into his room, he asked me if she was dead, and when I said yes, he sighed, and said that he had feared she must be. Then he said: 'Poor soul!' as though she had been a mere acquaintance. But when I told him that there was worse news for him to hear, I saw him brace himself. There was a painful look of anxiety in his eyes, and he lifted his hand, as if to

silence me. Then he let it fall, and spoke just one word—
Torquil?''

Kate caught her breath. "Philip, you don't mean—
Good God, did he *know* that Torquil was mad?"

"Suspected it. He told me that he had asked Delabole
for the truth more than a year ago. Delabole reassured him,
just as he tried to reassure me. Delabole is very plausible,
you know. I think my uncle *wanted* to believe him, perhaps
because he felt helpless, perhaps because the thought that
his only son was not of sound mind was so repugnant that
he couldn't bring himself to face it." He stopped, and said,
after a moment: "You know how it is with him—I told
you once! His nature is too gentle—too yielding! He can
never have been a match for Minerva, and after his health
broke down he only wished to be left in peace."

"I know, I know!" Kate said quickly. "And, indeed,
Philip, it is hard to see what he *could* have done for Torquil, when his health is so precarious, and my aunt was
determined that she, and she only, should rule the roast
here!"

He smiled gratefully at her, and said: "You do understand, and I needn't beg you not to think harshly of him."

"No, that you need not! I couldn't think harshly of him!
But go on! Did he guess that Torquil had murdered his
mother? Or had Tenby told him—prepared his mind for
the shock?"

"No, I don't think so. If that had been so, he must have
known that Torquil had strangled her, and he didn't know
that. When I told him that Torquil *had* strangled her, in a
fit of mania, he changed colour—looked so ghastly that I
obliged him to swallow some of his cordial. He was greatly
distressed—far more than by the news that Minerva was
dead! He said—oh, in an *aching* voice!—'Poor boy! Poor,
unhappy boy!' Then, when he had a little recovered he
asked me if I realized what it must mean: that Torquil

would have to be put away in some asylum. That was what upset him more than all the rest. When I told him that Torquil was dead, too, he was merely thankful. He said, very frankly, that he had never been able to care for Torquil, as he had cared for little Julian, but that to have been obliged to condemn him to spend the rest of his life in a lunatic asylum would have left him with nothing more to do than to have put a period to his own life. Then, after a little while, he asked me if you were still here, and when I told him, yes, and that you had refused to leave Staplewood, he instantly became more cheerful, and said that you were the silver lining to a very black cloud, and that he need no longer be afraid that he wouldn't see you again. When I left him, he was quite happily making plans for our wedding! He seems to have set his heart on leading you to the altar, and bestowing your hand on me himself— here, in the Church, as soon after the funerals as may be possible. I told him that I couldn't answer for you, and if you dislike the idea you mustn't hesitate to tell me so. It would be a private ceremony, of course: just ourselves, my uncle, Mrs Nidd to support you, and, if I could lure him back from his London dissipations, Gurney Templecombe to support me. Would you like it, or would you prefer to be married in London?''

"Oh, I should much, much prefer to be married here!'' she exclaimed, flushing with pleasure. "And for Sir Timothy to give me away! How kind, how *very* kind of him!''

He turned his head to look at Sarah, a question in his eyes. "The decision must rest with you, Mrs Nidd. It won't do for Kate to remain at Staplewood without you to lend her countenance: *I* know the sort of scandal-broth that all the tattle-boxes brew! Can you stay with us until you've seen us buckled, or am I asking too much of you? I know you have your own home to manage, and perhaps your husband might object to it, if you were to extend your stay? Not to mention your father-in-law!''

"Joe knows Miss Kate must come first," responded Sarah. "And as for Father, I don't doubt he'll cut up stiff, and make a great grievance out of it, but you don't need to worry about him, sir! He don't mean all he says: he's just naturally full of crotchets! I'll write a letter to Joe, explaining how it is."

"Thank you!" he said, holding out his hand. "I'm very much obliged to you! Kate, my uncle wishes us both to dine with him, in his own room: may I tell him that we'll do so?"

"Yes, indeed, you may!" Kate answered. "I—I was dreading having to sit down to dinner in that huge, sombre room, trying to be civil to Dr Delabole! It is so much cosier in Sir Timothy's room!"

"Dr Delabole," he said, "will be eating his dinner in the breakfast-parlour! But you are very right: the dining-room was never used, in my aunt's day, except for large parties. If we find ourselves obliged to take up our quarters here, I shall ask my uncle if we may revert to the old custom of dining in the Red saloon when we are alone."

"In the meantime, Mr Philip," interpolated Sarah, edging him towards the door. "I'll thank you to go away! If Sir Timothy wishes Miss Kate to dine with him, she must change her dress! And if you'll pardon me for venturing to give you the word with no bark in it, I'll prefer your room to your company, sir!"

He laughed, but said: "Must she change her dress? She looks very becoming to me!"

"Well, if you think she looks very becoming, with her hair in a tangle, and her dress all creased and rumpled, you *must* be nutty on her!" retorted Sarah acidly. "She looks like a hoyden, and let her go down to your uncle like that

I will not—not if you was to ask me on your bended knees! Get along with you, do, Mr Philip!''

She then thrust him out of the room, firmly shutting the door on him, and uttered, in accents of loathing: *"Men!"* However, she added grudgingly, as she passed Kate's wardrobe under rapid review: "Not but what it looks to me as though Sir Timothy knows a point more than the devil, as the saying goes. That's a very shrewd notion of his, Miss Kate! Once it gets to be known that it was him gave you to Mr Philip, in Church—and it *will* get to be known, make no mistake about that!—you'll have everybody that *is* anybody coming to pay you morning-visits. And as long as you don't get to thinking yourself first in consequence, and setting people's bristles up by condescending to them, which Mr Pennymore has told me your aunt was used to do, you needn't fear they won't like you. So just you sit down there, Miss Kate, while I brush your hair for you, and see if you can't pluck up a bit!"

"I'll try," Kate said, sighing. "But—oh, Sarah, it seems so fantastic that you should be dressing me for dinner when my aunt and Torquil are—are lying dead! It—it is almost indecent to wish to swallow a mouthful!''

"And when, miss, according to your calculations, *will* it be decent for you to eat your dinner again, like a Christian?" demanded Sarah somewhat tartly.

That made Kate laugh, and did much to lighten the oppression that weighed down her spirits. When she went down the Great Staircase, she found Pennymore hovering in the hall, with the very evident intention of conducting her into Sir Timothy's room. He smiled benignly upon her, saying that, if she would not think it presumptuous of him, he would venture to make so bold as to say that the sight of her would do Sir Timothy all the good in the world. "It's a long time since I've seen him take such a fancy to anyone as he has to you, miss, and Tenby says the same.

If you'll come this way, you'll find him and Mr Philip waiting for you.''

He preceded her to Sir Timothy's room, but although he opened the door for her, and bowed her in, a discernment which she recognized as being extremely nice made him forbear to announce her. She went in unheralded, smiled shyly at Philip, who had risen quickly, and had taken two steps forward to meet her, but went past him, to bend over Sir Timothy, softly kissing his cheek.

He took her hand, and patted it. "Well, my pretty!" he said fondly. "So here you are! Pour her out a glass of Madeira, Philip! Sit down beside me, my dear! I'm afraid you have had a very uncomfortable day."

She could not help feeling, as she recalled the events of the day, that this was a masterpiece of understatement, and she replied, rather faintly: "Yes, sir. It—it has been a *little* uncomfortable!"

He went on patting her hand. "Pennymore has been telling me that he doesn't know what we could have done without you. Thank you, my dear! Your nurse, too! You must bring her to see me tomorrow: she sounds to be a most excellent woman, and I should wish to express my gratitude to her. That's right, Philip! Pull up that little table, and set the glass on it! He and I have been discussing the future, Kate, and although it would make me very happy if you were to make Staplewood your home, you mustn't do so if you feel the least disinclination! I shall go on very well, and I daresay you will come to visit me, so that I shall have that to look forward to.'' He glanced across at Philip, with a melancholy smile. "I know you prefer the house your father built, my boy. Perhaps you will sell Staplewood, when it is yours: I shall be dead, so I shan't know.''

"No, sir: I shan't do that," Philip said.

"Well, I can't deny that I shall like to think that when

I've cocked up my toes there will still be a Broome at Staplewood,'' said Sir Timothy, more cheerfully. "You will have to decide, both of you, whether you will come to live here immediately, or wait until I'm dead. I shan't last for many more years, and I no longer have the health or the strength to manage my estates. You could do it, and I think it would be wise of you not to put off what I feel sure you think of as the evil day! However, I don't mean to press you, and we won't talk of it any more tonight.'' He smiled at Kate. "Drink up your wine, my pretty! I think we won't discuss anything that has happened today. We shall eat our dinner, and after that I shall challenge you to a rubber of piquet…''

Now that you've enjoyed
Cousin Kate
there's another treat in store for you.

Available in June 2000,
The Talisman Ring
by
Georgette Heyer
with a foreword by
award-winning author
Mary Balogh

Sir Tristram Shield never believed in true love—until
he became involved with the latest family mystery. But
who will win his heart? Impulsive cousin Eustacie? Or
the delightful Miss Sarah Thane? Discover the truth in
Georgette Heyer's wonderful novel,
The Talisman Ring!

For a special peek, turn the page....

"You're the last of your name," Sylvester, ninth Baron Lavenham, reminded his great-nephew Sir Tristram Shield.

"I know it. I've every intention of marrying."

"No one in your eye?"

"No."

"Then you'll marry your cousin Eustacie," said Sylvester. "Pull the bell!"

Sir Tristram obeyed, but said with a look of amusement: "Your dying wish, Sylvester?"

"I shan't live the week out," replied Sylvester cheerfully. "Heart and hard living, Tristram. Don't pull a long face at my funeral! Eighty years is enough for any man, and I've had the gout for twenty of them." He saw his valet come into the room and said: "Send Mademoiselle to me."

"You take a great deal for granted, Sylvester," remarked Sir Tristram as the valet went out again.

Sylvester had leaned his head back against the pillows, and closed his eyes. There was a suggestion of exhaustion in his attitude, but when he opened his eyes they were very much alive, and impishly intelligent. "You would not have come here, my dear Tristram, had you not already made up your mind.''

Sir Tristram smiled a little reluctantly, and transferred his attention to the fire.

It was not long before the door opened again. Sir Tristram turned as Mademoiselle de Vauban came into the room, and stood looking at her under bent brows.

His first thought was that she was unmistakably a Frenchwoman, and not in the least the type of female he admired. She had glossy black hair, dressed in the newest fashion and her eyes were so dark that it was hard to know whether they were brown or black. Her inches were few, but her figure was extremely good, and she bore herself with an air. She paused just inside the door, and, at once perceiving Sir Tristram, gave back his stare with one every whit as searching and a good deal more speculative.

Sylvester allowed them to weigh one another for several moments before he spoke, but presently he said: ''Come here, my child. And you, Tristram.''

The promptness with which his granddaughter obeyed this summons augured a docility wholly belied by the resolute, not to say willful, set of her pretty mouth. She trod gracefully across the room, and curtseyed to Sylvester before stepping up onto the dais where he lay in bed. Sir Tristram came more slowly to the bedside.

Sylvester stretched out his left had to Eustacie. ''Let me present to you, my child, your cousin Tristram.''

''Your very obedient cousin,'' said Shield, bowing.

''It is to me a great happiness to meet my cousin,'' enunciated Eustacie with prim civility and a slight, no unpleasing French accent.

''I am a little tired,'' said Sylvester. ''If I were not, might allow you time to become better acquainted. If yo want a formal offer, Eustacia, no doubt Tristram will make you one—after dinner.''

''I do not want a formal offer,'' replied Mademoiselle de Vauban. ''It is to me a matter quite immaterial, but my name is Eustacie, *not* Eu-sta-ci-a, which I cannot at all pronounce, and which I find excessively ugly.''

This speech, which was delivered in a firm and perfectly self-possessed voice, had the effect of making Sir Tristram cast another of his searching glances at the lady. He said with a faint smile: ''I hope I may be permitted to call you Eustacie, cousin?''

''Certainly; it will be quite *convenable,*'' replied Eustacie, bestowing a brilliant smile upon him.

''You may go down to dinner now,'' said Sylvester.

''You are all consideration, sir,'' said Shield. ''Shall we go, cousin?''

Eustacie assented, curtseyed again to her grandfather and accompanied Sir Tristram downstairs to the dining-room.

The butler had set their places at opposite ends of the great table, an arrangement in which both tacitly acquiesced, though it made conversation a trifle remote. Sir Tristram noticed that his prospective bride enjoyed a hearty appetite, and discovered after five minutes that she possessed a flow of artless conversation, quite unlike any he had been used to listen to in London drawing-rooms. He was prepared to find her embarrassed by a situation which struck him as being fantastic, and was somewhat startled when she remarked: ''It is a pity that you are so dark, because I do not like dark men in general. However, one must accustom oneself.''

''Thank you,'' said Shield.

''If my grandpapa had left me in France it is probable

that I should have married a duke," said Eustacie. "My uncle certainly intended it."

"You would more probably have gone to the guillotine," replied Sir Tristram, depressingly matter-of-fact.

"Yes, that is quite true," agreed Eustacie. "We used to talk of it, my cousin Henriette and I. We made up our minds we should be entirely brave, not crying, of course, but perhaps a little pale, in a proud way. Henriette wished to go to the guillotine *en grande tenue,* but that was only because she had a court dress of yellow satin which she thought became her much better than it did really. For me, I think one should wear white to the guillotine if one is quite young, and not carry anything except perhaps a handkerchief. Do you not agree?"

"I don't think it signifies what you wear if you are on your way to the scaffold," replied Sir Tristram, quite unappreciative of the picture his cousin was dwelling on with such evident admiration.

She looked at him in surprise. "Don't you? But consider! You would be very sorry for a young girl in a tumbril, dressed all in white, pale, but *quite* unafraid, and not attending to the *canaille* at all, but—"

"I should be very sorry for anyone in a tumbril, whatever their age or sex or apparel," interrupted Sir Tristram.

"You would be more sorry for a young girl—all alone, and perhaps bound," said Eustacie positively.

"You wouldn't be all alone. There would be a great many other people with you," said Sir Tristram.

Eustacie eyed him with considerable displeasure. "In my tumbril there would *not* have been a great many other people," she said.

Perceiving that argument on this point would be fruitless, Sir Tristram merely looked sceptical and refrained from speech.

"A Frenchman," said Eustacie, "would understand at once!"

"I am not a Frenchman," replied Sir Tristram.

"Ça se voit!" retorted Eustacie.

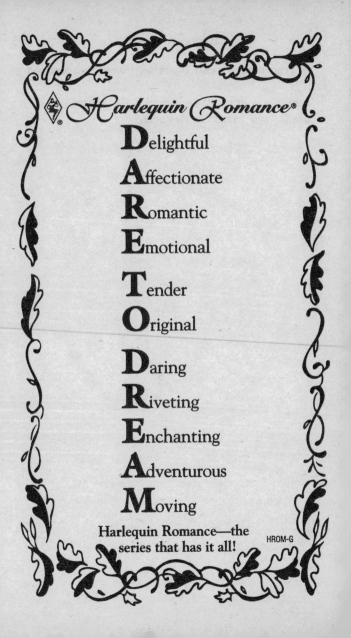

Harlequin Romance®

Delightful

Affectionate

Romantic

Emotional

Tender

Original

Daring

Riveting

Enchanting

Adventurous

Moving

Harlequin Romance—the
series that has it all!

HROM-G

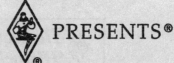

Harlequin® Historical

From rugged lawmen and
valiant knights to defiant heiresses
and spirited frontierswomen,
Harlequin Historicals will
capture your imagination with
their dramatic scope, passion
and adventure.

Harlequin Historicals...
they're too good to miss!

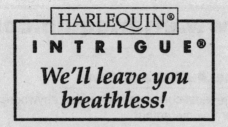

HARLEQUIN®

INTRIGUE®

We'll leave you breathless!

If you've been looking for thrilling tales of
contemporary passion and sensuous love stories
with taut, edge-of-the-seat suspense—
then you'll *love* **Harlequin Intrigue!**

Every month, you'll meet four new heroes
who are guaranteed to make your spine tingle
and your pulse pound. With them you'll enter
into the exciting world of Harlequin Intrigue—
where your life is on the line
and so is your heart!

THAT'S INTRIGUE—DYNAMIC ROMANCE AT ITS BEST!

HARLEQUIN®

INTRIGUE®